CONGO NIGHTFALL

JASON KASPER

SEVERN RIVER

PUBLISHING

Severn River Publishing
SevernRiverBooks.com

ISBN: 978-1-64875-604-7 (Paperback)

ALSO BY JASON KASPER

American Mercenary Series
Greatest Enemy
Offer of Revenge
Dark Redemption
Vengeance Calling
The Suicide Cartel
Terminal Objective

Shadow Strike Series
The Enemies of My Country
Last Target Standing
Covert Kill
Narco Assassins
Beast Three Six
The Belgrade Conspiracy
Lethal Horizon
Congo Nightfall
Rogue Frontier

Spider Heist Thrillers
The Spider Heist
The Sky Thieves
The Manhattan Job
The Fifth Bandit

Standalone Thriller
Her Dark Silence

To find out more about Jason Kasper and his books, visit
Jason-Kasper.com

To JB

"You know how most people say, it's you and me until it's you or me? Well my version is: it's you and me, until it's you and me in prison."

"Men, Special Forces is a mistress. Your wives will envy her because she will have your hearts. Your wives will be jealous of her because of the power to pull you away. This mistress will show you things never before seen and experience things never before felt. She will love you, but only a little, seducing you to want more, give more, die for her. She will take you away from the ones you love, and you will hate her for it, but leave her you never will, but if you must, you will miss her, for she has a part of you that will never be returned intact.

And in the end, she will leave you for a younger man."

-James R. Ward, OSS

"It's naptime in kindergarten, assholes."

-Cancer

1

"How you feeling about this one?" Worthy drawled beside me.

"Peachy," I casually replied, speaking over the hum of the twin engines outside our plane. "After the past few months without a job, I was afraid we wouldn't make it out the door again before my contract was up."

"Yeah?"

"Sure. And besides, when has anything gone wrong during one of our missions?"

Worthy examined my face, his own features an eerie crimson mask in the nighttime cabin lighting.

Then he said, "When *hasn't* something gone wrong?"

Ian must have heard us, because a moment later his helmet appeared as he leaned forward from his canvas drop seat to add his two cents.

"Or," Ian proposed, raising his voice enough to be heard, "to put a finer point on it, when hasn't almost everything gone wrong?"

I raised a fist, slowly extending my middle finger.

Taking the hint, Ian sat back to expose our medic seated beside him.

The fact that Reilly wasn't sleeping on infil was fairly well indicative that he too was on edge, and his words a moment later confirmed it.

"I'd say the stakes are a bit higher than we're used to. So far none of our missions have involved the risk of getting mauled by a leopard or getting our arms ripped off by a gorilla."

Cancer's face appeared beside him, half-lit by the red lights. "As long as we don't run into any cobras, who cares?"

"Just cobras?" Ian asked. "What about the mambas and vipers, because there's plenty of both where we're headed—"

"Fuck off," Cancer shot back.

I smiled politely, folding my hands over my chest.

"See?" I returned my gaze to Worthy. "The guys are all optimistic enough. Everything's going to be fine. Besides, you look great in your current getup. They should make a GI Joe action figure out of you—I'd buy it. And think of the royalties to supplement your contractor pay."

"I hate you sometimes, you know that? I feel ridiculous."

I smirked and admitted, "If we're being honest, so do I."

We wore rugged civilian hiking clothes in drab monotone colors that didn't blend in with the jungle quite as nicely as camouflage, but they were sufficient to provide some level of visual discretion while cultivating the appearance of adventure tourists if we were spotted during daylight hours.

That was, however, where the concessions to discreet appearance ended.

Our true intentions were betrayed by everything else we currently wore: MC-6 main parachutes tightly packed into bulky containers on our backs, with T-11 reserve parachutes across our abdomens. The tightly adjusted harnesses were uncomfortable under the best of circumstances, and less so when a modular weapons case was suspended from your left side, stuffed with a suppressed rifle in addition to a tactical vest with ammunition, grenades, medical kit, and radio.

The *coup de grâce* to the entire configuration was the heavy civilian hiking packs secured to our harnesses by virtue of a quick release system, and currently pressing down on our thighs as we sat on the aircraft's canvas foldout seats. And if the collective weight of all this equipment wasn't sufficient to motivate us to exit the aircraft in the most expeditious manner possible, then the fact that we all had to piss like racehorses after gearing up over three hours ago in Burundi most certainly was.

This type of thing was more or less standard fare during my time as an Army Ranger, albeit using enormous military aircraft like C-130s and C-17s instead of our current vehicle: an L-410 Turbolet, a twin-engine transport plane lightly modified by the CIA to insert operatives well before the crew landed to conduct an ostensibly legitimate cargo transfer.

"Don't get me wrong," Worthy went on, "I don't like high-altitude freefalls either. But at least it's civilized. I don't go in for this static line shit, man."

"Relax," I told him. "The OSS used to infiltrate with low-altitude jumps all the time."

"Yeah," he agreed, before countering my point with his own sage observation. "They sure did—*in World War II*. Beyond that, it's only worth the risk for airfield seizures. And I don't think we're in any danger of getting tasked with one of those anytime soon, do you?"

He wasn't wrong, I thought.

I replied, "I'm with you, brother. I tried explaining all that to her. But she wouldn't sign off on a freefall, so...here we are. And look at the bright side: the closer we are to our objective, the quicker we're on the way out. This still beats walking in, doesn't it?"

"It beats walking, but that's about it. Mayfly should've signed off on a freefall," Worthy said, using the radio callsign for my team's immediate supervisor, Meiling Chen.

"Look," I told him, "here was the convo. According to her, why risk an aircraft being detected on a cross-border incursion when the Agency routinely flies to and from various spots in the Congo? Because any cargo is inspected by Congolese authorities upon landing, says I. Then she said, so we'll have the pilots fly their usual flight path, lose altitude a bit earlier than usual, and drop us on the way. I told her a static line jump was noisy, noticeable, and comes with an untoward risk of landing in the trees. She asked if I wanted the mission or not—so it's either us jumping this way, or the other Project Longwing team that we're not supposed to know about."

Worthy heaved a sigh. "She just wants a low-altitude airborne insertion for her resume."

"That'd be my guess," I acknowledged. "And it's pretty hard to get that notch on her belt, because anyone with half a brain would be flying a lot higher right now to do a freefall—"

My soliloquy ended with a hand touching my shoulder, and I looked up to see our flight's designated loadmaster leaning down to announce, "We're about to descend. Ten-minute warning."

He returned to the rear of the aircraft, making way for a second member of the aircrew—our airborne safety—who moved in the opposite direction. I gave Worthy a helpless shrug.

"Well, that's my cue."

The aircraft descended as I struggled upright under the weight of my gear. I ran my hand down my static line, a length of yellow webbing that draped over my shoulder and ended in a snap link secured to the carrying handle of my reserve parachute. Unhooking the link, I reached up to clip it over a braided steel cable running the length of the aircraft. Then I formed a bite in the webbing so I could slide it along the cable as I waddled toward the tail, leaning forward so I didn't fall ass over teakettle as the bird continued its downward trajectory.

The loadmaster was waiting just aft of the closed jump door, and I handed him my static line before turning to face my team.

"Ten minutes!" I shouted, extending both arms with fingers spread.

My teammates echoed the command, leaving me to yell, "Stand up!"

They rose in unison, fighting their way to their feet and grappling for their snap links as I called, "Hook up!"

They did so in the manner that I had, securing their static lines to the cable. After jumping, the lines would tighten to extract deployment bags containing our main parachutes. Down we'd float under a canopy, leaving the loadmaster and safety to retrieve the lines and bags at the expense of considerable elbow grease.

"Check static lines!"

My men ran their free hands down the length of their static lines, a final inspection to ensure they were secured and free of twists or cuts before repeating the process on the harness of the team member to their front.

"Check equipment!"

They ran their free hands over their helmet chinstraps and harness connection points, and I paused to give them time to complete the process to their satisfaction.

The entire procedure was more or less akin to an airborne military operation, which made it seem absurdly out of place for a CIA paramilitary infiltration. It would never fly in a high-budget Hollywood screenplay, I knew, but the real world was a different matter altogether. When working in limited visibility on a no-fail mission where Special Activities Center Air Department crewmembers had exactly one shot to get you out the door before an exceedingly small jungle clearing below slipped by at 110 knots, you stuck to the basics and took nothing for granted.

I leaned back to remain upright under the weight of my equipment and parachutes as the airborne safety made his way down the line, inspecting each man before walking past me with a thumbs-up.

"Sound off for equipment check!"

Cancer yelled, "Okay." He slapped a hand against Reilly's hand to initiate a domino effect as the call was transferred down the line, ending with Worthy, who extended a hand toward me.

"All okay," he shouted.

I didn't respond.

He gave a frustrated shake of his head and clarified, "All okay, *Jumpmaster*."

"Was that so hard?" I asked, slapping his hand away and retrieving my static line from the safety before shuffling back to the number one jumper position. Once there, I turned to face the door.

"I hate this next bit," Worthy called out from behind me.

"Really?" I asked, feigning confusion. "This is my favorite part."

It wasn't that I was trying to fuck with him—that much was merely a fringe benefit—because in truth I loved jumping, and had from the first time I leapt out of a C-130 at the US Army Airborne School at the tender age of eighteen. Since then I'd racked up more static line jumps as a Ranger, one of which was in combat, followed by close to a thousand skydives and over a hundred BASE jumps. My team's initial and advanced freefall courses with the CIA had all been a high point for me, as had our routine training jumps and, most notably, our 24,000-foot leap behind enemy lines in Syria.

But that made me a rare bird amongst my team, and I sensed that only Cancer was actually looking forward to what was about to occur.

Within seconds, the pilots leveled out and began their deceleration to drop speed. I used my free hand to slide clear goggles down my helmet, adjusting them over my eyes before returning my palm to cover the opening flap of my reserve parachute container.

A moment later we reached the most sobering moment of any jump— and the one Worthy was dreading.

The loadmaster approached the interior fuselage to my left and unlocked the modified aft door, pulling it inward on hydraulic hinges as a hot whirlwind entered the cabin. By the time he'd slid the door to the rear and used a pin to lock it into place, the muted vibration of our flight transformed into a sweltering blast of humid jungle air tinged with the exhaust fumes of aviation gas. It was against this backdrop that the silhouette of the loadmaster, glowing scarlet beneath the interior lights, retreated toward the tail and gave me the thumbs-up.

I advanced once more, this time gripping the lead edge of the open jump door with my left hand before handing my static line to the airborne safety. Humid air whipped my face, the noise of the engines and wind deafening as I placed my right hand on the door's trail edge and swept my palm to the floor and then back up. If the metal had somehow sustained any damage during flight, it risked shearing our static lines and leaving us plummeting toward the jungle with a reserve parachute that we may or may not be able to deploy in time to save ourselves.

Once satisfied, I braced my hands on either side of the door and conducted my favorite part of jumpmaster duties.

Leaning outside the plane until my elbows were locked, I looked in the direction of flight; while the pilots were flying with night vision, mine was safely stowed, and the jungles ahead were little more than inky blackness that I visually scanned for other aircraft. I rotated my view upward at the stars, then rearward, down, and straight ahead before looking back toward our destination. The sky was clear enough for me to make out the lights of Kananga as a dim blur, far too distant for me to identify the airport where our plane would be landing without us.

My cheeks were flapping like a dog sticking its head out the window of a moving car, and once I'd satisfied myself that no other planes or helicopters would present a danger to my team, I momentarily looked down for any identifiable landmarks along our flight path. I could only make out a few crawling, glowing dots that represented headlights along the N41 highway to our east, along with a particularly prominent hilltop ahead—but the hilltop was enough. Once we flew south of it, we'd be approximately three minutes from our drop zone.

Pulling myself back inside the bird, I looked right to meet the loadmaster's gaze and flashed him three fingers.

He nodded. I repeated the gesture with my opposite hand, shouting to my team, "Three minutes!"

They shouted the time hack back at me, and a red light bulb flickered to life on a panel beside the door. In the absence of any further landmarks discernible to the naked eye, the loadmaster would issue all future time warnings with the assistance of the pilot's GPS. My job was to relay them to my team—only the two-minute, one-minute, and thirty-second warnings remained, after which we'd overfly the clearing of our designated drop zone. In a standard airborne training scenario, the jumpmaster would step back and order his men through the door before exiting last. But that role reversed in combat, and I'd be the first one to take the leap. I leaned forward once more, putting my face into the wind and repeating my scan for unexpected aircraft before assessing our proximity to the hilltop.

For a moment, I thought my eyes were playing tricks on me. The risk of ground-to-air fire by anything other than small arms along our flight corridor was assessed by the CIA to be zero. Not low, not extremely low, but *zilch*.

And yet, I saw flaming blots of orange emerge from the hilltop below, the sparks congealing into a single gleaming arc aimed directly toward our aircraft. My mind raced; this was supposed to be a covert insertion.

Who knew we were coming?

I pulled myself back through the door to shout, "*Incoming!*" a split second before the first rounds struck.

The cabin erupted into chaos as supersonic bullets tore through the plane's thin metal skin, cracking and whistling before going silent. The burst had mostly missed, but the rounds that found their mark did so uncannily close to the cockpit. I wondered if one or both pilots had been killed.

That thought was soon forgotten in the wake of a popping explosion outside. I instinctively knew that the right engine was hit, though my attempt to visually confirm this by peering out the door was met with a faceful of acrid fumes. I heard the churning screech of metallic parts grinding to a stop, followed by a drastic reduction in noise amid the cabin that was now filling with smoke, both of which assured me that my suspicions were correct.

The only input I could hear from my team came from Worthy, who shouted from his position as the number two jumper.

"Closing time!"

The tracer fire I'd seen arcing up from the hilltop didn't come from small arms or even a heavy machinegun, but a full-blown anti-aircraft cannon, and while the gunfire had ended as we flew past, our troubles were just beginning. We'd just lost one of two engines, and with a great distance remaining until the destination airfield, the L-410 Turbolet we'd so confidently boarded in Burundi was about to be wreckage scattered across the jungle.

The only question was if anyone aboard would survive the imminent crash, and if so, whether my team would remain inside to face it. Making it to our intended exit point was no longer an option, and even if it was, the odds of an enemy force waiting to interdict us were far too great in the wake of a premeditated aircraft shootdown.

As with all things related to this operation, we'd planned for every imaginable contingency in advance—if the aircraft was hit by ground fire prior to the drop zone, the pilots would do their best to hold the bird level. The decision of whether to conduct an emergency bailout or assume crash positions was mine alone as the ground force commander.

I had one second to make a choice, and I used it to whip my head rearward and assess the tail orientation. If the plane had pitched nose-up, we risked striking the horizontal stabilizer and quite possibly breaking our necks in the process.

But the tail held steady, at least for the time being, and no further commands were needed. If I jumped now, my team would follow without hesitation as surely as they would if I entered a doorway during close-quarters combat.

The airborne safety stood behind me, still holding my static line. I notified him of my decision with just two impulsive words, a universal phrase embedded in my psyche from my history as a BASE jumper.

"See ya," I shouted, and leapt into the vortex of whipping air over the Democratic Republic of the Congo.

Worthy's entire body had been gripped by a stranglehold of fear and dread the moment David announced incoming fire, and just as it seemed the dual emotions couldn't possibly rise to a higher crescendo amid the sound of bullets tearing through the cabin behind him, they managed to do just that at the exact moment the team leader jumped.

But Worthy's mounting horror did nothing to alter his actions one way or the other; he advanced toward the airborne safety as quickly as he could manage, pushing his static line forward across the braided steel cable. He didn't have to move far, perhaps three or four short steps toward the door, though that brief span of time stretched to a veritable eternity. As was so often the case in combat, this delay allowed his mind to race through a consideration that was nothing short of absurd given the circumstances: why had he, without any conscious thought, shouted "closing time?"

The last time he heard that phrase was when Cancer had spoken it in Libya, at a moment when the team's annihilation seemed particularly imminent. Worthy had impulsively said it seconds earlier as his last words, mainly because he fully expected the plane to disintegrate in mid-air. But the anti-aircraft fire had ended and the bird remained in shaky flight, leaving him to contemplate whether David had interpreted his comment as an invocation to conduct an emergency bailout.

By then he was handing his static line to the airborne safety, who appeared stunned by the team's reaction, but nonetheless grabbed the webbing and slid it backward along the cable as Worthy pivoted to face the roaring wind at the open jump door.

A single leap was all it took for Worthy to launch himself out of the plane, where he was ripped free of the fuselage by what felt like a gale-force tornado. Exiting on a static line jump was like grabbing hold of a rope trailing a moving freight train, only backwards—Worthy was sucked into the howling vortex of air like a rag doll, struggling to maintain an exit position with legs together, knees locked, and chin tucked as he gripped either side of his reserve parachute container.

The buzz of the aircraft and shriek of whipping wind faded to a rustling of fabric, and Worthy's velocity slowed as his parachute unfurled. He began a sweeping pendulum motion in the opposite direction, reaching up to find his risers twisted overhead. He pulled them apart and kicked, hearing another parachute blast open as he spun clockwise for two turns before his risers straightened out and he spun the other way in the harness.

Seizing control of his steering toggles, he yanked them free from the stows and pulled them down to the quarter brake position; there would be no time for a maneuverability check at five hundred feet over the jungle. A single sideways glance to see if the remainder of his team made it out yielded only a trace of reddish flame from the receding plane, whose angle made it impossible to determine if it was maintaining level flight or on its way toward the jungle.

He looked downward to assess his remaining altitude, and found the task impossible beyond a great certainty that impact was imminent. Ordinarily he'd yank the quick release to suspend his hiking pack fifteen feet along its lowering line, but that shit went out the window with an imminent tree landing where his testicles needed all the protection they could get.

Instead he pulled his toggles down to a half-brake position, wrenching his legs together from boots to hips in an effort to avoid a tree branch enema.

He swung his forearms in to protect his face as his feet crashed through foliage. Leaves and branches whipped across his entire body in a seemingly endless descent through the jungle canopy, and suddenly he was unmolested by Mother Nature but still falling, having passed clear through the trees. Nostrils now filled by air thick with humidity and rotting leaves, Worthy brought his toggles down to a full brake position in preparation for a parachute landing fall on the jungle floor.

His punishment for the attempt came a moment later, his parachute harness jerking him upright with so much force that he saw blotches of color. Worthy grunted in pain, impotently kicking his legs for purchase and instead finding that his boots dangled free. An instinctive self-assessment followed like the first seconds after a car crash. He was alive and, as best as he could tell, free of significant injury. That realization brought with it a rush of euphoria that faded as quickly as it had arisen, his thoughts pivoting to less selfish matters.

The fate of the plane and its occupants was chief among these considerations. Standard protocol for an aircraft going down was for any and all ground elements to secure the crash site and recover the crew. In this case there were two severe complications: first, he wasn't sure that his entire team had made it out of the plane in the first place. David had gone first, and Worthy had definitely heard Ian's canopy opening behind him. Whether Reilly and Cancer had safely exited remained unknown, and even if they had, there was no ironclad guarantee that anyone but himself had endured the subsequent parachute landing while remaining conscious.

And second, Worthy hadn't yet heard the plane crash.

Those thoughts were eclipsed by his own reality at present, hanging in the blackness at an unknown height over the jungle floor amid the thrum of crickets and the bloodcurdling screeches of night birds. Concerns about his teammates or the aircrew wouldn't mean much if he got shot by an unseen opponent while dangling like a human Christmas ornament, and he couldn't put his weapon, night vision, and radio into operation before getting down from here.

There was a very specific procedure for that sort of thing, and as with most things related to a static line jump, it was going to suck.

The first step was in many ways the hardest—Worthy felt across the bottom of the inverted hiking pack clipped to his harness, located a canvas pull tab, and yanked it free before throwing a knee forward in a sharp jab.

Sixty-plus pounds of weight vanished from his load as the pack sailed downward, the webbing of his lowering line extending to its full length before going taut and pulling on his harness like a suspended anvil. He'd been hoping to hear the thump of his pack making landfall well before that point, but the situation was what it was—he wrenched a clasp on his left side to release his weapon case, which slid free down the line before Worthy jettisoned the entire mess by unclipping his lowering line and counting.

Two full seconds elapsed before his equipment struck the ground with a percussive *boom*, leaving him in the harness sans critical equipment; this was the most vulnerable he'd ever been in combat, and things were only going to get worse from here.

Worthy found the quick release in his harness waistband and pulled it free, then placed one palm atop the reserve parachute strapped over his stomach. Applying pressure, he pulled a tab free and slid the opposite hand behind the first, pressing inward before yanking the rip cord handle and dropping it. If he let go now, a compressed spring would send his reserve parachute rocketing outward and very likely into the nearest tree, which wouldn't be much help considering what he was about to attempt.

He released the inward pressure gradually, using both hands to control the spring's extension and unfurl the slick ripstop nylon parachute cloth down between his legs. Once the parachute was fully out, he felt for the S-folded suspension lines secured by rubber bands against the rear of the parachute container, then yanked them free until his reserve was hanging from its risers below him.

Unclipping the reserve's left connector snap, he rotated the entire container sideways and secured it to a triangle link on his right side. He took a moment to set himself up for success, seating himself deep into the saddle of his harness before removing his chest strap. At this point the leg straps were the only thing holding him in place, and he grasped a canvas parachute riser like his life depended on it—it very much did, or at the very least his bone integrity. Then, holding tight, he used the other hand to activate his leg strap ejector snaps.

Worthy had wanted to freefall into the Congo, and he got his wish in the worst possible way now, dropping to full arm extension by his death grip on the riser before managing to take hold with the opposite hand. Now his upper body strength was the only thing keeping him from joining his gear somewhere below at maximum velocity, and he swept a boot across the suspension lines before cinching them in place with the opposite sole, forming a bite by which to control his descent.

Then, after testing his stability, he began to lower himself in a hand-under-hand slide that became tenuous the moment his palms cleared the canvas risers.

Official military doctrine for this sort of thing was remarkably brief: "climb down the outside of the reserve parachute." In reality he had to negotiate the suspension lines before getting to his reserve in the first place, and that proved much easier in theory than in practice. Those lines formed a tight bundle much narrower than a rope, and unlike a rope they were Teflon coated, which meant they may as well have been greased with cooking oil.

The only thing keeping Worthy from turning into a flesh missile was the friction created by his boots securing the lines, and even that was a dubious achievement given that gravity was playing a far greater role than he'd anticipated. He shifted his hands in ever faster movements until he surrendered to the process and glided downward, catching himself only when his feet reached the first billows of his inverted parachute.

After that he traded insecurity for indignity, making a controlled descent down the reserve canopy while low-porosity ripstop nylon parachute cloth swept across his face—less of an issue than it should have been, since he couldn't see a goddamned thing out here anyway. Ultimately, he felt his boots lose their purchase altogether.

Now his arms were the only thing keeping him in place, and he continued lowering himself until there was no parachute left to grab. Still his feet dangled free as he held himself by a dead hang, taking panting breaths as he reached acceptance with his situation.

Worthy had no idea how high he was off the ground, only that his fifteen-foot lowering line had been insufficient to span the distance, as had somewhere around two seconds of drop time after he'd jettisoned his equipment. The total length of his extended reserve parachute was unknown to him, as were any particulars of what awaited below. Leopards? Hyenas? Enemy fighters? Jagged rocks? All he heard was the pounding chants of insects and frogs, and he may as well close his eyes at this point because everything around him was a total blackout.

"Fuck it," Worthy muttered, and took the only action available to him.

He let go.

For the second time that night he went into freefall, once more assuming the position for landing with his feet and knees together, knees slightly bent, chin tucked, and forearms in front of his face. His stomach lurched with the sudden drop, a sickening feeling that brought with it the certainty that whatever his landing surface, it wasn't going to be a conveniently located pile of leaves.

On a daylight jump in calm winds, the five points of body contact elapsed in neat succession: balls of the feet, then sides of the calf, thigh, hip, and back, and Worthy threw himself sideways to distribute landing shock.

But tonight there were only three points of contact—*feet knees face*—and they all impacted in a near-simultaneous sequence that left him belly down atop a thorny plant that had been flattened under his weight. The wind was knocked out of him in an extended vacuous hiss, and he rolled to his side while pawing beneath his shirt collar.

Ideally he'd have a rifle close at hand, but that had been lost along with his tactical vest and radio when he'd cut away his weapon case. Only his night vision remained on his person, hanging from his neck on a lanyard and ensconced in bubble wrap beneath his civilian hiking shirt. Until he put that device into operation, he couldn't locate his equipment, and until he located his equipment, he couldn't radio to his teammates, or at least whoever among them had made the jump much less landed intact.

Then there was the issue of defending himself, which seemed to come second to the sheer necessity for air.

Worthy took hollow, sucking breaths as he yanked the bulge of bubble wrap free from beneath his shirt, feeling for the quick release tab of packing tape and pulling it apart. He extracted his night vision device, turning it on and bringing it to his eyes to take in his first glimpse of the fabled Congo from ground level. It turned out to be an underwhelming sight, because all he could see were leaves shrink-wrapping his view in all directions.

With a grunt he forced himself to sit upright, then to stand. Peering over thick vegetation, he made a 360-degree scan only to find monumental tree trunks rising skyward in all directions, crisscrossed by vines all the way to a black canopy high overhead. This was a jungle labyrinth, he realized, and one in which he was and would remain completely alone until he extracted himself from what was now a survival situation.

Or, he thought, until some bloodthirsty militia or another surrounded him and closed in for the kill—in the Democratic Republic of Congo, there was no shortage to choose from. After an aircraft shootdown, anything was possible. He may well be surrounded already and not yet know it.

Worthy looked down, expecting to find his equipment nearby and instead seeing only a tangle of brush in all directions. His pack and weapons case could have been one meter away or ten: there was no way to tell amid the undergrowth, and he probably wouldn't locate anything out here until he tripped over it.

Mosquitos descended on him then, an angry storm cloud that he swatted away. Bug repellant hadn't been high on the list of priorities when they were gearing up for a combat jump into DRC, and he sought to rectify that at the soonest possible opportunity.

First he had to find his gear, but where the hell was it?

Worthy's approach to the problem set was to identify a known point and begin walking outward and back in until he'd completed a tight cloverleaf pattern. He was starting to regain his breath now, and looked upward to find his inverted parachute suspended from the jungle canopy. This was the obvious starting point, the only notable feature amid this prehistoric landscape, and yet, visible as it was from his current position, he could easily lose sight of the landmark if he drifted too far.

So Worthy saved his location on his GPS before daring to venture out on foot, starting with a second cloverleaf maneuver and increasing his radius with each repetition as he fought his way through a snarl of plants, assaulted by mosquitos at every turn.

He was on round three of his ever-widening search before catching a glimpse of his hiking pack and, leaning atop it, his weapons case. Worthy raced toward the gear like a man possessed, as if a single blink could cause it to vanish amid the foliage once more. His thoughts were a racing checklist: put his weapon into operation, don his tactical vest, turn on his radio, and while waiting for it to power on, stuff the earpieces into place before making his first transmission to find out if anyone else had survived.

Cancer slipped through the jungle, sweeping his night vision for threats and finding that the only immediate danger was from insects.

He was well acquainted with the noise of mosquitoes from previous jungle excursions, but their tiny wingbeats were interspersed with a higher-pitched buzz that he assumed to be gnats. After waving a hand in front of his face, he slapped his palm on the back of his neck and made it three more steps before detecting a faint pulsing glow through the trees ahead.

In most settings, an infrared strobe would be a dead giveaway to any enemy with night vision; here in the jungle, however, no one would spot the glow unless they were navigating to a pinpoint location, and the necessity of assembling with all possible haste had taken precedence.

"Angel," Cancer transmitted, "I see your strobe. Coming in now."

"*Come in,*" Ian replied over the team frequency.

The intelligence operative was the middle jumper, making his current location the center point of their formation and obvious rendezvous point.

David and Reilly were already on the way, having confirmed they'd survived landing, which left only Worthy unaccounted for. Now, the remaining four men were about to launch the most under-resourced search-and-rescue mission in the history of the CIA.

Cancer continued moving as he keyed his mic and said hopefully, "Anyone heard from Racegun yet?"

"*Negative,*" Reilly answered.

"*No,*" David replied, "*but I can make out the strobe. Angel, I'm coming in.*"

Given how tightly they'd exited the plane, each man should have landed within 50 or 75 meters of the next, maybe even a hundred, but that meager distance counted for a hell of a lot more in the jungle than it did on the manicured drop zones of their training jumps.

Cancer was the last to exit, and approached Ian on the straightest-line azimuth he could manage without thrashing his way across thorn bushes; the sniper should have run into Reilly along the way, yet had somehow slipped past him without so much as a chance sighting. The jungle at its finest, Cancer thought—they could easily hide out here for a time, but every hour spent doing so would whittle down their effectiveness until they were either discovered by the enemy or degenerated into a *Lord of the Flies* survival situation.

Slipping between a final knot of brush and vines, Cancer found Ian peering over the vegetation from a standing position, his infrared strobe pulsing flashes of light as it dangled from its lanyard on a tree branch.

The intelligence operative shook his head. "Well, that was...fucked up."

Cancer dropped his hiking pack at his feet and turned to pull security in the opposite direction. "That's why you freefall."

"Time to evade?"

"Maybe," Cancer replied warily, "maybe not. Depends on what David saw from the jump door."

He'd been repressing the urge to interrogate his team leader over radio comms, ultimately deciding that each man was better left paying attention to their immediate security until everyone had linked up.

Ian hissed back, "Maybe? *Maybe?* What choice do we have? There's no way we can walk to our linkup point from here."

"No, we can't. But that doesn't mean there's no place to go."

Before Ian could ask the sniper to clarify what he meant, David arrived. Although he was stomping through the underbrush, the whistling, creaking, and croaking of nocturnal life formed a nonstop effect of jungle drums, and Cancer didn't hear the team leader's approach until he was practically on top of them.

David cursed as he peeled a thorny vine from his chest, taking his rifle into one hand to writhe out of his shoulder straps. His hiking pack thumped to the ground before he joined the security perimeter.

"You guys good?" he asked.

"Wonderful," Cancer replied. "Not so sure how Worthy's doing, though."

"Me neither."

"Where did those shots—"

That was as far as he got before Reilly transmitted, "*This is Doc, eyes-on strobe, coming in now.*"

"Come in," Cancer replied, assuring the medic that he wasn't about to get hit by friendly fire. At this point the consideration was more of a formality; the odds of any enemy fighters locating them in the proverbial haystack were slim to none, although the probability would swing violently in the other direction when the sun rose.

Reilly came crashing through the vegetation a moment later, depositing his pack and taking up a position with the muttered greeting, "Well, that sucked."

Cancer began again, "So where did those shots—"

As if to spite him, another transmission cut him off, this one from Worthy.

"*I'm good*," he gasped. "*What's our status?*"

Cancer keyed his mic to answer. "You're the last one to check in. Everyone's consolidating on Ian's position. What took you so long?"

"*Got hung up in a tree, had to climb down my reserve and then find all my shit in the middle of Jurassic Park. Send the grid.*"

Ian pressed a button to illuminate the screen on his wrist-mounted GPS, slowly relaying a ten-digit number so Worthy could enter it into his own device.

"*All right,*" Worthy confirmed, "*I'm 70 meters out, on the way.*"

Cancer asked David for a third time, "Where did those shots come from?"

"The hilltop to our northeast. Airborne Checkpoint Two."

"Triple A?"

"Definitely," David replied, confirming Cancer's assessment that anti-aircraft artillery had shredded their infil bird.

"Oh," Cancer said, relieved. "Good."

Reilly shot back, "*Good? We've got to go after the aircrew, like right-fuck-ing-now.*"

"Sure," Cancer quipped, "you hear the crash? Did anyone?"

When no one answered, he continued, "If we didn't hear it, we ain't walking to it. Besides, the pilots already sent a mayday to the Agency. We haven't, and we're not going to make satellite comms through triple canopy anytime soon. We're in survival mode now, and unless we pull ourselves out of the shit, we're going to die in it."

Ian spoke then, seeming to choose his words carefully.

"We set up evasion corridors for a reason. All we have to do is move along one—it won't be easy, I admit—and make it to an emergency exfil site."

"Where," David pointed out, "we have no idea how long it would take to get picked up, if Chen decides to send anyone at all."

Ian was flabbergasted. "There's no alternative."

"Sure there is. We can still get this mission back on the rails."

"We can," Cancer agreed. "You want to tell them, or should I?"

"Go ahead."

Only David knew what Cancer was about to say. It wasn't lost on anyone that the only two team members with a death wish were the first and second in command, but the remaining three men knew well enough by now that it was precisely that impulse for self-destruction among their leadership that had pulled their small team out of otherwise unsurvivable odds in the past.

Cancer knew that sometimes the only way to turn the tables was to do something so suicidal, so recklessly audacious, that no enemy in their right mind would anticipate it. Under such circumstances it was being overly cautious, not the reverse, that comprised the real danger to their continued existence.

He began, "An anti-aircraft gun can only be moved by vehicle. That means there's a truck with it, and if there's a truck, there's a road. We move to the hilltop, hit the shitheads who shot us down, steal their ride, and haul ass to our linkup."

"And," David added, "we do it before our asset waves off to bump the pickup by 24 hours. That puts the entire mission back on track."

Ian stammered, "That's...I mean, that's crazy."

Cancer slapped a mosquito on his throat, the force of his hand serving to both crush the insect and vent his frustration at having to explain every facet of their circumstances.

"It is crazy, and we better do it fast because as of right now, the bad guys *don't know that we jumped*. That's going to change come daybreak because Worthy's parachute will be visible to any aircraft flying over. We're not walking out of here before someone comes looking and finishes us off, I can promise you that."

He was caught off guard when his earpiece crackled with Worthy's Southern drawl. *"Coming in."*

In the hasty planning effort, Cancer had almost forgotten about the pointman entirely.

"Come in," he transmitted back.

Finally, Ian conceded, "You guys are right. Unless we want to quit now and take our chances on evasion, it's the only way."

Reilly gave a beleaguered sigh.

"Fine," he said. "Fuck it."

The moment of collective acceptance came and went then, soon disturbed by a rustle of leaves as Worthy fought his way through the brush like Bigfoot.

"Hey, guys," Worthy gasped, taking a knee and draping his assault rifle across his lap. "What'd I miss?"

2

Reilly's boots sank into the jungle floor as he fought his way uphill.

The jungle around him was a mix of dark and darker, but his night vision allowed him to keep Ian in view as he followed the intelligence operative up the jungled slope. Cancer was behind him, bringing up the rear as the team moved like a string of awkward, cursing pearls, united in the sole mission of getting up this damn hill.

The air was a cocktail of earth, sweat, and dank humidity against which nature's soundtrack never let up: the chatter of nocturnal animals was broken by the occasional calls of what sounded like a seriously annoyed bird.

"Even the wildlife's having a bad night," he muttered to himself, holding his HK417 in one hand to shift his shoulders and adjust the hiking pack that threatened to send him barreling back the way he'd come.

The abundance of jungle canopy on their satellite imagery obscured the view of any roads leading to the hilltop. Without that key input to their route planning, and eager to avoid any peripheral security surrounding the anti-aircraft artillery position, they'd decided to proceed up the least likely avenue of approach, and therefore the least likely to be defended: the steep side of the hill. The choice was born out of an abundance of caution, the only meaningful deference to the team's safety they'd yet made that night, and very likely the last one before daybreak.

And while the proverbial road less traveled made sense from a tactical perspective, it seriously sucked from a human one. Reilly was drenched in sweat as he lumbered up the slope. On the plus side, there wasn't much need for noise discipline when the jungle itself sounded like a nightclub: any radio communication had to be undertaken at near-conversational volumes just to be heard over the earpieces, a fact made evident when Worthy transmitted in his Georgia drawl a moment later.

"*Heads up: a mamba just took off in the vines to my left.*"

"*Quit fucking around,*" Cancer shot back.

"*I wasn't,*" Worthy clarified. "*Looked like a mamba, eye level.*"

David added his perspective as team leader to the proceedings.

"*Look at the bright side, Cancer,*" he offered, "*sure, there's nothing Doc can do to save you when...I mean if...you get bit. But we can all find out how he does with last rites. Could be entertaining.*"

Reilly keyed his mic. "Here's a sneak preview: 'Don't worry, it's not that bad. You're going to be fine.'"

A beat of silence on the radio, then Ian added solemnly, "*And then you bring the morphine.*"

"Then I bring the morphine," Reilly agreed. He followed Ian left, a sharp pivot that was explained when he saw an exposed rock face to their right, and continued, "Which is arguably preferable to this job. After all the fire-and-brimstone predictions about the world after Erik Weisz, I thought we'd be getting the band back together to go after someone in the Top 5. Instead we train for months and get assigned to Chiju...Chibongo...whatever his name is."

Ian supplied, "*Chijioke Mubenga.*"

"Yeah. Him. We could go from country to country in Africa and kill a Mubenga a day like a warlord Advent calendar, so why is this guy so important that we get sent to take him out?"

"*Welcome back,*" Ian said, "*to the world according to Chen. Just because Weisz is dead doesn't mean that his network isn't up and running. She thinks his man in the Congo was Mubenga, and we already know he's been active on the weapons market and bombing the military and civilians here to hell and back.*"

He's not in the Top 5, but we know from experience that the spokes of the Weisz wheel tend to be connected to each other. And that means a hell of a lot if it was Mubenga's people who took out our bird."

"The CLF isn't supposed to be this far south."

"Well, Kananga Airport doesn't exactly have a history of shootdowns, either."

"And Chen doesn't have a history of being honest with us," Reilly countered. "I think Mubenga's just the first gopher to stick his head out of the ground, and we're the running backs that she's handing 400 carries a year because when we go down, she's got another team to carry on."

Cancer responded impatiently.

"Quit your bitching, both of you. One step at a time, assholes. We're in the middle of the only plan we've got, and if it works out, we're done walking for the night."

Reilly reached for his transmit switch to respond—the word *amen* came to mind—when Worthy beat him to the punch.

"I can see the clearing ahead."

The news came as revelation to Reilly, who half-expected the climb to last forever. From his position near the formation's trail, he'd barely sensed the ground beginning to level out.

"Halt movement," David said. *"Last three, consolidate on my position to drop rucks."*

It was an order with which they were all too willing to comply. Ian, Reilly, and Cancer advanced until they'd converged with the team leader, taking turns to pull security and strip off their hiking packs before forming a tight standing perimeter to see over the undergrowth.

Once that was complete, David transmitted, *"Racegun, I'm coming forward."*

He slipped through the brush then, leaving Reilly to watch a motionless expanse of jungle; the medic knew that any approaching enemy would have to close within a few meters before being spotted. And here he would remain for some time, he thought, before Worthy and David got eyes-on the objective. The anti-aircraft gun had been employed with devastating effectiveness against a blacked-out bird: at least some of the fighters ahead had night vision, which necessitated a delicate advance to say the least.

But David transmitted again within ninety seconds of departing the formation, and in a seemingly impossible stroke of good fortune, he conveyed the sight ahead.

"*It's a small objective,*" he began, "*and there's a truck on the far side, thank God. Dirt road running north to south. Triple-A piece is at the center of the clearing. Four enemies with small arms that we can see. These guys are B team at best, looks like they're at a campout—there's a fire burning, tarps strung up as living quarters.*"

And that, Reilly thought, was another strike against Mubenga's purported importance according to Chen. If his Congolese Liberation Front really had been the ones to open fire on an ostensibly civilian plane, their anti-aircraft team should have been considerably more professional.

Not to mention dangerous.

Cancer said, "*I don't care if they're crocheting mittens and drinking cocoa. They just took out a bird, and the real pipe hitters might be on the way to break down the position and pull them out. We need to get this over with, fast.*"

"*Couldn't agree more. Our packs can stay where they're at. Cancer and Doc, move forward to establish overwatch. Angel, stay in position. Me and Racegun will swing back to get you, then we're flanking left for the assault.*"

"Moving," Cancer replied, cueing Reilly to take the lead in following the path David had taken two minutes ago. Moving without a rucksack on an increasingly level slope was like gliding on a magic carpet after the uphill slog required to get here.

He caught sight of David and Worthy spaced out ahead, both positioned behind trees, watching a gap in the foliage lit by the blazing glow of a fire. They held their positions until relieved by Reilly and Cancer, the four of them collectively upholding an unspoken combat maxim: once you got eyes-on an objective, you never took them off.

Then the team leader and pointman were gone, returning to Ian as Reilly assessed the clearing and realized they wouldn't have to wait long before initiating their raid.

To say that the objective was small was an understatement. The main gun was a ZU-23, one of the most common anti-aircraft weapons in the world and employed in every combat zone from Chechnya to the Sahara since its creation in the sixties. Its trailer now served as a stationary mount and a man occupied the gunner seat, reclined just above the ground as he scanned the sky with night vision. Twin barrels stood at a 45-degree angle, and if Reilly stood beside them he'd tower over the muzzles—the gun's presence was almost anticlimactic, like finally meeting a celebrity and realizing they're shorter in person.

Next to it was a military pickup that had seen better days, its camouflage paint peeling like a sunburn. Assorted tarps had been strung up haphazardly between spindly trees, serving as makeshift tents. The irony of it all was the security detail, if you could call them that. One man stood lazily by the anti-aircraft gun, grasping the hand mic for a radio on the ground beside him. Another two seemed engrossed in a card game next to the fire, their Kalashnikovs resting within arms' reach but otherwise forgotten.

The scent of woodsmoke meandered through the air, mingling with the earthy aroma of the jungle floor beneath him. Reilly scanned the tarps for any indications of slumbering fighters, unable to distinguish any from the black shadows below. No matter, he thought, because anyone now sleeping wouldn't be for long. The complacency of the slapdash base camp was palpable; whatever these men were expecting, it wasn't a ground attack. A careless laugh floated up from the card players, and Reilly braced himself against the tree to his front to take up a firing position against them. Cancer would take the gunner and his spotter, and after that point it would be a free-for-all of engaging further targets as they appeared, if they appeared at all.

Finally David transmitted, "*Assault element is in position, will need you guys to shift fire right once we move. And for the love of God, nobody hit the truck. Cancer, you have control.*"

"*Five seconds,*" the sniper responded, which was all the coordination they needed. On an objective this small, everyone's lasers would distinguish sectors of fire.

Or at least, that was the official solution.

In truth, the team had been operating as a five-man hivemind for so long that once the bullets started flying, each shooter would react to the actions of another with as much fluidity as fighting men were capable of.

He activated his infrared laser in near-unison with Cancer, each beam of white-green spearing toward the twin pairs of camp occupants. Reilly's laser blurred to the point of becoming indistinguishable with the fringes of the campfire's glow, but at this distance it served its purpose well enough— he depressed his trigger three times to send as many subsonic rounds into flight, causing one of the seated card players to topple over and sending the other scrambling for his rifle.

Reilly adjusted his aim as a new trio of lasers appeared to his left, the beams sweeping and trembling as the assaulters fired their opening salvo. The remaining card player was hit before Reilly could pull his trigger again, and he fired an additional two rounds before sweeping his aim right toward the anti-aircraft cannon. The gunner was still seated though certainly not alive, his arms splayed to either side and his chin on his chest, night vision staring into his lap.

His spotter had fared slightly better, but not by much. The man was still on his feet but just barely, now crouching and leaning forward with a hand on his belly before being lit up by Cancer, Reilly, and at least one man from the assault element all firing simultaneously.

That did the trick, sending the man into a falling faceplant. Reilly swept his rifle in search of additional targets, then conducted a magazine change in sequence with Cancer. Every visible opponent was downed within the opening eight seconds, and David waited several more for any unseen enemy to make themselves known before he transmitted over the team net.

"*Assault, assault, assault.*"

Ian cleared the vegetation, taking his first steps into the hilltop clearing amid the smell of wood smoke cut by the tang of diesel.

It was a simple objective, but nonetheless an extraordinarily dangerous one—the small campfire continued to burn, casting a glow that would subtly illuminate himself and his teammates as they moved perpendicular to Cancer's and Reilly's fields of fire.

Ian glanced left to ensure he was moving on-line with David and Worthy, then swept his rifle across four downed fighters who remained motionless, two beside the fire and two at the anti-aircraft gun. He directed his focus to the tarps ahead, each erected as a shoddy lean-to structure; the pickup truck on the left flank represented an equal or greater risk of harboring the enemy, but that was Worthy's problem to deal with.

There was a flash of movement to his front, a human silhouette appearing out of the trees on the far side of the clearing. Ian took aim and fired repeatedly, instinctively, having triggered his infrared laser without conscious thought.

The man doubled over, then was cut down altogether as David's laser merged with Ian's for two seconds of joint firing. Both lasers extinguished as each man swept their sectors, an effortless choreography born of countless shared repetitions in training and combat, and it was only after the clearance resumed that Ian realized this latest target had probably survived as long as he did because he'd just returned from a bathroom break in the jungle.

By then their collective line was coming alongside the campfire, with Worthy delivering a final headshot to each of the slain men out of an abundance of caution. They swept past the flames before Ian detected a subtle shift in the sloping tarp to his front; someone, he thought, had just noticed the recent silence that had fallen across the camp. Ian drove his aim toward the movement, sparked his infrared laser, and fired a cluster of subsonic rounds through the tarp before the material went slack once more.

Whoever was beneath it was now either dead or wounded, and Ian swept right before crouching to determine which outcome had befallen his most recent opponent of the night.

What he saw made him recoil as if he'd been the one to get shot.

Beneath the tarp was a dead man, or to put it more properly, a dead *boy*, his size indicating an age of ten to twelve. The bullet impacts left no doubt that he'd been killed instantly, one hand locked in a postmortem grip around an AK-47 that looked far too large for him to wield.

Under normal circumstances, Ian would have fired a controlled pair of bullets to ensure he didn't leave behind a wounded man before continuing his clearance. But now it was all he could do to kick the weapon away, turning his eyes from the sight out of a rising nausea as much as tactical necessity. Project Longwing made many demands of its servants, but none greater than this moment. Ian had the flashing thought, *I'm a child killer*.

And yet the emotion that followed his initial horror was a vague sense of relief that it hadn't been Reilly in his position. If it were, the big-hearted medic's lingering trauma would be worse than even Ian's.

Besides, there was no arguing the fact that bullets didn't care about the age of the shooters that fired them, and a child could kill him or a member of his team just as readily as an adult. The intelligence specialist in him clicked into place with a split-second conclusion that the fighters on this hilltop were expendable to the militia they belonged to—the anti-aircraft gunner and spotter were definitely somewhat expendable, but their security was made up of cannon fodder whose loss wouldn't be mourned in the event of a retaliatory airstrike.

Then Ian was moving once more, increasing his footfalls until he'd caught up with the advancing skirmish line of David and Worthy. Any shock Ian felt now faded, folded up and compartmentalized along with the thousand other horrors he'd witnessed as his mind reverted to survival mode amid the many immediate tactical necessities. His two maneuvering teammates could pick up on his sector of fire but not for long, and no sooner had Ian rejoined the advance than David fired into a second tarp before clearing beneath it.

What the team leader found, if anything, remained a mystery. Ian's efforts were consumed with forward security, covering down on David's sector as Worthy did the same on the opposite side. As soon as David rejoined the line, Worthy took a slight diversion to clear the camouflage-painted pickup truck, climbing into the bed and scanning the cab through the rear window without firing before leaping down.

All three teammates then advanced on the anti-aircraft cannon that had gunned down their plane. Its relatively modest size belied its lethality. The twin-barreled autocannon could send its 23mm rounds screaming through the sky up to two and a half kilometers, and a few hours ago it had done just that.

David had the honors of unceremoniously firing a pair of headshots into the downed fighters that had previously been an anti-aircraft spotter and gunner team, while Ian drilled a controlled pair of subsonic rounds into the man at the far side of the clearing.

Their small maneuver element had barely cleared the triple-A piece when David transmitted.

"*LOA, LOA.*"

Ian came to a halt and dropped to a knee before executing a tactical reload. David had just announced their limit of advance, which was where the resemblance to a normal raid would end. There would be no repositioning of the support-by-fire element, no searching of enemy bodies; they'd just slaughtered a handful of bad guys within twenty kilometers of their linkup with a local asset, and beating feet away from the scene of the crime took priority over all else.

David continued, "*Angel, kill the fire and help Doc and Cancer with the rucksacks. I'll hotwire the pickup. Racegun, you're on lookout.*"

Worthy rose from his kneeling position and moved out to his left.

He needed no clarification on his assignment as lookout—the assault had required him to move alongside a single muddy road that formed a C, cresting onto the hilltop before vanishing down the slope. It was the only feasible avenue of approach for enemy forces to reinforce the triple-A position, and therefore the one Worthy had to survey in both directions with nothing more than a 5.56mm weapon to his name.

The best tactical vantage point was partially obstructed by a broad mahogany tree trunk, and Worthy scrambled atop its gnarled root structure before checking his lines of visibility. Suddenly the glowing green nuances of trees beyond the road went darker in his night vision, the objective cast into near-total blackout as Ian kicked the campfire to embers. The pickup engine blasted to life seconds later—keys must have been in the ignition, Worthy thought, because no one on their team could hotwire a truck that fast.

But that moment turned out to be the high point of their good fortune.

The echo of the truck starting hadn't yet faded before Worthy spotted headlights to his right, their glow brightening as the yet-unseen vehicle moved uphill.

"Vehicle inbound from the south," he transmitted, then made a split-second judgment from the shifting dapples of white light and continued, "make that multiple vehicles."

The timing couldn't have been much shittier.

His team was as dispersed as they possibly could be, with Worthy near the road, David in the pickup, and the remaining three men occupied with moving everyone's equipment out of the jungle and toward their newly acquired getaway vehicle. Worse still, they were about to be caught at the site of slaughter for a half-dozen or so militiamen; even if they faded into the jungle, they'd be fleeing immediate pursuit and, therefore, in even worse shape than their emergency bailout from the plane had left them.

Worthy turned to retreat, instinctively looking for the best available position of cover and concealment behind him. What he saw made him simultaneously relieved and chagrined that he hadn't thought of it in the first place. He began sprinting and transmitted the only explanation required given the circumstances, preempting any decision from his team leader.

"You guys load up, I'll hold them off."

"*Copy,*" David replied, and a moment later the newly stolen pickup truck flew backward, rumbling over the remains of the campfire and at least one of the dead enemy fighters as David reversed toward the three teammates now occupied with locating their rucksacks and carrying them out of the jungle.

Worthy's darting run ended at the ZU-23 anti-aircraft cannon, where his first action was to grab the slain Congolese gunner with both hands before hoisting him sideways and onto the ground beside his dead radioman.

Then he shifted his rifle across his chest and assumed the throne, lowering himself into the gunner seat and glancing over the controls. He'd fired so many foreign weapons during his Agency training that trying to recall his ZU-23 orientation was difficult at best; instead, he relied on the commonalities on this type of Soviet hardware, which, to the USSR's credit, were remarkably straightforward and consistent across models. He reached to his right and pushed a lever to unlock the azimuth controls, then grasped the handles of twin rotary mechanisms for the quickest trial-and-error process of his life.

Spinning the left handle clockwise caused the barrels to elevate, and he quickly reversed the motion to bring his aim down. His right hand cranked the opposite handle and the entire gun rotated on its trailer mount with surprising speed, aligning on the road within seconds.

There was a moment of hesitation as he considered the foot pedals. One served as a brake to prevent recoil from rocking the gun backward and the other was, well, the trigger. He then recalled that this was like a car, though that didn't stop him from cringing as his left boot depressed the corresponding pedal. But the gun remained silent, leaving him to flip a lever and lock his barrels' elevation—or, in this case, lack thereof. With his opposite hand, he grasped the handle that traversed the cannon horizontally.

Worthy completed the process with surprising speed, yet found that it almost hadn't been quick enough. He could see the headlights of the lead vehicle cresting onto the high ground beyond the trees ahead, and caught a glimpse of an additional two trucks following it. He let his right boot sole rest lightly atop the trigger pedal.

Now mere seconds remained before he could open fire, leaving him just enough time to second-guess his entire plan.

He could only assume that the gun was loaded, based on its effectiveness against their infil bird and the fact that a gunner had manned it just before the raid. If he was wrong about that—hell, if the gun so much as jammed—then his entire team would have to bail on foot down the same hill they'd just spent considerable effort climbing. As the most exposed shooter among them, Worthy may or may not even make it that far.

But his team was now a cornered animal; they would either succeed with a Hail Mary play right here and right now, or face certain annihilation whether now or later.

And with that grim thought, the lead vehicle's headlights crossed Worthy's line of sight. He floored the pedal beneath his right foot, and everything happened quickly after that.

The gunner seat became a horizontal jackhammer, his vision erased completely by the dual muzzle flashes whose belching output merged into one glorious column of flame. A blast of scalding heat and choking gunpowder whipped across Worthy's face, and the decibel cutoff in his radio earpieces could only do so much to mute the tremendous shattering blasts before he ended his brief initial burst of fire.

When the twin muzzle blasts receded, his only indication of accuracy or lack thereof was that the lead truck had transformed into a cloud of smoke, though how much of that smoke was vehicular and how much incinerated bark and leaf litter from the jungle on the far side, he couldn't say. Worthy was already spinning his right hand slightly clockwise, cranking the azimuth lever to sweep the barrels to the right in an attempt to finish off the convoy before its occupants could react.

The second truck had braked to a stop, its headlights awash with a dark cloud from his engagement with the first vehicle. But the third truck, he saw, was already beginning to reverse out of the kill zone.

He gave the handle another quarter turn to align his gun with the retreating vehicle before tapping the right pedal once more. This time he was actively dreading the effects, although they were considerably better than the alternative of dying out here; once more the shrieking blasts sounded and his internal organs were rattling inside his ribcage as the gunner seat rocked him six times per second, once for every set of bullets passing through the twin barrels.

Worthy ended his second burst quickly, needing the lull in gunfire to see whether he'd actually hit the damn thing. And this time, the briefest glimpse of truck chassis was about the only indication a vehicle had been there at all—the entire thing rolled down the far side of the hill and into oblivion, either due to his rounds, the driver's hasty overcorrection while reversing, or some combination of both.

Spinning the azimuth lever counterclockwise, he leveled his barrels on the center vehicle with the expectation that its driver would be trying to accelerate or back up to clear the kill zone.

To his surprise, however, the truck was just *sitting* there, an inexplicably stationary target until Worthy dimly registered the flickering of muzzle flashes behind the headlights. The pops of incoming fire seemed absurdly inconsequential against the echo of his ZU-23 blasts, though any or all of his teammates could have been hit already, and if not, it would only take one bullet to turn Worthy himself into the second man to die in this gunner seat tonight.

Staving off either possibility came with the application of a few pounds of pressure against the foot pedal, and this time Worthy didn't satisfy himself with the discretion of his first two salvos.

Instead he kept the anti-aircraft gun firing, now confident in his accuracy at this short distance and determined to wipe every remaining fighter off the face of the map with 23mm rounds. The gunpowder grew so thick that breathing became impossible; so too, it seemed, was keeping his body from becoming much more than a rag doll in the jostling grip of seismic recoil. When he at last lifted his boot from the trigger pedal, it wasn't because he was holding his breath or pinching his eyes shut against the stench of gunpowder and oil—the mighty piece of Soviet-era nostalgia that was the ZU-23 had taken its last breath, both ammo cans going empty amid the clattering pelt of shells falling against the trailer below.

He peered left of the main gun sight to evaluate the effectiveness, unable to stop himself despite the fact that he should have been either huddling behind its metallic cover or distancing himself from the cannon before some unlikely survivor popped him in the face.

Beneath the billowing smoke, he could make out glimpses of a horrifically contorted truck frame between the trees, the view obscured by a branch that came crashing down. The lead vehicle was now a metallic heap, and where the third one had ended up was anyone's guess.

And yet, inexplicably, he heard the revving of a truck engine operating in full form. He barely had time to turn his head before the stolen pickup screeched to a halt beside him, its passenger window rolled down to reveal the upper receiver of Cancer's HK417 leveled at the remains of the enemy convoy.

Worthy pushed himself out of the gunner seat and tried to stand, then stumbled as a tingling numbness took hold of his limbs. It was all he could do to keep a hand on his HK416 while staggering toward the rear tire, bracing a boot on top of it as he tried to pull himself over the side and into the bed.

But that was all he needed to do. Reilly's hands were suddenly upon him, and the big medic hoisted him up with ease before Worthy found his legs scraping over the edge. Then he was deposited into a heap beside Ian, who had his rifle aimed over the cab; it was the last thing Worthy saw before the truck lurched into motion, speeding toward the road ahead and wheeling a left turn toward the north, away from whatever remained of the three vehicles that, minutes earlier, had threatened to kill them all.

Cancer retracted his HK417 from the passenger window frame, settling the suppressor between his boots and trying to steady himself against the pick-up's sudden acceleration.

"Well, that worked. ZU-23 turned that convoy into a fuckin' yard sale—"

"Hurry up," David snapped, rolling the steering wheel to keep a vehicle without the benefit of headlights from veering into the trees. "I'm flying blind here."

"Yeah, yeah," Cancer said, checking the screen of his encrypted phone and feeling devastated by what he found.

The old logging roads in Sankuru Province had been abandoned long enough for the jungle to re-stake its claim, which, in the immediate tactical sense, meant dodging branches that may or may not shatter the wind-shield. But in the navigational sense, it meant not only that their current back road wasn't visible on the CIA's satellite imagery, but that there was also no consistent GPS signal.

He turned to face the open window beside him and shouted to the men in the truck bed, "Signal?"

There was a brief chorus of replies in the negative, and Cancer glanced at his phone once more to confirm the nearest visible route, a two-lane dirt road south of the hilltop. If they could reach that, they could effectively navigate all the way to their linkup point, and if luck was on their side, they could do so before their asset departed.

"We need to get pointed south in a hurry. Take the first left you see."

"All right," David said. "You see that hood ornament?"

Cancer glanced out the windshield, seeing a blurry object at the end of the hood. "What is it?"

"Gorilla. Badass. I'm clipping it if we live."

The truck was plummeting downhill now, their path from the triple-A position winding on an ever-downward trajectory.

Cancer put his encrypted phone away, then flipped his night vision upward and turned on the red-lens headlamp around his neck before tilting its beam to illuminate his portion of the cab.

The face of a snarling cartoon leopard glared back at him, its head atop a soccer ball on a badge-shaped sticker affixed to the dash. And since that wasn't weird enough, he thought, a string of dried chili peppers was suspended from the rearview mirror, bouncing wildly with every bump in the road.

Cancer checked the console beside him, finding nothing more than a crumpled pack of cigarettes atop Congolese franc coins. A glance between his legs revealed that his HK417's suppressor was resting atop a layer of old bullet casings and food wrappers, leaving him to open the glove compartment in the last-ditch hope of finding what he was looking for.

And there, lit by the crimson glow of his headlamp, was paydirt.

"Map," he announced, extracting the paper and unfolding it with delicate reverence. He scanned the topographic lines, following the terrain to locate the hilltop representing an airborne checkpoint before their plane got blown out of the sky. Upon finding it, he muttered a curse—the map bore no hand-drawn markings whatsoever and certainly no roads that hadn't been visible on satellite imagery.

Cancer crumpled the map into a ball between his hands, dropped it onto the floor, and angrily pulled his night vision device back down over his eyes.

David quipped, "So it'll be a guessing game, then?"

"Pretty much," Cancer admitted, extracting a handheld compass from his kit and flipping it open. The accuracy of such things was dubious inside a vehicle cab, where electrical systems, to say nothing of the metallic frame, could present magnetic interference. But until one of his teammates in the truck bed acquired a GPS signal, assessing direction along with time traveled was his only option.

He held the compass close to his chest to glance at the display without moving his night vision device, then spoke without enthusiasm.

"We're veering northwest. Better than north, but still not south."

"Yep," David agreed. "How much longer in our linkup window?"

Activating the button to illuminate his watch face took Cancer three attempts—the pickup's suspension had given up on life long ago, and every divot in the road turned the chassis into a mechanical bull. Finally, he said, "Fifty-seven minutes."

"Are we going to make it?"

Cancer replied, "We could make it with time to spare or miss it by hours —depends on what the roads do. You realize I'm going off cardinal directions here, right?"

"I'm not asking about the roads," David clarified. "I'm asking about your intuition."

"In that case, I'm not sure."

"If you can dredge up any false optimism, feel free to lie to me."

Cancer kept his gaze out the windshield, looking for any break in the foliage that would indicate their next intersection, as he replied.

"Optimism ain't my specialty. But within a few minutes we'll know if we're going to make our linkup or not, and that's the next decision point. If we can't get there in time, bringing this pickup any closer isn't worth the risk of compromise. You know what that means?"

David nodded. "Three-step contingency plan."

"Uh-huh. Ditch the truck before dawn—"

"Go feral—"

"—and make the Bataan Death March toward our linkup site."

"Without getting killed...guess that's a fourth step."

Cancer gave an affirmative grunt. "Hard to overstate the importance of that last one, so yeah. Four steps. And hope to God that our asset remembers to repeat the linkup process like he's supposed to."

"Is that a fifth?"

"Step 4a, maybe. No need to overcomplicate—left, *LEFT!*"

Reilly nearly flew out of the pickup bed as the truck braked sharply and careened sideways, his standing position maintained only at the full flexion of an arm clinging to the cab.

David rolled back on the gas before the rear end had completed its fishtailing slide, and the tires regained traction in time to send the pickup flying down a side road that had barely been visible until the last second.

Reilly scanned for targets, ascertaining from the thumps behind him that Ian or Worthy or both had just been laid out by the speed of the turn. Until they could reacquaint themselves with gravity well enough to take aim again, he was the only one who could spot and react to threats.

But the dirt road extended 40 meters through the jungle before veering right, the entire length free of visible enemy fighters, much less incoming vehicles. Once that fact became apparent, Reilly shouted, "A little hard to pull security back here when I've got whiplash."

"You're a medic," Cancer boomed. "Grab a neck brace."

Amid the muggy air whipping past his face and tires rumbling over the uneven strip of dirt and mud, Reilly repositioned his HK417 over the cab and called out, "You guys all right?"

"Barely," Ian grunted.

Worthy's response was more composed.

"Yeah," he said, then yelled loud enough for David and Cancer to hear. "We're headed south. Should be a straight shot to the main road."

That victory was short-lived, however; as soon as David steered the pickup around the next curve, the path resumed its southerly azimuth before splitting in a Y-intersection.

Both routes were equally worn, effectively removing any possibility of choosing the road more traveled. They diverged wildly from one another, and Reilly intuitively knew that to choose the wrong one was to miss their linkup entirely. Either could connect to their destination, and either could run off into oblivion; it was a fifty-fifty shot, and no map, compass, or GPS could save them.

David hurtled the old pickup through the intersection and to the left without a second's hesitation.

There followed, however, a shocked and immensely sobering period of utter silence, ending when Worthy resumed, "I had us going due south, how'd you know to go left—"

"We were," David yelled, "and I didn't."

The words, "Got it," were the only response from the pointman, who by doctrine should have been riding shotgun instead of the team sniper. Then again, Reilly thought, the last person who should be driving was the ground force commander. And yet there was David behind the wheel, piloting the vehicle by virtue of the fact that he'd been the one to steal it. Given time to reshuffle their task organization, they would have, but time was one thing among many they simply didn't have at present.

"Trending west?" Reilly asked.

"Definitely," Worthy answered, "and if this connects to the two-lane road we're gunning for, we can haul ass and maybe make our linkup."

"And if not?"

"No chance," Ian confided. "We'll have to turn around, take the other fork in the road, and get as far as we can by twilight. Once that happens, we better be with our local asset or hiding in the jungle."

Reilly braced himself as the pickup bucked over a bump in the road. "We all know the jungle's not big enough to hide five guys after Worthy's little murder spree at their triple-A site."

Ian added, "Or once they spot his parachute in the treetops."

"Guy's been nothing but a pain in the ass this whole mission." Then he added, "Didn't the cavalry at that hilltop seem a little insufficient for the CLF?"

Worthy sounded pissed.

"It didn't *feel* insufficient."

But Ian took a more pragmatic approach, speaking quickly over the whipping air. "Doc, you're right—could be there's something Chen's not telling us, or it could be there's something she's not aware of. Something doesn't add up, I just don't know what it is."

"Due west," Worthy yelled. "If that doesn't change in thirty seconds, we'll have to flip a bitch."

Reilly added, "And the great and mighty David would have to admit defeat."

Cancer shouted back, "Yeah, well, it won't matter for long because we'll all be dead by sunset anyway."

"Cold consolation," David admitted, "but probably accurate. Ten seconds remaining?"

There was a brief pause before Worthy responded, his instincts as pointman serving as the best guess that anyone on the team could make.

"Fuck it," he said. "Give it another thirty."

Reilly gave a low whistle, holding on as the pickup negotiated a series of curves that didn't change their westerly orientation in the least. "Sun's coming up quick, brother. Truckful of white guys in the DRC isn't going unnoticed after twilight."

"Maybe they don't profile here."

"Pretty sure they do," Reilly noted, studying the winding curves of the road ahead and trying to intuit any future changes of direction by sheer force of will.

But the pickup's creaky frame and rock-hard suspension continued to rattle parallel to the two-lane road they needed to reach; not a problem if they were headed toward their linkup, but the westerly course was taking them in the opposite direction, and that disparity grew with each passing second.

David finally snapped, "That's enough, I'm turning around."

"Ten more seconds," Worthy insisted.

"You already had an extension. If I give you another one, Cancer's going to accuse me of playing favorites..."

His words trailed off as the road drifted right; it was only a slight change toward their desired direction of movement, but the view beyond the curve revealed a patch of sky as the jungle gave way to a small clearing.

David sped toward it, and as he did so, Reilly felt the truck arcing from west to southwest and, gradually, toward the southeast.

As the canopy of treetops receded to clear sky overhead, Cancer shouted preemptively out his window.

"Do we need to stop?"

"Hang on," Worthy replied, yelling over the screams and chants of nocturnal creatures. Then he continued, "I've got the GPS reading—we're a few klicks from the two-lane road, and headed in the right direction."

The team leader was already accelerating as Worthy concluded his announcement with urgent euphoria.

"Go, *go!* Floor it and we might have a chance of making the tail end of our linkup."

3

The sun was nearing its crest on the horizon—not a good thing.

Ian had been pleased to note nothing in the way of incoming traffic from his vantage point in the pickup bed, but daybreak was about to bring the civilians out in full force, and once the bloodbath at the triple-A site was discovered, the militias as well.

Cancer leaned out the open passenger window, shouting to project his voice over the humid morning air whipping past as the truck jostled down the dirt trail.

"One minute out."

The three men had previously been hunched down in the bed to avoid detection by any passersby, and Cancer's announcement caused them to shift into a security posture: Worthy at the driver's side of the bed, and Reilly kneeling at the tailgate to address any threats to their six o'clock.

Ian began to rise as well, catching himself only at the last second to retrieve a foot-long handheld wand from the outside pouch of his rucksack.

He pulled the device free as Cancer asked, "Bonafides?"

"I got it," Ian yelled back, slipping the wand into his tactical vest before assuming his vigil with his rifle in hand, leaning into the pickup's rear window while taking aim over the cab.

Worthy asked, "You sure?"

"Yeah," Ian replied. "I am sure."

The pointman's concern wasn't unwarranted. Doctrinally speaking, confirming a local asset with bonafides was the team leader's job alone, but with David occupied behind the wheel and thus responsible for team egress in the event of a setup, someone had to pick up the reins. And while any of the three men in the back could technically do so, Ian considered himself as close as the team had to a human lie detector.

And besides, he thought, both Worthy and Reilly were better gunslingers than he was, and establishing security at the linkup would be of paramount importance, to say the least.

Provided, of course, that the asset was still waiting for them.

Ian momentarily flicked his eyes from the road to check his watch, seeing that they were now three minutes from the end of their linkup window.

Then he returned to security, gaze sweeping his sector of fire from the empty road ahead to the wall of jungle on his right side, a tangle of moss-strewn tree trunks and emerald vegetation from which a cluster of muzzle flashes could erupt at any moment. At this point, he thought, the exhaustion was almost more mental than physical—his team had gone from aircraft shootdown to offensive raid, then from completely lost to miraculously on course to arrive in the final moments of their linkup window, all in the span of six hours.

Now, the delineating factor between success or failure hinged primarily on whether their local asset would wait until the bitter end as instructed, and if so, whether or not his wristwatch was running a few minutes fast.

Ian glimpsed a flash of white beyond a bend in the road, zeroed in on it to see the panel of a stationary 4x4 Mercedes Sprinter van bearing a red Vodacom logo. The vehicle faced away from them, angled to reveal a raised hood. Beside it stood a tall Congolese man in an incongruous scarlet company polo. He was easy enough to recognize at a glance from the photographs in his dossier.

The pictures, however, had done nothing to convey the unflinching confidence that Ian observed now—the asset had been expecting a single American in civilian clothes to emerge from the undergrowth, exchanging bonafides before calling the rest of the team forward.

Instead he was witnessing the last-minute arrival of a speeding truck full of armed marauders cannonballing toward him, the spectacle providing precious little assurance that he wasn't about to get shot in the face...and still his jaw was set, eyes broadcasting a preternatural sense of calculated calm.

David braked the truck to a stop five meters from the van; they were fully committed now. The only assurance that they hadn't stumbled into a trap was the lack of incoming gunfire, a dubious comfort that could vanish at any second.

Everything after that point was unscripted, automatic; Ian *knew* that Worthy would leap out and sweep the left flank and Cancer the right, *knew* that Reilly would secure the rear while David remained in the idling pickup to exfil his men, shield them from incoming gunfire, or run over enemy combatants as the situation warranted. And all these things occurred just as he anticipated, all while Ian's own actions likewise occurred without much, if any, conscious thought.

He bailed off the left side of the truck bed a moment after Worthy, who had already made landfall and was now advancing along the trees to ferret out any hidden fighters.

Ian's boots impacted in a slick of mud and he advanced while orienting his suppressed HK416 at the Congolese driver, who kept his hands visible while nonetheless regarding the scene before him with a cool and discerning gaze that shifted into a rueful grin at the sheer ridiculousness of the team's arrival.

The proper use of bonafides was one word as challenge and one as password, both concealed within a nondescript sentence of the partici- pants' choosing...but the team leaping out of the pickup to seize the van at gunpoint removed the need for discretion.

"Mechanic," Ian said.

The man before him responded in a deep, authoritative timbre, his words colored by a subtle Swahili inflection.

"Lukonga."

He then extended his arms for the inevitable search, doing so not as a panicked gesture but rather with casual aplomb, as if allowing a tailor to help him into a bespoke dinner jacket.

Cancer had posted himself on security by the time Ian arrived, and the intelligence operative swept his detection wand over the Congolese driver's extended arms and body—ostensibly to search for weapons, but in reality sweeping for location transmission devices. Then Ian began his questioning.

"Were you followed?"

"No."

"Any threats in the area?"

"Only militias to the north."

Fuckin' A, Ian thought. "What about on our route to the safehouse?"

"Nothing that I know of. It should be clear."

Ian completed his sweep and replaced the wand in his kit to assume a two-handed grip on his rifle. "Open the rear doors and show me what's inside."

The driver didn't hesitate to comply, striding to the back of his vehicle with an urgency that seemed more out of concern for the team's safety than his own. He'd scarcely swung open the twin rear doors of the Sprinter van, allowing Ian the briefest glimpse at a cavernous cargo space, before the engine of the stolen pickup revved and grew in volume at a breakneck pace.

David whipped the truck into a perpendicular turn just shy of the van, blocking the road from any pursuit from the rear and killing the engine.

"Wait here," Ian said as his team leader leapt out to assume positive control of their local asset—but not, he observed with contempt, before breaking a silver hood ornament off the stolen truck and stuffing it into his dump pouch.

Leaping into the back of the van, Ian swept the ceiling for radio frequency emissions that would indicate a device broadcasting their location with or without the driver's knowledge. When he found none, he exited in time to avoid being struck by the hiking packs that Worthy and Reilly were transferring from the pickup to the van as rapidly as possible. Ian hastened to run his wand over the driver's seat, console, and open engine bay before slamming the hood and proceeding to the passenger side. He swept the remaining exterior surfaces of the Sprinter van, which garishly displayed an arrangement of magnetic signs with the red Vodacom logo.

While the team's previous local assets had ranged wildly in experience when it came to transporting CIA elements, Azibo Okoye had a lengthy track record backed by what was quite possibly the best imaginable cover as a telecommunications consultant for the largest mobile service in the DRC. Conducting surveys to establish telecom services in remote areas was his literal day job, and brought with it both a service vehicle and a viable reason to travel almost anywhere he pleased without drawing undue suspicion: even Congolese militias needed cell phone connectivity to effectively operate, and would no sooner harass a Vodacom van than a Stateside gang would interfere with an internet service vehicle making its rounds.

Ian completed his exterior sweep without detecting the slightest hint of radio frequency emissions or satellite communication beacons, a positive development that seemed to have been a foregone conclusion to David. The team leader was already loading himself into the passenger seat, while Cancer stood near the rear bumper as the final dismounted security. Threading his way past the sniper, Ian clambered once more into the rear and negotiated a path between Worthy and Reilly, both positioned near the back, and the hiking packs now heaped atop the floor.

His crouched movement ended at the folded partition between storage area and cab. Ian knelt and slid it open to reveal Azibo keying the van to life. Then the cargo doors slammed and Cancer called out, "Go."

The only delay in compliance was the momentary shift to put the van into drive, at which point Azibo pressed the accelerator and wheeled onto the road to begin their escape. There was a rustle of men and equipment as the team shifted into their typical configuration for a vehicle piloted by a local asset.

Ian didn't need to look behind him to know that Reilly was positioning himself at the rear driver's-side corner with Cancer beside him, and Worthy at the opposite corner. The slots for dealing with an enemy checkpoint and/or roadblock had been established long ago and tested on multiple occasions since then, and while Ian would flow behind Worthy in the event of an emergency dismount, his role at present was far less auspicious—he waited as David stripped off his tactical vest, then accepted the team leader's kit and rifle before positioning them behind the open partition.

"If we get stopped," David said to the driver, "I'm a lost adventure tourist you found on the side of the road. Leave the engine running and tell them whatever you have to so they let us pass."

Azibo nodded without speaking, and David continued, "They tell either of us to step outside the van, or to see what's in the back, negotiate a bribe and I'll pay it. If they don't go for the bribe, I want you to keep your head against the seat because I'm going to shoot through the driver's window while my guys jump out to eliminate the threat. Get your head down, keep your foot on the brake, and wait for my guidance to move. Okay?"

"I understand," Azibo replied, giving no indication that he was either uncomfortable with the instructions or surprised to hear them. It was a refreshing change of pace, Ian thought, to be working with an experienced local asset.

He felt a dense object tap against his shoulder, and he looked back to see Cancer offering a Glock 19 in a Kydex holster. Ian passed the item to David in the passenger seat, then repeated the process for a duo of sheathed pistol magazines with a belt clip.

David lifted his shirt tails and was in the process of tucking the Glock inside his waistband as he probed for whether or not Azibo had detected the plane crash. "Did you hear anything unusual while you were waiting for us?"

"No."

"Nothing at all?"

Azibo glanced from the windshield to David, then back again.

"You have been in this jungle at night. What else could I hear?"

Ian offered, "FM."

"Turn on the radio," David instructed him. "I want any local news for the area, anything related to our infiltration."

The driver complied, filling the cab with the voice of a woman speaking in the Tshiluba language. Until they could stop to establish encrypted satellite communications with Meiling Chen at the Project Longwing operations center, open-source news was their best chance of garnering information. In a nation with as many remote areas as the DRC, FM radio was the single most important means of communication, and news traveled fast here. The only question was whether an initial report of the crash had yet made it out.

Azibo flicked through radio stations, stopping when he landed on one without a song or advertisement. Two broadcasters were speaking in rapid-fire French.

"Anything?" David asked.

"Football scores."

"Keep going through the stations. Tell me anything out of the ordinary."

The only delay in compliance was Azibo wheeling the van through an intersection on the dirt road, after which he continued checking stations. David turned to face the rear and spoke one word.

"Angel?"

Ian didn't need any further clarification.

Now that the team's immediate safety was achieved, concern shifted to the fate of the remaining four Americans currently unaccounted for: the airborne safety, loadmaster, and two pilots who'd gone down when their L-410 Turbolet had been shot out of the sky.

To say that the matter was a delicate one would be an understatement.

If any of the aircrew had survived long enough to flee the crash site and begin evasion, then Ian's team was their only hope of extraction. If all four had been killed, however, any attempt to recover their bodies from wreckage that had surely been surrounded by militias would accomplish little more than adding his own team to the list of American dead in the botched infiltration.

Complicating matters was the fact that they didn't know where the crash site *was*. And while the vector between the shootdown point and Kananga Airport would give some indication, it nonetheless covered a considerable swath of jungle before ceding its grasp to increasingly urban terrain.

But the team knew the pre-established evasion corridors that any survivors would use, namely because they shared the same ones.

"We need to get tucked in first," Ian said, referencing their upcoming entry, clearance, and occupation of the safehouse. "You check in with higher, and—"

"And if she doesn't let us go for it?" David interrupted.

A fair inquiry, Ian thought, and one that had been burning through his mind.

Meiling Chen had a single-minded focus on the team's primary mission, in this case the targeted killing of Chijioke Mubenga. Whether the aircrew's situation would factor into her decision-making process was up for debate; many operational CIA officers within the Special Activities Center were definitionally unattributable, though no one seemed as keen to accept that as Chen herself. She had a hard-earned reputation for hanging her operators out to dry, which the team had verified firsthand on their last mission to Yemen. Even if Chen knew the location of the crash site, whether there were any survivors and, if so, where they were currently at, that didn't mean she would transmit any of that information, much less authorize the team to go after them.

Which was fine with Ian, so long as another CIA or military element could reach them first. But knowing Chen, that probably wouldn't be the case.

He replied, "I'll be able to cross-reference the intel reports with any beacon pings. Might be able to get enough information for a decision point on which corridor to commit to."

David paused, then spoke just loud enough for everyone in the back to hear him as well.

"Once we get to the safehouse," he began, "we're going to do a hasty refit."

Then, staring fixedly at Azibo, he continued, "And I'll need you ready to take us back out for an immediate follow-on operation."

4

Reilly threw open the front door of the house, stepping aside as Worthy raised his rifle and broke left before disappearing inside.

I was second in the stack, flowing in behind him and cutting right to clear my first corner. The foyer was unassuming, covered by a worn mat in bright and clashing colors that I slipped across while transitioning the aim of my rifle to an open doorway ahead. Beyond it was a living room that I visually cleared as much as I could while on the move, halting beside it amid the sound of footsteps going silent.

My peripheral vision registered the shapes of Worthy and Cancer coming to a stop before a doorway on the opposite wall of the foyer. A hand alighted on my shoulder and gave a light squeeze before I slipped inside the living room, clearing my first corner and moving toward it while twisting my upper body to collapse my sector.

Reilly performed a simultaneous mirror image of my actions on the other side of the room, our barrels sweeping over wooden chairs and an overstuffed sofa against walls adorned with abstract local art that I only vaguely registered. My focus was on identifying human threats or, barring that, potential hiding places for the same, and it took mere seconds to rule out both as I aligned my suppressor with a closed metal door.

I'd barely reached it before Reilly arrived on the opposite side, dipping his barrel and giving me a nod. Testing the handle to find it unlocked, I flung the door open and paused until Reilly was halfway through the doorway before closing with his backside.

We button-hooked in near succession, him right and me left. I made it exactly one step toward the next corner when a door to my front swung inward and a man entered with surreal speed. I lowered my rifle upon seeing it was Worthy.

Cancer and Reilly were already at the far corners, and all four of us took in the same sight.

Crudely assembled bench seating faced a row of plywood desks, the latter adorned with a few serviceable computers and lined with a tangled mess of charging cables. A windowless wall held two oversized posters of the DRC, the first a political map highlighting roads, cities, and provincial boundaries. The second was a satellite image presenting at a glance a tactically foreboding nightmare: savannahs and grasslands in the south and west transitioning into dark green, impenetrable rainforests sliced by the carving path of the Congo River before jagged mountains dominated the eastern periphery.

No sooner had I taken in the sight than I noticed Cancer and Worthy moving to my left.

They closed with four ruggedized, extra-large Pelican tough boxes, and set about opening the lids with the thumps of thick plastic clasps.

"Azibo come through?" I asked.

Worthy stepped aside, leaving Cancer to reply.

"And then some."

I approached the open boxes to see the rubber-lined interiors brimming with supplies: civilian clothes, camouflage fatigues, satellite communications equipment and encrypted laptops, loaded magazines, demolitions, Glock 19 pistols in holsters, and MP7 submachine guns with suppressors. The gear had been sent in various shipments that Azibo had collected and placed here well ahead of our arrival.

Reilly came to a stop behind me, barely glancing inside.

"How's the kitchen?"

Worthy pointed to the door behind him and said, "See for yourself."

The medic departed then, leaving me to send my first radio transmission since making entry.

"Angel," I began, "we're good here. Coming out."

Moving through the side of the house that I hadn't seen on the way in, I passed three sparsely furnished bedrooms and two bathrooms that appeared minimally functional—I could tell at a glance that the water pressure would be questionable at best. Then I crossed through the kitchen where Reilly stood dumbfounded before an open fridge packed with eggs, milk, deli meat, and the like. The counters were stacked with mangoes, papayas, passion fruit, and bananas that I strolled past on my way to the foyer and then the front door.

I stepped outside beneath an overcast sky whose soft, diffuse light shone on a tree-dotted dirt yard surrounded by a six-foot-tall perimeter fence constructed from ubiquitous local bricks that blocked outside view without screaming "top-secret facility." It was covered in places by climbing plants, and the gate closed above an unpaved driveway where a white Toyota Land Cruiser was parked beside the Vodacom Sprinter van.

Azibo was in the process of exiting from the driver's side. Ian was nowhere to be seen, and I'd almost reached the van before the intelligence operative swung the cargo doors open and stepped out from the back, locking eyes with me with a look of content relief.

"Disappointed?" I asked.

His face soured in response.

"Yeah. Sure. Devastated."

I smiled as he pulled his hiking pack toward the rear bumper, genuinely wondering what went through Ian's head in the minutes it took us to clear the safehouse. His only role during that time was to wait with gun in hand, and if so ordered, to shoot Azibo in the head.

It wasn't anything personal. My team had developed several edicts in our years of working together, one of which was the decree that if one of our local guides ever led us into a trap and death was imminent for us all, then the offending asset would be the first to go. Granted, it wouldn't save us. It would, however, make our final moments at least somewhat gratifying...and since Ian was the least experienced in matters of building clearance, the role of potential executioner fell upon him.

He shouldered his hiking pack and asked, "How'd it look?"

"All the standard safehouse kit is there, everything we shipped is there...he even stocked the fridge."

"Nice."

"Yeah," I agreed. "Too bad we won't be staying."

Ian took the hint and replied without further prompting, "I'll get started on trying to locate the aircrew."

He departed as I located my own hiking pack. Rather than haul it back into the house, I opened the top flap and slid my hand into an interior pouch to retrieve the one thing I was looking for.

A cocktail of military regulations, operational policies, and international law barred the use of forbidden items on a combat mission. A dirty secret of America's military industrial complex was the number of servicemembers who faced UCMJ action when a privately owned pistol was discovered among their deployment bags.

And while I understood the impulse—who didn't want an heirloom to pass down like their grandfather's old 1911 that had presumably killed a few Nazis—I was well past the experience threshold that gave a shit about nostalgia.

But I did have one highly unauthorized item that could land me in solitary confinement if discovered. The CIA was particularly touchy about security leaks stemming from unencrypted and therefore unauthorized communications devices like the Iridium Extreme 9575 Satellite Phone I pulled out of my hiking pack now.

Cancer appeared at my side then, looking first at the phone and then at me.

"Tell him I said hi."

"I will," I muttered, stepping out of his way and thumbing the Iridium's power button.

Cancer recovered his pack and departed just as Worthy arrived, eyes narrowing at the sight of me rotating the phone's satellite antenna upward.

"You calling who I think you're calling?"

"Mm-hmm."

"Think there's any action on his end?"

"Half of me hopes so," I replied, holding the phone at arm's length to check the signal, "and the other half hopes to God not."

He donned his hiking pack, paused for a beat, and then said, "Give him my regards."

"Yep," I replied distractedly, watching the Iridium display as it searched for satellite connections.

By the time Reilly arrived, I was gazing upward, irritated to notice a few tree limbs overhanging the fence of the property.

"Can you take my shit inside? I've got to make a call."

"Yeah," the medic said, "sure. I'll come get you once SATCOM is up."

I was already walking toward a patch of ground with open sky overhead, stopping when the reception spiked enough for me to dial.

"Hey," Reilly called.

"What?"

He bore his hiking pack and mine by single straps over the same shoulder, the otherwise immense load rendered diminutive by virtue of his size.

"Tell him I said what's up."

"Sure." I nodded, then returned my gaze to the Iridium, located the only programmed number, and pressed the call button.

An interminable wait ensued until the call connected at last. I heard what sounded like an infant screeching in the background a half second before a man spoke.

"Yeah?"

"Suicide Actual," I said.

"Talon Actual," the man replied. "You guys all right?"

Brent Griffin was a living personification of all the reasons we couldn't trust Chen.

For one thing, he was the commander of a second Project Longwing team, one whose existence she'd never informed us of. And when his team had gotten captured in Yemen, she'd not only *not* sent us in to rescue him and his men, but ordered us to complete the mission without so much as a word of warning that the last men attempting to do so were incarcerated.

Gradually we learned all of the above, after which it became clear that a) Chen actually lied to us more than we'd lied to her, which was no small feat; b) she'd cut loose an entire Longwing ground team; and c) they were going to die in captivity if we didn't do something.

So we proceeded to execute a spectacularly violent prison break, freeing Griffin's entire team. I'd demanded one and exactly one concession in exchange: namely, that if we were ever in the same country and my men were in trouble, his team would turn their back on their mission, along with God and Country if required, to save our bacon.

And after we used burner phones to set up a communications protocol up to and including undeclared satellite phones with Chen being none the wiser, Griffin stood ready to make good on that promise.

I replied, "We're okay. But she doesn't know that yet, and there's a fair to decent chance that she thinks we're all dead. Any chance your guys got activated?"

"No. And if we haven't gotten spun up yet, I don't think we will."

Shit, I thought, trying to keep my voice level as I mused, "I figured she'd stuff you into the breach like she did with my guys last time. Historical precedent and all that. And we could use the support this time around."

I heard a shrill cry on the other line—definitely one or more kids running around at Griffin's place. When my team went on a mission, he'd erected a portable satellite antenna outside his home with a wire running to his Iridium, and if the time zone difference was any indication, I'd interrupted him trying to put his newborn back to sleep.

"Support?" he asked. "Is the area worse than you thought?"

"Bird had a bad night. We're about to see if we can kick out on recovery."

"Damn. How many in the wind?"

"Four."

Griffin heaved a dismayed sigh, sounding pained as he continued, "I'm sorry to hear that. Wish we were going, but God willing there's someone closer she can send."

"We both know she won't."

"No," he agreed. "Probably not."

Reilly called out behind me, "Hey, boss."

I gave him a thumbs-up to signal that I'd heard him.

"Got to run," I said to Griffin. "Sorry to interrupt your time with the baby."

"She's an insomniac. Probably more peaceful over there than it is in my house right now."

"For sure. I'll fill you in on everything once we get back."

"Stay safe out there."

I almost hung up on him, then brought the phone to my ear once more. "Hey."

"Yeah?" Griffin asked.

"My guys send their regards."

Ending the call, I turned to face Reilly standing in the front doorway of the safehouse, jerking a thumb over his shoulder.

"SATCOM is up," he said. "You should probably check in now."

5

CIA Headquarters
Special Activities Center, Operations Center F2

"Quiet in the OPCEN!"

The chatter of sixteen individuals ceased at once, the collective gaze of everyone in the operations center focusing on the intelligence officer who'd just made the announcement.

Meiling Chen leaned forward, palms flat on her desk at the center of the highest seating tier. The peripheral details of a half-dozen staff sections spread in descending levels facing oversized screens displaying all pertinent mission data faded in her vision as she stared at the back of Andolin Lucios' head.

He didn't look away from his computer screen, his Spanish accent reverberating loudly enough for everyone to hear.

"Report received at 11:02 Central African Time: Chijioke Mubenga received a radio transmission that a CLF anti-aircraft site was attacked at an unspecified location in Sankuru Province. His men are breaking down camp and relocating, and Mubenga is fleeing at this time with his personal security entourage of unknown composition."

Lucios turned in his seat to face Chen. "His destination is Mbuji-Mayi. End report, no further information."

She looked from her intelligence officer to the largest screen in the OPCEN, studying the high-resolution satellite map of the Democratic Republic of the Congo. The digital canvas, devoid of any UAV or aircraft feeds, was marked with the flight path of the L-410 Turbolet terminating at the point it was hit with anti-aircraft fire, ringed by concentric circles representing the maximum estimated movements of the ground team at two-hour intervals.

An inverted teardrop icon appeared over the city in question, the graphic summoned by a member of Lucios' intelligence staff. Mbuji-Mayi was far southeast of the flight path's end, well outside the dark emerald rainforests and almost directly in the center of Kasai-Oriental Province.

Chen asked, "ETA range?"

"Could be as high as eight hours if Mubenga avoids the highways for as long as he can. Given the circumstances, I assess he'll take the quickest route possible. In that case, we're looking at approximately six hours minimum, ma'am."

She narrowed her eyes at the screen, trying to make sense of this news and, given all the information at her disposal, finding herself unable to do so.

After a frustrated breath, she began, "Mubenga's had uncontested reign over the CLF for years now. In that time he set up an anti-aircraft position we didn't know about, opened fire at an Agency plane, and had his entire shootdown team wiped out a few hours later. He knows we've come for him and has no reason to stick his neck out anytime soon. My question is, why go to an urban bed-down site rather than deeper into the jungle?"

Lucios didn't hesitate.

"If he suspects the Agency is behind this—and he has every reason to—then he also knows we're bound by mitigating collateral damage. Disappearing into a population center is his best chance of avoiding a ground assault or a drone strike."

"I suppose that checks out," she admitted, her thoughts turning to the operational picture. "And once he goes underground, he's going to stay underground. Does anyone disagree?"

There was no spoken dissent, though her operations officer swiveled in his chair and began typing at his workstation.

Chen went on, "We all know an interdiction attempt in the meantime is a shot in the dark at best—"

"Particularly," her operations officer added, speaking over his shoulder, "since our team has yet to check in. Even if they make it to the safehouse right now, they'd only beat him into the city by an hour or two. Most likely, they'll be out of the fight completely or, at best, arriving well after Mubenga."

Chen was annoyed both by the interruption and the fact that he routinely dropped the word "ma'am" from his comments to her.

Wes Jamieson had served and served well, first in the Marines and then Ground Branch, and knew damn well he had a longer leash because he was a tactical wizard whose input could either confirm or crush their best-laid assumptions. Everyone else in the OPCEN had blinders on for the sake of their specialty, while Chen was responsible for keeping their collective effort moving in the right direction.

But Jamieson was the only one whose tactical knowledge rivaled that of her ground team.

She conceded, "We're going to prepare for the most time-sensitive possibility. Best-case scenario, they reach the safehouse in time to depart on an interdiction attempt. How can they best accomplish it?"

Jamieson didn't respond at first, instead returning to his computer to take control of the main screen at the front of the OPCEN.

The view of DRC shifted to the satellite imagery of a sprawling cityscape, a dense mosaic of buildings intersected by a web of roads. From this altitude, the city's bustling markets and residential areas were mere specks against the vast backdrop of the Congo's wild landscape.

"At first glance," Jamieson said, "it's a no-go. Mbuji-Mayi city is fifty square miles with a population of three million."

Then he zoomed in on the city, its gridded network suddenly brought into stark clarity and, she noted as he directed a laser pointer from the upper left to lower right, bisected by a pronounced highway.

Jamieson continued, "But there's only one main route running through it: National Road Number 1. The odds of Mubenga using NR1 to enter the western edge of the city are close to a hundred percent because any attempt to use local roads will increase his travel time considerably. So tactically, the team's only got one option."

"Which is?" she asked impatiently.

"A hasty low-visibility operation. Civilian clothes, weapons hidden, and blending in to local traffic to the full extent they can. They have a pair of vehicles at their disposal, so they can split into two elements. The first has to stake out the highway at the western edge of the city—if we're lucky, we'll be able to establish Mubenga's exact destination, get a description of his vehicle, or at a minimum find out his ETA in the time it takes him to make the trip. That would put the team's first element on standby to establish visual contact and follow him in."

"And the second?"

He directed his laser pointer to the city center and drew a tight circle.

"The second element stages further east in Mbuji-Mayi to vector as needed based on intel hits. Depending on how precise that intelligence is, they might be able to intercept him at or prior to the bed-down site. Then it's a surgical kinetic strike at best, or positive identification of Mubenga's final location at worst—provided, obviously, that we get sufficient information in the meantime."

Chen nodded.

"Draft up everything the team will need to execute that, with an emphasis on recommended staging locations. They won't have much time to plan."

"We're on it, ma'am. But at this point I think we should consider forward-staging our second team as a backstop. If Griffin's men assemble now, they could be on a plane within—"

"Out of the question," she cut him off. "One team can win or lose, but the failure of two teams would be a black eye that this program can't afford. Not after Yemen. And my worst nightmare is a Top 5 target popping up while one team is chasing down a lower-priority terrorist. Griffin's team will remain on standby for that eventuality."

Jamieson frowned but nodded nonetheless, turning back to his computer as she addressed the remainder of her staff.

"Switching gears to the worst-case scenario: we get no further intelligence, and Mubenga goes off the grid entirely. The next course of action is authorization to extend our mission to DRC by two weeks at a minimum." She cut her gaze right, zeroing in on an older man with a salt-and-pepper beard and a business suit. "Legal?"

Gregory Pharr rose from his seat, his expression conveying bad news even before he'd said a word. People outside the world of covert operations tended to assume a free-for-all of espionage and assassinations, while those within it knew damn well they were boxed in on all sides by byzantine legal restrictions that could only be reviewed in their entirety much less interpreted by a seasoned Agency lawyer like the one standing before her now.

Pharr began in an unapologetic tone, "Ma'am, I can assure you we won't get a two-week extension if there's no forward movement on terminating Mubenga."

"Mubenga," Chen replied hotly, "is a third-tier target at best who wouldn't have even been on our radar if every other terrorist in our target matrix hadn't vanished after Erik Weisz's death."

"I understand that, ma'am, but—"

"That was six months ago, and we need a victory to secure continued funding in order to survive long enough to go after Weisz's replacements as they emerge. Our higher-priority targets won't stay hidden forever." She omitted the fact that she'd provided the ground team with a significantly overstated version of Mubenga's importance, siding instead with the words, "And those targets had better start emerging soon, because our exposure is getting worse. If we keep sending in the team on inconsequential missions, eventually there's going to be an article in *The New York Times* and Senator Gossweiler will get called on to the carpet. Right or wrong, Pharr?"

Pharr's response was unflinching.

"No contest. I agree with you, ma'am. We're running out of time to wipe out bad actors in the vacuum because the powers that be won't keep this program around until we run out of luck."

Chen relaxed, right up until he began speaking again.

"Now here's the Catch-22. Killing Erik Weisz was a landmark achievement for the Agency, much less Project Longwing...but the seventh floor has a short memory when it comes to continued funding, and we've been at a standstill since March. Everyone in this room knows that all the bad guys are regrouping for international network 2.0.

"But to the strategists and the bean counters, it looks like Project Longwing has run its course while the bulk of US and Allied counterterrorism efforts have succeeded valiantly in keeping terrorism in remission. We can certainly request two weeks in case I'm wrong, but I've been doing this long enough to know what'll come back down the pipe. They'll give us an extension, but not two weeks' worth. Not for a minor player like Mubenga."

She swallowed. "How much?"

"Seventy-two hours at best. At that point they'll cut their losses at a botched infil and a totaled Air Department plane."

"Which wouldn't have been totaled," she said, "if they'd listened to us in the first place."

Pharr gave her an exasperated look as if her comment was too obvious to reiterate, which it probably was. She'd originally requested a freefall infiltration in alignment with her J3's strongest recommendation, only to find that her superiors felt it preferable to leverage the existing cargo flight schedule rather than launch a dedicated special operations C-17 from Djibouti.

Then Pharr said, "That's exactly right, ma'am. But upper management isn't going to hold themselves accountable when they can—"

"*Raptor Nine One,*" came a crackling voice from the speakerbox, "*this is Suicide Actual.*"

Everyone in the OPCEN froze in unison, and Chen grabbed her hand mic to reply.

"Send your status."

David Rivers continued, "*We just reached the safehouse. All men, weapons, and equipment accounted for, we're finishing refit and ready to launch on CSAR.*"

"CSAR?" she asked, bewildered.

"*Combat search and rescue,*" he clarified. "*We just need to know which evasion corridor they're using, provided there were any survivors.*"

Chen was livid.

"Survivors of *what*?"

David sounded equally incensed when he answered. "*Our infil plane getting blown out of the sky. Aircrew, remember? Two pilots, safety and loadmaster. Did. Any. Of. Them. Survive?"*

"Copy," she said, breathing a relieved sigh. For a moment she thought the team leader had lost his damn mind. "The aircraft didn't crash."

"It didn't?"

"No. The pilots reported your emergency bailout and limped the plane to Kananga Airport on one engine. They touched down without incident. The aircrew is fine, we're already pulling them back to Burundi."

"Well..." David hesitated, a rare moment of indecisiveness punctuating his otherwise fast and furious radio update. *"I feel sheepish."*

Keying her mic, she explained, "We just picked up chatter about an attack against a CLF anti-aircraft site. I'm assuming that was your team?"

"We needed a vehicle," he said matter-of-factly.

"Well in the process of getting one, you spooked Mubenga."

"What do you mean, we 'spooked' him?"

"He just received word of the raid. Now he's fled his hideout along with his security entourage, and is on the move."

"Forgive me for not being surprised," David replied snarkily. *"But he'd still be stationary if you hadn't sent us on a suicidal low-altitude static line jump that nearly got my entire team killed, first by triple-A fire and then bailing out over the goddamned Heart of Darkness—"*

"Suicide," she cut him off.

"What?"

"Shut up."

He went silent then. Chen had a moment of reprieve to remind herself that under no circumstances could she correct him, for the same reason she couldn't pass the blame to her superiors when she originally told David about the static line mandate: because if and when something went wrong, the satellite communications transcript would be scrutinized in its entirety. The CIA didn't take kindly to program directors throwing their institution's higher leadership under the bus, and taking the blame herself was far preferable to what would happen if—or, more likely, when—the hotheaded team leader ran his mouth about Agency leadership over SATCOM.

Keying her mic once more, Chen redirected the exchange to more pressing matters.

"Mubenga is currently headed toward Mbuji-Mayi."

"He's headed in that direction," David asked warily, *"or you're sure it's his destination?"*

"It's his destination, and he'll be traveling on NR1 eastbound to get there. We don't know where he's headed within Mbuji-Mayi, but it's probably an urban bed-down site sufficiently distant from his usual area of operations to wait out what he now knows is a targeted killing attempt."

"Do we have time to tail him?"

"You can beat him into the city if you move now. You'll need to split up in two vehicles, one to wait at the western outskirts and the other positioned deeper to stand by for possible updates on his vehicle and location."

Chen immediately regretted her choice of words, and true to form, David called her out on the disparity.

"'Possible' updates?" David asked. *"If you want us to do this thing, I need his vehicle make and model backstopped by the usual cellular tracking. You've got both, right?"*

She mentally ran through her response before speaking. The last thing she needed to do was divulge any sensitive information to David that could be compromised in the event the team was captured alive.

And at the moment, the Agency's assistance from a human intelligence source in Mubenga's entourage was at the top of that list.

"You'll get all the information on this late-breaking development as soon as I have it. Your current mission is to achieve visual contact and pinpoint his bed-down site without getting made. We've got no assets in the city so if you miss him on arrival, we could lose him altogether. My J3 will send over all the information you need."

"All right." Another pause. *"But five white guys don't exactly blend in here. I need the authority to take him out as soon as we have positive identification."*

If that chance arose, she thought, his point was almost a bygone conclusion. Even if she told him no, he'd likely do it anyway and manufacture some story about self-defense within clearly delineated rules of engagement.

But in this case, her and David's goals were perfectly aligned.

"If you get the shot," she replied, "you'll need to take it."

Chen drew another breath and explained, "Because if we lose Mubenga now, we're not going to get another chance."

6

Worthy peered out the passenger window, taking in the stark contrasts of the Democratic Republic of the Congo as Azibo navigated the Sprinter van along National Road Number 1.

The road, a vital artery cutting through the country, was bustling with a variety of vehicles, from overloaded trucks and rickety buses to a United Nations SUV. Worthy checked his side-view mirror, scanning through the cloud of fine red dust drifting up from the road and catching a glimpse of the Land Cruiser containing Ian, David, and Cancer as it swerved around an ox cart.

"Azibo," Worthy said, "I've got to say that your reputation preceded you. Still, I can't thank you enough for waiting at the linkup point until we made it to you."

The driver's face was expressionless, one powerful arm draped across the console as he steered with the opposite hand.

"It was my job to wait."

Silence ensued as the landscape rolled past, a panorama of verdant green interrupted by patches of cultivation and small villages. Worthy noticed the vibrancy of the roadside markets, where locals sold everything from fresh fruits to handmade crafts. Women in colorful wraparound garments carried baskets on their heads, while men pushed bicycles laden with goods.

"And," Reilly added, speaking from the open partition behind the cab, "we appreciate you getting all of our equipment staged in the safehouse. There was only so much we could carry in, and we'd be in a world of hurt if anything was missing."

Azibo steered right to allow the passage of a motorcycle, locally known as a boda-boda, as its driver weaved through traffic while balancing an improbable load. The sun beat down mercilessly outside, casting sharp shadows and creating a glare off the windshields of oncoming vehicles.

After a few moments of silence, the driver cleared his throat and responded to Reilly. "I surmised my work was helpful when you loaded that equipment into the vehicles and we departed as quickly as you arrived. What you have not told me is why."

Worthy quickly supplied, "The situation is fluid, and we're waiting to get more information from our headquarters. But we've got a long drive to Mbuji-Mayi to figure out the rest."

"I understand that," Azibo said. "But you are risking my life as much as your own, and the risk to me extends long after you have left the Congo. I have a right to know what you know."

The van's air conditioning struggled against the heat, a warm draft sneaking in through the windows, as Worthy considered that there was an art and a science to dealing with local assets. Sure, they were vetted, recruited, and paid quite well, but no amount of financial compensation altered the fact that Azibo was wading into tremendous personal danger for the sake of his duties. His paycheck would remain the same whether he provided the minimum level of acceptable service or went above and beyond his duties to support Reilly's team, and the difference between those two ends of the spectrum hinged upon personal rapport more than anything else.

As was the case with every local asset, Reilly and Worthy needed to massage his ego a bit without being insincere, demonstrate their own professionalism and competence without becoming unlikable, and pay tribute to the hardships he'd endure over the course of the mission without scaring the shit out of him.

And, at present, to avoid keeping him in the dark without detailing the full scope of their covert mission to the DRC.

Worthy offered, "We'll stop at the western outskirts of the city and set up a stakeout. We need to watch NRı for the arrival of a particular vehicle."

"A vehicle containing...who, exactly?"

"A bad guy. We'll try to spot him on his way in, then trail him into the city. At a minimum, we need to figure out where he's headed. Best-case scenario, we take him out upon arrival. With any luck the lead vehicle will be able to intercept him and do most of the shooting—I'll reinforce their assault, and Doc will load any casualties into the back for treatment. Then we'll get the hell out of Mbuji-Mayi."

Diesel fumes permeated the cab as Reilly added, "And we might need to lie low for a while before heading back to the safehouse."

"Right," Worthy said. "I'll provide all instructions, and all I ask is that you trust me and follow them immediately. Given your background, I don't think that'll be a problem—you're about the sharpest local asset we've ever worked with."

The van passed a small river, its banks crowded with people washing clothes and collecting water. Beyond the immediate roadside, Worthy could see small fields of cassava and maize, the backbone of local agriculture.

Azibo spoke his next five words abruptly.

"You are going after Mubenga."

The statement caught Worthy off guard, though he gave no indication of it. The problem with Azibo being an experienced asset, he thought, was that it was difficult to pull the wool over his eyes.

Azibo's dossier was bolstered by extensive documentation of his previous involvement with the CIA. Chief among these was the particularly harrowing transport of a Ground Branch team to recover a case officer trapped by the Kamwina Nsapu insurgency, after which Azibo had spirited all the Americans involved across the border into Angola. The entire mission had spanned five days and involved several firefights in a conflict that had seen 40 police officers decapitated in a single insurgent ambush; given that level of experience, it was far better to redirect the current line of questioning than get caught lying outright.

Worthy looked over at Azibo casually and asked, "What makes you say that?"

"The location of our meeting place and the safehouse. The closest terrorist threat is the Congolese Liberation Front, and the leader of the CLF is Mubenga. Am I wrong?"

Worthy wasn't sure what to say to that, and Reilly mercifully saved him by asking, "What's your take on him?"

Azibo's grip tightened on the steering wheel.

"I have much in common with Mubenga."

"Oh?" Reilly asked innocently.

"We were both raised in the Kivu region. My father served in the local government, and his was a leader in the KL Militia. The army killed his father, and in response the KL Militia killed many—my father among them."

"Damn," Worthy said, affecting genuine sympathy. "I'm sorry to hear that."

None of this was news to Reilly's team, however; whether Azibo consciously realized it or not, his background was a chief factor in compelling the CIA to initially recruit him.

There was, in fact, very little about the man that the Agency didn't know in detail; they re-vetted every asset quite extensively before every operation. Devoid of any need to respect personal privacy, Azibo's dossier contained everything from his bank balances—particularly important to check for obvious bribes from bad actors—to bizarrely specific details about his medical history. The team knew, for example, that he was allergic to penicillin, his blood type was A positive, he'd been diagnosed with high blood pressure three years earlier, and his wife was pregnant; her OB/GYN reports were even included in the file, though Worthy had no earthly idea what purpose they were intended to serve.

Azibo went on, "If I believed in my government, I would have joined the army. But I do not, so I did not. Mubenga did neither. He started his own army with the Congolese Liberation Front. Everything he has done since then has been to overthrow the government."

"And," Reilly began, "to end foreign exploitation, right?"

"This is correct. I cannot say I disagree with him on the desire for either.

But not through guerilla warfare. And not," he continued with emphasis, "by slaughtering good people."

As Azibo spoke, Worthy's gaze fell on a group of children playing soccer with a makeshift ball by the roadside, their laughter a stark contrast to the somber conversation within the van.

Then he continued, "Only death will ease the pain of losing my father. It is the same with Mubenga. And that is why he must die."

Reilly reached forward to pat him on the shoulder. "Maybe that'll happen sooner than you think."

"I hope so. My country would be much better off without him. But I am sorry to tell you that he is a symptom, not the disease. The CLF, like many others, has left deep scars across the Congo. It is a cycle of violence that has torn many families apart. Including mine."

Worthy sighed. "I can't imagine what you've been through."

There was a brief silence as Azibo reflected on that, his gaze momentarily distant.

"My wife and I..." He hesitated, then went on, "We have seen the worst of it. These militias, they do not just fight. They destroy lives, entire communities. And it is the people who suffer most because of this. Mubenga is one of many such men...but he happens to be one of the worst."

Worthy's thoughts drifted as the landscape shifted subtly, the bustling activity of villages giving way to more isolated stretches of road. Azibo's words painted a vivid picture that was all too common in regions like this, the harsh realities familiar to the team after their years of successive operations.

Then he said, "But you're more than just a bystander, Azibo. You've got your ear to the ground working with Vodacom, and that's a valuable position for making a difference."

Azibo's voice was tinged with pride.

"Yes, my job gives me information. And access. This is why I agreed to help, and have for years."

"There's no shortage of Congolese citizens who know the land and its people. Very few will take risks to build a better future for the DRC, and we thank you for that."

Azibo's response was a nod, his focus returning to the road as they approached a bustling town, the cacophony of daily life momentarily pulling them away from the gravity of their mission.

"The Congo needs change," he said. "We need stability. If helping your country can bring some peace, then it is worth it. And, of course, the extra money...it helps. My wife deserves a better life."

Worthy perceived a darker subtext, something that wasn't being said, although he couldn't put his finger on it. Everything Azibo said aligned with his own thoughts, and yet an air of unease hung between them.

But this wasn't the time to pursue the matter.

Instead, Worthy's thoughts turned to the tactical particulars of the mission ahead as the van continued its journey eastward, toward the city.

And toward Mubenga.

7

"Copy, Raptor Nine One," David transmitted from the passenger seat. "Send it."

Cancer was seated directly behind him, rolling his neck to release tension that had built over the course of a multi-hour drive leading him here, to Mbuji-Mayi.

He gazed out the Land Cruiser's rear passenger window, continuing to take in the sights of the city they'd spent the better part of thirty minutes aimlessly cruising around as they waited for Chen and/or Worthy's stakeout element to detect any sign of Mubenga.

The streets of Mbuji-Mayi spread out like a bustling montage, alive with color and ceaseless movement. Women in bright headwraps balanced baskets skillfully atop their heads, their graceful forms navigating through a maze of honking mototaxis, rickety bicycles, and the occasional lumbering truck. The air was filled with dust stirred into a swirling dance by the relentless traffic, sidewalks lined with civilians in market stalls setting up for the evening rush.

And above all, no sign of anything unusual whatsoever.

David concluded, "Copy all, relocating now."

Then he transmitted over the team frequency, his voice audible both from the front seat and, with a split-second delay, over Cancer's radio earpieces.

"Net call, we just got word that Mubenga is headed toward Kabila Street. She's working on further info, but it's a short side street so we shouldn't have any problems covering it."

Then, looking toward the driver's seat, he ordered, "Take a left here—it's on the north side of the city."

Ian complied, wheeling the Land Cruiser through the next intersection as Cancer withdrew his team phone and pulled up the imagery of Mbuji-Mayi. David keyed his mic again.

"Racegun, have you and Doc seen anything yet?"

"*Negative*," Worthy transmitted back. "*We've been looking at civilian traffic with regular spacing. Short of having a vehicle description to go off of, we haven't seen anything suspicious.*"

By then Cancer had found the street in question on his satellite imagery, and began swiping up and down the length of it to get his bearings.

"All right," David acknowledged. "Hold position and stand by for my word to move. We're circling around to Kabila Street, will drop Cancer for street surveillance."

"Yippee," the sniper muttered, zooming in on the imagery while David continued feeding directions to Ian.

When they'd fitted the Land Cruiser with a discreet satellite puck antenna to maintain communications with Chen, Cancer had expected more detailed information to be forthcoming at some point in the day.

Instead they'd been met with a whole lot of radio silence broken only by David's periodic requests for updates, each of which was met with a negative response. And now that she'd actually sent more information, it couldn't have been more vague—that street name could have represented a waypoint along Mubenga's route, a destination he wouldn't arrive at for another eight hours, or merely a piece of bad intel altogether.

"This is bullshit," Cancer observed.

David helplessly replied, "Wish I could come up with something to make you feel better, but you know as much as I do."

"Yeah, well, I'd feel better if Chen wasn't keeping us in the dark."

Ian began, "I'm telling you, based on what she's given us—"

"You mean," Cancer interrupted, "what she *hasn't* given us?"

"My assessment stands," Ian insisted, following the shortest route to Kabila Street. "I think Chen's only surveillance on Mubenga since he left his camp is single-source human intelligence. That means she's got exactly one person reporting to her, and we're at the mercy of how much he knows and when he can send her updates."

"Wouldn't she have told us who he is? I mean, if we wipe out everyone who's with Mubenga, we kill her source."

"True. But saving his life isn't high on Chen's list of priorities."

David groaned.

"I don't disagree, and that's what concerns me. If her source is a plant, then Mubenga could be pulling the strings to lead us into a trap. Trusting a single human source is like taking your life savings to Vegas and putting it all on red—hang on. Raptor Nine One, send it."

Cancer waited for him to complete the satellite exchange with Chen, after which the team leader spoke quickly.

"All right, looks like Kabila Street has some run-of-the-mill businesses and apartment buildings, then transitions into a minor industrial area. Nothing out of the ordinary there, only wild card is that two-story building halfway down the block on the west side of the street. Looks like a warehouse, but she doesn't know what it is."

Cancer found the structure on his phone imagery, eyes narrowing at David's statement.

"What do you mean, she doesn't know what it is? She's got an OPCEN full of intel geeks to figure it out."

"They're working on it."

"Sure. Fine." He scanned his phone, talking aloud. "Warehouse is a good bet—there's an alley for vehicle access to a closed parking lot at the backside, looks like a loading dock." Swiping upward, he continued, "And it'd look a hell of a lot less out of place a few blocks north in that industrial area."

Ian glanced toward the backseat. "I can't exactly analyze it while I'm driving. What do you make of it?"

Cancer grinned, pleased that both the intelligence operative and team leader had the common decency to trust the instincts of their team's most seasoned man.

"It's what I don't make of it," he began. "Someone put it there for a reason, but it ain't a terrorist safehouse."

"You want a drive-by first?"

"No. Drop me a block south of it, on the opposite side of the street. Get your look when you drive past, and don't bring the truck past it again. Circle around to the south; I'll head that way if I'm in trouble."

David relayed directions to Ian as Cancer continued studying his phone, now scrutinizing the buildings on both sides of the street and checking the reassuring placement of his concealed Glock with a patting hand.

As the truck made the next left, David announced, "Here it is—Kabila Street."

The Land Cruiser slowed as Cancer put his phone away, removed his radio earpieces, and tucked the cords inside his shirt collar. Then he said abruptly, "Tell Worthy to bring the Sprinter van this way. They already missed Mubenga."

"How do you know?" David asked.

"I just do. Call my cell when you have any info."

"Same," the team leader replied as the truck came to a stop. "Happy hunting."

Cancer exited the vehicle, setting his boots down on the gritty pavement.

The air was rich with a blend of street scents: spicy grilled chicken and roasting maize from scattered food stalls. He slammed the door shut and David pulled away, the Land Cruiser's engine noise fading as the city's soundtrack enveloped him: the persistent honks of mototaxis navigating through traffic, the melodic calls of market vendors selling their wares, and the laughter of children echoing from a narrow alley to his right.

It took him a few steps to survey his surroundings, eyes shielded by sunglasses as he methodically scanned from near to far. He passed an electronics shop that hummed with the chatter of televisions and radios, glanced across the street to see a fabric merchant displaying a kaleidoscope of Congolese textiles that stood in stark contrast to the dusty road. The crowd around him was a melting pot, and he was pleased to note that he wasn't the only non-Congolese among the city's pedestrians. In addition to locals in colorful traditional attire, he identified a white couple in safari shirts and cargo pants—probably aid workers—along with a few Indians and Chinese who most likely represented foreign business interests.

Cancer scrutinized each passerby and street vendor, looking for the tell-tale signs of militia supporters waiting to receive Mubenga: bulges of concealed weapons beneath clothing, backpacks and duffels carried for quick access, window and rooftop spotters, anyone with the unnatural focus of someone surveilling the area. He noted each vehicle, observing the drivers for any sign of militant affiliation or covert cargo. There was a seemingly endless list of indicators that blended into his intuitive assessment, countless details that would cue him into Mubenga's reception party.

And he saw none of them.

Dismayed, he continued up the sidewalk until he could make out the second story of the mystery building hovering above the flow of vehicle and pedestrian traffic. His attention intensified as he neared it, and the biggest factor that caught his suspicion was how utterly unremarkable it was—its stout gray facade blended into the urban landscape between a barber shop and a restaurant.

Not until he got close enough to make out more details did the hair on the back of his neck stand up.

First he saw sparse, tinted windows, and then the jet-black half-orbs of surveillance cameras. Then he identified the vehicle access lane on the building's left side, just as the imagery had indicated. But he couldn't tell from the satellite view that the lane was sealed by a locked gate, nor that it was oversized enough to accommodate double the width of a standard vehicle—too narrow for a full-sized cargo truck, but definitely wide enough for an armored vehicle. Whatever was moving in and out of the loading dock on the opposite side was valuable enough to warrant armed transport and sensitive enough to justify being hidden in more or less plain sight.

How the combination of these factors related to Mubenga remained irritatingly outside his grasp. It wasn't a bank and it definitely wasn't a prison, nor was it anywhere near subtle enough to indicate an outstation for either a Congolese or foreign intelligence service.

His senses sharpened to the details—the sun's heat on his skin, the street dust on his clothing, the faint smell of diesel in the air—as he looked for clues to fill in the gaps of his understanding and found nothing. Cancer moved with calculated steps, scanning to the point of overload, a deep-seated intuition assuring him he needed to stop.

The aroma of robust coffee and fried beignets wafted toward him from a cafe to his front, and taking a seat outside seemed a no-brainer. For some reason he didn't like that idea either, but committed to it for a dearth of alternate options. He felt that if he took his eyes off the warehouse structure for one second, something bad would happen.

Cancer had just pulled out a chair at an unoccupied table when he heard a chorus of shouts from across the street. He looked up to see a black Land Rover running aground on the sidewalk, causing the civilians in its path to scatter as it shrieked to a stop in front of the warehouse building.

And if that weren't enough cause for alarm, the vehicle reversed three meters, then pulled forward one meter to stop at a pinpoint location known only to the driver. This was yet another disparity that caused the hair on the back of Cancer's neck to rise, his mind reaching one unalterable conclusion about what this sudden course of events signified.

Then the driver's door flung open as a Congolese woman blocked his view, stopping in front of his table to stare at the commotion.

Cancer leapt from his chair and tackled her from behind.

They hit the ground in unison, her face down and him pinning her down, trying to smother her body with his as she screamed and writhed violently.

He looked up, now uncertain whether there was more mayhem in front of the building where an SUV had just stopped, or around the cafe where he'd just assaulted a citizen of the DRC for seemingly no reason at all.

A crowd of bystanders surrounded him as shouting men assured Cancer he was about to get the shit kicked out of him. Without letting the woman up, he drew his Glock with one hand and angled the pistol across the street. The vigilantes scattered before him, clearing his line of sight to the recently abandoned Land Rover and its former driver, now on foot and sprinting toward him, holding an AK-47 and attempting to distance himself from his vehicle as fast as possible.

The driver was a Congolese man in jeans and a camouflage fatigue jacket, his face covered in a red headscarf—no naive and expendable young martyr sweating profusely with visions of paradise, but instead a hardened veteran who, by his steely gaze, was no stranger to having a gun pointed at him.

His eyes flashed a moment of decision—continue running or defend himself—and he sided with the latter, skidding to a halt and bringing his rifle to his shoulder to send a barrage at Cancer and the helpless woman beneath him.

Cancer fired four 9mm rounds at the man's chest, but the lack of a stable position and his one-handed grip caused the shots to career low and left, a single bullet striking the man in his pelvis and causing him to double over and fall sideways.

A chorus of screams erupted as Cancer struggled to keep the woman down, angling for a follow-up shot before his target could return the favor.

Then his vision was eclipsed by a fiery orange blaze, the Land Rover detonating in one massive fireball in the flashing moment between seeing the explosion and pinning his head down over the woman.

An earth-shattering concussion washed over his backside with a scorching shockwave of heat, a shuddering earthquake tremor reverberating across the ground as his hearing turned into one endless cathedral bell. Cancer had known what was going to happen, was the only person on the street besides the driver who did, and was nonetheless stricken with a horrified sense of shock. Nothing rendered a man so helpless as a catastrophic explosion in close proximity; there was no way he could think, shoot, or fight his way out of this situation, nothing to do at all but cower in its wake, keep his index finger off the trigger of his exposed Glock, and hope he'd saved the life of at least one civilian.

He kept his head down over the woman's shoulder as debris showered down his backside, an endless hailstorm of stinging bits of gravel and hot metal fragments. A gradual lessening of the deep vibration beneath him was his only indication that the blast was receding—his entire head was ringing now, and he dared not expose his face until the shrapnel had stopped flying. He'd already lost his sense of hearing and his smell was going too, nostrils filling with dust and vaporized brick and plaster. The only notable scents he could make out were diesel, smoke, and smoldering rubber from incinerated tires, and only when a full second passed without a projectile hitting his back did he roll his head sideways to look.

The walkway and street were covered in a thick snowfall of sandy grime and bits of paper and cloth that continued to descend, the view overhead blocked by a pale gray cloud that drifted sluggishly between buildings. It was impossible to see the opposite side of the street, though his backward and sideways glances revealed the fallen dust-coated bodies of men and women that had been upright pedestrians seconds earlier. There were flashes of blood and most incredibly, *movement*, some of the people managing to grope and writhe amid shattered glass from the storefronts around them.

But he knew the real victims would be on the other side of the street.

"You're welcome," he said, unable to hear his own voice as he rolled off the woman beneath him and rose, crouching low and assuming a two-handed grip on his pistol. A strip of cloth snagged across the toe of his boot with the first step, and his attempt to shake it free knocked enough dust off it to reveal that it was a once-vibrant tapestry of the type worn by Congolese women and girls. He'd just recovered his footing when his opposite boot struck an object, and he saw a man's shoe skittering away from him with enough heft to assure him that a human foot was still intact inside.

Then Cancer caught sight of the fallen driver to his right. He momentarily dropped to a knee to finish the job he'd started only to find it wouldn't be necessary: the man was face down and motionless, a foot-long metal shard impaled in the small of his back. Advancing nonetheless, he holstered his Glock and snatched the AK-47 from the man's side, rolling the body and stripping three magazines from a chest rig beneath the fatigue jacket.

Slipping the mags into a cargo pocket, Cancer darted across the street to see if any civilians there had survived long enough to be saved.

Reilly's ass suddenly began to tingle, the effect of leaning against the hiking pack behind him for too long.

He drew in his legs to sit cross-legged in the Sprinter van's cargo area, then fished through a pocket of the tactical vest beside him as Worthy spoke to Azibo.

"Once we hit the next intersection," he said, scanning the phone in his hands, "I want you to make a right. That'll bring us north of Kabila Street where Cancer is on foot, and we'll start running parallels until we get further guidance."

"No problem," Azibo replied.

Reilly's hand froze as his fingertips hit paydirt. He smiled, then withdrew a king-sized Snickers bar from the pouch.

Most missions didn't allow for such indulgent luxuries—the team usually had to carry in whatever they could, then carry it out again. The adage that ounces turned to pounds and pounds turned to pain was never as accurate as when humping a rucksack uphill through the jungle, and besides that, space for combat equipment was at too high a premium for culinary delights.

For this DRC op, however, Reilly had been able to pack a wholesale box of candy bars into one of the team shipments destined for Azibo to emplace in the safehouse. He started with 24 Snickers bars in total to sustain him over the course of the mission, which made each one a precious commodity to be reserved for those dark moments when a morale boost was most desperately needed.

He'd already consumed two in hasty succession before the team had departed for Mbuji-Mayi, stashed most of the rest in his hiking pack, and slid three more into his tactical vest for rapid access.

The bar in his hand was the last of the trio, and he peeled the wrapper down before bringing it to his nose and drawing a deep, luxuriant inhale of the heavily processed chocolate.

Reilly steadied himself against a bump in the road, then moved to take his first bite.

The air around him felt like it was momentarily compressed, a sensation that occurred near simultaneously with a deep, thunderous rumble that he felt in his chest.

He threw the bar over his shoulder and scrambled to his knees as a sharp, echoing boom rippled through the van and caused the metal frame to subtly vibrate. The sound was muted and yet distinctly jarring, leaving no question as to the source.

"VBIED," Worthy transmitted, "sounds like it's along our route. What do you got?"

David replied over the team frequency.

"We heard it, continue movement, break. Cancer, check in."

Reilly found the suppressed HK416 beside him and handed it forward to the passenger seat as Worthy issued his instructions.

"Drive as fast as you possibly can without getting us killed," he began, accepting the rifle and sliding it barrel-down between his legs. "I'll provide all directions, you just keep us moving. Forget about cops—you're cleared to ram vehicles, drive on sidewalks, whatever you have to. Anyone tries to stop us, we'll take care of it."

By then he was turning to grab the tactical vest that Reilly had set beside him, while the medic was in the process of donning his own without bothering to relocate his concealed radio and pistol.

"Yes," Azibo agreed as the van picked up speed. "Okay. But...VBIED?"

"Car bomb," Reilly declared, siding with the simplest non-acronymized explanation as he buckled his vest.

The obvious next question for the uninitiated was how both Americans knew exactly what the sound was, but Azibo left that one unasked.

And at any rate, the explanation was simple enough.

Amid the myriad sounds of warfare from grenade detonations to rocket impacts, nothing outside of an aerial bomb—and a big one, at that—came close to rivaling the raw power and sheer concussive effect of a VBIED. Roadside bombs were smaller because they had to be concealed; a small to medium-sized vehicle, however, permitted a few hundred kilos of explosives to be transported unseen and detonated in one horrifying split second of chaos.

"Racegun," David transmitted, *"be advised, Cancer's not answering his cell. We're moving toward Kabila Street from the south, I need you to approach from the north. Case of beer to whoever picks him up first."*

"Three minutes out," Worthy confirmed.

Reilly's HK417 was tucked between hiking packs. He lifted the weapon and pinned the reassuring mass of its buttstock beneath his arm as Azibo sped through every turn. Reilly knelt before the partition, watching Mbuji-Mayi whipping past as the van weaved its way through traffic.

Minutes earlier, David had ordered them to end their stakeout; he told them that Mubenga was already in the city, and when probed for further details of what Chen had said, he confirmed that she hadn't called at all. Instead, he'd offered three simple words: *Cancer said so.*

Reilly didn't question the sniper's instinct or his experience. But he couldn't bring himself to feel particularly aroused amid such a vacuous dearth of intelligence updates, either.

Now the situation had gone from banal to dire with the sound of an explosion whose general direction, paired with Chen's previous mention of a single street, left no doubt as to where it had occurred. The fact that Cancer was on foot and not responding to communications indicated that he was either unconscious—dead or alive, who could say—or for some reason gainfully employed past the point of giving his teammates the slightest confirmation as to his fate.

"*Cancer,*" David transmitted, "*check in. I'm inbound from the south, Racegun's coming in from the north. We're both headed for the blast site unless we see you first, so get your ass moving.*"

"Take this right," Worthy directed.

Azibo slammed on the brakes instead, bringing the van to a halt as a Toyota sedan blasted through the intersection. Reilly was instantly furious—Azibo should have been pummeling cars out of the way if required, and he damn well knew that after Worthy's guidance. Then he saw a Hyundai SUV following the Toyota sedan so closely that impact seemed inevitable.

And in the following seconds, Reilly's heart sank as he realized what he was looking at.

A Hilux pickup followed the Hyundai, then a Mitsubishi SUV and a Ford Ranger, all speeding nearly bumper to bumper with each driver wearing scarlet headscarves. A Toyota Land Cruiser and Isuzu D-Max followed, the interspersion unquestionably a blend of shooter delivery SUVs spaced by pickups to load casualties. The convoy ended with a

Hyundai Santa Fe, another Hilux, and finally a Volkswagen sedan that swept through the intersection.

"Hold here," Worthy said to Azibo, then transmitted, "Cancer, head south and get out of there, now—run. Enemy assault force inbound from the north. Ten vehicles, two-zero bad guys minimum. Anyone with a red headscarf is hostile. Cancer, run. South. Now. Confirm."

Without waiting for a response, he said, "Take the right and follow them, keep your distance. We can't afford to get burned."

David transmitted back, "*Racegun, copy all—I want a support-by-fire position at the north end of Kabila Street.*"

"On it," Worthy replied, clearing the net for David's next instruction.

"*Cancer, I'm coming in hot from the south to get you out of there. Advise on your injuries, status, over.*"

"Doc," Worthy called back, "I want you in the prone facing the front edge of the sliding door. We're going to reverse the van until it's got just enough clearance around the corner for you to see the blast site. I'll crack the door open for you. Azibo, you're going to dismount and direct civilians out of the way so Doc can have a clear line of sight. I'll post behind the rear bumper, take out nearby targets and anyone who shoots at us. Doc, you just worry about the long shots. You're on sniper duty."

Reilly was already in front of the sliding door, positioning a hiking pack to serve as a shooting rest from which he could drastically incline or decline his barrel as needed. Once it was in position he laid his HK417 atop it, the action causing him to notice that his hands were trembling. It was his first conscious indication that his pulse was hammering as well, and the only way to mitigate both was by regulating his breathing cycle.

He dropped onto his belly, extending one leg as far as he could with the inner sole flat against the van's floor and pulling the buttstock into his shoulder. Then he began box breathing—inhaling, holding, exhaling, and holding again in two-second intervals, extending to three seconds as he brought his vitals under control amid the shifting frame of the Sprinter van.

Reilly felt his body slide as they cleared another intersection, and after another few seconds, Worthy said, "Azibo, turn us around and start reversing. Target street is dead ahead."

By now Reilly was breathing in four-second cycles, squeezing in his final moments of air regulation before the door in front of him opened and everything else in his world gave way to moment-by-moment reaction.

"Cut the wheel right, slow us down—I want us parked at an angle with the engine bay behind cover."

"Yes, sir," Azibo said.

"Doc, ten seconds."

The vehicle began accelerating in reverse as Worthy continued, "Slow down...another meter...half meter...stop!"

A wave of screams entered the cargo space as the driver and passenger doors swung open and then slammed shut to restore a muffled, eerie white noise. Azibo was already shouting at fleeing bystanders, first in an African dialect, then French, then another unintelligible language that grew in volume as Worthy cracked the sliding door just far enough for Reilly to take in his first sight of the chaotic scene.

The explosion had transformed the street into a landscape of confusion and terror. Thick clouds of dust billowed through the air, blanketing everything in a heavy, ashen shroud, and any civilians that remained standing were now covered from head to foot in gray dust. They stumbled and staggered amidst the rubble, their expressions a mix of shock and fear, wailing as they tried to locate friends and family who had been with them moments earlier. Shattered glass from storefronts littered the ground, glinting in the weak light filtering through the rising dust cloud. The air was tinged with the acrid smell of burning debris, stinging his nostrils and throat even at this distance.

Shifting his body position to adjust his aim, Reilly saw the trucks from the convoy in a loose semicircle around the warehouse facade; they enshrouded a pillar of black smoke that was undoubtedly the smoldering remains of whatever vehicle had been used to deliver the explosive.

In stark contrast to the bewildered civilians, he glimpsed figures moving with deliberate intent near the stopped convoy. These individuals navigated the pandemonium with unsettling focus, clearly distinguished from the innocent bystanders caught in the fray by their red bandanas and fatigue shirts. The militia-style uniforms were unquestionably worn to distinguish their own and prevent friendly fire amid the chaos, but for Reilly, they removed any danger of inflicting collateral damage.

He was lining up his sights for a precision shot when a spark of flame twinkled beside one of the trucks, the sound of automatic gunfire reaching him a split second later and immediately joined by others as the attackers began gunning down any visible civilians.

Reilly pulled the slack out of his trigger until it broke cleanly, sending a 7.62mm round spearing through the air toward a militia shooter standing in the open beside the Mitsubishi SUV. The man was firing sporadically across the street before his rifle went silent and tilted toward the ground, followed by his body as it careened over.

Reilly transitioned to search for his next target before the first one hit the dust-covered street, and found a figure darting behind the Ford Ranger. He emerged within seconds, spraying bullets in a wild arc as Reilly exhaled and pulled his trigger again. The shot went wide, punching into the truck's right side, and the impact went unnoticed by his target, who jolted and collapsed with the impact of a second, successful shot.

The next militant he spotted was crouched between a pickup and the Hyundai SUV, reloading his AK-47 with mechanical precision. Reilly lined up the shot, felt his buttstock recoil before he consciously realized he'd pulled the trigger. The militant jerked violently and then slumped over, his weapon and its loose magazine clattering to the ground.

He'd barely begun his sweep when a flash of red appeared, the headscarf of another militia shooter as he emerged between vehicles, aiming not across the street but instead directly at the Sprinter van. Reilly broke three frantic shots in succession, one clipping the man's shoulder and spinning him around with a spray of blood. The impact dropped the man but didn't kill him, and the medic slid his knees upward to decline his point of aim, firing twice more before the shooter could alert his comrades. At least one of those bullets succeeded, though Reilly had no idea whether his most recent kill had occurred in time to prevent word of his location from reaching the rest of the assault force.

But that was Worthy's problem to worry about for the time being—Reilly's focus narrowed to his next target, his next breath, his next decision. His rifle went empty, and he rolled to one side to procure a fresh mag and reload before settling back and continuing to shoot. The air outside the van was still thick with dust and debris, the sounds of chaos and fear permeating every moment, David's voice reverberating over his earpiece although Reilly didn't listen to what was being said. The raw terror and desperation of the civilians permeated the space between him and the militia convoy, whose fighters continued their calculated violence as Reilly fired his next bullet, then another. There were too many bad guys to kill, and he was instead desperate to stem the tide of brutality one shot at a time while he still could.

The Sprinter van rocked subtly, and Reilly was dimly aware of the front doors slamming shut as he tensed his finger for another shot. His newest target was relocating between vehicles to fill the gap left by a fallen comrade whose death must have seemed inexplicable thanks to the team's suppressors. The world around Reilly narrowed the line of sight between himself and the running militiaman when he abruptly jolted for no reason at all, his view suddenly a flat wall of brown as he rocked in a violent motion that caused him to pull the trigger involuntarily, sending a bullet thwacking into a surface of brick that swept past as the van accelerated in a wild, careening turn.

He struggled to put his weapon on safe as a series of high-pitched metallic pops sounded toward the rear of the van, his first indication that they'd been spotted and then fired upon.

"You all right?" Worthy shouted from the passenger seat. The Sprinter van's top-heavy frame rolled as Azibo floored the accelerator in a desperate bid to put distance between them and the carnage on Kabila Street.

"Yeah," Reilly said, rising to a knee and pulling the sliding door shut.

Only then did he notice that the slab was pockmarked by a half-dozen pinpoint bullet holes. A rearward glance revealed a half-dozen more along the passenger side, a sight that he gazed at in numb disbelief as Worthy transmitted.

"Suicide, we got made. Support by fire is out of the fight."

"*Copy,*" David replied breathlessly, gasping for air between his next words. "*Coordinate with Angel—I'm making my way to Cancer on foot.*"

The edge of the wall before me exploded in a wave of incinerated plaster.

I flinched and pulled my head back, the incoming gunfire only the latest factor that had me questioning the efficacy of my plan. Aborting my attempt to peer up the street, I retreated along the inner wall of the pharmacy instead, searching for an alternate exit. Against enemy forces in these numbers, any progress I made was directly attributable to my luck or their ineptitude.

Finding a side door, I flung it open to reveal a narrow alley.

I raised my HK416 to visually clear the space as far as I could in both directions before committing, then knelt at the doorway and repeated the process while partially exposed. No enemy to be found, no civilians either, and certainly no Cancer.

I darted across the alley, my boots slipping on the debris-littered ground. The space was narrow, the walls of the buildings on either side close enough to touch. I moved in a crouch, my rifle at the ready. Every sense was heightened; I could smell the acrid stench of explosives and burnt metal mixed with the sharper scent of blood.

The nearest window was partially shattered as a result of the VBIED detonation and I glanced inside for threats, instead finding the interior of an abandoned bakery. Using my buttstock to clear the remaining shards from the window frame, I hoisted myself over the side and touched down to the sound of people screaming in alarm to my left.

Whirling sideways, I found four civilians crouching in the corner, three men and one woman cowering with their hands outstretched, several of them bleeding from minor wounds, all pleading for their lives in French. Their shrieks scared me about as much as my sudden appearance must have scared them, and I lowered my rifle apologetically. Doing my best to assure them I meant no harm, I bellowed the full extent of my applicable language skills.

"*Bonjour! Excusez-moi. Merci, s'il vous plaît. Merci.*"

It was impossible to tell if my hasty attempt at international relations had achieved its intended effect, though they were sure as shit confused enough to stop screaming.

Moving to what had once been a storefront, I saw that the smoke and dust from the blast still provided concealment that was thinning rapidly.

Kabila Street was unrecognizable.

I raised my rifle toward the opposite side of the road, scanning for any sign of my missing teammate. Doing so wasn't so simple as assessing skin color for gringo presence, as every human I saw was uniformly coated in pale dust. But the people crouching inside shattered storefronts were far too disoriented to be Cancer, and everyone outside was dead. At this point in our workings together I was reasonably confident that my war junkie second-in-command couldn't be killed.

I was still south of the enemy convoy, though judging from the sharp cracks of rifle reports I'd made considerable progress toward the blast site. Turning to face the bewildered civilians, I located the nearest door on the north side of the bakery and continued my approach.

Each step was more or less calculated as I slipped through back doors and broken windows, crossing through dimly lit rooms and overturned offices. Many of the buildings were interconnected, representing a maze of potential ambush points. Continued militia gunfire was a constant reminder that I needed to find Cancer, and every second counted.

And regrettably, there was only a 50/50 chance that I was proceeding up the correct side of the street.

But if Cancer was currently on the far side of the blast, there was a fair-to-decent chance that he was already moving away from the scene and simply unable to make comms. I had a sneaking suspicion that I'd encounter him in short order for one reason more than any other: the stupid bastard had an unenviable habit of running toward the sound of guns. He'd have had ample time to approach the blast site before the enemy convoy arrived, and once they did, I wouldn't put it past him to try and schwack a few bad guys despite the fact that he was armed only with a pistol.

I made my way through a hardware shop and found a side door leading to a particularly long corridor. Following it closer to the street, I stopped at another door and paused, listening. The sounds of the street filtered in, a chaotic symphony of terror and violence. I cracked the door open to see an alley and then came up short, looking down at smeared blood and drag marks through the dust leading to my left.

And there, feverishly manning an impromptu medical treatment area in the narrow alley with an AK-47 at his side, was Cancer.

He was hunched over a teenage boy with his limbs grotesquely twisted and there was a middle-aged woman to his left, holding one end of a belt wrapped around her upper thigh, where a three-inch-long gash was oozing bright blood. The makeshift device was staunching the flow of blood enough to keep her alive but not much more.

"I've got him," I transmitted. "We're in an alley on the west side of the street, probably fifty meters south of the blast. Casualty collection point."

Then I called out, "Cancer." No response.

"CANCER," I shouted, with similar effect. Finally I moved forward to touch him.

His shoulder dropped out of my grasp as he performed a lightning-fast cheetah flip of sorts, rolling over on his back and swinging a Glock at my face before I had time to react.

Raising one hand in mock surrender, I managed, "Nice to see you too, asshole."

He looked immeasurably relieved to see me, though not for the reason I expected. Rising to holster his pistol, he used both hands to strip away the pair of tourniquets affixed by rubber bands on either side of my mag pouches.

"Fix them," he yelled, jerking his head toward three additional casualties with less critical injuries.

Assessing them at a glance, I determined the priority of care and how I could best allocate the limited medical supplies at my disposal.

Moving first to a young woman, I knelt and opened my aid pouch, removing an Israeli dressing and stripping the wrappers off. She was peppered with shrapnel wounds across her left side, the worst of which was hidden beneath a wadded piece of cloth that she clutched over her left bicep. A dark red stain was spreading through her fingers; her eyes were wide with shock. I pulled her hand away and peeled back the cloth to reveal a wide gash, her misshapen upper arm confirming that something had sliced through her flesh and fractured her humerus. Probably shrapnel, though Cancer had already removed the object.

She jolted in pain as I laid the sterile gauze of my dressing over the wound, then pulled the elastic wrap once around her bicep before routing it through an opening in the attached C-shaped cleat. Yanking the elastic in the opposite direction, I pulled the cleat tight over the point of injury. Routing the wrap through the closure bar, I reversed the elastic and wrapped it around her bicep in ever-tighter loops until there was no more material to stretch, then affixed the closure bar before Cancer stopped beside me, grabbed something from my aid pouch, and left again.

Next, I turned my attention to a shirtless older man seated against the alley's crumbling brick wall, his face etched with lines of pain. He had a makeshift bandage—his shirt in its entirety—pressed against a wound on his lower leg. Dark blood had soaked through the fabric, indicating a significant injury but not arterial bleeding.

Kneeling beside him, I carefully removed the bloodied cloth to assess the damage. He had a deep laceration on his calf, about four inches long, oozing blood steadily but not spurting. The edges of the wound were jagged, likely caused by a large piece of twisted metal.

I reached into my aid pouch and pulled out a packet of hemostatic gauze, ripping it free of its wrapper and wadding a portion into a tight ball that I pushed as far into the wound as I could. Then I worked my way outward, shoving more of the material in. The hemostatic agent in the gauze would help to accelerate clotting and control the bleeding, and the man winced but remained stoically silent as I worked.

Once the wound was packed, I took a second Israeli bandage from my kit. Unlike the treatment I gave the young woman, this wound didn't require the pressure of a cleat but needed a secure, absorbent dressing to cover and protect it. I placed the non-adherent pad of the bandage over the wound, then wrapped the elastic portion around his leg, ensuring even pressure was applied but not tight enough to cut off circulation. Securing the bandage with its built-in closure bar, I then moved to my final casualty.

Finally, my eyes settled on a young girl, about eight or nine years old, sitting slightly apart from the others. She was trying to be brave but clearly terrified. As I approached, she watched me with wide, cautious eyes. I smiled at her and offered a cheerful, "*Bonjour, mon ami.* English?"

She gave a small nod.

"All right, sister," I began, "let's see what we've got here."

My initial glance told me there was nothing I could feasibly do that would improve her situation, and upon closer examination I saw that I'd been right.

Her biggest wound was a fractured tibia, evident from the swollen and misshapen mass of her lower leg. The artery was intact, I knew, because otherwise the swelling would have been catastrophic and she'd already be dead.

"I know it hurts, but keep your leg still until the ambulance gets here. Can you do that for me?"

Another nod.

I turned my attention to the superficial cut on her forehead and several smaller abrasions on her arms. The forehead cut was bleeding, but it was more of a trickle than a flow, indicating it wasn't deep. But the head could bleed a lot even from minor injuries, and it must have been nearly as frightening for her as her broken leg.

I used an alcohol wipe to dab the wound, causing her to flinch slightly as she watched my every move. At this point I was providing comfort more than anything else—if Cancer needed my assistance, he would have grabbed me by now.

"I've got a daughter about your age," I said, opening a small package of antibiotic ointment and applying a thin layer on the cut. "Never thought I'd see anyone braver than my daughter until I met you—"

The sound of slamming car doors caused me to look up sharply—engines were revving to the north, and I looked sideways to find Cancer facing away. He couldn't see me and definitely wasn't going to hear me, so I grabbed a rock from the alley and whipped it into his back.

He turned around with murder in his eyes. I pointed forward and then jerked a thumb behind me to indicate the convoy was about to move, then repositioned myself between the girl and the street before kneeling to provide some cover for her in the event of stray bullets.

Keying my transmit switch, I said, "Angel, get off the road—they're exfilling to the south."

I counted vehicles as the convoy sped past, waiting for the tenth to vanish before rising to sprint to the corner of the building behind me.

A Volkswagen sedan was bringing up the rear, barreling into a cloud of dust stirred up by the convoy's first vehicles as I took aim and rotated my selector lever from safe to fully automatic.

I ripped through my thirty-round magazine in a series of short bursts, shattering the rear window but probably not accomplishing much else before the car fishtailed into a left turn and followed the convoy out of sight.

The din of approaching sirens reached me in the time it took to reload, and I transmitted quickly.

"They're gone. Angel, get your ass up Kabila Street to pick up me and Cancer. I can already hear the sirens."

"*Good copy, thirty seconds out,*" Ian replied.

Cancer grabbed my arm and spun me around to face him.

"Hospital," he demanded, pointing at the casualties.

Shaking my head, I said, "Ambulances on the way."

His brows furrowed as he squinted at my mouth in confusion.

"Am-bu-lances," I repeated, pointing up the street.

He gave me a nod of confirmation, and I took one more glance across the casualties before settling my eyes on the little girl, deciding there was one more thing I could do for her.

I knelt beside her and said, "This'll help with your leg."

Reaching into a dump pouch on my kit, I withdrew a king-sized Snickers bar—I'd seized Reilly's entire stockpile from his hiking pack and distributed it more or less evenly among the other team members while we were loading equipment. Then, I held it out to her with a smile.

She accepted the candy bar with a weak grin. I heard the squeal of brakes behind me, turning with the mild fear of seeing a cop car and instead finding the ass end of the Land Cruiser before Ian reversed and brought it to a stop.

I emerged onto the street and scrambled for the passenger seat, loading as Cancer slid into the back with his stolen AK-47. Ian floored the gas before either of us could close our doors.

"Pinpoint VBIED," Cancer shouted, retrieving his tactical vest and primary weapon from the storage space behind him. "Driver went to the trouble of fine-tuning his parking spot, and he was a seasoned fighter in his thirties. Not exactly expendable, and he wasn't interested in becoming a martyr. What was that building—what did they attack?"

Ian whipped the truck onto the next street and called out over his shoulder, the very attempt at communication infuriating Cancer.

"Hey fucksticks," he responded, still yelling. "I can't hear shit. Write it down. Charades, something."

But I'd heard my team's intelligence operative well enough, though what he'd said was so incongruous that I found myself second-guessing whether or not I understood the words. Ignoring Cancer, I leaned toward Ian and demanded, "Say that again."

Ian repeated himself as I went from confusion, to understanding, to shock in the span of five seconds.

"You're sure?" I asked.

"I'm sure," Ian replied. "We've got Mubenga's sudden departure from the jungle, the significance of Mbuji-Mayi, and the assault force's time onsite...one coincidence is rare, two is unheard of. But we've got three, and that puts us in the realm of certainty or as close as we're ever going to get."

Forcing myself to turn and face the backseat, I locked eyes with Cancer, who had already donned his vest. Shaking my head, I spoke slowly enough for him to read my lips.

"Not an attack."

Cancer threw up his hands. "Then what was it?"

I paused with a grim look then, preempting any inquiries as to whether my next words were a joke.

Then I spoke again.

"Robbery."

8

Chen addressed the OPCEN, seeking validation or contradiction for her worst suspicions.

"Our source has access and placement in Mubenga's inner security entourage. I don't see how it's possible that he didn't know about this attack in advance, which renders anything he feeds us from this point forward highly suspect."

Only Wes Jamieson spoke, delivering his brusque commentary without the slightest trace of self-doubt.

"Ma'am, our source has put his neck on the chopping block with every transmission. In my estimation he didn't inform us in advance because he didn't know; otherwise, we'd have had multiple leaks in the lead-up to sending our team into the DRC. Given everything else about the attack, it's fair to assume a high degree of compartmentalization up to and including an experienced raid force on standby outside Mubenga's main camp."

She glanced at Lucios a split second before David's voice came over the satellite speakerbox.

"Raptor Nine One, Suicide Actual."

Chen lifted her hand mic. "This is Mayfly. Go ahead."

He responded flatly, *"All men, weapons, and equipment accounted for, no injuries, we're moving generally eastbound on minor roads in Mbuji-Mayi to distance ourselves from the blast site and inbound first responders."*

The information brought her a brief respite from the chaos that had followed the explosion, although she sensed that her troubles were just beginning.

"Copy," she said. "Be advised, we assess that the attack was against a foreign-owned consortium as a means to punish colonial powers."

"Angel says it was a robbery, considering how suddenly Mubenga left the jungle and how long his men were on-scene after the VBIED blast. Probably diamonds, based on the local mining operations."

The comment gave her pause, though she couldn't fathom the team's intelligence operative making an off-the-cuff hypothesis that would in any way best her own staff.

"We have no information that would corroborate that assessment."

David responded as if she hadn't spoken at all. *"We need guidance on our next move, over."*

"Wait one," she said, "I'm working on it."

Then she turned her gaze to Christopher Soren, her communications officer, and asked, "What's the latest?"

"Still southbound on the N1, just past Kabwa."

"Fidelity?"

Soren nodded. "As good as we're going to get—we're still triangulating our source's location via cell phone towers now that he's moving in a built-up area. Pending any further phone activations—"

She held up a finger to silence him, then transmitted, "We've got dual-source intel that Mubenga has passed Kabwa and is currently southbound on the N1. I want you to head that way, blending in with the flow of traffic until told otherwise."

"Copy all," David replied. *"We'll move to N1 and will continue south until we get further word. Keep us updated when able."*

Then he added, with a tone of smugness, *"Looks like our raid on the triple-A site didn't 'spook' Mubenga as much as we thought."*

Before she could speak, he transmitted, *"Suicide Actual, out,"* and vanished from the net.

Prick, Chen thought, though the clang of metal locks disengaging behind her erased the thought in the same instant.

Chen spun her seat around to see the OPCEN door swing open, held by a member of her intelligence staff.

A slight woman in khakis entered with a tablet in hand, her glasses and tousled hair affecting the look of an introverted librarian.

"CTMC," the woman said, scanning the room uneasily before her gaze settled on Chen. "I have our initial report on the VBIED blast. Would you like me to brief you individually, or…"

"Everyone," Chen said without standing. "This is time-sensitive in the extreme." When the mousy woman didn't speak, Chen added, "Please."

Raising her voice, the woman announced, "Barbara McLane, CTMC. Everything I'm about to say is contingent on the accuracy of ongoing police reporting. However, based on that information, the explosive used in today's bombing was Composition C-4. The Congolese Liberation Front has conducted 32 bombings to date, 16 of which used C-4. But that's where any historical precedent begins and ends—all prior attacks were indiscriminate, unfocused blasts against military targets or civilian population centers."

She shifted her tablet to hold it in both hands, reading off the display as she continued.

"The explosion created a significant breach in the building's facade, and the blast pattern indicates careful placement and angling of the explosives within the vehicle to concentrate the effects in their desired direction. Bottom line, we're looking at a highly sophisticated shape charge."

Son of a bitch, Chen thought—the use of a shape charge irrevocably tilted the balance of probability from a targeted attack on foreign business interests to a robbery of some kind, just as Ian had speculated.

McLane continued, "That fact leaves no question that the CLF possessed both the depot's blueprints and the expertise to use them in reverse-engineering the demolitions we saw today."

Chen blinked rapidly. "Blueprints—why?"

"The point of detonation destroyed a non-load-bearing section of wall. If that blast had occurred on the opposite side of the main entrance, or much closer to the vehicle access gate, it would've compromised the structural integrity of the entire building. Then there's the amount of explosive material used: too little would fail to create a breach, and too much would affect the nearest load-bearing joists and cause a partial or total collapse that would prevent the raid team from making entry. Whoever designed this charge didn't just know the type of material used in the building's construction and the wall thickness, he knew the exact spot to target and how to calculate the exact amount of explosives needed to create a breach."

That final statement was too much for Chen to ignore, and she spun to face Lucios and his intelligence staff.

"All signs are pointing to robbery—"

"Unquestionably," McLane interrupted her, swiping her tablet display. "The CLF breached a vault inside the building."

"A vault?"

"Yes, ma'am. They used a thermal lance. It requires a relatively low level of expertise, and could have been conducted by any number of professionals involved in metal cutting or welding, shipbuilding, specialized construction, or military engineer units."

Looking up from her tablet, McLane continued, "As far as quick and failsafe ways to get inside a vault go, I'd say they picked the right tool for the job."

"Robbery it is," Chen concluded, spinning to face Lucios, "and since Mubenga is heading away from his normal area of operations, we can reasonably assume he's attempting to offload the merchandise. I want a full assessment of airfields and possible transfer points south of Mbuji-Mayi. Cross-reference with any reporting from the Congolese ANR and national police as well as any chatter from government channels—given the extent of this operation, he's got to have officials on the payroll."

When Lucios nodded, she turned back to McLane and ordered, "Proceed."

The woman went on, "All available facts indicate expertise that, based on historical data and to the best of our knowledge, the CLF doesn't possess. Conclusion, Mubenga had extensive consultation with, or contracted employment of, an outside demolitions expert."

"Outside," Chen asked warily, "as in, from outside the DRC?"

McLane's expression softened to a near-smile, and she replied with a sympathetic tone a half-step removed from condescending.

"Ma'am," she began, "I've analyzed hundreds of VBIED blasts from around the world. I assure you there is no precedent for this on the African continent. Given the level of sophistication, we're looking at a current or former military technical expert from the Middle East, if not Europe or beyond."

Chen asked Lucios, "Any precedent of the CLF using international contractors?"

"No, ma'am," he replied.

"And is there any precedent," she continued, "of the CLF using theft to fund their operations?"

Lucios shook his head adamantly. "No, ma'am. Looting and kidnapping for ransom, but that's it."

The extent of this raid was making Chen's head spin. Even this preliminary amount of information pointed to one incontrovertible truth. This felt, she thought, like déjà vu.

"Anything else?" Chen asked McLane.

The woman shook her head. "This concludes our initial report, pending your questions."

Chen spun to face her staff in the OPCEN and, when no one spoke, turned back to McLane.

"That'll be all for now."

"Very well. All further updates will be sent electronically. If you'd like a CTMC rep to come back and answer any further questions, just let us know."

"Thank you," Chen said impatiently, anxious to continue her staff brief without an outside observer present.

McLane showed herself out, and Chen saw that her intelligence officer was focused on his computer.

"Lucios?" she asked.

He finished reading something on the screen, then spoke without looking up.

"New update: the Mbuji-Mayi Police Service has located the CLF vehicles. Ten in total, all abandoned at an unused industrial facility three kilometers east of the robbery."

Briefly turning to face her, he went on, "This confirms our assessment that Mubenga's raid force already transferred vehicles and will likely do so several more times over the course of their escape. And I've received a transcript of the Provincial Police report regarding the contents of the vehicles."

"Go ahead," she replied. "If it's relevant."

He looked back at his computer screen and narrated, "Looks like they all stripped off fatigue tops and red scarves. The vehicles also contained explosives and detonators, hydraulic spreaders and cutters, oxy-acetylene torches, manual door breaching kits, and protective equipment required to use everything. I assess that this equipment was intended to facilitate widening the entry point or bypassing damaged areas of the building. All of it was untouched."

"Owing, I assume, to the precision of the initial explosion."

"Concur, ma'am. But this indicates not only that they were prepared to stay on site for as long as it took, but that they've been planning and stockpiling equipment for weeks if not months. This information dovetails with the CMTC's data. I'll pass that over to Lynn, who has been running point on liaising with the Directorate of Analysis."

Chen shifted her gaze to Lynn Ensey, a member of the J2 staff.

"Ma'am," Ensey began, "I just received a report that corroborates that Ian was correct."

She consulted her notes. "The target building was a depot owned by Central Congo Holdings. They receive the rough diamond parcels from eight mines, three industrial and five artisanal. Depot ships to the intermediate holding company, Primary Trade Solutions NV, based in Antwerp—"

"Go on. I don't need the business particulars at the moment."

"Yes, ma'am. The depot received eleven shipments over the past two weeks, with the last four delivered yesterday. Armored transport was scheduled to transfer everything at nineteen-hundred local time tonight. Bottom line, the depot was maxed out prior to distribution. Their holdings were at a six-month high, which indicates beyond a shadow of a doubt that Mubenga had access to the same data and selected the time and date of the robbery accordingly."

Chen steeled herself for her next statement with a sip of coffee, setting her mug down before she spoke.

"Dollar amount."

Ensey drew a breath and replied, "It's worth stating that the rough parcels arrive in their natural, uncut, and unpolished state. The lots aren't sorted until they reach Antwerp, so the DA's estimate is a general one."

"And their estimate is...what, exactly?"

Ensey looked uneasy at this question, though she responded with confidence.

"Industry markup ranges from one hundred to two hundred percent or more. Given current market conditions, the wholesale value ranges from 7.3 to 11 million USD. Retail value, up to 22 million."

Chen swallowed, looking to Lucios for the answer to her next question.

"Is the CLF capable of fencing that? Any of it?"

"Frankly, ma'am," Lucios said, "no. And any attempt to do so would both minimize their profits and exponentially increase their risk of detection by Congolese intelligence. My assessment is that they will conduct a bulk transfer to someone with the ability to launder and distribute that kind of volume. In exchange, the CLF will get a fixed percentage that will far exceed what they'd earn if they attempted to sell themselves. That arrangement is a win-win for both parties, and would explain a lot of the loose ends we don't have an alternate explanation for."

Chen observed, "This has got all the workings of insider assistance."

Ensey quickly added, "The DA is still screening employees and their communications history, so we can't make a definitive assessment. However, their preliminary data shows no recent employee turnover. The few managers who had access to the exact vault contents at any given time are all long-term employees."

Chen's eyes narrowed suspiciously. "I imagine that one or more of those 'long-term' employees has or is about to vanish, which would serve as all the confirmation we need of an inside source."

Wes Jamieson abruptly interjected loud enough for all to hear and then some. "Ma'am, we better hope you're right on that. If Mubenga had a man or woman on the inside, it means our job will be a hell of a lot easier going forward."

Unable to repress her curiosity, Chen took the bait. "Why is that?"

"Because," Jamieson continued, spinning a pen between his fingers, "it took the DA no small amount of time and effort to procure the historical information we're discussing now. No one in the CLF has anywhere near that capacity for hacking or data mining. If Mubenga didn't have an insider at the depot, he's received assistance from well outside the DRC. Demolitions expertise is one thing, but now we're talking advanced hacking to say the least."

Chen didn't want to contemplate that possibility, much less give voice to it before she had all available information.

Instead she asked Ensey, "Is there any company along the business hierarchy that would stand to benefit from the robbery? Financial troubles, any indicators for an insurance scam?"

"No, ma'am. Not according to the DA."

The sum total of factors was congealing in Chen's mind, forming a single incontrovertible truth that she didn't want to face.

But judging from the tense expressions across her staff, she wasn't the only one thinking it—Jamieson in particular was watching her expectantly. He'd abandoned his pen and sat with his arms crossed, one thumb rhythmically tapping his chest.

Chen started to reach for her coffee mug, stopped herself, and then stared blankly at the front wall of the OPCEN with its myriad screens. All of the data displayed was meaningless white noise when weighed against the particularly ominous thought swirling through her mind right now.

"So we have," she ventured, still looking straight ahead, "a robbery perpetuated by the CLF that far exceeds their capacity to do so or even conceive of it. No history of operational or technical expertise that would indicate otherwise. Meticulous planning and months of stockpiling equipment without the slightest information leak, and execution on the best possible day to maximize a payload of diamonds that they can't possibly fence."

She paused to let her words sink in. "Does anyone have a reason to suspect this robbery is *not* the outcome of significant international support to Mubenga?"

She waited for a response only to be met with silence, then went on.

"Then we've got twenty million dollars' worth of diamonds on their way out of the DRC, and given all available facts, one or more undetermined terrorist groups are standing by to take possession. Does anyone disagree?"

Again, no one spoke.

A flash of movement caused her to focus on Jamieson, who'd now folded his hands behind his head in a broad-chested expression of agreement.

Chen glanced up at the ceiling, swallowed, and considered the obvious. There had been six months of total silence from an unprecedented international terror network since its leader was slain in Yemen.

Now, she had another inexplicably complex terrorist victory on her hands.

"Does anyone else," she mused aloud, "feel like Erik Weisz has risen from the dead?"

9

Ian held his jerrican steady, listening to fuel gurgling into the dark maw of the Land Cruiser. The sound was almost meditative after seemingly endless hours of driving. Hell, he thought, merely standing with his legs fully outstretched was sheer ecstasy, and he reveled in the pleasure as he breathed in the earthy, wet smells of the surrounding forest mingled with fuel. Highway R610 stretched into darkness to either side, a vein of civilization in an otherwise wild landscape.

The reverie was broken when a flash of movement appeared at the edge of his night vision, a large figure approaching from the open tailgate so fast that Ian startled.

"Hey, motherfucker," Reilly hissed.

The medic clamped his hands onto Ian's shoulders, shaking him hard and nearly causing a spill.

"Get off me," Ian protested, setting the can down with a thud. "What the hell?"

Reilly leaned in. "I just opened my pack for some Snickers bars. And guess what, they weren't there."

"What has that got to do with me?"

"Did you take them?" Reilly said accusingly.

"No," Ian replied, elbowing Reilly out of his way and hoisting his jerrican.

He glanced sideways to see if anyone would back him up if this went bad—Reilly wasn't to be trifled with when he got hangry, which was often —but he saw only Cancer refueling the Sprinter van, fatigue evident in his slumped shoulders.

Reilly persisted, "Did. You. Take them?"

Ian tilted the jerrican to resume filling, dismissing the accusation with logic. "How am I supposed to know where your candy is?"

"You're the intel guy, not me," Reilly countered.

Ian heard a surging burble that indicated his top-off was complete and set the can down again, wiping his hands on his pants to remove the gasoline residue clinging to his skin.

"All right," he conceded, still trying to reason with Reilly. "How many—"

"Twenty, give or take. I sent a wholesale pack to the safehouse, but I ate some and stashed some more in my kit," Reilly explained. "Everything's been kind of a blur since the VBIED, but definitely around twenty."

Ian shook his head with conviction.

"No way you misplaced that many bars. You must've forgotten to pack them."

"Impossible," Reilly gasped.

"Think about it, man. We were in a hurry to get out of the safehouse. Or... or maybe you put them in a hiking pack, just not yours. Have you checked with the other guys?"

"No, that's...that's a good idea." Reilly's tone softened, the urgency dissipating into the night's silence.

Finally the medic retreated, leaving Ian to cap the fuel tank and enjoy a few moments of relatively quiet night as a reprieve from the constant hum of the engine.

They'd been on the move all night, rotating driving duties with sleep shifts and topping off all their jerricans at gas stations when the opportunity arose.

Since nightfall they'd loosely trailed Mubenga from NR1 to R606 to R610, and none of those transitions had made a lick of difference—aside from passing through the occasional town or sleepy village, they were still traveling along a bumpy two-lane strip of dirt carved into the countryside. The first hour was uncomfortable, the three after that were brutal, and the last stretch was sufficiently miserable that he wouldn't have wished it on his worst enemy.

He loaded his jerrican into the back of the Land Cruiser, and was almost immediately accosted by David.

"You seen Azibo?" the team leader asked, swinging his night vision to either side.

"No."

"What did Reilly want?"

"He says his Snickers are missing."

David pulled a half-wrapped bar out of his pocket, taking a bite and replying with his mouth half full before hiding it again.

"You think he suspects anything?"

"I think," Ian said, "that he's more concerned about your theft than the damn diamonds. It's going to come out at some point, man."

"Yeah? Well, not right now, it isn't. Don't forget: everyone got a share."

There was a rustle of brush from the forest beside them, and both men turned to scan the trees. A shadowy form emerged from the darkness, appearing in the faint green glow of night vision.

"Where were you?" Ian asked.

Azibo gave an elegant bow. "*Déféquer, monsieur.*"

"Ah. *Très bien, monsieur.*"

As the driver headed back to his Sprinter van, the crackle of the SATCOM radio broke the quiet. Chen's voice was distorted but urgent, seeking David's response.

"Where was he?" David asked.

"Taking a shit." He nodded toward the cab. "And it sounds like Chen's trying to reach you."

"She can wait."

David whirled away, transmitting over the team net. "Everyone good?"

When the crew of the Sprinter van responded in the affirmative, everyone loaded up to resume the trip. Ian slid into the driver's seat— they'd been swapping sleep and driving shifts all night. With sunrise approaching there would be no more sleep, so he and Azibo were restored once more to permanent driver status.

David mounted the passenger seat and the Land Cruiser rocked as Reilly folded himself into the back. Keeping a medic in the trail vehicle was more or less standard, although that was where their concessions to protocol ended. Cancer was riding as an extra gun in the Sprinter, reversing the usual arrangement where the ground force commander was up front and his second in command in the rear. Such were the judgment calls required of a five-man team.

Besides, Ian thought, it wasn't the most grievous breach of protocol the team had achieved thus far: in Mbuji-Mayi, their medic had acted as a sniper while their sniper acted as a medic.

Ian watched the Sprinter van pull back onto the empty dirt highway, its sides now bearing misaligned Vodacom magnet panels that concealed the bullet holes it earned in the course of Mubenga's depot raid.

He accelerated forward, hearing Chen try to reach David once more before the team leader finally graced her with a reply.

"*Suicide Actual,*" her voice called out again over the speaker, "*Raptor Nine—*"

"This is Suicide," David cut her off. "We just got back on the road after a refuel. Send it."

Whether Chen believed him or not wasn't evident in her tone; she spoke, Ian thought, with a somewhat clinical detachment.

"*Mubenga is still headed south toward the Copperbelt. But we received a high-fidelity report that he just turned off R610, and is currently heading westbound on an unnamed local road that connects to a network of smaller routes. Could be for another vehicle switch, an exchange point, or he could just be cutting across to the N39 highway to make an alternate approach to Kolwezi.*"

David clicked on a red headlamp around his neck, preparing his notepad. "Copy, send the grid."

After transcribing the numbers of Chen's response, he checked his phone.

"Okay," he said, "we should reach that intersection in the next ninety minutes. You want us to follow it?"

"*If he continues toward N39, yes.*"

"Copy, keep us posted."

Transitioning to his team radio, he transmitted, "All right, boys, the Queen Bee herself has spoken: Mubenga has turned off R610 for a local road fifty klicks south of us, probably to cross over to N39, and we're going to follow him. We'll do one more stop before then and top off our jerricans before we commit to leaving the highway—if you can call this piece of shit a highway—and hopefully she'll have some more info for us by then."

Ian wondered if Reilly would smell the chocolate on David's breath after such a long transmission, and sure enough the medic abruptly leaned over the console.

"You notice that ever since we got on the road, she's got a 'high fidelity' update for us every hour?"

"Sit back," David ordered. "You're making me claustrophobic."

Ian saw the Sprinter van whip left, and adjusted his steering to bypass a gash in the road deep enough to swallow a tire. Then he responded to Reilly's comment, "They're triangulating the source's position with cell phone towers."

"Yeah?" Reilly asked, now leaning back and, Ian hoped, out of range from David's Snickers-laced breath. "How come they couldn't do that before Mubenga blew up a diamond depot?"

"Because it's all wilderness north of Mbuji-Mayi. The assault force took back roads, so her contact's phone was only pinging one cell tower at a time. That's the trouble with single-source human intelligence. Chen was forced to rely on maddeningly short updates when her source had the chance to do so without getting killed. Now he's on a major highway, surrounded by towers and probably able to send messages a lot more frequently than he could in the jungle."

Reilly noted, "Right up until Mubenga offers him a cut of the diamonds that exceeds his Agency informant pay."

David clucked his tongue.

"Not gonna happen," he insisted. "Whoever had that info and paid Mubenga to get the diamonds knows *exactly* how much to expect and can probably hire an army big enough to make the CLF look like a pick-up basketball team. I guarantee you no diamonds are going to go missing."

Ian replied, "I'd say that's about right. Now Mubenga just has to make his transfer point."

"You're still thinking Zambia?"

"Yes, but not directly. If he wanted to get out of the DRC as quickly as possible, he'd be in Angola by now."

"Right," Reilly said. "So why's he spending all that extra time and effort heading into the Copperbelt?"

"Because it's the safest."

"I thought the quickest way would be the safest."

Ian groaned.

"Look, the DRC has more natural resources than any country in the world. Most of them are concentrated in the Copperbelt. Tantalum, cobalt, tin, gold, you name it. Most of those resources are sent south into Zambia, then on to Tanzanian ports that carry them to China. That means a 24/7 flow of cargo trucks across the border, a few of which are probably waiting for Mubenga right now. He can blend in with cross-border traffic to get into Zambia, then ride that supply chain as far as he needs to link up with his buyer."

Reilly sounded impressed. "Cool. So how come you haven't mentioned any of that to Chen?"

David interjected, "Chen knows, she's just not telling us."

"If she knew," Reilly countered, "she wouldn't need us to tail Mubenga."

Ian cut them both off. "Mubenga's punching way too far outside his weight class to have planned any of this. His buyer set everything up, and the DRC government is too corrupt to not be involved in some meaningful capacity. But the Zambians have some semblance of political order, a strong military, and better diplomatic relations with the US. I guarantee you Chen's already got them set for interdiction on their side of the border."

David yawned and offered groggily, "For sure. Which means the only reason she's keeping us in play at this point is in case Mubenga's buyer has a Plan B."

"Such as?" Reilly asked.

Ian shrugged behind the wheel. "Probably a bush plane, or a helicopter waiting somewhere."

"But you don't think he does."

"No."

Reilly was silent for a moment before responding, "Because it's way too easy to pinpoint when there's a tidal wave of cargo headed south every day."

"Every *hour* of every day," Ian clarified. "Exactly."

He scanned the road ahead, his night vision illuminating the endless road heading southward, and on it, the Sprinter van containing Azibo, Worthy, and Cancer.

"And my money," Ian concluded, "says that our mystery buyer is waiting in Zambia to get positive control of those diamonds as soon as possible."

10

The first light of dawn bathed the landscape in a soft golden hue as David's voice crackled over Worthy's earpiece.

"*New hit on Mubenga: he took the local roads to N39. But then he went north, not south.*"

"North, north," Worthy muttered, his gaze fixed on the sparse woodland visible from the Sprinter van's passenger window. He scanned the routes on his phone, trying to piece together Mubenga's sudden change in direction.

Keying his transmit switch, he thought aloud, "Local roads are a quicker connection to N39 than taking the 610 all the way to Kolwezi to reach it. Mubenga's not heading for Zambia at all—N39 transitions due west. He's making a run for Angola."

"*That's what Mayfly thinks,*" David confirmed from the Land Cruiser trailing behind them. "*And whether he is or not, going off the highway is the only way we'll keep up with him.*"

"Take that local road, then?"

"*Yeah,*" David replied. "*And kit up. If there's a checkpoint out here in the sticks, it won't be police and we won't be talking our way out of it.*"

Cancer transmitted from the cargo area, "Agreed. Once we're off the highway I'll take the driver slot and you guys can take the lead in the Land Cruiser."

The sniper handed Worthy his tactical vest and, once he'd donned it, his HK416 as well.

Worthy heard Cancer adjusting his kit in the cargo area as he checked the road ahead and then his phone. Then he transmitted, "Half-kilometer to right turn, westbound."

In the rearview mirror, he caught a glimpse of the Land Cruiser with Ian, David, and Reilly inside. It trailed them at a steady distance, blending into the increasing flow of civilian traffic on the highway. The normalcy of the scene, with locals going about their morning routines, felt surreal given their purpose—and then the next turn was upon them.

Azibo guided the van off the R610 with a steady hand, steering onto a narrow dirt track that wound its way westward. The change was immediate and jarring, the bumpiness of their previous highway suddenly seeming as smooth as ice compared to the jolting, uneven rhythm of the single-lane dirt road. Dust billowed up, swirling in the early morning air. Driven by instinct, Worthy rolled down his window to better hear the world outside. Before he could instruct his driver, Azibo wordlessly did the same.

The cool, dusty air of dawn rushed in, carrying with it the calls of birds from the surrounding trees. Worthy looked through the windshield, scanning the road's snaking path through an undulating landscape bordered by thickets of varying density and occasional rocky outcrops.

Cancer waited until they'd reached the middle of an empty straightaway with good visibility forward and rear before speaking.

"Stop here," he ordered Azibo.

Worthy keyed his mic and said, "Driver swap," as the two men changed positions. It was the right call, he knew, and spared him the trouble of having to explain the particulars of such back-road travel to Azibo: take the blind curves at a crawl, react to ambushes by speeding through the kill zone if at all possible, ram any vehicles at the rear quarter panel rather than the engine block, et cetera. Azibo was certainly no slouch, but even if he'd had all the requisite training—which he didn't—there was no telling how he'd react on a moment-to-moment basis while under fire.

Cancer, by contrast, had proven himself in more gunfights in more countries than Worthy cared to speculate.

The sniper slid into the driver's seat, wedging his rifle beside his right leg as David transmitted, "*As soon as the road's wide enough, pull over to let us by.*"

Placing the Land Cruiser first in the order of movement would be helpful for several reasons, least of all the vehicle's ability to confirm every kilometer of road was negotiable by the top-heavy Sprinter van.

But the single-lane strip of dirt was so closely flanked by trees on either side that they couldn't make the adjustment yet, a detail that hadn't been discernible on their satellite imagery. This road was, Worthy considered, some real third-world shit. If two vehicles came from the opposite direction, the larger of the two had right of way and would proceed while its smaller opponent reversed until it could back out of the way entirely.

They pulled forward once more, the dust and light of the sunrise creating a hazy aura as Worthy slid one leg beneath him, angling his seated position and his rifle to fire out the passenger window if necessary.

"Azibo," he said, "you plant yourself behind the console and watch the road. I want to know if you see anything suspicious."

"How would I know?" Azibo replied. "You are the experts."

Worthy sighed. "Yeah, well, we're also foreigners, and that's the problem. Every back road we take in a new country gives us bad guy vibes. Some more than others."

"And this one?"

"I'm not sure," he admitted. "You?"

"Everything seems fine to me."

Now concerned with the lack of input from the new driver, Worthy asked, "Cancer?"

The sniper's hands were firmly on the wheel as he navigated the van with focused precision.

"To be honest," Cancer began, "I haven't had a good feeling about anything since about thirty seconds before the diamond depot went up in smoke."

The road narrowed as they delved deeper, the van's tires occasionally skirting the edge of steep hills that dropped off into shadowed valleys. Worthy's gaze darted across the landscape, where dense underbrush and uneven terrain would make it difficult to spot an ambush until it was too late. Perhaps equally disconcerting was the lack of any wide section or cutout that would allow the vehicles to switch positions, or even let an oncoming car pass. It was all too easy to get boxed in here, and even the simplest of roadblocks would present a serious obstacle.

But they were committed now, and had done everything possible to prepare themselves for this detour through the wilderness: their final stop had been used to inspect and refuel the vehicles, both of which were laden with freshly refilled jerricans. Everyone was as well-rested as they could be after a ten-plus-hour drive, and if Mubenga's convoy had successfully navigated this route, then so could they.

Cancer slowed the van as another blind curve approached, the sloping elevation on either side of the road precluding any forward visibility until they hit the following straightaway. And while the way ahead was clear, they almost immediately encountered another blind curve as the road wound uphill.

The Sprinter van was halfway around that second curve when Worthy knew beyond a shadow of a doubt that something was wrong. Everything looked just as it had a millisecond before, but through the window came a sudden perversion of the forest scents, an acrid stench that caused his stomach to churn.

"Stop," he shouted, keying his transmit switch. "Back, back!"

Cancer complied without hesitation, but even at their slow pace, the van's forward momentum persisted with the wheels locked before they lurched to a sudden halt.

They could suddenly see around the curve, and in the center of the road not ten meters to their front were the scorched remains of a human body.

Its flesh was blackened and unrecognizable, skin a brittle, cracked shell that peeled away in places to reveal the ghastly sight of charred muscle and bone underneath. Intense heat had caused the limbs to contract and contort into unnatural positions, locking them in a haunting pose—and staring at them was a face melted and warped beyond recognition, mouth agape in a silent scream, vacant eye sockets staring hollowly into oblivion.

Worthy knew exactly who it was.

The sight beyond it was far worse: a felled tree blocking the path and serving as cover for a half-dozen men in a mishmash of civilian clothing, all of them kneeling before a pickup containing additional militants.

Cancer was already reversing as Worthy abandoned his effort to lean out the window and instead opened fire over the dash, spraying on full automatic in rapid bursts as the windshield spiderwebbed into opacity with incoming and outgoing bullets. The sound of unsuppressed gunfire from their front was interspersed with crackling pops of the van's hood and front bumper absorbing bullets.

The chaos ended as abruptly as it began. Cancer had wheeled the van back out of sight, leaving Worthy to frantically scan their flanks for the inevitable muzzle flashes of a hidden ambush line.

But there were none, a seemingly impossible stroke of good fortunate that came and went with the next curve in the road as David transmitted, *"Enemy convoy at our six—"*

Cancer slammed the breaks and threw the van into drive, accelerating forward as the team leader continued.

"Left side, left side, rucks only. Cancer, go high."

Any other instruction would have been redundant for lack of alternative options. Death awaited at their front and rear, and all they could do now was temporarily get out of sight of both elements before running for their lives.

"Azibo," Worthy instructed, translating the instructions, "put on Cancer's ruck and throw mine out the back. We're bailing out and moving uphill to our left. Stay behind me and keep up—Cancer will be shooting bad guys off our back the whole way up."

The man's reply was overshadowed by the screech of brakes as the van came to a stop between the curves, a fleeting sanctuary free of enemy observation that wouldn't remain so for long.

Worthy leapt out of the passenger seat and scrambled around the back in time to see his hiking pack fly out of an open cargo door. It bounced off the Land Cruiser's grill as Ian pulled the vehicle in tight, and Worthy had barely recovered his equipment when Azibo jumped out of the Sprinter's cargo area with his backpack and a rucksack.

There was a frantic scramble as the five men shouldered their packs in an adrenaline-fueled blitz, leaving only one unaccounted for.

Cancer had taken off like a shot, already heading up the hillside and out of sight.

Each of Cancer's steps was a battle against the uneven sloping terrain, his boots digging into the soft earth, pushing through underbrush that varied from thin, spindly branches to thick, entangling foliage.

It was that latter possibility that concerned him now.

Cancer's route selection was based on a second-by-second assessment of the terrain ahead, the difference between life and death for his team coming down to the simple absurdity of whether or not he could avoid becoming ensnared by a thorny vine. He navigated around the tangle of vines with practiced agility, expecting to hear gunfire from below at any moment.

Complicating matters was the necessity of finding a suitable sniping perch with a relatively clear line of sight toward the road below. That was no easy task when moving as close to a sprint as he could manage, and certainly not when the forest was a chaotic mix of shadow and light with the early sun filtering erratically through the canopy. He veered left, angling toward a rock-strewn patch of hillside. The game now wasn't to move far—quite the opposite, in fact—but to achieve a foothold from which he could cover his team's withdrawal, remaining in place until they'd established defensive positions of their own. Once that happened it would be his turn to run again, after which the two elements would continue to leapfrog backward until free of immediate pursuit.

And then, he thought, the real running would begin.

His breath came in heavy gasps as he maneuvered around trees and overgrown shrubs, keeping an upcoming patch of rockfall in sight. The weight of his suppressed HK417 seemed impossibly heavy as he maneuvered the suppressor around vegetation, his tactical vest snug yet seeming to drag him down with each step. With enemy forces converging on both sides of his team's former vehicles, his teammates burdened by hiking packs and their fate unknown, he simply couldn't move fast enough.

The incline grew steeper as he approached the rocks, the vegetation more dense. Cancer pushed forward, his muscles burning with exertion, his mind singularly focused on reaching a vantage point. Finally he broke through the trees with an unhindered view of the sloping patch of rockfall he'd been aiming for—far from a natural sniping nest, but as good as he was going to get.

The pop-hiss of rocket-propelled grenades sounded from below, his peripheral vision registering fiery flashes of light and the rumbling quake of explosions through the trees as he scrambled behind a jagged slant of rock, lowering his bipod only to find that a treetop blocked the road almost completely.

Darting right, he tried twice more until his third attempt placed him between a gnarled tree trunk and a hulking boulder. A cacophony of secondary blasts continued to ring out below, the combination of the enemy's munitions along with the team's demolitions and jerricans sparking a series of explosions so intense that even if his team had made it into the trees, he questioned whether one or more had just been killed in the attempt to flee.

From this new position, Cancer could make out the glow of flames through the vegetation, open patches of the dirt road, and most importantly a 45-degree sector of fire to his left that would allow him to overlook the slope that his team would hopefully be moving across at any moment.

Cancer dropped into the prone, situating his bipod and conducting a more detailed naked-eye visual sweep as he fought to catch his breath.

The rattle of explosions had given way to metal crackling and glass popping amid flame. There was no sign of his team but no pursuers, either, which led him to scan the dirt track winding its way through the forest, a narrow ribbon partially visible through a sea of dirt, rock, and greenery. The first indication of movement caused him to bring his cheek to the buttstock and his right eye behind the scope, a magnified view appearing as automatic gunfire rang out.

For a moment he thought he'd been spotted, but the sight below revealed no such thing—a trio of men in civilian clothes were proceeding at a lackadaisical pace toward the team vehicles, firing into the trees on either side of the road without aiming.

He held his fire, watching four additional men proceed toward the vehicle wreckage. All had ubiquitous olive drab AK-47 chest racks found the world over, and were carrying rifles and firing sporadically. The fighters represented undisciplined, untrained local talent at best, and Cancer thought that when it came time to take them out in the greatest numbers possible, he'd have a field day.

The only question now was when to begin shooting.

"Suicide," he transmitted.

No response, so he tried again.

"Suicide. Anybody. I'm in position, need your status."

There was no return transmission, which complicated matters considerably.

If his team was alive and free of pursuit, opening fire now could do more harm than good.

But there was a better than passing chance that he was already the final survivor, and if that was the case, he was going to start thinning the enemy ranks out of cathartic release if nothing else.

"Suicide," he transmitted.

Nothing.

Finally he offered, "Somebody check in or I'm gonna start smoking motherfuckers."

Without waiting, he swept his aim across the trees, finding a cluster of five stationary men forming a tight semicircle that must have delineated the outer fringes of scorching heat from the team vehicles.

He'd take them from farthest to nearest, feeling reasonably confident that with his suppressed weapon and their lack of any discernible tactical awareness, he could drop three or four before the closest one realized what was happening.

Most of his rifle ammo was stashed in the hiking pack he'd never see again, but he had three magazines on his vest. Combined with the one in his weapon, that meant 80 rounds with which he'd begin picking off militia fighters one by one, relocating uphill until he'd fired the final bullet. Then he'd go to his pistol, and finally, his Winkler fighting knife, raging against the enemy until his inevitable death in a blaze of glory.

Lining up his reticle on the sternum of the farthest man, he rested the tip of his index finger against the trigger.

"...*again*," David panted breathlessly, "*don't shoot. I say again, don't shoot. Do not—*"

Irritated, Cancer removed his finger from the trigger well and used his left hand to key his mic.

"Status."

"*Thank God. Whatever you do, don't shoot.*"

"Yeah, I heard you. Now explain yourself."

"*Been...been trying to reach you. We...we went to ground. On the hill. They're shooting up both...both sides of the road. No effective fire...break.*" He paused. "*No pursuit, yet. Might...might think they got us with the rockets.*"

"Copy. I'm in the rocks to the left of our initial direction of movement. It's a good spot. If you need to run, go straight uphill so I can pick 'em off."

"*Got it. Thanks.*"

With that, Cancer continued watching the road. The gunfire had stopped, and he watched the visible fighters lowering their weapons and beginning to march back the way they had come.

The rattle of a vehicle engine reached him, and he cut his barrel right to find the source.

A white, dust-covered Toyota Hilux reversed through a gap in the trees and vanished again, followed by a similarly colored Isuzu D-Max pickup that backed into view and stopped.

The Isuzu's passenger door paint was chipped, metal surface crinkled with some impact—probably the same one that had sheared off the missing side-view mirror—and Cancer distantly wondered if all that damage had occurred in the process of making the thirty-point turn necessary to turn a vehicle around on the narrow road.

He caught sight of dismounted fighters loading the Isuzu while a file of others proceeded up the road to some unseen vehicle, the slam of tailgates and doors dimly audible over the ongoing crackle of flames as the contents of jerricans continued to smolder.

The Isuzu pulled out of view, followed by the Hilux, and then there were no indicators of human presence at all. Cancer lifted his gaze from the scope and then returned it, continuing to sweep for any stragglers or stay-behind forces.

David transmitted, "*We can't see any more movement. You?*"

"No," Cancer replied. "Looks like they cleared out. Doesn't mean there's not a bigger force on the way."

"*Concur. We're going to move, straight line to the high ground.*"

"Good. Keep an eye out for spotters. I'll remain in place until you guys are clear."

Only then did he hear the first sounds of movement downhill to his left, the rustle of brush closer than he anticipated—the crackling flames below had obscured any previous sign of his teammates.

Cancer tried to spot them through the trees, and when it became apparent he couldn't, he transmitted instead.

"Audio contact. Good position, stay on heading."

"*You got it.*"

Returning his gaze to the scope, Cancer continued sweeping his barrel across the low ground, searching for any threat to his retreating team.

11

_____

"*Boss*," Worthy transmitted, "*I think this is it.*"

I replied, "Hold in place. I'll be there in a sec."

My tone was calm and pragmatic, totally in control; it had taken me serious effort, however, not to sound like a wheezing bag of shit.

I climbed the last few meters to the hilltop clearing, my breath coming in short gasps from the exertion. The early morning sun, now an hour past sunrise, bathed the landscape in a soft, warm glow. As I reached the top, the dense forest gave way to a spacious clearing, the grass still wet with dew. The air was fresh, the somewhat panoramic view of the surrounding low ground breathtaking compared to the maze of trees, slopes, vines, and thorns we'd negotiated to get here.

The clearing was alive with the sounds of wildlife, with birds chirping and whistling from the nearby trees. I spotted a couple of brightly colored sunbirds flitting from branch to branch, their iridescent feathers catching the light as insects buzzed and hummed in the tall grass. The rustling of leaves in the gentle breeze added to the chorus, creating a sense of peace that was a comforting and temporary illusion.

Worthy was on a knee at the far side, pulling security toward the low ground. I made a quick loop around the small clearing's edges, assessing its suitability and coming to the same conclusion that my pointman had. We were far from roads and natural lines of terrain drift that an undisciplined enemy force would gravitate toward, on high ground ringed by trees with lines of sight down the hill in all directions. Easily defensible with 360-degree avenues of egress should the need arise and, as the lowest priority, clear sky to establish satellite comms with a woman seven thousand miles away who couldn't help us in the least.

Moving to pick up a sector of fire until my team was set, I keyed my mic.

"Cancer, let's circle the wagons—we've found our Alamo. Keep an eye on Azibo."

"*Yeah, yeah*," the sniper replied with his usual degree of enthusiasm.

The rest of the team filed into the clearing after me, spreading into a defensive perimeter without a word. Ian emerged first, followed by Azibo, who had done a heroic job of keeping pace with Cancer's not-insubstantial hiking pack until the sniper linked up with our formation on the move. After that came Reilly, and finally, my second in command.

Cancer performed a quick assessment of the area. If there was any flaw to be found in Worthy's and my mutual decision to stop here, this was when we'd hear about it; but no one was approaching us without being seen, and Cancer began adjusting our team's defensive positions to establish interlocking sectors of fire.

When he relocated Ian within a few meters of me, I retreated to the center of the tight clearing, dropping to a knee and waiting for the two words I'd been dying to hear. My hamstrings felt threadbare, quads and calves jellified. Both knees felt like they were being hammered from all sides.

"We're set," Cancer transmitted. "*Drop rucks.*"

I heard the soft thumps of men easing their hiking packs to the ground, then the rustle of movement as they positioned themselves behind the newly shed equipment and picked up security once more. Once these sounds subsided, I dropped from my kneeling position, letting my ass hit the ground, followed a moment later by the bottom edge of my pack. My legs were unburdened at last, and I stretched them out with painful relish.

Leaning back, I writhed my arms free of the straps and leaned against the soaking back pad with my weapon beside me. Then I took a long pull of warm water from the hose leading into my ruck, a final shot before getting down to business. It was time to come up with another of my patented dumbass plans, and I palmed my Agency phone to assess our greater surroundings.

In truth, there were no good options: the trick now was to find someplace we could procure a vehicle with the least possible chance of enemy interference. Villages were the priority, followed by a well-traveled road where we could conduct a hijacking as a last resort. The route was just as important as the destination—we were in no condition to make another death march uphill, and exploiting low ground was preferable for speed as much as it was in passing a water source. Dehydration could kill us more quickly than anything else save actually stepping on a landmine or getting shot, and we were running on dwindling water supplies after our speedy movement away from the ambush site.

After a minute of checking and double-checking, I keyed my radio switch.

"Cancer, come check this out."

I was preparing my mobile satellite antenna by the time he arrived, diverting one hand to pass him my phone.

"There's a small mine about three kilometers from here. Multiple streams on the way for water resupply, and if the mine is closed we'll divert west and head another four klicks to the nearest village. Unless," I added, positioning my antenna in the proper orientation and testing for signal, "I'm wrong about any of that."

"There's a village on the north side of the mine."

"Look closer—it's a shantytown."

"Shit. All right, your plan it is."

"How's Azibo doing?"

Cancer shrugged, handing my phone back. "He's shook up."

"Send him here." When the sniper's eyes narrowed in silent reprimand, I quickly followed up. "We've got to let the guys rest anyway. There's time. Besides, are you really that excited to get any more updates from Chen? Maybe another hot tip on a 'local' road that's so 'local' that all the civilians know not to use it?"

His face turned to a scowl that I could read as easily as if he'd spoken— at this point in our shared history, our communications bordered on telepathy. The grizzled sniper knew I was right but equally furious that he couldn't smoke with possible enemy fighters nearby. We both knew his nicotine tablets were nowhere near as satisfying to him as puffing away at a cancer stick.

"Have a tablet," I advised sagely. "You can light up at the mine."

"I'll get Worthy started on making a route and brief the guys."

I watched him depart and then appraised my surroundings, unable to keep myself from appreciating the beauty of the place despite the circumstances. The sun climbed higher, casting its golden light across the clearing, turning the dewdrops into sparkling jewels on the grass. No matter how fleeting, the tranquility of the scene was the closest thing to peace we'd have in the foreseeable future.

Azibo approached and stood over me.

"Yes?"

"Have a seat."

He lowered himself to the ground and sat cross-legged, his powerful form coming to rest in a relaxed posture but his eyes alert.

I said, "You'll be compensated and then some for the loss of your Sprinter van. You'll just need to tell Vodacom it was stolen."

He didn't reply, instead watching me with guilt-ridden intensity.

"You look like you've got something to say."

"It is my fault," Azibo confessed without hesitation, his voice deeply conflicted. "I should have sensed something was wrong. No other traffic on a route between highways...I should have known."

I exhaled, trying to think of what I could say that would keep his head in the game.

Then I offered, "If anyone should have known, it was us. Keep your chin up, Azibo, because we're going to need you all the more from here on out."

"How?"

"We've still got to make it out alive," I pointed out. "There's a mine three kilometers from here."

He blinked quickly, unable to decipher my meaning. "We are in Lualaba Province. There are mines everywhere."

"Well, we can walk over twice that distance to a village and have you buy a vehicle. Or we can stop at the mine and steal one, maybe two if we're lucky."

"Steal?"

"Normally we don't condone theft, mind you. But when it's between dying out here and getting everyone home in one piece, we're pretty damn good at stealing. We don't have wheels, so we're taking someone else's."

"I understand," he said. "But if we go to a mine, you must not interfere with the workers."

"We'll try not to interfere with *anyone*, management included. Best-case scenario, we make it in and out without being noticed. Why?"

Azibo looked pensive, struggling to find words that would do justice to what he had to say. "Because when a resource is discovered, entire villages are destroyed to dig the mine. The people then have no jobs but to dig. This is their only income, and if they believe we are coming to take it away...let me say they will not view us as freedom fighters. You must keep this in your thoughts if we get seen."

I nodded. "The last thing we want is an open rebellion. We'll be sure to get a good look before committing to go in. If we can't keep it low key, we'll bounce to the nearest village. Anything else I should know about?"

He thought for a moment.

"No, but there is something I must know. The man at the roadblock... the burned body. Who was he?"

I'd almost forgotten that Worthy had informed me of the corpse, and yet no one explained the significance to our local asset. It was, of course, nothing he needed to know about. Chen had compartmentalized the information even from us, although that hadn't stopped my team from figuring out the obvious. Under any other circumstances, I would have used lies and half-truths to dissuade Azibo's curiosity.

But at this point, I decided, I could be perfectly honest. After everything we'd put him through and all that he'd endure in the coming hours, he deserved that much.

"A lot of our intelligence information," I began, "came from an inside source. Looks like Mubenga figured that out, and...well, you saw the rest."

Azibo's eyes went wide, lips parting in a horrified recognition that went far beyond what that simple and somewhat obvious information would warrant. I could see his interpretation playing out in his features: being burned alive was the fate of informants in this country, and that same treatment awaited him—and quite possibly his pregnant wife as well—if Mubenga ever figured out his involvement.

Quickly changing the subject to something more hopeful, I added, "But there's one piece of good news that came out of all this."

"What is that?"

"Our only mission now is finding a way back to the safehouse, and then you're going home."

"Yes," Azibo agreed, his voice ringing hollow. "Home...home sounds nice, right now."

It was one thing to contemplate the theoretical consequences of his involvement as a local asset, but he'd never experienced them firsthand. However the rest of our operation played out in the Congo, I knew we were all witnessing Azibo's final job for the CIA.

"All right," I said with genuine gratitude, "thank you, Azibo. Go and help the guys keep watch, if you don't mind."

He nodded, then left me to the least enviable part of my duties.

I keyed my command mic and spoke.

"Raptor Nine One, Suicide Actual."

Only the slightest delay before her response. *"This is Mayfly. I've been trying to reach you for the past two hours."*

"Yeah," I transmitted back. "We've been a little busy. And I regret to inform you that stopping the diamonds will come down to you, not us."

"Clarify. Over."

I wondered how well I'd be able to control my temper, and decided that the raw facts were punishment enough for Chen.

"Mubenga turned your source into a human torch and had some local militia ambush us on that 'local' road you told us about. We're on foot with whatever we could carry on our back."

"Then you shouldn't be contacting me on our primary frequency," she scolded. *"And I need a list of all sensitive equipment that fell into enemy hands, starting with radios."*

"That list," I informed her, "consists of nothing because both of our vehicles were incinerated by rockets. And they didn't pursue us, so they either think we're dead or didn't care enough to finish the job. I'm not sure which."

"Injuries?"

"Nothing notable. Stand by for our current location."

I transmitted the grid coordinates from my GPS, and after she confirmed receipt, her tone finally indicated a sense of penance for our circumstances.

"I'm not sure what type of extraction I'll be able to line up. And it's going to take time."

"Yeah," I said, "we figured that. So we're extracting ourselves."

"Meaning?"

"There's a mining operation three kilometers north of our current location. We're going to head that way and liberate a truck or two."

A long beat of silence followed.

"I need you to stand by while I get this authorized."

She was, I knew, worried about protecting herself from backlash if there was any exposure or collateral damage. The only way to move things along was to paint myself as belligerent, and I was all too happy to do so.

I was sick of putting my men in harm's way all over the world, and doing it for a faceless bureaucracy that may or may not give a shit if we got killed trying to achieve their stated objectives. For the first time, I was beginning to realize there was nothing in the Congo worth sacrificing the lives of my men, least of all a payload of diamonds that my team could no longer do anything to stop.

Keying my mic, I said, "All due respect, Mayfly, following your orders got us into this mess. Now we have to get out of it, and we're going to do it our way. I'm not asking your permission to go to the mine; I'm *telling* you that we're going. The decision has been made. If you have any information that will help, give it to us now because we're burning daylight and I don't intend on waiting around to see if Mubenga has sent an assault force to comb the hills looking for us."

She hesitated. *"All we have on that mine at present is the same satellite imagery you have. It may take a half hour or more to get further information, if we can at all."*

"Then we're stepping off. Daylight's wasting. If the mine's abandoned, we're continuing to the village four kilometers to the west. I'll come up on comms when able. The first vehicle we clip will have to be swapped with a local purchase, probably several times over before we're clear. Then we're taking the shortest possible route back to the safehouse, so you can start planning our exfil from there. Suicide Actual, out."

I broke down my satellite antenna, then keyed my team mic. "Cancer, we're all set. Once the guys are ready, we can move."

"*They're ready*," he replied at once.

Heaving a sigh, I made one last visual sweep of the peaceful morning scenery around us. I really, *really* didn't want to continue our march, and no one else on our team did either.

But the sooner we got to a vehicle, the sooner we'd be done rucking across hell and back.

"All right then," I said with an air of resignation. "Here we go."

12

As Reilly knelt in the forest, the crackle of the radio in his earpiece broke the natural stillness around him. He listened intently, his senses heightened, as Cancer transmitted the layout of the mine.

"*I'm set. Good overwatch. My position is gonna have to be the left flank.*"

Worthy had halted the team's formation just as the trees cleared out enough to see the way ahead, after which Cancer had free rein to establish his sniper overwatch. As the team's long-distance marksman, it was Reilly's job to set up a supporting position, which meant, unfortunately, going more or less wherever the hell Cancer ordered him.

"*Doc, I want you to set up to my right, find a position within talking range, and don't get spotted—lot of eyes down there.*"

Reilly looked behind him to lock eyes with David, who headed a kneeling perimeter composed of Worthy and Ian, with Azibo in the center.

David gave a nod.

Reilly transmitted, "Moving," and began creeping forward at a low crouch with his rifle, wary to avoid open patches that could potentially be observed from below.

"So," David radioed back, "*the mine is manned, eh?*"

Cancer sounded like he was smiling as he replied, "*Oh, it's manned, all right. Wait until Doc is in position before you come forward and take a look.*" He paused, then added with a trace of eager anticipation, "*This one's gonna be delicate, boys.*"

As Reilly stalked down the slope, he felt a sense of trepidation rising within him.

The word "delicate" wasn't one he'd ever heard leave Cancer's lips, and Reilly surmised that whatever the view below, it involved heavy security. But he hadn't told David that they'd need to bypass the mine and head to the village, either, which meant there was at least a chance they'd be able to avoid additional hours of walking and all the risk of enemy contact that involved.

Reilly crept through the dense Congolese forest, his steps muted by the thick underbrush. The air was thick with the scent of earth and greenery, the dense canopy above him filtering the sunlight into a dappled patchwork of light and shadow on the forest floor. Reilly used this to his advantage as much as he could, glimpsing the soles of Cancer's boots through the brush ahead as the sniper continued his transmission.

"*We're on the backside, main entrance catty-corner to our left—security shack with a few dump trucks, plus motorcycles and a couple pickups. Road wraps most of the way around with a few offshoots. Entire mine is fenced. We've got some trailers to our front, and that's where things get good.*"

"*Talk dirty to me,*" David commanded.

Cancer happily obliged. "*Fucking parking lot down there. Five trucks that I can see parked outside the fence at our two o'clock, next to the trailers. Could be more, looks like that's their security HQ. I see a couple guys coming and going.*"

Reilly's boots sank slightly into the soft, damp earth as he moved, the forest's dense foliage brushing against his gear. The tranquility was undisturbed up here, even as Cancer's descriptions painted a starkly different picture of the low ground before him.

"*Security's all over the place, dismounted inside the fence. All armed. Good news is they're worried about keeping the workers in—looks like everyone's facing the mine. These people ain't used to getting fucked with.*"

Pausing, Reilly peered around a large fern, its fronds trembling as a gentle breeze passed through. He glanced from Cancer's position to the terrain before him, then decided on a thick mat of decomposing leaves to aim for. Shifting the pack on his shoulders, he stayed low and continued moving.

"*The way I see it,*" Cancer continued, "*me and Doc can stay right here and cover your movement. Assault element can move downhill through the trees, get within twenty meters of the vehicles before needing to break cover. As long as we're not spotted before then, this thing will be a piece of cake.*"

Reilly stopped short of his destination, unslinging his hiking pack and rolling sideways to deposit it quietly beside him. Then he laid his weapon across the crooks of his elbows and slithered forward to visually confirm his sectors of fire before he committed in full, his movement churning up the earthy smell of the forest floor.

By then Cancer's tactical vision was in full swing. "*Even if someone gets compromised at the vehicles, we'll be able to pick off guys from the high ground long enough for a hotwire. Best case, no one spots us and we've got time to slash tires on anything we're not taking. Either way, bring the truck left, me and Doc will link up at the road, and we're off like a prom dress—road network to the village, ditch the vehicle and buy another couple if there's time, steal them if there isn't. Then it's off to the safehouse.*"

Ending his crawl when he was suitably assured that he'd have a panoramic view, Reilly flipped down his bipod legs and aligned the optic to his line of sight, adjusting his elbows to decline his barrel and take in the scene before him.

He was struck by a wave of uncomprehending disbelief, removing his cheek from the buttstock and looking left to address Cancer in a hushed whisper.

"Jesus Christ," he began, "you seeing this?"

For a moment all he heard was the sounds of the forest—the distant call of a bird, the rustle of a small animal somewhere in the underbrush—and, concerned that he was outside of Cancer's earshot, said, "Hey, Cancer—"

"It's the Congo, brother," the sniper cut him off. "If they weren't here, they'd all be doing the same thing somewhere else."

As if in anticipation that Reilly was rendered near-speechless, he sent a transmission on the medic's behalf.

"Suicide, Doc is set. Go ahead and bring the others behind us real careful-like...they're not gonna get a better view of the objective."

"*On the way*," David replied.

Peering through his optic, Reilly swept his gaze over the ground below, taking in everything but the details that Cancer had concerned himself the most with.

The mine was a scar on the earth, a sprawling pit of unearthed soil and rock surrounded by a hive of activity as workers, drenched in sweat, dug and hauled amidst the clatter of metal against stone.

The brutality of the working conditions defied comprehension. Men and children wearing tattered clothing hanging loosely from their bodies, their faces and clothes caked with a relentless accumulation of dirt, dug into the earth with rudimentary tools or simply their hands. Their movements were mechanical, a testament to the soul-crushing monotony and despair of their daily toil.

A shallow stream basin, its waters clouded with sediment, was filled by women and girls. Their hands were perpetually submerged in muddy water, moving with a practiced, resigned efficiency as they methodically washed extracted chunks of earth for the resources within. Some of them were barely in their teens, others younger still, more than a few wearing makeshift slings with infants swaddled to their chests.

Throughout this churning mass of human suffering were men in civilian clothes untarnished by the dirt and dust of the mine. They brandished assault rifles, periodically stopping to berate the workers or, as was the case with one armed teenager, to deliver a buttstock blow to the neck of a man he deemed to be working too slow.

The brush rustled behind him, the sound followed by David's whispering voice.

"Azibo, hold up right there."

Reilly heard the others creeping forward. He knew what was about to transpire—David would survey the site with his compact binoculars, then hand them to Worthy and, finally, Ian, allowing them to get a look at the objective.

"Ian," Reilly hissed over his shoulder. "What the fuck?"

"Cobalt," Ian said quietly, his voice conveying unbridled disgust. "Vast majority of the global supply comes from the DRC, all dug by civilians working for a dollar or two a day whether they want to or not. Foreign companies pay Congolese politicians for the mining rights. Politicians pocket the cash, private enterprise supplies the world with cobalt, we all get our smartphones and laptops and electric vehicles. Everyone wins but the population that's forced to dig—"

"We get it," David cut him off. Then, speaking a bit more softly, he continued, "Look, it's a slave operation and we all know it. But this is the norm for DRC, and we need a ride. Everyone down there is still a civilian. No lethal force unless absolutely necessary for self-defense. Cancer, get a good look at those trucks and figure out which will be the best candidate for our exfil."

Cancer replied casually. "Yep, stand by."

David went on, "We don't have time to fuck around. Azibo stays here, the rest of us move downhill to the trucks. Worthy, you and I are going to cover Ian while he does the hotwire."

Worthy protested, "You don't want to take two vehicles?"

"Not if it means dropping a man from local security. This could get dicey in a hurry—"

"Suicide," Cancer said.

"Hang on—"

"I know that fucking truck."

That got the team leader's attention, and he went silent as Reilly cut his sights toward the vehicles parked beside the trailers: two Hiluxes, an Isuzu, and a couple Mitsubishis, all pickups and none appearing out of place in the slightest.

"Which one?" David asked.

Cancer's voice had gone from surprised to incensed.

"White Isuzu D-Max pickup, damage to the passenger door. *Missing side-view mirror*. It was with the convoy that came up on our six. Probably some of the others, I can't be sure." He paused. "Whoever's securing the mine are the same people who almost killed us."

Reilly gasped with recognition. "So that's how Mubenga had a ready-made militia to do his bidding."

"Exactly," David said.

But Ian had a different view, voiced with pragmatic levelness. "You're both looking at it all wrong: Mubenga lured us down that specific road *because* of that militia."

And that, Reilly realized, explained everything about Mubenga's detour.

"I stand corrected," David said. "If we can make it in and out without spilling blood, that's what we'll do."

He hesitated before speaking again; probably, Reilly thought, because after losing the entirety of their vehicle stockpiles, ammo was in very finite supply.

Emotion, of course, got the better of him.

"But if we get compromised, we go kinetic. Anyone has to fire a shot, then we take out as many of them as we can." Then, in a cleverly conceived justification reverse-engineered to fit his bloodlust, the team leader added, "Otherwise they'd be pursuing us anyway."

"Good," Cancer concluded, satisfied with the guidance. "Fuck 'em. And since you asked, both Hiluxes look to be in about the same condition. Hotwire the closest one—if there's anything that will run until the wheels fall off, it's a Hilux."

David spoke quickly.

"Azibo's staying here. I'm taking Worthy and Ian into the low ground with me. Straight shot in and out. Cancer, you and Reilly meet us at the road curve directly to your left for exfil. Questions?"

Reilly swallowed hard but said nothing; the decision had been made, and regardless of the horrors playing out at the mine beneath them, his only role in life now was to cover his team's carjacking attempt until they'd all fled somewhere safe. He would, regrettably, have the rest of his life to question his utter lack of any meaningful contribution to the denizens of the Congo.

Finally David said, "Let's move."

13

Worthy led the way toward the edge of the forest, his movements becoming more calculated as he approached the open ground before him. The morning sun filtered through the canopy, casting webbed rays that danced across his path as he searched for human presence from a hidden spotter to a roving guard stopping to take a piss. Both were possible, along with everything in between. Adrenaline spiked his senses, now tuned to every subtle nuance around him—the rustle of leaves underfoot, the distant call of a bird, the gentle sway of the trees. All were noted and cataloged without conscious thought.

David and Ian followed closely behind, mirroring Worthy's cautious approach. The tension in the air was palpable, a silent current that ran between them as the minutes and seconds ticked down toward their inevitable exposure to steal a truck while they still could.

And while the precision firepower of Cancer and Reilly counted for nothing until the assault team had departed the forest, their watchful gaze counted for more with each passing moment.

Worthy keyed his mic and whispered, "Ten meters out."

"*Copy,*" Cancer replied. "*No movement, will provide all updates in real time.*"

Worthy's pace slowed as he neared the mine, increasingly confident that sound wouldn't give him away in the slightest. A distinct white noise emanated from the mine: a continuous hum of conversation from the throngs of miners beneath the constant, metallic clinking of tools chipping against rock. An occasional shout of warning or call for assistance penetrated the din as Worthy moved from tree to tree, using the thick trunks as cover. The vegetation brushed against his hiking pack as he paused, crouched low, and closed the final distance to a tree that he knelt beside, peering through the foliage at the mine's outer edges.

Worthy's eyes scanned the area, taking in every detail as Cancer's voice crackled in his earpiece.

"Four guards approaching the fence to your twelve, looks routine."

The fence enclosing the mine was unremarkable. It was made of chain link, about two meters high, topped with barbed wire in some sections. It was more a symbol of control than a formidable barrier, its rusted links accomplishing little but preventing the miners from fleeing their worksite during daylight hours.

The militia security appeared to be a stopgap to that possibility.

He glimpsed four of them just inside the fence, all wearing a mix of civilian clothes: faded T-shirts, torn jeans, and makeshift uniforms. Their weapons were as varied as their attire: an old rifle he couldn't identify, an AK-47, and a couple of shotguns. They conversed while retrieving plastic bottles of water from a crate at the base of the fence, then returned to their duties inside the pits and vanished.

"Four guards departed," Cancer advised.

Cutting his gaze right, Worthy found the pickups lined up in a rough formation. Dust covered their surfaces, a testament to the harsh environment they operated in. All bore the scars of rough use: dents, shoddy spray-painted patches over body damage, and cracked windshields. None were out of place in the DRC. If they made it to the highway in any one of them, Worthy thought, the militia would have a hell of a time trying to find them among local traffic.

The last part of his assessment were the trailers to his left.

They were a haphazard collection of rusted metal and peeling paint, relics of a bygone era repurposed for the mine's administrative and security needs. Most of them sat unevenly, propped up on blocks and mismatched tires, their windows either barred or covered with grimy, faded curtains. The closest one was also the largest, presumably a central office. It looked like a third-world version of an Airstream, bearing a faded logo whose original purpose was long lost to time and weather. Behind this trailer, almost hidden from view, was a Range Rover. Its sleek modernity cast a sharp contrast to the decay around it, black paint almost completely obscured by a thick layer of red dust.

Worthy took in these details with a practiced eye, each element adding to the mental map he was constructing. The layout of the trailers, the positioning of the trucks, the demeanor of the militia—all of these factors would play into his reactions as the situation unfolded, and all that remained was to get the rest of his assault element up to speed.

Without taking his eyes off the scene to his front, he transmitted.

"Suicide, Angel, bring it in."

His teammates arrived on either side of him, and he remained silent as they took in the layout of their target.

"Hold on," Ian said, speaking just loud enough to be heard over the racket of the mine. "Check out that Range Rover."

David asked, "Upper management?"

"Definitely. If I can get in there for an intel snatch, we might be able to find out who's running this mine."

Worthy nipped that idea in the bud. "Doesn't matter to us at this point."

"They're connected to Mubenga," Ian shot back. "So it matters a lot, if not to us then the Agency. Don't forget there's twenty million in diamonds en route to finance international terror. I've got a feeling about this, David. I need to get in that trailer."

"We can't delay getting transportation out of here," Worthy pointed out.

"If it were Cancer saying to go, you'd both have agreed already."

It was clear from David's lack of response that the team leader was seriously considering it. Worthy quickly noted, "It's a bad idea."

But when David replied, it was as if this entire change to an already risky plan was a bygone conclusion.

"Ian needs to be on the inside to identify intel. Worthy, you're the fastest shot. You go with him and keep him alive. I'll hotwire a truck and pick you guys up on my way out."

Shaking his head, Worthy said firmly, "Think about this, David."

"I am. How often has Ian been the one telling us to go in harm's way? Drop your rucks; I'll haul all three of ours to the pickup bed. We might not have time to come back and get them on the way out."

"Yeah," Worthy said, reluctantly stripping off his hiking pack as Ian did the same.

David moved behind them, arranging the packs for hasty donning as he transmitted, "FRAGO."

Worthy knew that Cancer and Reilly were probably cringing just as much as he was; in military parlance, a fragmentary order was used for notifying everyone of a change to the existing orders.

In David's hands, however, a FRAGO meant something more akin to *buckle up, we're about to go off the rails.*

The team leader continued, "Angel identified a headquarters trailer. He and Racegun are going to make entry and gather intel."

There was a brief pause—disbelief, probably—before Cancer replied.

"Do I need to tell you that—"

David interrupted, "That it's a bad idea? Racegun beat you to it. We're doing it anyway."

Then, to the men beside him, he said, "Give me one frag each. In case this goes bad."

"Sure," Worthy muttered, yanking one of the two hand grenades on his kit from its pouch and depositing it into the team leader's open palm. "Just 'in case.'"

He handed over a second grenade from Ian, using the opportunity to scowl at the intelligence operative while he had the chance.

"Door is on the far side of the trailer," Worthy pointed out, "so thanks for that. We'll be fully exposed to the pits on our way in and out."

"You want me to breach, or—"

"I'll handle it," he replied testily. It would be wonderful to have someone get the door open for him to enter, but they didn't exactly have a breaching shotgun on hand. If the door was locked, he'd have to improvise by firing 5.56mm rounds at the point where the locking bolt met the door-frame. That meant choosing his angle carefully to mitigate the risk of shrapnel—the least of his concerns at present—along with a few other factors that he didn't put past Ian fucking up one way or another in the heat of the moment.

"So," David asked cheerfully, "you guys ready?"

"We'd better be."

The team leader transmitted, "We're about to break cover and do a simultaneous break—Angel and Racegun to the largest trailer, me to the trucks. Advise, over."

Cancer allowed, "*No movement out of the ordinary. No one approaching the fence. And I 'advise' you not to do it.*"

"Moving."

Worthy and Ian rose in unison, slipping forward as David fumbled to slide an arm through the straps of two additional hiking packs. He could afford to move with glacial slowness, Worthy thought, having less ground to cover and almost nonexistent exposure to anyone in the pits.

The same luxuries didn't apply to him or Ian, now designated to enter and clear a trailer under the watchful eye of anyone in the mine who happened to look up and see a couple white men in full kit wielding suppressed weapons. Any one of those elements was sufficient to trigger a compromise, and the three together were preposterous to the point of tactical arrogance.

By the time he reached the forest's edge, Worthy's gaze was locked on the trailer looming across twenty meters of open ground. Its aluminum body glinted under the harsh African sun, the very sight of its rounded shape and reflective surface making it an incongruous sight against the backdrop of the mine and its attendant horrors.

With a final breath, he broke cover and launched into a run.

His boots kicked up small clouds of dust as he traversed the open ground at a sprint, each step a regrettable risk. Worthy was prepared to slow if necessary to engage targets on the move, scanning with wide-eyed alertness for any emerging threats with a focus toward Cancer and Reilly's many blind spots amid the trailers ahead.

The security posture they'd witnessed thus far made it clear enough that the militia wasn't expecting an attack: there would be no boobytraps, no armed sentries inside aiming at the trailer door. His team's biggest threat right now was getting spotted by militiamen in the pits, and the surest defense against that was speed. The irony wasn't lost on him that he was moving as if this were a hostage rescue, when in truth, the only thing they actually needed to free was a truck.

But he reached his destination without enemy contact, rounding the back of the trailer and staying low beneath its windows as he approached the door. His heart pounded in his ears, a rhythmic counterpart to the distant, muffled sounds of a vast mining operation that he was now fully exposed to.

With no time to lose, Worthy closed the last few meters to the trailer's door. A small generator hummed outside as he reached the entrance, finding the flat aluminum handle hot to the touch as he performed a cursory test with the full expectation that it was locked.

Instead there was an abrupt clacking noise as the door pulled free in his grasp.

He flung it open and leapt inside the trailer in one fluid motion, bursting into the dim interior with his HK416 at the high ready. The sudden shift from blazing sunlight to shade momentarily disoriented him, the air inside stale and heavy with cigarette smoke.

There were three men seated at makeshift desks, each manning a laptop. Two were smoking and none appeared managerial, instead glancing up with the blank expressions of worker bees inconvenienced by a sudden interruption to their work. A pair of them were Congolese and the last appeared Chinese, the latter's purpose intriguing but unknowable— there was no time for questioning, and certainly none for taking a live prisoner.

The tight confines of the trailer and unarmed nature of his opponents presented all the tactical difficulties of shooting fish in a barrel. Worthy had an immediate sense of almost overwhelming relief at the sight. He was severely pissed off at this intel diversion and far more so at the abysmal conditions he'd seen in the pits.

Now he had an opportunity to gain payback for both offenses, and he wasn't going to waste it.

Worthy fired from left to right, delivering two suppressed shots into each of their chests. His barrel completed the arc in mere seconds with zero misses before he felt his bolt jam as the final bullet's casing failed to eject.

He performed remedial action with blinding speed, slapping the bottom of his magazine and racking his charging handle while simultaneously tilting the weapon to his right to clear the piece of brass. Then he fired a single headshot to his last target before reversing his sweep to repeat the process with the first two men whose shoulders were still sagging from the initial shots.

The entire engagement was over within seven seconds of entering the trailer, and he whirled to establish security at the open door, nearly running into Ian in the process.

Ian barely cleared the doorway before Worthy pushed past him on his way back, drawling three frustrated words as he moved.

"Make it fast."

Ian stepped aside and gained his first look at the bodies inside the trailer.

On the plus side, he wouldn't have to take time to photograph faces of the dead—the contents of their skulls were splattered in high-velocity impact spatters all over the interior. Their faces hadn't fared much better, with entry wounds ranging from the bridge of the nose, to the right eye, to an upper lip split apart to reveal shattered teeth in a hideous grimace.

Ian let his weapon hang free on its sling, reaching into his dump pouch for an item he'd pre-staged there.

Reilly dictated the minimum contents of everyone's aid kits, and common sense lorded over things like night vision, radios and spare batteries, and the quantity of rifle magazines. Ian's contribution to the team loadout was lighter and more compact than all of the above, consisting of a pair of heavy-duty trash bags.

He procured one and whipped it open before employing it in its intended purpose, slamming the covers shut and unplugging a trio of gore-covered laptops before depositing them into the bag. An Iridium on the left desk followed, along with two iPhones lying in the open. He had to fish in the pockets of one of Worthy's victims for the third, calling out the moment this last device was in his hand.

"We're good."

Ian had time to collect two blood-soaked notebooks as Worthy transmitted, "Suicide, we're good here—need exfil now."

The only response Ian heard was the blast of an explosion outside the trailer, followed moments later by a second.

Cancer settled his crosshairs on a man clumsily pulling himself up the chain-link fence with a shotgun pinned under one bicep. It was a valiant effort to stop the newfound invaders, and one that was almost comically simple to put a stop to.

A single 7.62mm round went slightly lower than Cancer had intended, ripping through the man's abdomen and sending him into a short and violent freefall. Sweeping his aim right, Cancer found a teenager higher up, having chucked his AK-47 over the top to free both hands for climbing. After a quick jolt of the buttstock against his shoulder, the sniper watched his quarry jolt and slide down the fence with his face reverberating against the chain link all the way down.

He transitioned right again, locating his next target and firing with predictable results.

There was no telling exactly *how* the assault element had been compromised, only that they had. The security operation at the pits had gone from business as usual to complete pandemonium in the course of seconds, triggering the closest thing Cancer had ever seen to a zombie apocalypse.

But this was even better: human targets didn't require headshots to go down, a fact that he'd proven nearly ten times over in the minutes since the alarm had been raised.

The first fighters to react had come streaming through a gate in the fence, an easy chokepoint for death and mayhem that he gladly ceded to Reilly.

Cancer instead performed a scanning overwatch for the next wave of targets, these ones presenting a slightly more challenging proposition as they clambered up the sections of the fence that weren't topped with barbed wire. Picking off the climbers one by one was an effortless yet immeasurably satisfying process, and within his first few kills of the day, Cancer found himself wishing his team raided cobalt mines more often.

A sideward glance revealed one of the Hiluxes pulling out of its parking spot and stopping, followed by David exiting the vehicle and scrambling around the hood.

Worthy transmitted, "*Suicide, we're good here—need exfil now.*"

Cancer returned his attention to his targets, dropping two more militiamen before hearing exactly what he knew he would: a series of low, barking explosions signifying that David was rolling fragmentation grenades under the front axles of the remaining pickups.

He was almost disappointed that his involvement as a sniper was coming to an end, and had the sense of closing time at an all-you-can-kill buffet. Cancer was far from full, but had to settle for whatever he could get.

By then David was back in the driver's seat, pulling forward to the trailer and skidding to a stop to leave behind a drifting dust cloud that rivaled a smoke grenade. Worthy and Ian appeared, the latter carrying one of his dumbass trash bags over his shoulder. Both men clambered into the truck bed as David transmitted.

"*We're pulling around the bend—divert 45 degrees left for exfil.*"

No shit, Cancer thought. As if he'd consider a tactically undignified sprint pell-mell toward the total anarchy at the mine.

The Hilux pulled forward again, Worthy and Ian now firing from the back. Without any more climbers to drop, the sniper found a militiaman standing in the open outside the pits, frozen with indecision as he stared at the carnage before him.

Cancer fired his final round of the engagement, watching his target fall —wounded but not killed, an indignity that there was no time to rectify. No matter, he thought; if the blood loss didn't get the downed militiaman, the infection would.

"Overwatch is down," Cancer transmitted. Then he shouted, "Let's go," before wrestling his hiking pack over his shoulder.

14

Chen stood at her desk, watching Lucios closely and impatiently waiting for the intelligence officer to finish scrutinizing his screen.

When he spoke at last, his monotone voice indicated neither victory nor defeat. "Phone cluster has departed Kolwezi and is heading north. The incoming could have been the order for Mubenga to move."

"What's your level of certainty?" Chen asked.

At this point, Lucios stalled.

"Ma'am, it's important to note that our 'chain of contacts' isn't much more than a series of dominos—whether or not the first one to fall belongs to the buyer is the key question here. If it was, we're on the right track. But all we know for certain is that someone with a Marseille-based number placed a call to a phone that is peripherally linked to what we *think* is a network affiliated with Mubenga."

Jamieson interjected, "Whether that originating call is significant or a coincidence will make or break us. Because beyond that, we're at the mercy of assumption. We know from triangulation that Mubenga's first set of burner phones was genuine, but they all went dark after the mine was raided. The new phone cluster we're tracking could just as easily be a decoy to throw us off the trail."

She flicked her gaze to Lucios, who admitted, "He's not wrong, ma'am.

If Mubenga is on the move, then we've got a lead that stretches all the way to the buyer. If not, we're seeing the results of a counterintelligence effort. Either way, we don't have the personnel or equipment in place for an audio grab that could provide certainty one way or another."

Chen's head was spinning now—the only thing worse than a massively sophisticated intel effort resulting in nothing more than dubious information was having no idea what the tactical implications were, and she needed to rectify that before David Rivers checked in.

"Jamieson," she said, "give me Mubenga's courses of action, and what they mean for our team."

All too eager to supply his opinion, her operations officer shot back, "Option one, we've got a genuine trace. He's relocating the northeast border region in conjunction with the buyer moving to receive the diamonds. We can keep our team in the fight in a supporting capacity and marshal Ground Branch for the actual takedown."

Her breath hitched as he went on. "Option two, the mine raid blew everything out of the water. Mubenga activated a false set of burners and put them on vehicles heading north. He'll stay in the vicinity of Kolwezi in preparation for an alternate ground crossing into Zambia, if not Angola. Personally, that's what I think we're looking at. Reversing course with twenty million in diamonds is too risky, given how far he's come."

"Lucios?"

"It's impossible to know for sure, ma'am. We could make a convincing case one way or the other."

When she found her mind at gridlock, Jamieson supplied, "No matter what's actually occurring, it behooves us to assume course of action number one. Because if Mubenga's still planning on a border crossing to the south, it's going to be complete before we can do a damn thing about it."

Chen was almost speechless, finally summoning the presence of mind to ask, "How long will it take Mubenga to reach our zone of concern at the northeastern border?"

"Twenty-eight hours to the southern edge. If he goes all the way north, closer to 40."

There was no such thing as a lucky break in this business, she thought, and the last thing she wanted to do was put all her eggs in one basket. But out of a dearth of alternatives, she did just that.

"We're all in," she began, "on the possibility that Mubenga is heading north at this time. You know the drill: I want an assessment of possible transfer points rank-ordered by probability. We need to get ahead of this thing as much as we can."

Wes Jamieson was already watching her expectantly, an eager schoolboy hoping he'd be called upon.

She said, "I'm thinking a team re-route to the N2, then stage in South Kivu. Objections?"

He shook his head. "None whatsoever. I'd say that's exactly the right play."

She took her seat, setting her elbows on the desk and steepling her fingertips.

It had been just over 15 hours since the team's raid at the cobalt mine, an operation she only learned about long after the fact.

David's two updates since then had confirmed the impossible: not only had they emerged unscathed, but they'd driven their stolen vehicle to a village before using Azibo to purchase two more. Now they were moving back to the safehouse, northbound on NR1. And somewhere in that process they'd managed a brief stop to send satellite data shots containing the preliminary data from their impromptu raid—photographs of a few dozen blood-soaked documents, along with data from an Iridium and three cell phones—while advising they had as many laptops in their possession whose contents would be forthcoming when time allowed.

But so far, the phones alone gave their only possible leads.

Providing teams of CIA analysts with recovered intelligence was like tossing scraps of meat to a pack of wild dogs. They'd converted the transmission into data and then devoured the information, all of it representing an intelligence windfall that could have meant everything or nothing depending on what the Directorate of Analysis, along with her staff, could make of it.

Her speakerbox came to life.

"*Raptor Nine One, Suicide Actual.*"

She recovered her hand mic. Devoid of regular comms—the team's mobile satellite antennas had gone up in smoke along with the vehicles themselves—she'd been at the mercy of David's periodic roadside stops to update her on their location.

"Suicide Actual, this is Raptor Nine One. What's your status?"

"Oh, you know, still northbound. We went south, followed your directions, and got our ass handed to us. Now we're headed back to the safehouse. Over."

"Your location," she demanded.

"Funny you should ask. We're about twenty minutes from Mbuji-Mayi, where this whole shitshow started."

A map appeared on the central OPCEN screen, complete with a pin drop approximating the team's location.

"Okay. Listen, I need you to proceed to the N2 interchange, then follow it northeast."

Long seconds of delay followed, probably David checking his imagery. During that time, the screen was populated with data from the J2 section— distances and travel times for her to reference.

Finally David said, *"Northeast...how far?"*

"All the way."

"Mayfly, this thing goes all the way to Rwanda."

"I know."

Another pause.

"You have an alternate exfil waiting for us that I should know about?"

"Not yet. But we've got a promising lead on Mubenga."

The team leader sounded unimpressed. *"I thought he'd be in Zambia by now. Or Angola."*

"So did we, but not anymore."

"Why? What's changed?"

Chen couldn't tell him that everything she was about to say hinged on a coin toss of probability; all that remained was the decision on whether to convey the fallibility of her information or present it as if it were an iron-clad truth.

She sided with the latter.

"The cell phones you captured appear to be the missing link. One of them received a call whose timing was consistent with an order for the militia to depart the mine and stage a roadblock and ambush for your team. We ran a full network analysis and have found no cause to dispute that assumption."

"You're sure about that?" he asked.

Perhaps the only thing she truly liked about David Rivers was that he didn't care about technical details, only the certainty of her assessment.

Processing phone data entailed analyzing call patterns and contacts, looking for anomalies and connections to known individuals, and scrutinizing the phone's interaction with cell towers to map the user's movements and frequented locations. Every lead illuminated a new portion of a network for the procedure to begin all over again, and if a connected phone remained active—as several had—then ongoing monitoring and interception of communications continued. This was complemented by cybersecurity analyses for counterintelligence indicators suggesting that the targeted individuals were actively running deception operations.

But in spite of this well-oiled process mastered in the course of decades of experience by the CIA, Project Longwing was now at the mercy of whether or not a decoy effort was in play by their adversary. It was entirely possible that she was now ordering David and his men to the wrong location.

"I am sure," she replied. "Bottom line, we gained leads on three phones in Mubenga's entourage. All appear to be moving together from the diamond depot raid up until now at geographic intervals indicating vehicle movement."

David sagely replied, *"That's wonderful. But all those phones will go dark when Mubenga figures out the mine was attacked and a few devices went missing."*

For a knuckle dragger, Chen thought, David could certainly surprise her every now and again.

"Those phones all went dark shortly after your raid."

"And yet you're still happy about this," he noted.

"Only because there's a wild card: two incoming calls from separate numbers. The first caused Mubenga to go stationary in Kolwezi. This occurred before you'd even arrived at the mine."

"So he abandoned his border crossing before our raid?" David noted with delight. *"Sounds like you spooked him."*

Chen saw a flash of movement in the OPCEN, zeroing in on Wes Jamieson spinning his chair to face her, his face aglow with a playful expression of delight. The team leader had just thrown her own words back at her, apparently holding a grudge from her accusation that his raid at the triple-A site had scared Mubenga into departing his jungle hideout.

She glared at Jamieson until he turned around, then keyed her mic again and allowed, "We assess that someone, probably the buyer, got wind of our interdiction efforts at the Zambian and Angolan borders."

"*Mm-hmm,*" David replied knowingly.

Chen went on, "After the first cluster of phones went dark, Mubenga activated a new set. One of which received the second contact about ten minutes ago."

"*But you said it was from a new number.*"

"I did."

"*Mubenga had a new phone. So how did you connect the dots?*"

"The first call," she explained, "triggered a network analysis of associated numbers. One of them was linked to both incoming calls through a series of phone cutouts."

"*So the buyer is calling the shots behind the scenes.*"

Maybe, Chen thought, although the alternative—Jamieson's aptly described first domino in the chain—could just as easily have been a standard international phone call.

She said, "In as many words, yes. Almost unquestionably."

What she didn't add was that even *if* the originating call had been a genuine lead to the buyer's network, the CIA in all its glory had very nearly failed to trace the chain of communication. Doing so required a suite of cutting-edge tools unknown to even the most well-informed terrorists and the vast majority of intelligence services worldwide.

Even Chen had been unaware of some of these means until the Directorate of Analysis presented their findings: quantum cryptanalysis to break encryptions in a long chain of burner phones, advanced AI algorithms to identify trends and irregularities in communications stemming from Zambia, and stingray devices that mimicked cell phone towers to trick phones into connecting with them. All that had led them to dark web internet traffic used to communicate with cutouts, after which satellite-based deep packet inspection allowed them to intercept and analyze data to trace communications back to the source—or at least, what she hoped was the source.

Sidestepping the compartmentalized minutiae, she went on, "That second incoming call put us onto Mubenga's new set of phones, which, as of ten minutes ago, appear to have left Kolwezi. We assess that the stationary time was for the buyer to set up a new exchange, which just occurred and triggered Mubenga to move. And now he's headed north."

Sounding skeptical, David asked, "*Then why can't we try to take him on the road?*"

"Since we can only keep tabs through triangulation, we don't have enough precision for you to target him on the move. Anticipating his destination is the next best thing until we have more information, and right now his destination is to the north."

"*North doesn't mean he'll be shooting for the eastern border. So why do you want us taking the N2?*"

There was, she thought, an ironclad catch-all excuse to keep information from the ground team. Since they could be captured and interrogated at any juncture in the mission, Chen could simply refuse to provide specifics and, in doing so, give the perception of total certainty.

"If anyone asks," she said, "it's a hunch. Beyond that, you're going to have to trust me."

"*That's a tall order. But fine.*"

With that out of the way, she projected a tone of confidence as she read off the lines of text appearing on the central OPCEN screen now, all of them being typed by Lucios in bullet points.

"So we'll settle for the assumption that Mubenga is on the move to an exchange point somewhere along DRC's eastern border. We don't yet know exactly where that will be, but the process of elimination tells us a lot. Lake Tanganyika covers 400-plus miles, and if he sends the diamonds by boat we'll be able to interdict them upon landfall in Tanzania."

David wryly observed, "*Mubenga isn't dumb enough to put twenty million in diamonds on something that could sink. And even if he was, the buyer wouldn't let him.*"

Lucios typed, *CONCUR.*

"We're in agreement on my end," she said. "That means Mubenga would have to travel farther north to a ground crossing, and it's very unlikely he'll make a run all the way to South Sudan. That leaves us with Burundi, Rwanda, or Uganda."

"*So we take N2 all the way to the border, and then what?*"

"By the time you make it there, we hope to have an idea of the exchange point. At this point we're lucky to have reasonable fidelity on Mubenga's location."

"*The last time you used the word 'fidelity,' it didn't end well for us. Is there another 'local' road network you're dying to tell us about?*"

She defended herself as best she could. "We're running with new intelligence now. It appears Mubenga has his orders to bring the diamonds somewhere along the northeastern border. He just departed Kolwezi, over 400 miles south of your current position."

Narrowing her eyes at the screen, she narrated a hopeful line of text, this one undoubtedly written by Jamieson with the intent of keeping David's head in the game. "Your team has just gone from out of the fight to back in the middle of it with *at least* a ten-hour head start."

When David didn't immediately reply, she offered, "I thought you'd be thrilled."

"*If you turn out to be right,*" David allowed, "*I will be. But after the couple days we've had in the Congo, you'll understand if I'm not leaping to my feet with wild applause.*"

After a brief pause, he added, "*But far be it from me to question orders. I need to give my guys a break, though. We're going to find someplace to hole up for a few hours, and we'll send over the laptop info then.*"

Chen nodded to herself, grateful that the team leader had stumbled upon her next request before she'd had the chance to speak it.

Then, continuing her hopeful ruse, she replied, "Considering the results from your captured cell phones, believe me when I say that we couldn't be more eager to receive that data."

15

Reilly moved down the dim second-story hallway in full combat attire, clutching his rifle.

A door behind him opened, causing the medic to spin in place and confront the man who appeared a moment later.

Cancer stepped into the hall in his tighty-whities, wad of dirty clothes under his arm and an unlit cigarette dangling from his lips.

"How's the shower?" Reilly asked.

"Freezing," the sniper replied, sparking his cigarette and blowing a cloud of smoke upward. "If my balls were any smaller right now, I'd be you."

Reilly stammered, "Well, that was...unnecessary."

But Cancer was already on the way to his room, making way for Worthy as he headed toward the shower.

The pointman was clad in boxer briefs and nothing else, sauntering with a towel draped over his shoulder. "Don't take it personally. It's a steroid joke."

"I don't use steroids," Reilly protested, but ultimately he was talking to himself—Worthy vanished into the bathroom, closing the door behind him.

Unbelievable, he thought. They finally had a few hours of respite, and everyone was still on edge. Reilly felt like he was the only one actually enjoying their current arrangement: a local guesthouse with 100 percent vacancy.

Situated on the outskirts of Mbuji-Mayi, the building was a quaint two-story home constructed with sunbaked clay bricks and a sturdy, corrugated metal roof. Azibo reserved the entire guesthouse under the guise of being a travel guide for a group of adventure tourists seeking an authentic local experience, and the Congolese couple who owned it had offered neither objection nor suspicion to the team's arrival just after midnight. They'd happily ceded the entire second floor to their new guests, and the wife had even whipped up oversized portions of Congolese cuisine—cassava leaf stew, doughy balls the size of his fist loaded with plantains, grilled fish and yams—before going back to bed.

All in all, it was a godsend.

Sure, Reilly thought, the entire second floor was lit only by the faint glow of exposed bulbs powered by a generator outside. And yes, the building's plumbing was only a recent upgrade, the toilet was three sizes too small, and the shower was, apparently, far from warm.

But after thirty hours of driving punctuated by an ambush, killing a bunch of people at the cobalt mine, and then fleeing again, the opportunity to bed down for a few hours with minimal security was a blessing beyond imagining. Everyone was willing to push their road trip limits when the final destination was the safehouse; now that they were heading for the eastern boundaries of the Congo, however, this diversion was well worth the slight reduction of their head start against Mubenga.

Reilly approached the room at the top of the stairs, pushing open the door to find Ian in full intelligence-guy mode within.

He'd already dragged the rickety table beside the window, and was in the process of aligning the tripod of a satellite antenna connected by wire to a radio lying next to his open Agency laptop.

"Hey, man, what're you up to?"

"Working," Ian said. He busied himself with the radio now, testing his signal and making small adjustments to the antenna.

Eager to make conversation, Reilly offered, "Forgot to tell you, Worthy and I had a good conversation with Azibo on the way to Mbuji-Mayi. He was open about everything in his dossier, really cares about his country. Seems genuinely motivated to help us."

When Ian didn't reply, he concluded, "I just thought you should know."

"Azibo is used to working with Agency types," Ian said, finally satisfied with the alignment of his antenna. "He knows what we want to hear. But don't think for a minute that his loyalties are so pure."

Reilly's shoulders sagged. "He seemed pretty genuine to me, Ian."

Ian retrieved the first of the three captured laptops from his hiking pack, laying it on the table beside his Agency computer and using a cable to plug it in as he replied.

"I'm not saying he's a scumbag. He's not, and I wish every asset we worked with was half as good as he is."

"Then what *are* you saying?"

"That money speaks louder than words." Ian was now opening digital windows filled with indecipherable code on his screen. "The Congolese don't trust outsiders because foreign powers have been pilfering the Congo since the late nineteenth century. First it was ivory, then rubber, then copper and conflict minerals. Now it's cobalt."

"We're not here for natural resources."

Ian shook his head. "No, but we *are* foreigners and we *do* work for the Agency, which is arguably worse. You know the only hope that the Congo has had in the last sixty years? It was one man, Patrice Lumumba. He was the first Prime Minister of the DRC, and the last politician of any rank who put his country's interests ahead of his own. If he'd had his way, the Congo's resources would have benefited his people instead of foreign powers."

Reilly shrugged. "Yeah? And?"

"And everyone who benefited from pilfering the DRC tried to kill him. The Belgians threw their weight behind a military official who launched a *coup d'état*, then put himself in charge of a one-party state. That was the start of the kleptocracy here. Lumumba was imprisoned and executed by firing squad in '61, with plenty of assistance from the US. But we gave it one hell of a shot ourselves."

"We?"

Ian abandoned his keyboard, looking over his shoulder.

"The CIA. We backed the Belgians in starting a secessionist movement in the Copperbelt, all because we couldn't allow someone whose goal was independence and unity to maintain control over his country's own natural resources. And with the West trying to take him down, Lumumba asked the Soviets for military assistance. We used that to say he was pro-Soviet and needed to die, and delivered a tube of poisoned toothpaste to the CIA station chief here. The only reason we didn't go through with it is because the Belgians came up with a better plan."

The medic swallowed. "No shit."

David appeared in the doorway, attired in full kit with his rifle slung. He said nothing, observing the proceedings with an indifferent expression.

Ian turned to face the medic at last, concluding, "No shit, Reilly. So if you think Azibo looks at us like the second coming of Christ for his country, think again. He doesn't trust us or the CIA, and he shouldn't. He's doing this for money, and we're lucky to have that. Because if any of us were in his position and some case officer tried to recruit us, we'd have told him to fuck off or worse."

Reilly's eyes narrowed. "If America's so bad, why are you still in this line of work?"

Ian scoffed.

"I'm not saying America is bad. But she's far from innocent. And there's a lot of selective memory that goes into thinking otherwise, particularly with regard to the CIA—"

"Whoa," David intervened at last, "it's a little late in the evening for accurate historical observation to cloud the fervor of blind patriotic obedience, isn't it, Ian?"

Then, cutting his eyes to Reilly, David stepped inside the doorway and gave a forceful nod toward the hall behind him. "Doc, you're up for the shower. I'll take security."

David waited until Reilly departed, then closed the door.

"You're in rare form tonight, Ian." Moving to the desk, he set an object down with the words, "Here, this'll cheer you up."

Ian grabbed the Snickers bar and unwrapped it, absentmindedly taking a bite with one hand as he typed with the other.

His mental gears shifted from anger to focus on the task at hand, repeating a version of the process he'd used to transmit his data shots to Chen nine hours earlier. The sequence was relatively simple then: he'd photographed the paper documents, then plugged the captured iPhones into the ruggedized Agency laptop that extracted, compressed, and encrypted the data. A transceiver converted this digital information into a format suitable for transmission, and the antenna beamed the sum total to a US satellite overhead. The only real difference now was time.

Not even the CIA was free of the bandwidth restrictions inherent in this method, and while sending photographs and a trio of 256 gig phone rips off into space took a matter of minutes, the laptops contained a cumulative six terabytes of data.

That meant a multi-hour transmission that he began with the tap of a final key.

"Is it sending?" David asked.

"Yeah," Ian replied, watching his screen. He took another bite of Snickers bar and chewed as he confirmed, "It's sending."

Then he whirled to face his team leader and said accusingly, "Why'd you take so long to get to Azibo at the asset linkup?"

"What? I didn't."

"Sure you did. Swiping a hood ornament was apparently more important than getting out of there."

David dropped his gaze to the floor. "Oh. That. You would've taken it too."

He reached into his dump pouch and procured a silver object that Ian accepted, turning it over in his hand. It was crafted in the style of the iconic Mack truck bulldog, with one notable exception—it was a gorilla.

Ian handed it back. "That better be going in the team room."

"Course it will," David replied, accepting his trophy and taking a seat on the bed. "And hey, man, you all right? You seem a little..."

"A little what?" Ian said testily.

"Oh, I don't know. Dark."

He shook his head, speaking in a low tone. "If that isn't the pot calling the kettle black, I don't know what is."

"Sure," David conceded, setting his rifle down and leaning back with both elbows on the mattress. "But darkness is really more my area, so it concerns me to see it in you. We go back a long way, Ian. Longer than anyone else on this team, so don't try and bullshit me. What's up?"

Ian didn't answer, instead taking successive bites of the candy bar until it was gone, then wadding the wrapper.

David waited patiently. When Ian accepted that he wouldn't be able to shake the team leader's focus, he conceded defeat and finally spoke to the heart of the matter.

"I killed a kid back at that triple-A site."

"Yeah," David said without hesitation. "I got one too."

Ian looked up sharply, spinning to face his team leader. "When you were on the left flank?"

"Mm-hmm. Shot him through the tarp. He had a weapon and all, but...I didn't find out he was a boy until it was done."

"Same."

How had David carried the weight of this sin without providing the slightest indication? Ian, for one, had felt his thoughts and his mood spiraling ever since that engagement on their first night in-country. The prospect of dying troubled him less and less than ever before, and he'd found himself questioning whether he'd have demanded the extremely dangerous entry at the mine trailer if he hadn't shot that boy.

And what could he possibly say to David, a teammate who knew the same soul-crushing pain that he did?

Ian had no idea, and settled on a numb and wildly insufficient comment instead. "I'm sorry, man."

David lay back on the bed, folding his hands over his stomach. "Be sorry for both of us. I don't know what to tell you, brother, or what to tell myself." He hesitated. "TIA—this is Africa."

"TIA," Ian agreed, the shared acronym a tacit acknowledgement of the obvious. They were operating on a continent where some militias held more child soldiers than grown men, and many of the latter in their ranks had once been the former.

Then he added, "I really wish legality helped."

Sitting up with a groan from the mattress, David agreed.

"Shit, man, me too. You know what an Agency lawyer or a chaplain would tell us? Both kills were perfectly legal, rational, and moral. Zero risk of civilians being camped on the hilltop beside a triple-A cannon, and shooting through tarps made a hell of a lot of sense after they'd blown us out of the sky. I mean, both those kids were armed combatants, right? And we'd both do anything to keep one of our guys from getting killed."

"Yeah," Ian allowed. "Yeah, that's right."

David inhaled deeply, held his breath, and then let out all the air in his lungs in one protracted sigh. "And I might actually be able to delude myself with some of that logic if I wasn't a parent."

Ian felt a chill run down his spine.

He hadn't even considered the fact that David already had one child and another on the way. If he, Ian, had nearly been annihilated with the fallout of his reactions at the anti-aircraft site, then how was his team leader feeling at the moment?

None of that, he quickly reminded himself, changed the fact that there was a mission in progress. Ian knew that the memory was best packed away into the infinite void within him, a black hole of a burial site for things he couldn't yet digest without compromising his ability to fight.

He'd often pondered what would follow his retirement from the fighting profession—a life spent killing filled a man with demons whether he wanted to admit it or not.

"You know my dad," he ventured.

"Of course I do," David replied. "His career was damn near sufficient to earn himself a statue at Fort Bragg. He's a legend, a living legend."

Ian snickered. "Well, I grew up watching him crawl inside a bottle to deal with his demons. Now I've earned a few of my own, and I'm going to have to face them." He paused. "Sometimes I get the feeling that after we leave the CIA, we've all got a long, hard road of therapy ahead."

"You think? Doesn't take an intelligence operative to figure that one out."

Then David threw his head back and continued, "Enjoy your retirement, fellas—you've got the rest of your lives to try and sort through all the horrible shit you've done."

He met Ian's eyes once more. "So yeah, brother, I feel the same way. And we'll see how well the God and Country narrative holds up then. We've all spent careers accumulating baggage, and we'll all spend retirements trying to unpack it. I'd say a long, hard road is just about the right way to put it."

He looked away and then back again, his expression brightening with playful aplomb.

"Or," he said theatrically, "we could all get killed in the next few days, and not have to worry about a thing."

16

Worthy carried his equipment outside the guest house, seeing the first hints of sunrise painting the sky with strokes of orange and purple.

He breathed in early morning air that was cool and carried the fresh scent of the earth, a welcome reprieve from the stagnant interior of the second floor his team had spent the last five hours in. Still groggy from his recently interrupted sleep, Worthy approached a nondescript Suzuki Vitara and opened the rear hatch. Depositing his hiking pack beside a row of jerricans in the cargo area, Worthy moved to the rear driver's seat to stage his tactical vest and HK416 for the journey ahead.

The compact SUV was one of two vehicles that Azibo had negotiated the purchase of after the team ditched their stolen Hilux from the mine. Reilly and Cancer were loading their gear in the second truck, an enviably more spacious Nissan Patrol SUV that would bring up the rear of their small convoy.

Seeing a flash of movement from the guest house door, Worthy turned, expecting to find David and Ian, but Azibo exited instead, trotting down the steps and striding out to the Suzuki. He casually tossed his backpack in the cargo area and approached Worthy with an invigorated expression.

"All right, sir, where are we headed?"

The driver was, Worthy thought, particularly bright-eyed and bushy-tailed because he'd had the first shower and gone directly to bed. No guard shifts, no equipment preparation, just pure, blissful rest from start to finish of their brief stay.

Worthy replied, "We'll take the N2 all the way to Kavumu."

Azibo's expression soured. "I do not think Mubenga will be going there."

"Neither do we," Worthy quickly acknowledged. "But we need someplace to stop in that area until we receive further orders. Kavumu has an airport and is just outside one of the biggest national parks in the country. That means a lot of white tourists and local guides for us to blend in with. Besides, the closer we are to your backyard, the better."

He regretted the words as soon as he'd spoken them. A long beat of silence followed, Azibo's menacing gaze fixed on Worthy's.

"How do you know where I live?"

The entire team had, of course, read Azibo's lengthy dossier in depth. His home was in Mugenderwa; not exactly next to Kavumu but not far, either.

After seeing the rising anger in his face—understandable, Worthy thought, given the man had a pregnant wife to worry about—he sided with a more general explanation.

"You mentioned growing up near the KL Militia's zone of operations. You know the area well, and that'll come in handy for spotting anything out of the ordinary."

"Yes," Azibo allowed, the tension in the space between them abating, if only slightly. "Okay. But we will not go near my home."

Worthy gave a gracious nod. "Of course not. We'd never ask you to do that, Azibo."

There was no response; instead, Azibo moved to the driver's door and leaned against it, crossing his arms as he watched the other team members at the Nissan.

Still no sign of David or Ian, though, and that began to concern Worthy. The contents of the captured laptops had all been transmitted by now; they were supposed to be making one final transmission to Chen before breaking down the satellite antenna, but the task was taking far longer than expected. He immediately suspected they'd received word of some late-breaking complication to the mission, and that concerned him greatly.

Worthy used the opportunity to fish a small plastic pillbox out of his pocket, then opened it to retrieve a capsule that he swallowed without water.

He'd barely finished stashing the box away when Reilly sauntered over.

"It's day three of our cycle. You take your microdose?"

"Yeah," Worthy replied. Antibiotics, vitamins, supplements—all could be forgotten from time to time. But microdosing psilocybin seemed to have a more positive impact on everyone's sleep, focus, and stress—aside from Cancer and David, who preferred to do the same with LSD—and ingesting a carefully measured sub-hallucinogenic quantity every third day never required a reminder from their medic. Reilly was, after all, the one who'd gotten the entire team started in the first place.

Hell of war, Worthy thought. A hell of a war indeed.

David and Ian finally emerged from the guest house, both men looking cryptically at their teammates as they moved. After staging their gear, David called out in a somewhat stern tone.

"Racegun. Doc. Over here."

They both followed the team leader a short distance from the vehicles, during which time Ian pulled Cancer aside to whisper something. Worthy tried and failed to get a read on what was happening by David's cross-armed posture.

"We in trouble?" Reilly asked.

David recoiled. "What? No. Chen had an update, and it's a big one."

He lowered his voice. "One of the buyer's people slipped up when he was talking over the cell network. We've got a fix on the diamond exchange. Thirteen-hundred tomorrow. Location is Goma, North Kivu Province."

Worthy frowned. "How far is that from where we're headed?"

"Six hours further north, right on the border with Rwanda. Kavumu is on the way and we'll stop there as planned to check in with her."

"If Chen knows about the diamond exchange this far in advance, I'm guessing this means we're relegated to support."

"More or less," David admitted, glancing around the pair to make sure Azibo was still out of earshot. "Tentative plan is we try to pursue Mubenga.

Everything's low-vis, and under no circumstances do we prevent the exchange—otherwise they might never find out who the buyer is."

"Yeah?" Reilly asked incredulously. "And then what?"

"She's moving Ground Branch into position now. One of their elements will secure an exfil on the Rwandan side, and the rest are going to set up surveillance in Goma ahead of the exchange. The buyer's representative is the priority for a live capture as soon as the diamonds are handed off. Once that happens, Mubenga becomes the second string. If we're lucky we can take him on his way out, maybe a street shooting. But our priority is to make it to the exfil point in Rwanda, where Ground Branch will hopefully have the diamonds and the buyer's representative in custody. They 'extraordinary rendition' his ass out of the country to find out who commissioned the heist and why, and then we get on a bird home."

Worthy had more immediate concerns in mind, thoughtfully rubbing the stubble on his jaw as he spoke.

"This sounds a bit fast and loose, even for us."

"The situation is fluid right now," David said. "It's on Chen to fill in the details over the next thirty hours. Apparently Mubenga doesn't even know the specifics of the meet yet, which means we're still ahead of the game. But we'll need to shake up our load plan. Ian drives the second truck with me and Cancer so we can go over the imagery of Goma. Reilly, you're in the lead vic with Worthy and Azibo. And don't mention any of this to him—he'll find out when we need him to."

Worthy held his breath, considered keeping silent, and then decided to speak his mind before they split up for the long drive ahead.

"Boss, I don't like this. Something feels off."

"Good," David said without a trace of humor in his voice. "That means it'll probably come off without a hitch, because your judgment has been suspect this entire mission."

Worthy recoiled. "What's that supposed to mean?"

David gasped, as if the answer should've been obvious. "It means our infil bird was totally fine, and you made the decision to jump anyway."

"*I* made the decision? It was your order!"

The team leader gave an unforgiving shrug.

"You're the one who said 'closing time,' Worthy. Not me or anyone else."

"Well I didn't mean we had to jump. I thought we were about to die, and I don't know, it just...it just sort of came out."

David shook his head in disgust. "Plus one point for steely-cool final words. Minus ten for context. If you want to play it safe, think it through next time. What was I supposed to do, discount my pointman's guidance?"

Reilly put a hand on Worthy's shoulder and gave it a light shake, speaking solemnly. "He's right. We didn't have to jump. You did this to us, Worthy."

"I most certainly did not. Besides, if we didn't jump we would've been found and arrested by Congolese authorities at Kananga Airport. Our faces would be all over the news."

David threw up his hands. "And he finally cops to it."

"I'm not 'copping' to anything, I'm just stating the facts—"

"Then," David cut him off, "you disrespected one of our own. You called Ian a moron, right to his face."

"What? When?"

"No need to play dumb. When Ian suggested we raid that trailer at the mine, look for a little intel, you said it was a bad idea. Tried to talk me out of it."

The pointman was apoplectic.

"That *was* a bad idea, plain and simple. We're lucky none of us got killed."

Reilly said, "Ian was just doing his job."

"And," David added, "if you had your way, we'd already have lost Mubenga *and* the diamonds."

Then Reilly was back in the mix. "Whose side are you on, Worthy? Us, or the terrorists?"

"They're not wrong," Cancer said abruptly, appearing behind Worthy and tapping a fresh pack of cigarettes against one palm. He looked at David. "I swapped my gear and Reilly's for the new load plan. We're all set to go, boss. Better get moving."

17

Rain pattered rhythmically against the window of the Nissan Patrol SUV, drawing Cancer's gaze to the blurred world outside. Through the veil of rain, the dark, dense expanse of Kahuzi-Biéga National Park loomed, its canopy a seemingly impenetrable fortress against the dull, late afternoon sky. The heavy fog that clung to the treetops added an almost mystical quality to the view—mist danced between the trees, creating a scene that was both haunting and beautiful.

"Looks like Skull Island," Cancer noted, leaning toward the door to get a better look.

David didn't get the reference.

"What's that?"

Ian supplied the explanation before Cancer could. "Place they found King Kong."

"Oh."

"Actually," Ian went on, somewhat eagerly, "Kahuzi-Biéga has one of the only populations of eastern lowland gorilla left. All the subspecies are limited to a few Central African countries, whereas Skull Island...well, it's depicted in the Indian Ocean or South Pacific, depending on the source."

Cancer sat back, finally vindicated. "I always wondered about that. No gorillas in the fuckin' ocean, right? It's like they weren't even trying."

"That always bothered me, too."

Shaking his head from the passenger seat, David noted dryly, "For how much you both bicker with each other, it's fascinating what you actually agree on."

The transition from the Copperbelt to Kavumu couldn't have been more stark. The southern part of the DRC was nearing the end of its dry season but the roles reversed in the north, which had a month to go before the frequency and intensity of its rainfall decreased.

Worthy transmitted, *"It's up ahead here, on the left."*

"All right," David replied. "Let's stop."

Cancer glanced through the windshield, where the Suzuki Vitara was pulling off the road and into an enormous gravel strip.

The parking lot at the western fringes of Kavumu was strategically positioned for tourists embarking on or returning from their journeys into the park: the lot was mostly filled with mud-splattered SUVs interspersed with vehicles adorned by tour guide logos. Directly across the street to the east, a row of restaurants and shops faced the parking lot, offering a variety of local and international cuisines, souvenirs, and essential supplies for trekkers.

If his team was going to blend in anywhere, Cancer thought, this was it.

Ian and Azibo reversed their vehicles into open spaces next to one another, front bumpers facing the town.

Cancer stepped out of the Nissan, feeling the cool drizzle and humid air brush against his skin, a welcome relief after the long drive from Mbuji-Mayi. He looked across the open field now separating them from the park's boundaries, a barrier between civilization and the wild that was both literal and symbolic. The dark forest seemed to absorb all light, its expanses rising into mist-capped hills.

The team consolidated at the rear of the vehicles, stretching their limbs to ease the stiffness that the journey had imparted. Their tactical vests and rifles remained discreetly stashed, which, in addition to relaxed manners and civilian hiking clothes, left them looking like a group of tourists.

They opened the SUV hatches to recover lightweight rain jackets as David announced, "First order of business: food run."

"I'll go with Azibo," Cancer volunteered, as if the thought had just occurred to him.

In truth, the men in his vehicle had spent much of the drive analyzing the streets of Goma in preparation for tomorrow afternoon's diamond exchange. David needed to brief Worthy and Reilly on everything they missed, Ian needed to fill in any intelligence gaps, and Azibo would need to be kept busy until the cross-leveling of information was complete.

"Before you go," Reilly said, addressing Cancer in a confrontational tone, "know that I'm only eating what the rest of you guys eat. So don't try to feed me grilled rat meat or any shit like that. Azibo, you hold him to it."

Cancer grinned as he retrieved his jacket and slipped his arms into it. "Experience is making you wiser, Doc."

Then he checked the placement of his concealed pistol and spare mags before withdrawing his phone and checking the display.

"I've got two bars."

"Same," David replied. "Don't go far."

Cancer turned to face Azibo, who had pulled on a slicker and now stood stoically, waiting for the sniper's word.

"Let's go."

The two men ventured across the muddy road behind the parking lot, approaching the western fringes of Kavumu.

The town exuded an ethereal vibe, its subdued colors a sharp contrast to the dynamic life they had left behind in the urban sprawl of Mbuji-Mayi. Cancer was pleased to see tourists and locals moving between buildings despite the inclement weather.

"You been to that park?" he asked.

"Many times."

"How is it?"

Azibo glanced over his shoulder at the rainforest behind them. "You have seen it, my friend—it is beautiful."

The streets of Kavumu were lined with modest shops and eateries, and Cancer let his local asset lead the way. The colorfulness of the buildings, though dimmed by the overcast sky, still held a certain charm.

"Spot any gorillas?"

"Once."

"That's it?"

Azibo chuckled. "You must buy a permit and go with a guide. Then you trek to find them, and stand about twelve meters away for one hour."

"And? What's it like?"

"The babies are curious about visitors. The adults are indifferent—they eat leaves, they groom one another, they sleep."

"Not scary, then."

"I felt only joy. It made me wish humans could live so peacefully."

And there was the seed of a Hallmark card, Cancer thought.

As they continued their walk, the unique olfactory palette of Kavumu enveloped them. The mingling scents of rain-soaked earth and local cuisine wafted through the air, and Azibo dismissed several dining options in the search for a good meal.

With its blend of modern and traditional elements, the town reflected the diverse cultural fabric of the Congo. Small, brightly painted shops neighbored more subdued, older structures, creating a visual mosaic that captured the essence of Kavumu. The occasional laughter of children playing in a nearby alley, undeterred by the rain, added a layer of normalcy to the otherwise tense atmosphere.

"Here," Azibo said, pointing ahead. "This place. Excellent food."

It appeared to be a quaint, inviting establishment, nestled among a row of businesses. A simple, hand-painted sign displayed the restaurant's name in bold, friendly letters above the entrance.

Cancer pulled out his cell phone only to find that his reception had dropped to a single bar.

"I've got to wait outside," he said, finding a wad of cash in his pocket and handing it over. "Get as much as you can, as fast as you can."

"Yes, sir," Azibo replied, taking the cash and stepping inside.

Taking up a position beneath the hanging plants suspended by a narrow outside roof, Cancer retrieved his cigarettes and lit one. Smoking allowed him to instantly look like he belonged almost anywhere in the world, one of the fringe benefits to the invigorating consumption of nicotine.

A local couple exited the restaurant as Cancer texted an update to David, and the team leader's immediate response served as confirmation that they had good comms despite the weak signal. Then he leaned against the wall near the entrance, drawing on his cigarette as he watched his surroundings. Pulling security in a low-visibility context required a few adjustments—looking complacent was a major one, as was appearing to stare at his phone as much as possible as he drew on his cigarette.

There was little vehicle traffic but civilians continued to traverse the streets, hurrying through the rain. The older locals were easy enough to identify by the bright colors of their clothing, though the younger crowd was mostly in Western-style dress as they tended to be all over the world. Tourists were impossible to miss, and their attire spoke to how much money they'd burned in preparation for a trip to the Congo. At the lower end were worn boots, cheap cargo pants, and bulky jackets, while the visitors of means wore overpriced hiking clothes with high-end brand labels, bright GORE-TEX jackets and the like, boots that far exceeded those of special operators in terms of both price and flashiness.

Cancer reached the end of his first cigarette and lit another, the smoke curling up into the damp, foggy air. The rain had slowed to a fine mist, its patter a rhythmic backdrop as his thoughts drifted to the mission at hand—one night of rest followed by a high-stakes movement into Goma the following morning, where the grandest plans of his team and a planeload of Ground Branch operators would reach their ultimate conclusion one way or another.

He was halfway through his second cigarette when he felt an uneasy tugging sensation in his stomach. It was a sensation he knew all too well, and he scanned the area to identify whatever was out of place enough to trigger it. A group of three men approached from his left, all white and all in exorbitantly priced hiking clothes, bantering good-naturedly with one another in British accents. They greeted him and he nodded in return before they entered the restaurant.

Cancer had dismissed them as a threat almost at first sight, and the rest of the town wasn't much different. It was a scene of tranquil normalcy: a few locals meandering, the soft patter of rain, the dim glow of building lights struggling against the fog.

A nondescript white Hyundai sedan appeared at the far end of the street to his right, its appearance in stark opposition to the mud-spattered

4x4s and worn-down local models. It was simply too new, cruising slowly through the intersection, its driver indistinguishable through the rain.

Cancer dialed and brought the phone to his ear, watching a second vehicle follow the first—another sedan with notable cleanliness, moving at a crawl to allow its occupants to scrutinize the area. He waited for it to pass, then pushed off the wall and flicked his cigarette away.

"We're burned," he said as the call connected. "Get ready to exfil to the highway, I'm heading back now."

"Got it," David confirmed, and then Cancer was pulling open the door and entering the warm restaurant interior. He quickly scanned the diners amid the murmur of conversations and laughter, the clatter of dishes, and the sizzle of food being cooked.

Azibo was seated at an empty table near the kitchen, waiting for a to-go order that would never be filled.

Cancer approached him at a controlled yet swift pace, senses on high alert, overcome by frustration that the driver hadn't spotted him yet. He didn't look up until Cancer had nearly reached his table.

"Come on. We're leaving."

Azibo appeared oblivious to the urgency in his demeanor.

"The food is almost—"

"Now," the sniper replied, turning to leave with or without him.

The two men moved quickly toward the exit, their departure drawing a few curious glances from the other patrons.

As they emerged onto the street, Cancer's eyes instinctively swept the area. There was no sign of the suspicious vehicles he'd spotted earlier, but the unease they had instilled in him remained. He led the way back toward their vehicles, steps quick but measured in an attempt to blend in with the evening rhythm of the town.

Sensing the gravity of the situation, Azibo quickened his pace. Cancer placed a hand on his shoulder, slowing him down. "Stay nonchalant," he muttered under his breath. "They're already here."

Any ambiguity in his words was gone as they crossed the next street.

Two blocks to their north was a Toyota SUV with police markings parked in the center of the intersection, flanked by a pair of cops with berets and rifles stopping traffic. Cancer glanced the opposite direction to see a multi-purpose truck so hideous that it could only be a Mercedes Unimog heading west, its bed filled with men in fatigues. Both sights were a profoundly disturbing development in their situation. His team could likely evade a few suspicious vehicles running surveillance in the town, but they couldn't outpace a sudden marshaling of official forces in such numbers.

Placing his next call on the move, Cancer adjusted the plan.

"Police have the roads blocked, military dismounts inbound. Break down weapons, stuff everything into our packs. Only place we can hide is the rainforest."

He heard David relay a verbal order to the others, then respond, "How'd they find us so quick?"

"Must've gotten word before our arrival and taken this long to get here. They're on someone's payroll and it ain't the Agency's. That means the local chapter of KL Militia is in play, so we've got a three-front war on our hands if we don't move now."

"Perfect. Anything else?"

"Yeah, don't wait for us. Carry our gear into the park, assemble rifles, and cover our movement across the field—there's a better than passing chance that me and Azibo will be sprinting across that motherfucker."

"Done. We're stepping off asap."

Cancer had barely ended the call when a distant shout erupted down the street behind them.

"*Simama! Simama sasa hivi!*"

"Don't look," he hissed. "What are they saying?"

"Stop."

The voice continued, "*Polisi!*"

Azibo's voice was strained, a half-step from panic as he duly informed him, "That means he is police—"

"I get that," Cancer cut him off, identifying every possible route ahead and prioritizing them from best to worst. He was a scant two blocks from the team, but breaking into a run now would result in a radio call heralding positive identification to every authority in Kavumu, and that wouldn't do at all.

The suspicion invoked by a single gunshot, by contrast, was a far lesser evil. Now he had to find the best spot to kill a cop with as little fanfare as possible, and let his reflexes and his Glock do the rest. Cancer would inherit an additional weapon from the proceedings but raise the stakes against himself and Azibo considerably—but necessary business was necessary business.

He identified an alley to his right, picking up the pace to reach it ahead of the cop who, from the increase in the volume of his shouts, was now running.

But fate intervened seconds before he committed to the turn.

A crowd of eight or ten tourists emerged from an establishment a few meters ahead, laughing uproariously as they poured into the street for a mass crossing. Cancer saw that they'd just left a bar, and that spelled opportunity.

"Stay close," he said, slipping into the crowd and working his way toward the far side through the stench of beer. They were conversing in the elevated tones of drunkenness that he called the "Irish whisper," preventing him from hearing whether or not the cop was still yelling and, if so, from how close. Two men in the group tried to engage him and Azibo in rapid-fire French. Cancer ignored them as he crossed the road with the full expectation that a sudden hand on his shoulder would require him to spin, breaking the grip with one hand and drawing his concealed pistol with the other, and aim point-blank at a police uniform before executing him in the middle of the crowd.

But he reached the far side of the street without incident, and Cancer seized the moment to veer off into a narrow alleyway. The channel was draped in shadows as his steps quickened, putting distance between himself and the main street. A glance over his shoulder confirmed that Azibo had followed, and he raced ahead to take cover behind a pile of construction debris.

Azibo was only a second behind him, and Cancer pulled him behind cover, signaling him to crouch as he tore his Glock from the holster and knelt facing the street.

He peered out from behind the heap of concrete blocks, broken tiles, and wood scraps partially covered by a tarp, waiting to see if his detour had been spotted.

A policeman appeared a moment later, darting past the alley in pursuit of the drunken Frenchmen. He saw a second cop do the same, then a third, before everything went quiet.

Cancer looked over his shoulder, seeing the alley extend to a series of offshoots behind him, the evening light casting long shadows through the pattering rain.

"You good?" he asked Azibo.

"Yes."

Rising from his kneeling position, Cancer holstered his Glock and turned toward the maze of alleys, hoping that a serpentine route would lead back to the dirt road separating him from the parking lot. With any luck, his team was already moving away from it on their way across the field and into the rainforest.

"Let's go," he said, leading Azibo deeper into the labyrinth as the distant hum of the town receded, leaving only the sound of their running footsteps echoing off the walls.

18

I moved through the dense underbrush at the edge of the rainforest, following Reilly as he led the way parallel to the field.

The late afternoon light filtered through the canopy in a shimmering veil of greens and browns, the stagnant air impossibly thick with the scent of damp earth and vegetation. Rain was falling in waves now, its patter through the canopy an intermittent backdrop to the chorus of wildlife all around us.

Crossing the field to the jungle had come off without a hitch, and now we could remain as concealed as we needed to be. Kahuzi-Biéga National Park was significantly larger than Rhode Island, and any tourists would be located along a sparse road network that was far from our current location. Our civilian clothes and gear had drab coloration to blend in with the wilderness, although playing civilians demanded that our vests and weapons remain stashed out of sight—a practice we had to remedy as soon as possible. Just because we hadn't been followed into the park didn't mean that Cancer and Azibo wouldn't be spotted and pursued by cops, the military, or both.

But first, our acting sniper needed to select his firing position.

"Here," Reilly called out, stopping abruptly.

Worthy raced past him to find a vantage point a few meters away, and I looked left to confirm that Ian had picked up the left flank.

"We're good," I shouted, cueing a mad rush to transition into a tactical configuration.

I dropped my pack, unclipping the retention straps and ripping the top flap open as my teammates did the same. My tactical vest rested at the very top of the storage space, and I set it aside to recover my HK416.

The weapon was broken down into the upper and lower receiver, both ends connected by the sling. I aligned them together and pushed the pins into place, quickly loading a magazine and chambering a round before placing the rifle beside me.

Next I lifted my tactical vest, donning it with a sideward glance to see how my teammates were faring.

Reilly had hauled Cancer's pack in addition to his own, for two reasons. First, he was a big bastard and could handle the weight; and second, as the team's long-range marksman, he was next in line to assume sniper duties. Worthy had already grabbed and assembled Reilly's next-most accurate weapon, repeating the process with his own as a backup.

After securing the tactical vest over my torso, I turned on my radio and inserted both earpieces, using the time it would take my radio to boot up to close my pack and tighten the straps. Using it as a shooting rest was a fool's errand given the underbrush, and I instead took up a standing firing position beside the substantial tree trunk I'd selected for the purpose.

Then I transmitted, "Comms check in sequence."

"*Racegun up.*"

"*Angel.*"

"*Doc, I'm up.*"

Angling my body to test the limits of my field of fire, I took in the sight before me.

The lushness of the jungle was both a sanctuary and a barrier, separating us from the wide expanse of grass and mud that we'd just crossed. The field was dotted with puddles that reflected the cloudy sky and ended in the parking lot where we'd abandoned our vehicles.

Beyond the parking lot lay Kavumu.

The town seemed almost peaceful from this distance, belying the chaos we knew was transpiring within it. Small houses and buildings with tin and thatched roofs painted the picture of a typical Congolese tourist town, now with a few stark exceptions. Streets that had been bustling with activity only minutes earlier were now eerily quiet, the normal civilian movement halted by the influx of military and police.

I scanned the main road that snaked through Kavumu, now dotted with checkpoints. The roadblocks were manned by soldiers and police silhouetted against the occasional headlights of a passing vehicle. The authorities were controlling all movement in and out of the town, turning the place I had briefly known as a bustling community into something resembling a militarized zone.

But none of them had yet fixated on the parking lot; instead, they seemed to be reacting to a general notification of our presence by corralling the entire town. I could make out armed figures moving systematically through the streets, their purposeful strides and occasional stops at buildings indicating a crude search pattern that was nonetheless effective due to their sheer numbers.

Checking my phone, I saw no reception—predictable, I thought, and yet something Cancer and I hadn't considered in the rush to revise our tactical plan. A call would be my only assurance that he and Azibo weren't already in custody or dead, and I was beginning to understand how Chen felt in between each of my satellite transmissions.

The reality of our situation settled in as I shifted my gaze back to the field.

That open expanse was the no-man's land between us and our missing teammates. Given the ever-massing hostile presence, it felt like an ocean that Cancer and Azibo needed to cross on a life raft. If they could manage to do so unseen, we'd have salvaged a major victory despite our compromise.

Keying my mic, I transmitted our courses of action.

"COA 1, Cancer and Azibo make it here without getting spotted. We hole up overnight in the rainforest and keep eyes on the town. The cops and military will think they already missed us and leave, so we can move back to our vehicles once the coast is clear."

Worthy cautiously transmitted back, *"And if the authorities don't leave?"*

"We move deeper into the park, set up along a road, and hijack a tour vehicle at first light. We'd still have a chance of making the exchange in time, and if not, the Ground Branch team will have to pick up our slack."

Reilly had a more grim take on the circumstances.

"*Cancer and Azibo are playing live-action Pac-Man right now, and the odds don't look great. What if we never see them cross the field?*"

"That's COA 2," I replied. "We go in after them."

Ian interjected, "*No, we make comms with Chen and see if she got any traffic about their capture. If not, then we go in after them.*"

"Right," I allowed. "And we'll cross that bridge when we come to it."

But Ian wasn't done. "*There's a COA 3: we don't see them cross the field, but we do see a military contingent come after us. We're here now because Cancer told us to, and Azibo heard that. Cancer's not going to talk if he gets rolled up, but Azibo might—*"

Reilly's next transmission cut the conversation dead in its tracks.

"*There they are.*"

I looked across the field, seeing the impossible.

Amidst a backdrop of military and police swarming like hornets in the town beyond, two figures strolled out of the parking lot and into the field.

Cancer and Azibo were moving casually enough not to draw attention, yet quickly enough to cover the distance as fast as possible without breaking into a conspicuous run. The sheer audacity of the sight was staggering—there was almost no way they could've made it out of the town, and yet if anyone could find a way, it was Cancer.

Now he was gliding across the field with Azibo a few meters to his side, just far enough that they wouldn't both be cut down by a single automatic burst.

I checked their angle of approach, seeing that Reilly's search for a sniper position had taken us twenty meters off the shortest straight-line trajectory that our missing teammates now walked.

"Angel," I transmitted, "*bump left to link up with them as soon as they make it. The rest of us will hold fast.*"

"Moving," Ian replied.

I re-focused on Cancer and Azibo, pulse pounding as they closed the remaining distance. There was no change in the disposition of the authorities behind them, which was a promising sight.

Then I saw an influx of new vehicles—dark, rugged 4x4s streaming into the parking lot, all of them unmarked. It spelled only one possibility, and Cancer had predicted it with eerie accuracy when he told me that the paid involvement to stop us wouldn't end with the Congolese police and military.

The KL Militia had finally arrived.

"*Hey*," Reilly transmitted, "*you guys seeing this?*"

"Militia," I replied tersely, hoping against hope that their arrival was a random event and that they were called in to isolate any escape to the rainforest. "Angel?"

The intelligence operative replied at once.

"*Cancer and Azibo are burned. The police and army aren't here to kill us. They're official forces and don't want five dead Americans on their hands. So they called in the militia to finish us off.*"

Ununiformed men disembarked the 4x4s with alarming speed, flowing out of the parking lot and into the edge of the field.

Cancer seemed to spot this at the same moment I did, his walk transitioning into a darting sprint along with Azibo before the militiamen had a chance to fire.

"*Suicide?*" Reilly asked.

I analyzed the distance remaining between all actors in this unfolding tragedy, assessing at a glance that both our missing teammates would make it to the treeline with a few minutes of lead time at best. No police approached the field, and no military.

"Hold fire," I said. "We start dropping bodies in the open, they'll send the army in after us. The militia thinks they've got us dead to rights, so let's not ruin that now. We'll deal with them in the jungle. Racegun, peel left and lead us toward the others."

Worthy ran behind my position a few moments later, followed by Reilly as we dropped men from the firing line one at a time.

I was last, our three-man formation moving as quickly as we could toward Ian and, judging by the next transmission, Cancer and Azibo as well.

"*I've got them,*" Ian said.

"*Eyes-on,*" Worthy replied.

By the time I arrived, Worthy had already made a 90-degree turn and was leading the way into the rainforest. Reilly and Cancer conducted a frenetic gear exchange, the sniper grabbing his pack and rifle and pulling security back toward the field.

I managed only the briefest of insults to Cancer—"Where's the food we sent you for?"—before breaking left and picking up Worthy's trail. Ian picked up the order of movement behind me, followed by Azibo and Reilly.

Cancer brought up the rear, transmitting the information he'd gleaned from his final seconds of visibility across the field.

"*Ten-man hunter-killer team, plus a commander and a radio operator. Could be more on the way. All KL Militia.*"

Our pursuers clearly had carte blanche from the authorities and had seen exactly where Cancer and Azibo had entered the park.

And that was just the start of our troubles.

Rain meant even wetter ground than usual in the rainforest, and wet ground meant we could easily be tracked by a militia that was unencumbered by the hiking packs we carried, and therefore had the advantage of speed. They'd be on us before long no matter what we did.

"Racegun," I transmitted, "find us an ambush spot. We can't outrun them for long and there's no way they'll lose our trail. Our only chance now is to hit them hard, then break contact and evade until nightfall."

19

Worthy plunged ever deeper into the rainforest, navigating through the dense undergrowth with speed born of adrenaline; for the time being, the weight of his hiking pack, tactical vest, and suppressed HK416 did little to slow his movement. The vegetation limited his rate of travel more than anything else, a handicap that applied equally to the KL Militia fighters in hot pursuit.

The rainforest of Kahuzi-Biéga National Park was a living, breathing entity, its thick canopy a shield against the sporadic downpours of early evening. His senses were on high alert, attuned to the orchestra of the jungle—the chirping of insects, the rustle of wet leaves as he moved, the pulsing calls of birds overhead. Amidst this cacophony, an odd white noise lingered at the edge of his perception, elusive and out of place. He pushed forward, his eyes scanning for a kill zone through which he could lead his team for the oldest ambush technique in the book: a buttonhook maneuver to lay an ambush on their own trail.

But first, he had to find a patch of relatively open terrain.

Suddenly the dense vegetation began to thin out, a promising development. Worthy quickened his pace, eagerly following the path of least resistance that would provide the most open fields of fire once they swung back around.

"Halt movement," he transmitted urgently, unsure of what he was seeing ahead and proceeding with caution until he could identify what lurked in the clearing.

The sight beyond took his breath away.

Before him lay a natural pool, its tranquility disrupted by the majestic force of a 25-meter waterfall. The water cascaded down in a powerful, frothy deluge, crashing into the pool with a resonant roar that echoed through the clearing. The surrounding cliffs were draped in lush greenery, embracing the waterfall in a tight semicircle that formed the natural bowl of low ground in which he now stood.

The roar of the falls required him to speak loudly as he continued his transmission.

"It's a waterfall, perfect ambush spot. You guys need to make a right turn and lead the formation two-zero meters due north, then run the same play due west and due south. Break brush all the way, make it obvious. You'll come out at the basin and by then I'll have spots set for assault and overwatch—they'll walk right into us."

The ultimate decision came down to David, who could either incur a one-minute time penalty to come forward and confirm the assessment, or trust Worthy's judgment and move now.

The team leader didn't hesitate. *"You heard the man—let's do it. Racegun, set the table for us."*

Worthy broke left, splashing across a stream runoff and rounding the basin's edge.

The more he saw of the area, the more he liked it. The slope he ran up was elevated over the enemy's angle of approach whether they followed the team's detour or stumbled directly into the clearing, and the jumble of vegetated rockfall through which he jogged provided ample cover and concealment for a ten-man assault line, much less the few shooters the team would need to employ.

He stopped twice to reappraise the kill zone, visualizing intersecting fields of fire in every possible variation. Then he continued uphill, circling toward the cliffs in the hunt for advantageous positions for Cancer and Reilly's precision fire. In an engagement against a numerically superior force, longer-range kills were far preferable to the alternative—but, he reminded himself, they didn't have to slaughter the entire hunter-killer team, only drop as many as possible before fleeing deeper into the rainforest.

Worthy halted halfway up the slope, reappraising the basin from his new vantage point. Any higher would isolate Cancer and Reilly from the assaulters without providing a correspondingly advantageous view of the kill zone. Without moving, he looked back the way he'd come to identify the twisted and knotted root structure of a fallen tree. It was almost equidistant from the assault line to the overwatch, resting in a natural divot that any approaching enemy wouldn't be able to see. A perfect place to drop and later recover their hiking packs, from which they'd have an almost 270-degree arc of egress options.

"*Racegun,*" David transmitted, "*we're almost there.*"

Worthy looked across the basin in time to see Ian emerge into the clearing, the movement causing every interlocking field of fire to appear in his mind as he envisioned the militia's pointman leading his men into certain death. This was perfect, he thought, utterly perfect.

Waving one arm overhead as the rest of the team spilled out of the brush, he transmitted, "Cancer, Doc, and Azibo up here."

As soon as Reilly confirmed receipt of the message, Worthy backtracked to the gentle ridge overlooking the tree roots, then stopped and keyed his mic.

"ORP is just behind me." In truth, the term "objective rally point" was best reserved for staging rucksacks on the way to a target rather than unceremoniously dumping five hiking packs behind an ambush, but universal brevity was easier.

He used a straight-arm point to trace an arc back and forth over the downslope and transmitted, "Assault line."

"*We got it,*" David replied.

Worthy remained in place until Cancer, Reilly, and Azibo were approaching up the slope, then pointed and transmitted, "By those tree roots."

All three men detoured then, Cancer and Reilly arranging their packs beside each other while Azibo dumped his backpack into the mix.

Once they'd departed and continued moving uphill, Worthy darted down to the packs and dropped his own in line with the others while leaving space for David's and Ian's—when departing an objective in a hurry, the ability to know which ruck was your own was both critical and best facilitated by leaving them spaced out in the same order that the team patrolled in.

Both men arrived, staging their packs before departing as a trio for the ambush line.

David took a position at the right flank, with Ian selecting his cover and concealment in the middle before dropping to a knee.

Worthy picked up the left side, spacing himself at roughly the same interval and dropping down behind a sloping and moss-covered rock big enough to offer protection from incoming 7.62mm rounds. After tearing out a fern in his path, he had enough visibility to cover the kill zone from an elevated prone shooting position, by which time David was on the team frequency.

"*Assault line is set,*" he began. "*Overwatch, how are you looking?*"

Reilly replied, "*I'm good; Cancer is getting into position now. We've got Azibo hiding a few meters behind us.*"

"*I'm up,*" Cancer said as cool rain penetrated the treetops once more. "*Ready to rock and roll.*"

There was a none-too-subtle bloodlust beneath the sniper's words, and for good reason. They'd just made the switch from fleeing rabbits to predators lying in wait, and all that remained was to wait for the hunter-killer team to arrive before executing a little population control.

It was a smart move on all fronts. The militiamen had no reason to slow down on the trail unless they'd been punched in the face and forced to deal with some wounded and dead in their ranks. If they kept pursuing after that, it would be at a far slower and more cautious pace, by which time Worthy and his teammates would be running out the clock until sunset and, with it, the advantage of superior night vision, which allowed them to vanish altogether.

David answered, "*We'll wait fifteen minutes. If they haven't found us by then, they've either lost our trail or given up.*"

Truth be told, Worthy actually *wanted* the enemy force to stumble out of the vegetation he now watched closely on the opposite side of the basin.

His team could afford to let a few fighters trickle into the open before hitting them hard, evening the numerical disparity at least somewhat before running once more.

And in the meantime, views from an ambush line simply didn't get any better than this.

The waterfall was a magnificent force of nature, dominating the clearing with its power. Water cascaded down in a massive, unbroken sheet, crashing into the basin below with a resounding roar. The sound was a constant, thunderous rumble that filled the air and reverberated through the dense foliage surrounding the area, almost comforting in its regularity.

It was only out of the loosest consideration for rear security that he looked behind him.

When he did, Worthy immediately registered the sway of taller plants that rose above the waist-deep carpet of brush below.

He keyed his mic.

"Shit, they're behind us. Coming up fast."

He scrambled to reverse his position, slithering on his belly away from the gentle crest on which he'd been positioned as David transmitted back.

"Get this line turned around. Cancer, what can you see?"

"Jungle's too thick. Relocating."

Worthy was gripped by a sense of abject disbelief at this turn of events. The militia hadn't simply turned the wrong way at the clearing, they'd veered wide around it and very deliberately approached the ambush line from behind. They should have either followed the team's trail into the kill zone or hit the basin head-on—there was simply no universe in which they could anticipate what his team was going to do before they themselves knew, and yet that seemed to be exactly what was occurring now.

Then the answer hit him hard, a gut-wrenching realization of something so obvious that it seemed impossible he or anyone else could have missed it.

This was the KL Militia's backyard; they knew the terrain, knew from his team's general direction of movement what they would encounter along the way. It was possible that the militia had used this waterfall as a navigational landmark dozens of times before, and there was only one way to maximize the effect of an ambush here. The hunter-killer team had anticipated all this, then countered it so elegantly that Worthy couldn't help but appreciate their skill.

Now his team faced an attack from the worst possible angle—they were backed up against the water basin, an open area that would be suicidal to flee across. The cliffs blocked another angle of retreat, leaving a downhill sprint back toward Kavumu as their only way out. Hell, he thought, at this point they couldn't even make a run for their hiking packs without running headlong into a dozen bad guys.

Every advantage Worthy had meticulously identified was now turned against them, and he maneuvered into a low crouch to initiate the battle before the enemy tripped over him.

He rose slightly from his squat, identifying an enemy fighter to his front and two more further back, staggered in an echelon to the right.

Worthy fired on the nearest target, stitching a sloppy, rapid burst of single shots across his arm and abdomen before the man dropped his rifle and went down.

Diverting his aim sideways, Worthy drilled the next man with a trio of better-aimed bullets that seemed to have the desired effect, the body falling out of sight as he transitioned to the third man and opened fire again, the sound of his suppressed shots lost amid the din of the waterfall.

His newest target unquestionably saw him, making a barely audible shout that ended when Worthy released five more subsonic bullets his way. Before he could appraise his shots, a burst of automatic fire roared from his left.

The sound preceded an explosion of colorful birds overhead as Worthy dropped beneath the foliage and darted three steps sideways, popping up again to locate who had shot at him and instead finding that Ian and David were already well within their own gunfights, the dark shadows of militia fighters barely visible among the trees. Worthy swept his weapon from left to right and back again, firing rapid double taps at any and every possible movement in the brush until his magazine was expended.

Dropping out of sight once more, he made another lateral bound while reloading in preparation for what had to come next. There was no time for David to issue an order and no need—the three shooters had found themselves in a reverse near-ambush, and with bullets ripping through the leaves around them, the only option was to assault forward.

Worthy slammed his bolt forward and made his next bound, lurching toward the enemy formation while staying low.

But he'd only made it a few footfalls into his advance when a freight train barreled into him from the side, an enemy fighter knocking him down as he lost his grip on the HK416. He hit the ground panicking as he attempted to figure out what the hell had happened.

He recognized the man atop him now as the first one he'd fired on, now gut shot but not out of the fight. One of his arms was useless after being fractured from Worthy's initial, poorly aimed shots. The fighter's remaining hand was pinned on Worthy's throat, and the pointman broke the grip with a blow from his forearm and pinned the man's leg with his own to roll sideways.

The momentum carried him too far, putting him on top and then on the bottom again in a clumsy barrel roll of human bodies. Worthy rotated sideways once, finally using the weight of his body to pin his opponent to the ground.

His Glock was still in its concealed holster beneath his shirttail, too risky of a position for him to chance reaching for it.

Worthy drew his Winkler knife instead, aiming for the heart until the man's thrashing diverted the tip of the blade a few inches right of his sternum. Worthy tried to drive the knife home only to find that he'd struck bone; angling the blade beneath the rib, he applied a full measure of strength and plunged it in up to the hilt.

Air whooshed out of the man's lung in a ragged, desperate rush. It made a harsh, guttural sound, a deflating tire struggling against its last resistance as Worthy ripped the knife out. Then he stabbed twice more, this time into a kidney, before rolling off his victim and landing on his back in a desperate struggle to regain control of his rifle.

The sight that awaited him was nightmarish in its sudden appearance —brush was suddenly pushed aside as another militiaman materialized from the jungle, a man nearly as large as Azibo with a thick, unkempt beard, towering over him with a predatory grace.

He wore mismatched military fatigues that were stained and torn from untold skirmishes, the fabric soaked from the jungle air and clinging to his imposing frame. Strapped across his chest was a bandolier of ammunition, his hands maneuvering an aged yet well-maintained AK-47 whose surface was marred with scratches and dents.

Worthy's perception of time had ground into slow motion, each detail vivid in stark clarity as he brought his HK416 to bear with a distant hope that his assailant's weapon would possibly jam with the first trigger pull. Neither man could miss at this range, and all that mattered was the better angle of a rifle barrel, an advantage that his opponent had in full.

The bearded fighter jumped slightly with a movement that could only be absorbing the recoil of his weapon, and yet there was no muzzle flash nor sound of a gunshot—he looked momentarily bewildered, his eyes that of a man stung by a hornet he never felt alight on his skin.

His arms fell limply to his sides, AK-47 tilting downward until it was vertical as he dropped to his knees with two bloody rosettes forming on his left side. Worthy still hadn't aligned his barrel before his opponent's head kicked sideways in a spasming tic that ended with a cratered hole in his temple, a macabre exit wound that disgorged fleshy chunks of brain matter through a pale fog of pink and gray.

By then Worthy's index finger was seated on his trigger, prepared to pull off the first shot in a one-on-one engagement that hadn't existed a second and a half earlier. He held his fire as the dead man toppled over face first, then cut his eyes toward a flash of movement a meter to his right.

A massive form effortlessly vaulted the body, the figure disappearing into the undergrowth with an HK417 as quickly as he'd appeared.

Reilly bowled past Worthy's position on his way eastward, the urgency of reinforcing his team pulsing through him like an electric current.

His goal was to move in semicircles, weaving behind the lines of his team's counterattack, ready to reinforce wherever he was most needed. Simple enough. But where that line actually *was* remained open for debate —Worthy should have been two or three bounds into his assault, and instead Reilly had stumbled upon him almost immediately upon reaching the basin's edge.

Now he ran east amid the undulating chatter of automatic gunfire, scanning the ever-shifting expanse of jungle for any sign of his remaining teammates. Tactical prudence dictated that he bound from one covered position to the next, but Reilly instinctively ceded his fate to Lady Luck given the tremendous abundance of trees, and relied on sheer momentum to remain a ghost in the jungle.

He spotted Ian behind a tree trunk, firing around one side before being forced behind cover by incoming gunfire. The intelligence operative was pinned in position in a game of cat-and-mouse gone wrong, and Reilly could make out enemy fighters closing in with a mix of caution and aggression. They moved through the dense underbrush, intermittently visible between the patches of foliage and shadow in a violent countdown to their inevitable kill.

As grim as the sight was, the team had bigger problems.

A conspicuous lack of enemy fighters at the right flank told him that most of the bad guys were massed to the east, near David, in a flanking maneuver to drive the team toward the cliffs. Reilly had to get there as soon as possible—if the militiamen managed to get behind the team, they were all as good as dead. But there remained the small issue of keeping Ian's brain intact rather than splattered all over the rainforest.

Faced with two competing priorities, the medic resolved to do both. The very attempt would require extreme precision and, more importantly, extreme speed.

Fortunately, Reilly had both in spades.

There was a raw, primitive rage that medics knew better than most, the hardwired instinct to save the lives of their men extending beyond casualty treatment. Combat medics joked that they killed better than most simply because they didn't want to do the work of fixing wounded teammates, but the outcome was very real and very, very effective.

Upon seeing the chaos erupting in the bushes below his long-range shooting position, Reilly felt boiling hatred well up inside him; his rush down the hill occurred with an odd sense of detachment. He'd suddenly become a spectator more than a participant, seeing his view transition as if he were watching a movie. The act of gunning down Worthy's assailant had occurred almost devoid of any physical sensations at all; he was totally in the zone, a peak state of combat performance that required no conscious effort.

And now, having made the split-second decision to save Ian, his body took over the rest.

The interplay of light and dark in the dense jungle shifted around him as he diverted to an oblique approach toward his teammate, eyes registering the movements of enemy fighters and adjusting his course in a fluid play-by-play. He darted behind a tree and brought his HK417 up, delivering three rounds to a crouching target as a second fighter looked over to identify this new American combatant.

By then, Reilly had slipped behind the trunk and taken aim again off the opposite side, reacting a fleeting second faster than the man who now had to shift his point of aim accordingly and received a controlled pair of subsonic 7.62mm bullets before he could complete the process.

Then Reilly was on the move again, understanding that both targets were down without visually confirming either, his legs driving him ever further toward his next covered position.

An unnatural movement caught his eye and he came to a full stop in the open, swinging his aim 45 degrees right and seeing nothing, yet unable to move. A head peeked over a fern bed ten meters away, and Reilly fired three times into the vegetation, his suppressor aligned with where a corresponding torso should be.

His ejected shell casings were still airborne as he turned and ran, no longer toward Ian but behind him, intuitively knowing beyond all doubt that the time to make a break for David and the left flank was precisely that moment.

Ian finally caught sight of him and shouted something that Reilly didn't hear, instead maintaining a wide-eyed laser focus on David's anticipated position. No visible fighters to his side, which meant that he was correct about the flanking maneuver; he should have called Ian to follow him, should have reloaded on the move because he only had nine rounds remaining in the mag—how could he possibly know that?—but Reilly did neither. He traded both actions for speed as he was forced further east by whatever impulse had been driving his actions from start to finish in this gory spectacle.

He caught sight of David bounding away from him, assaulting eastward toward the encroaching enemy and fighting like hell. The hisses and cracks of incoming bullets persuaded Reilly to slow his aggressive charge, moving instead from tree to tree as he swept toward David's left side. It was a more precarious choice than the opposite direction; Reilly was now placing his back to the basin, which removed the majority of angles to retreat and risked silhouetting him against the open ground.

But a far greater risk was allowing the enemy to succeed in their flanking maneuver.

Reilly instinctively came to a stop behind a weathered tree trunk from which he could make out a spread of militiamen on either side of his team leader, who was now stationary behind cover and reloading. Reilly fired a three-round volley at the leftmost target, then swept right to repeat the process with the next fighter he could identify by the spark of his muzzle flash. A thwack of bullets impacting his cover caused him to duck behind the tree, crouching low before he emerged on the opposite side.

He only had three rounds remaining, reserving two for an advancing fighter before taking aim at a man who was little more than a fleeting shadow amid the undergrowth. Reilly fired his final bullet and felt his bolt lock to the rear.

Slipping behind the tree trunk, he conducted a textbook emergency reload with uncanny speed and prepared for his next move. He'd just engaged four targets in rapid succession, having no idea whether he'd hit much less incapacitated any of them; his current position was burned, but a cursory check was necessary before he bounded forward and left.

Moving to the opposite side of the trunk, he angled his body sideways and took aim only to find that further bounding wouldn't be required at all.

There were hardly any militiamen left to see. The few traces of movement he could make out consisted of fighters who were retreating with very good reason.

Chunks of bark were exploding off trees, the enormous leaves of tall bushes whipping as bullets sheared through them. Worthy and Ian had arrived and dealt themselves into the fight, resulting in a four-man-strong last stand that had accomplished its desired effect in full.

Then the gunfight was simply over, a final shot of unsuppressed gunfire fading to the roar of the waterfall that prevented any assessment of whether or not there were wounded survivors in the brush. That didn't much matter, he realized, because there would be no time to search bodies or conduct a combat resupply.

David transmitted. *"Consolidate at the ORP."*

"I'll cover the withdrawal," Reilly volunteered.

He trailed David, Ian, and Worthy northward, checking his backside and the western flank often while keeping a deliberate distance from his teammates.

The supercharged fighting instinct then faded, abruptly leaving Reilly in full control of his own actions although adrenaline continued surging so powerfully that he could feel his temples throbbing.

How could he explain what had just occurred? His single greatest performance of valor had come and gone almost without him thinking in the slightest, the vast majority of the act relegated to some reptilian portion of his brain that didn't allow for second-guessing in the wake of raw action. Reilly almost felt like he'd wake up at any moment from a particularly vivid dream, and he forced his mind to more pressing matters.

"Med check in sequence," he transmitted.

"Racegun, no injuries."

"Suicide, I'm good."

"Angel, no injuries."

The responses ended there, prompting Reilly to order, "Cancer, check in."

When no response came, Reilly repeated the process more forcefully.

"Cancer, med status."

But the net remained silent, prompting the medic to pick up his pace toward the ORP and, beyond it, the semicircle of high ground that ringed the basin. It was the last place he'd seen the sniper before reinforcing the assault element, and he registered a sinking fear that Cancer's long streak of emerging from gunfights uninjured had finally come to an end.

Cancer maintained his firing position, his rifle carefully perched in a notch among the exposed tree roots at the ORP. He caught another sight of the shadow between trees before it vanished again, altering his point of aim in eager anticipation of another appearance as Reilly transmitted to him a third time.

"*We're on our way. Hang in there, buddy.*"

He ignored the message, focusing instead on continuing to track the fleeting target that he'd only get one shot at, if that.

Upon realizing that the enemy was coming up on the ambush line's six o'clock, Cancer had taken far too long disentangling himself from the brush at his initial sniping position. By the time he was in a position to join the assaulters, it was too late to help them; instead, he'd set up at the ORP for long-range support. As expected, there wasn't much opportunity to be had in the dense foliage between the treetops and the undergrowth, but he'd soldiered on regardless, firing a grand total of seven shots during the engagement. All of them were extremely complex, technical shots and none of them, frustratingly, were identifiable as hits or misses. The vegetation was too damn thick, the trees far too numerous for him to be sure.

And while a majority of the surviving enemies must have fled together, there remained one singleton separated from his comrades—an inexperienced fighter by the looks of it, making a panicked rush in the hopes of outrunning any opposition. His confidence that he'd been successful in that endeavor was probably increasing with each passing second, and Cancer remained hopeful that he'd have the opportunity for a miracle kill after the conclusion of the bloody engagement.

He heard someone approaching behind him, the sound of a man crashing through the undergrowth audible over the waterfall's constant hum.

Worthy said, "Cancer, we've been trying to—"

"Shut up," the sniper said, glimpsing another flash of the retreating fighter before he disappeared amidst the trees.

Then Ian's voice as he arrived: "Whoa, we thought you were—"

"Shut up," Cancer repeated, hearing a new transmission being spoken.

"He's fine," Worthy said. "I'm co-located at the ORP."

Another crash of brush preceded David's voice.

"Hey, man, is your radio down—"

This time he was spared the trouble of responding.

"Quiet," Ian said. "He's got something."

Cancer was desperately trying to block out the noise of his teammates donning their packs—until Reilly arrived, he still had a chance of getting one last shot in under the buzzer—when he finally got the opportunity he was looking for.

The retreating fighter was visible once more, appearing in a tight gap between trees.

But this time he was loping directly away from them, the angle perfectly aligned for Cancer to maintain his visual. Adjusting his aim, he completed his exhale and used the natural respiratory pause to settle his sights.

The trigger break was clean, his weapon's recoil subsiding as Cancer lined up for a follow-up shot and instead saw the barely visible target drop out of sight amidst the bushes.

"Got him," he announced without fanfare. "You guys can run your mouths now."

The only response came from Reilly, who was panting for breath as he arrived and said, "Man, I was afraid you were bleeding out."

Cancer glanced over his shoulder to see the medic grabbing his hiking pack, the second to last one that remained in the middle of the tight perimeter established by the rest of the team.

Squinting at Reilly's left side, he said, "You're shot," before returning his gaze to his sector of fire.

"Hilarious," Reilly replied sullenly.

"Oh shit," David gasped, "you actually are. Jesus, sit down."

There hadn't been much of a wound to see—Cancer had merely spotted blood seeping through a hole in the narrow space between the medic's radio and med pouches, although the view would be considerably worse once the point of injury was exposed.

He heard Reilly sit, followed by a shuffle of equipment as David helped him remove his tactical vest and asked, "How bad?"

"Not bad," Reilly said, "yet."

Cancer listened to the click of a plastic buckle—Reilly opening his med pouch—followed by the crinkle of plastic as he removed a chest seal from its packaging.

The sniper looked back again to assess the injury, now visible as the medic held his shirt up with one hand and used his teeth to peel off the backing of the transparent, pancake-sized chest seal.

He used a gauze pad to wipe the blood away before laying the adhesive side directly over the wound, pressing it into position as he continued, "Worst case, a hemo- or pneumothorax could be forming. I should know ahead of time if that happens, but if I drop, you guys will need to be ready with a chest tube kit and a needle decompression."

Cancer returned his gaze to the jungle, scanning for movement.

"Hey, Reilly," he began in an accusatory tone, "aren't you the one always telling us to *look* for injuries instead of just assuming? Might not feel it because of adrenaline, you said. Full visual sweep, you said...fuckin' hypocrite."

Worthy shot back, "Take it easy—he saved my ass."

"Mine too," Ian offered.

David was next. "He saved all of our asses because they were about to break through our left flank."

Cancer rolled his eyes, addressing the medic over his shoulder.

"Guess you were hungry, you fat fuck—only time I've seen you get mad. When did you get hit?"

There was a rustle of gear as David helped Reilly back into his tactical vest.

"No idea," he said with astonishment. "Must have been a ricochet, because I never felt it. Don't even feel it now—"

"Yeah, well, that'll change once we start moving. Better pop some pills while there's time."

David spoke impatiently.

"Cancer, get your shit on—we'll grab Azibo on the way out and patch up Reilly once we get some distance. Let's move."

20

"That," Ian said with trepidation, "is pretty gnarly."

Reilly grimaced at the sight, agreeing in a pained tone.

"Yeah, it...it is. Makes your job easier, though."

They were roughly 45 minutes northwest of the ambush position now, having completed an evasive route designed to slow down enemy pursuit—but after the bloodbath at the waterfall, it seemed that no one had bothered to follow them as of yet.

This time, their stopping point was wisely chosen for its sheer mediocrity.

Their team's perimeter ringed a minor, unremarkable hill that provided good fields of fire in a near 360-degree arc of the surrounding rainforest, with particularly good visibility along their backtrail. The elevated position was bordered on one side by a stream for a much-needed water resupply and, most importantly given the latest confrontation, far from any key terrain that the KL Militia would be intimately familiar with.

The only real surprise was that upon arrival, Reilly had refused to treat his own injury. He prided himself on providing his teammates with rigorous medical cross-training, and given they were at the beginning of a far-overdue rest break, he decided to put their skills to the test. David,

Cancer, and Worthy had promptly recused themselves, citing the need for heightened security so soon after stopping.

And that was how the unenviable task fell upon Ian.

The intelligence operative worked quickly in the waning light, kneeling over Reilly's prostrate and shirtless body while removing the chest seal from the medic's ribs. Having delicately peeled the clear dressing all the way to the wound itself, he saw the seemingly impossible sight that greeted him now—the bullet was visible, barely stuck to the adhesive seal, and Reilly reached down to pinch it between his fingers.

"Go ahead and pull it off," he said.

Ian peeled the remainder of the seal off as Reilly freed the distorted piece of metal, its shape altered by the impact with bone. It was no longer the sleek, cylindrical object that had sailed from an enemy barrel; the tip was flattened from its violent impact, the once smooth and shiny surface now marred and slick with blood.

Cleaning the wound with alcohol and betadine, Ian asked, "How did that happen?"

Reilly grunted. "Round hit the rib, penetrated slightly over the top. Must've worked its way back through the wound tract during our movement."

By then Ian was applying a bulky gauze dressing over the bullet hole, prepared for Reilly to correct his treatment plan at any moment.

But the medic laid his head down instead, breathing shallowly and still clutching the bullet as Ian taped his dressing into place.

"You okay? Your breathing sounds rough."

"It's *been* rough," Reilly corrected him. "Diaphragm is having trouble contracting, but it's just the pain. What next?"

Sitting back on his heels, Ian thought for a moment. "Tape your ribs all the way around, potential fractured rib in the middle."

"Right you are."

Reilly lumbered to his knees, lifting both arms to allow Ian to complete the procedure while providing the minimum possible guidance.

"A little tighter...that's good, you've got it."

By then David was making his rounds, collecting the water bladders

from each of his teammates' hiking packs along with the bottles carried by
Azibo.

The team leader tossed the containers in the center of the formation,
speaking as Reilly put his shirt back on.

"Doc and Cancer on security. The rest of us are on resupply."

Azibo started to rise until David stopped him.

"Stay up here—we've got guns, you don't. Help them keep a lookout."

"As you wish, sir."

After the water containers had been split more or less equally between
the three men, Ian followed Worthy and David down the hill and toward
the stream they'd spotted on their way in.

The jungle around them seemed to transform with the onset of nightfall, the bright greens of daytime fading into deeper, darker hues. Overhead, the canopy was a dense weave of leaves and branches that filtered the
remaining daylight, casting a dim, shadowy glow over the forest floor.

And while the slope itself was a gradual descent, the terrain was
uneven, littered with roots and rocks that made the journey treacherous.
Every step Ian took was cautious and deliberate, his boots occasionally slipping on the damp earth and wet leaves.

The sounds of the jungle seemed to intensify, the chirping of crickets
and the croaking of frogs forming a natural chorus that grew in volume as
they neared the stream.

As he approached, the sound of running water grew from a soft
murmur to a clear, soothing cadence, guiding him closer with each step.
Upon arriving at the stream, Ian felt like he had uncovered a hidden world
within the rainforest: tall grass bordered a narrow, pristine ribbon of water
that flowed gently. Even the air here was cooler, bringing a welcome respite
from the humidity of the jungle.

They lined up at the edge and began filling the water containers. No
one spoke—the stream's tranquility provided a stark contrast to the day's
earlier violence, and Ian suspected that each man was allowing himself a
moment of peace.

Finally Worthy said, "Guys, I fucked up with picking the waterfall.
Didn't even occur to me that they could've known the spot and anticipated
our ambush."

David sighed wearily.

"Yeah, you fucked up," he began. "But so did I. Didn't matter whether I confirmed your plan or not—I would've done the same thing. If anyone can smell a rat it's Cancer, and I didn't hear him objecting once he got eyes-on the kill zone."

Ian finished topping off a water bladder, adding a pair of chlorine dioxide tablets before screwing the cap back on and speaking. "We all did the best we could. Enemy always gets a vote, too. Those guys were good, better than we gave them credit for. But we can't exactly think of everything when we're running like hell, can we?"

"No," Worthy said. "No, I guess not."

Then David concluded, "We've already used up eight of our lives on this mission, and now our luck is running on fumes. We've just got to make it last a little longer...that being said, the decision to jump three nights ago was still your fault."

He grabbed his water containers and moved out a few meters to the left to pull security as Worthy called out after him, "Prick."

Ian had recoiled at David's comment, then relaxed. There was only one explanation for a ground force commander accusing his pointman of botching such a monumental decision as whether or not to conduct an emergency bailout, and that was some kind of inside joke he was unaware of.

So much had happened since their infil bird was crippled that Ian had nearly forgotten about the cataclysmic event altogether. It was, in hindsight, merely the first in a series of pitfalls that had befallen them since entering the DRC. Driving straight into an ambush in Kolwezi was next, and he hoped that their most recent compromise in Kavumu would be the last.

He capped another bladder and grabbed one of Azibo's bottles, dipping the mouth beneath the stream's burbling surface. Water flowed into the bottle along with an unintended passenger: a tiny, speckled aquatic frog that struggled valiantly to escape the riptide within its new prison.

Ian smiled, lifting the bottle and observing the panicked creature for a moment before pouring it back into its natural habitat, where it was swept downstream with kicking abandon.

Looking up, he saw that Worthy had finished his refill and was facing right, augmenting the security afforded by Cancer on the hilltop. Ian tilted his head, finding David was still doing the same to his left. He looked back into the stream, noticing for the first time that smooth stones were visible at the bottom. Some were as small as pebbles, others as large as a man's fist, each nestled comfortably against its neighbor to form a bed of smooth, undulating shapes beneath a veil of sand.

Ian rose abruptly and took a step back, feeling Azibo's water bottle slip from his grasp and land in the wispy grass of the streambed.

He made a beeline for David, kneeling beside him with the words, "We have to talk."

21

Reilly lay in the prone behind his HK417, hearing the return of the water resupply element up the hill behind him where Cancer's watchful eye had covered their movement to and from the stream.

The medic heaved a breath and released it in a ragged sigh, continuing to survey his sector of fire with dull fury pulsing through his veins.

The emotion wasn't wholly explicable as adrenaline from the gunfight, although that certainly lingered despite the time and events that had since lapsed. But when he searched for further causes all he could come up with was his wound, an unbecoming affliction for any combat medic. The bullet had penetrated the intercostal space between his sixth and seventh ribs along the mid-axillary line, and his combat pill pack—Tylenol, Meloxicam, and Avelox—had only done so much to take the edge off.

A large part of his frustration, Reilly guessed, was that he was devoid of the usual myriad chances to second-guess his actions over the course of the gunfight. In the aftermath of such events it was normal, almost unavoidable, to seek flaws in his actions that could have been avoided for a better outcome. But now there was no way to criticize himself for a missed opportunity to emerge uninjured, largely because he had no idea when the fuck he'd actually been hit. Had the round that ricocheted into him come from a poorly aimed shot fired by a militiaman who'd spotted him running? Was it just a random bullet bouncing through the jungle? Either could have been the case.

Beneath his anger was a nervous energy about returning home. How was he going to explain getting shot to Olivia, who already wanted him out of the gruesome job he'd somehow come to regard as totally normal? Do anything long enough, he supposed, and it would begin to seem reasonable. The entry of a woman into his life had changed all that, and when Olivia said she wanted children, his entire worldview was annihilated with the implications. David had somehow managed to make the otherwise mutually exclusive ecosystems of combat and kids coexist in an uneasy sort of harmony, but could he, Reilly, ever do the same?

As if reading his mind, David approached and knelt beside him.

Reilly grinned. "Speak of the devil—I was just thinking about you."

"Thought I felt my ears burning," David quipped, "but there's only four others out here, so I suppose the odds weren't too bad. How are you feeling?"

"Fine, I guess. I just...I need to talk to you about something. Olivia's been—"

"Not now."

Reilly felt a resumption of his previous anger overtaking his tumultuous introspection.

Speaking through gritted teeth, he said, "We can't move until we've transitioned to night vision, and seeing as we've got a few minutes before that happens, I thought I'd share one moment of actual human vulnerability, David. Just one."

Rather than apologize in the slightest, the team leader squatted lower, leaned in, and whispered briefly in Reilly's ear. The statement was so out of place that the medic briefly wondered if David was attempting the world's most ill-timed practical joke.

"Seriously?" Reilly whispered back.

David nodded and rose, leaving the medic with no chance to question him further.

Luck was a fickle thing, Reilly decided, bestowing minor blessings at the most curious of times. Here he was, wallowing in self-pity, wishing there was some outlet for the simmering anger that had only increased after David cut off his attempts at a normal conversation, when a peculiar and serendipitous opportunity presented itself.

Reilly let his rifle rest on the bipod and, rising to his considerable height, rolled his neck to either side and rotated his arms at the shoulders to loosen up. The pain in his side was still there, all right, but he'd manage.

Then, in the most unnatural of acts that ran counter to every instinct, he left his weapon behind.

Turning to face the inside of his team perimeter, he saw that everyone was pulling security except himself and Azibo, who sat in the center, stuffing his now-full water bottles in his backpack.

Reilly lunged forward and tackled the man, his body crashing into Azibo's with all the force he could accomplish.

The impact was immediate and crushing, causing Reilly's side to erupt in a searing jolt of pain, the agony momentarily clouding his vision. Azibo was taken by surprise but reacted in a flash, grunting as he bucked and twisted his body in a desperate attempt to free himself from Reilly's grasp as an intense and chaotic struggle ensued.

Azibo's size and strength made him a formidable opponent even from a compromised position, and his movements were fueled by a raw, primal need to escape. Reilly, grappling with both Azibo and his own pain, fought to maintain control and keep the man pinned to the ground.

David, Worthy, and Ian rushed in to assist, each grabbing hold of Azibo to subdue him. The team worked in unison. David and Worthy grabbed Azibo's flailing arms, struggling to keep them still, while Ian applied his weight to Azibo's legs, preventing him from kicking out.

The sound of the scuffle was a mix of grunts and heavy breathing, the forest floor churning beneath them in a blur of movement and struggle. Reilly was pleased to note that Cancer, true to form, had entered the fray and was now viciously and repeatedly kicking Azibo in the ribs without the slightest clue as to *why* he was doing it. The sniper had as much control over his actions now as a shark in a feeding frenzy.

"Roll him," David said, cueing Reilly to release his grasp just enough to flip Azibo onto his chest with the assistance of his teammates.

Finally, with a concerted effort, they managed to secure Azibo's arms behind his back and flex-cuff his wrists and ankles together.

Reilly panted and winced with pain, and as he slowly dismounted the man, his side throbbed with each heartbeat. He was the only one big enough to tackle Azibo and was paying for it dearly now, the immediate agony fading as he realized the battle may have just begun.

For a few seconds, it seemed as if Azibo would break the zip ties through sheer force of will.

The Congolese man rolled onto his back and sat up, struggling violently against the restraints. Veins popped to the surface in his forearms and neck. If he got free, Reilly thought, they were going to have to shoot him. In the leg, perhaps, but shoot him nonetheless, and in the process expend more precious medical supplies.

But Azibo's struggle began to subside, his movements slowing as the reality of his restraint set in.

Worthy ripped open Azibo's backpack, searching the contents as David frisked the man from top to bottom.

The team leader completed his sweep, then patted the interior of the restrained man's left thigh.

"Right here," he said.

Ian sprang into action with his medical shears, cutting Azibo's pants to expose a black Spandex sheath wrapped around his leg. Extracting a rectangular device from a pouch in the material, he flipped it over and narrated what he'd just found.

"It's passive," he said. "Looks like it's not set up to continuously transmit a location."

Continuing to examine the object, he continued, "But that's where the good news ends. This thing doesn't use cell towers—it runs on a combination of low-orbit satellite connectivity and short-range encrypted mesh networks."

Looking up at Azibo, he concluded, "This is a $50,000 piece of hardware to accomplish untraceable voice comms. *We* don't even use this tech. Where did you get it?"

The man didn't answer, and David waited a beat before saying, "Cancer, Racegun, pull security. Doc, sit down—you look like you're about to pass out."

Reilly complied, noticing as he did so that Azibo was subtly flexing against his restraints.

"Knock it off," the medic said with menace in his voice. His pain was now almost forgotten—the fact that a Congolese asset he'd previously trusted was trying to get his entire team killed was too much to bear. "We could execute you, we could torture you, we could tie you to a tree and let you see how long it takes the leopards to find your ass. You can't do a damn thing about it."

Ian intervened, "But we're not going to do any of that. Instead, we're going to have a nice civil talk about why you betrayed us."

Azibo's first words were an inquiry.

"How did you know?" he asked hollowly.

Ian gave a bland smile.

"We've had three catastrophes on this mission, starting with an aircraft shootdown. You must have told the CLF we were coming, and what our linkup point was. It was too far inland for us to get there except by parachute. Mubenga had to take us out to preserve his diamond heist. So he found one of the only clearings in the jungle we could've landed in, and had it surrounded by fighters to take us out in case we arrived by freefall. But the flight paths to Kananga Airport were too close to be a coincidence, and he hedged his bets against a low-altitude static line jump by placing an anti-aircraft gun to shoot us down before we reached our exit point."

Reilly cut in, "Fortunately for you, the aircrew survived. Otherwise this conversation would be going down a whole lot differently."

"Second," Ian continued, "when we were refueling before Kolwezi, you vanished into the woods for a few minutes. *Déféquer, monsieur*, remember? You were sending a message to Mubenga just like you've been doing all along; but the fact we'd followed him that far meant he had an informer in his ranks. So he found the source's phone and kept sending updates, turned off R610 onto the local road to lead us into a trap."

Azibo offered no objection, instead staring at the ground beside his bound ankles.

"We weren't attacked at the guest house because you couldn't get outside alone to find a signal and transmit—we were on the second floor and had guard shifts all night. And you were supervised from the time

Worthy told you our next stop was Kavumu until the time we got here. But as soon as you had a few minutes alone at the restaurant, boom, the cavalry shows up for catastrophe number three. That means you must have gone out the back door to make a call."

Reilly could tell from Azibo's silence that they had him dead to rights, and there was a long pause before he responded at last with an expression of guilt and shame.

"I kept my reports as general as possible."

Reilly shot back, "Well that didn't seem to work out, did it?"

"It did," he said, now glaring at the medic. "Back in Kavumu, if I had specified the parking lot instead of the town, we would all be dead."

Ian nodded quickly. "And we appreciate that. But what's going to happen now is that we're going to find an area with a clear signal. You're going to tell your handler that we flushed out of here, and are moving deeper into the park for exfil at first light."

"I will not," Azibo insisted. "And you cannot fake this. I have words I use to assure them I am cooperating. I have words I am to use under duress. And I will not reveal these things, no matter what you do. I will *never* cooperate."

The response assured Reilly that Azibo's threat, as well as his resolve not to compromise his service in the slightest, were very real.

Ian said, "You never struck me as a fanatic."

"I have become one."

Cancer replied in a singsong voice, "I've got my Winkler..."

"No," Reilly shot back, fixing his gaze on Azibo. "After this fuck almost got you guys killed, I'll do it."

While ordinarily mild-mannered, he meant exactly what he said. The team could easily claim that their local asset had been killed in the previous firefight, and Chen would be in no position to dispute that assessment.

Azibo swallowed, eyes growing wide as he looked imploringly from one team member to the next. "My wife is pregnant."

David shook his head unapologetically. "We already know that from your dossier. But it's way too late in the game for mercy, Azibo. What I want to know now is—"

"They have them," Azibo interrupted.

"They have who?"

"My wife," he said, eyes reddening and filled with tears. "And my unborn child."

The admission hit Reilly like a sucker punch.

He'd been so blinded by rage that he hadn't so much as considered why a local asset with a sterling record and consistent income from the Agency would suddenly break bad. If Reilly had managed to consider the contradiction, he probably would have discovered the answer before Azibo had a chance to say it—the man's dossier indicated that his wife was pregnant, though he'd never admitted that fact to anyone on the team. The combination of those two factors alone seemed damning evidence that he wasn't lying now.

Ian made a fist, tapping his knuckles against the forest floor. "When?"

"Two days before you arrived," Azibo said. "They must have known I was an asset. Men came to my house and...put a gun to my wife's belly. I had to tell them everything. Then they gave me the device, and told me they would not leave my home until your team was dead, one way or another."

David asked, "Mubenga's people? The CLF?"

"Yes," he managed, tears spilling down his cheeks. "Mubenga's people."

Ian gave a knowing nod and clarified, "With assistance. They couldn't hold off on the depot raid without missing out on most of the diamonds. Whoever commissioned that heist knew we were coming, and provided this"—he held up the communications device—"in case the CLF didn't get us on infil."

Reilly felt himself deflate, the anger washing out of him at once and in full. He placed himself in Azibo's position, considering how he'd react if Mubenga had Olivia hostage—and only one answer came to mind.

"All right," Reilly said abruptly. "We can fix this."

Seconds earlier the medic was ready to carve Azibo into pieces; now, he was almost serene, total logic restored to his voice as he went on, "The barricade in Kavumu will have ended by now. We can surveil the town to be certain, then move in and recover our vehicles now, tonight."

David replied tentatively, "I don't disagree...but we're not carrying Azibo out of here."

The unspoken implication was that they'd have to execute the uncooperative man, reclaiming control of their fate and coming up with a cover story for Chen later on. No one seemed to object to this possibility save Reilly, who had a grander plan in mind at the moment.

The medic looked fixedly at Azibo. "Let me get this straight: they're holding your wife hostage in your house."

"Yes. They have men outside, too, all over the neighborhood. If I do not cooperate, they will...they will do things to my wife. They will burn down my home and all the others. You know the CLF. They threaten much, but they do not lie."

"No," Ian said, glancing at the treetops. "They don't."

Reilly swatted a hand impatiently at Ian, then addressed Azibo once more.

"And you live nearby."

"Mugenderwa, yes. The village is only a half-hour drive from Kavumu, which is why I did not want to return here."

Cutting his gaze to David, Reilly saw total recognition in the team leader's face.

Rather than object to the medic's forthcoming plan, David asked, "How far along is your wife?"

"What does that matter?"

"I'm not just passing the time, asshole. How far along is she?"

Azibo hesitated. "Five months."

"Good."

"Why?"

"Because my wife's at seven, and she can still walk reasonably well."

"But what is your point?"

David gave Reilly a nod and said appreciatively, "Go ahead. It's your plan."

"Check it out," Reilly said. "You're not going to cooperate. I get that, because I wouldn't either—they've got your wife. But you just said Mugenderwa is a half hour from our trucks."

"So?" Azibo asked, now growing enraged. "So what? What is your point?"

"My point is," Reilly declared, "we can get out of the rainforest, drive to your village, and set up surveillance. If what you say checks out, if the CLF really is there, we can get your family back."

He shook his head gravely. "The police have already been paid. And I told you that the CLF has security. Not just in my home, but the entire neighborhood."

"You were with us at the cobalt mine, weren't you? You've seen what we can do. And in this case, we don't want to take down all their security, just the guys inside your house. Otherwise the red flag goes up and Mubenga knows we're onto you."

Azibo sounded fearful now. "You will get my wife killed."

It was Ian who spoke next. "I hate to tell you this, Azibo, but you saw what happened to our source once Mubenga found out about him."

Cancer volunteered helpfully, "Human barbecue."

Ian continued, "After this thing is done, Mubenga isn't going to give you a free pass."

"You think I do not know this?" Azibo shot back. "I am already dead. My only concern is for my family."

After releasing a remorseful sigh, Ian looked down, avoiding Azibo's eyes and speaking quietly. "He's not going to give your wife a free pass, either."

Azibo was silent, staring into the middle distance with his nostrils flaring. If denial had thus far kept him from accepting the obvious, Ian's words were clearly getting the point across.

Reilly quickly added, "We don't want her to get harmed any more than you do. But the only chance either of us has of saving her and your child is to get them back."

Azibo offered no argument; he was stock-still, probably coming ever closer to acceptance of his family's fate and what could be done to stop it.

"So here's the deal," Reilly went on. "We rescue her now, tonight. When she makes it back to you alive, you cooperate fully. Send a false update to Mubenga making it look like we lost some guys, and are carrying our dead to a vehicle pickup deeper in the park. That buys us some time to keep moving until they figure out your wife is gone. No matter what, you remain our local asset until the mission is complete. When we exfil the hell out of DRC, you and your wife come with us. The CIA will relocate you both."

Staring back at Reilly, he asked, "And if your mission fails? If she doesn't make it out alive?"

"Then we're all fucked anyway. But that's not going to happen."

David leaned forward to place a hand on Azibo's shoulder.

"Like I said, my wife is pregnant. My team will treat this rescue as if we were saving my own family. You have our word."

22

Cancer warily approached the edge of a clearing, sweeping his suppressed HK417 across the gaps in the trees ahead.

His night vision transformed the woods around Azibo's neighborhood into a sea of green hues, the shapes and movements of the night rendered in a monochromatic palette. Being the furthest from the team's starting point, he would be the last to get into position; but any urgency he felt was mitigated by the very real possibility that there could be one or more guards at the edge of the clearing before him.

A dark silhouette flashed across his field of view, causing him to momentarily freeze—the bats had been messing with him all night. Then he continued stalking forward, senses heightened under the cloak of night.

Gradually the thick, earthy scents of the forest were interspersed with the fresh, clean scent of open air, the trees to his front too spread out to risk proceeding further. Instead he moved laterally until his view improved, sweeping left toward a low fallen tree. Cancer flipped down the bipod legs on his rifle and set them atop the coarse bark, settling into a cross-legged firing position with his weapon aligned on the area he'd been selected to cover.

The main entrance to the neighborhood consisted of two concrete posts on either side of the road, where three men were spread out in a state of casual complacency. He could make out automatic weapons in his night vision's eerie luminescence, and performed a quick scan to determine if anything was amiss. Any new guard arrivals for shift changes or, God forbid, reinforcements, would have to pass through this crucial checkpoint.

He keyed his mic.

"I'm in position at the northwest, have a good line of sight to the neighborhood entrance. Three stationary guards, nothing suspicious." With grave finality, he transitioned to the formal nomenclature of numbered observation posts. "OP 1 is clear. Let's get this party started—any objections?"

"*Hold,*" Reilly answered. "*I've got a bogey lingering at the intersection leading to Azibo's house.*"

Cancer desperately hoped this would be the last delay as he was struck by the sheer irony of the situation at hand. In the rainforest they'd been trying to survive until nightfall—and now, outside Azibo's neighborhood, they were fighting sunrise.

The time crunch was unavoidable ever since they'd made their pact with Azibo. Since they were stranded in the jungle, there were no nearby villages to purchase vehicles and no time to wait for daybreak in order to hijack one along the park's trails; instead, they'd been left with the sole option of getting their original trucks back.

Which was, of course, much easier said than done.

Patrolling through dense vegetation at night was far more time-consuming than doing so during the day, and extricating themselves from Kahuzi-Biéga National Park had taken almost twice as long as the sum total of their movement into it. Then they'd spent an hour at the jungle's edge, surveilling the outskirts of Kavumu for any indications that the authorities were waiting for them.

Even when the coast seemed clear, they'd stealthily moved back to their trucks and taken off with the full expectation that they'd have to kill some Congolese cops and/or army soldiers along the way—instead, they'd slipped out of town wholly uncontested. Then they'd parked outside Mugenderwa, slipping through the woods outside Azibo's neighborhood to confirm or deny his story about a CLF lockdown.

That much had been easy enough to establish due to an initial sighting

of a pair of roving guards, which warranted an approach to Azibo's house...
at least, after they'd fully assessed the Congolese Liberation Front's level of
security.

Which was, of course, relatively excellent.

Reilly's voice came over his earpiece.

"*OP 2 is clear.*"

"*Hold,*" Ian replied over the net. "*Main road has two bogeys heading north.*"

Cancer sighed in frustration, continuing to watch the three bored
guards through the trees.

The real issue wasn't how many bad guys were present, but *where* they
were: patrolling the neighborhood perimeter, walking between the houses,
and finally, as was the case for two CLF fighters, stationed outside Azibo's
front door. Fortunately the woods wrapped tightly around the cluster of
homes, presenting ample opportunities for the team to observe them unnoticed. This was, at heart, a simple problem set: the team needed sufficient
observation posts to guide an assault element from the woods to the house
and back again.

But as with everything in this godforsaken mission, there was a catch.

Ian transmitted, "*OP 3 is clear.*"

Then Reilly was on the net again.

"*Hold, I've got a new bogey cutting down the side street.*"

Cancer's vantage point in the northwestern part of the woods was
required to establish a clear line of sight to the neighborhood's main
entrance. Another was necessary to the east to watch the backside of
Azibo's house—where the entry would, with any luck, soon be taking place.
Still another was needed to the southeast, where an observer could clearly
view the neighborhood's main thoroughfare. Finally, the southwestern part
of the woods presented an obligatory location for an observation post from
which to monitor a wide street intersecting with the assault team's journey
to the target, as well as a portion of Azibo's front door.

Which was, of course, hidden from the view of any other possible
location.

All that was well and good, except for the minor hitch that they only
had five shooters in the first place. That meant they could either establish
proper surveillance at all four positions and send in one man to attempt a

rescue, or roll the dice on dropping multiple observation posts of equal importance to send in a proper assault element. The former option was suicidal while the latter was, for lack of a better word, also suicidal.

And while both choices were equally fucked, David had the final say.

"*OP 2 is clear,*" Reilly said excitedly.

"Hold," Cancer said through gritted teeth, describing the latest development in his sector of fire. "My three guys just consolidated at the neighborhood entrance, one on the radio. Could be replacements are about to arrive or it could be nothing. But I have to be sure."

There was no response—what was left to say? They could easily go back and forth like this until sunrise necessitated a total mission abort.

And that was arguably a better outcome than the actual plan. In the end, David had cited Azibo as the determining factor—their Congolese asset-turned-traitor had provided the general layout of the neighborhood and surrounding woods while they were walking out of the rainforest, and once the team arrived, they'd confirmed that his information was true with staggering accuracy. He'd further specified the exact cellar door behind his house through which the assault element could enter without getting spotted at a door or window.

Cancer knew the decision on how to proceed with a hostage rescue was preordained from the start. No self-respecting team leader would ask his men to do anything that he himself wouldn't, and that logic could be and was twisted to determine which poor bastard would serve as a one-man assault element.

Because the truth was that David, whether he knew it consciously or not, *wanted* to go in alone.

Cancer watched the three guards spread out before him, keying his radio before there was time for a new complication to arise.

"The guards just dispersed. OP 1 clear."

"*Hold,*" Worthy transmitted. "*I've got a bogey passing the backside of Azibo's house.*"

The disappointment was overwhelming; this was a puzzle that required four blindfolded participants to assemble it by verbal communication alone. No one individual could call the shots. Between the guards, the neighborhood layout, and the split-second updates required to guide a lone assaulter into the target, this entire operation was an unavoidable collaboration of the worst kind.

Then Worthy spoke with urgency.

"OP 4 is clear—check in."

Cancer keyed his mic. "*1 clear.*"

Reilly was next. "*2 clear.*"

Then Ian.

"*3 clear.*"

At the very moment Ian went silent, Worthy transmitted again.

"All OPs clear. Suicide, go, go, go."

I ran from the edge of the woods with my rifle, the unfamiliar neighborhood of Mugenderwa spread before me as a maze of shadows. My previous observation from Worthy's post was limited to a narrow slice of the village, and now I was barreling into it at a dead sprint.

I ran in a straight line, remaining a few meters to the right of Worthy's line of sight to the cellar door that represented my final destination. Only twenty meters separated me from the nearest homes, but under the circumstances it felt like as many kilometers.

My last wink of sleep had occurred at the guesthouse roughly twenty hours ago, to say nothing of the driving, fleeing for our lives, and slaying motherfuckers in the rainforest before moving back out of it that had transpired since then. I was now running on adrenaline and two Snickers bars from my previous theft, both consumed while I waited at Worthy's observation post.

The citizens of Azibo's neighborhood were mercifully asleep, but there were enough guards around to obliterate any sense of comfort that simple fact could offer. My only guidance now was the live updates from four observation posts, each of which represented a lifeline in this unknown territory. My night vision goggles bathed everything in green light, turning the mundane into something otherworldly. Houses, fences, and parked cars appeared as ghostly shapes, their details blurred and distorted but nonetheless the best view I'd get. A veil of clouds blocked out the stars, and aside from a few scattered exterior lights among the homes, the Congo nightfall was absolute.

My heart pounded in my chest, not just from physical exertion but the weight of the task at hand. Every step was a calculated risk, every turn ahead a potential encounter with the roving guards I knew were out there but couldn't see. The air was cool and damp against my skin, carrying faint sounds of barking dogs and, at periodic intervals, the crowing of an insomniac rooster.

But the silence over my earpieces was the most unsettling thing of all. My team's radio chatter had gone from constant to nonexistent; no one would transmit now unless they had some update critical to my progress, and when that occurred, I had better react without the slightest hesitation.

Unfortunately, the first such report arrived when I was still five meters out from the nearest houses.

"*Hold,*" Reilly warned me. "*Two bogeys inbound to the intersection along your route, ten seconds out.*"

I sprinted the remaining distance, scanning the immediate vicinity for cover. Against the house to my right stood a large, cylindrical water tank, a common sight in the DRC.

It was my best bet.

Decelerating so fast that I nearly fell on my ass, I dropped to a crouch and pressed my back against the tank's cool metal surface, feeling the slight vibrations of the water I'd disturbed within. The tank was large enough to conceal my presence but I crouched further, wedging myself against the side of the house.

The low murmur of a conversation in progress reached my position. I held my breath, trying to still every part of my body. The seconds stretched out, each one longer than the last, the guards' voices growing louder as they neared the intersection, footsteps a rhythmic thud against the dirt road. Through the green haze of my night vision goggles, I watched two oblong shadows flit past the dimly lit ground beside me. They seemed to be moving with casual alertness, their voices and footsteps receding into the night.

I was damn well going to wait until instructed otherwise, but another ten seconds passed before Reilly finally came back on the net.

"They're north of the intersection, continuing to move. OP 2, clear."

Without any of my teammates telling me to hold in position, I quickly rose and continued my advance toward Azibo's house.

The neighborhood was a labyrinth, and I was acutely aware of how easy it would be to stumble into the path of a patrol. This was uncharted territory, and one misstep could compromise everything.

I'd barely resumed my forward movement when Cancer came over the net.

"Heads-up," he said, *"the three guards at the neighborhood entrance just got a whole lot more alert. One's on the phone."*

Had I already been detected? If I committed to ducking behind another water tank, I'd be exposed to any of the crisscrossing guards who happened to pass by; my options boiled down to retreating to Worthy's observation post, or continuing to move forward in the hopes that I could make it into Azibo's cellar before the situation got any worse.

So forward I went, slipping past the wall of the house beside me, darting across an open space to the next one, and then proceeding toward the open road ahead.

Cancer transmitted, *"Yep, there it is—cargo truck pulling into the neighborhood now. Either they got tipped off or there's about to be a guard rotation. It's southbound on the main road...I've lost visual."*

Ian spoke a second later.

"I see it, truck is still headed southbound."

I stopped at the corner of the final house before the dirt street. By now I could hear the throaty growl of a diesel engine along the main thoroughfare a scant block beyond Azibo's house. Raising my rifle to clear the road in both directions, I saw no guards and sprinted across while there was still time to do so.

Ian continued, *"Cargo truck stopped at the main bend...it's making a three-point turn...now it's facing back north. Tailgate's dropping."*

I knew what came next, and this time I didn't let up on my sprint. Each passing second brought me closer to my destination, and Azibo's cellar was the only refuge I'd find given what was happening now.

Ian continued, *"I've got a dozen or so men dismounting, no one's in a hurry.*

Assess they're switching shifts. Suicide, wherever you're at, you better go to ground until this blows over. OP 2, what can you see?"

Reilly replied, "*Nothing yet, stand by...okay, I've got—*"

"*Break break break,*" Worthy interrupted. That kind of transmission was never a good sign, I thought. He continued, "*Suicide, two bogeys have doubled back. They're on course to pass Azibo's house. Get your ass in the cellar, now.*"

By then I had no choice.

I was crossing Azibo's backyard, the sound of the cargo truck's idling engine growing louder, my gaze fixed on the cellar door that was partially concealed by overgrown bushes. There was no time to adjust the focus of my night vision for close-proximity work; I scrambled to a stop before the low door that was angled 45 degrees from the ground, dropping to my knees as I felt for the handle. Finding it, I flipped open a rusty latch and pulled the door open by a few inches, momentarily startled enough to freeze—the creaking noise was a step shy of ear-splitting in the stillness of the night, a detail that Azibo had failed to mention.

"*Fifteen seconds,*" Worthy said, cueing me into action. The approaching guards would probably hear me open the cellar, but if I didn't, they'd definitely see me. I pulled the door ajar enough for me to slip inside, stumbling on the concrete steps within and losing my grip.

The door banged shut over my head, so loud that it may as well have been a gunshot.

Clumsily descending the steps, I aimed my rifle forward across an inky blackness that presented a veil of flat green darkness in my night vision. I triggered my infrared floodlight to illuminate my surroundings, more of a cramped storage space than a room: wooden shelves appeared, covered in spiderwebs and laden with jars, along with a stack of worn-out furniture piled haphazardly to my left.

My floodlight clearance only lasted a moment, long enough to assure myself there were no targets down here, before I spun around to aim at the cellar door through which two guards were about to enter after hearing my noisy grand entrance.

Sidestepping to use the furniture as cover, I was crestfallen to discover it consisted of a set of rickety chairs and a table that had seen better days, none of which would do much in the way of stopping incoming rounds.

With any luck, however, the pile would serve to conceal me long enough to shoot a couple inbound fighters.

Or at least, I hoped so.

When my earpiece crackled to life, I fully expected the message to be redundant—I'd see the cellar door swinging open clearly enough without any update from Worthy. Sure enough, the transmission came from him.

"They passed by, headed for the main road."

How could that be? It seemed impossible that they didn't hear the door slam shut a few seconds ago, which sure as hell seemed too loud to be obscured by the engine noise. Had they been conversing too loudly to notice? I had no idea and rejected my pointman's assessment out of hand; surely they were about to return, possibly with more men.

But Reilly's next message caused the thought to evaporate in the midst of a far greater threat.

"Five new arrivals approaching Azibo's house from the west."

I heard footsteps thumping overhead and turned around, igniting my infrared spotlight once more to see that the low ceiling was crossed with beams. Cobwebs clung to them, and in one corner, a small, rusted water pipe ran along the ceiling, disappearing into the wall.

Identifying the stairs leading up to the house's main level, I centered my floodlight on the door overhead and approached it with cautious steps. The floor beneath my feet was uneven, made of packed dirt that had hardened over time. A few old rugs were strewn across it, and I lifted my boots to avoid snagging the edge of one as I inhaled musty air filled with the mildewy tang of old wood.

I kept my aim trained on the center of the door, kneeling as I reached the base of the steps and killed my infrared floodlight. If that door swung open I'd have to shoot whoever was at the top before racing upward in the transition to an emergency clearance.

There were more footfalls overhead, the movements quicker now, as Reilly continued, *"Front door to Azibo's house is opening, and...wait one...three guys entered the house, two switched with the outside guards. Stand by...three guys exiting. That's the shift rotation. Suicide, you've got at least three guards inside, plus two outside the front door, how copy?"*

I keyed two bursts of static to let him know the message was received, and listened to a new flurry of heavy boots on the main floor. When the footsteps stopped, I lowered my rifle and considered how long I should wait. A few minutes at least, I thought, enough for their curiosity at the new surroundings to dissipate. But I couldn't afford to stall much longer than that: the complexity of moving into the neighborhood would be compounded exponentially when reversing the journey with a pregnant woman in tow.

Provided, of course, that I could rescue her in the first place.

The arrival of new guards also presented a fresh complication I hadn't anticipated, the results of which were more curse than blessing. I'd been hoping to encounter a small enemy force that had been in position for hours and reached the apex of complacency. Instead I was about to face off against fully alert militiamen, and that fact alone increased my risk by a factor of ten.

On the other hand, I had no idea how long the guard shifts were. Eight hours, twelve, twenty-four? No matter what, a successful raid now would maximize our time to escape before another crop of guards arrived to find their predecessors slain.

We'd set ourselves up for success as best we could, prioritizing surveillance in the interests of me making it into and out of Azibo's house uncompromised. The rest fell upon me alone. But I knew the layout of the single-floor house well, had made Azibo sketch it out and answer my every question about which way the doors swung, which ones could lock and which ones couldn't, where the windows were and what sectors of visibility they'd afford to any guards outside.

I also knew the location of the bedroom, where his wife was most likely being kept. If this all went to shit I'd get there as fast as I could to defend her, then try to exit out a window before making a panicked rush for the woods in the hopes that my teammates could take down enough guards to give us a fighting chance of escape.

A heady rush fell over me then, some primordial instinct assuring me that the time to initiate my clearance was now.

I rose and climbed the first stair, testing for creaks before committing my bodyweight and moving to the next. Any sense of fatigue had evaporated in full, replaced by unshakably steadfast confidence.

The door ahead was rimmed with faint light, and I flipped my night vision upward on its mount upon reaching the top of the stairs. Angling my head so my ear was just off the door, I paused to listen. A faint rhythmic beat of Congolese music seeped through the cracks, something energetic and pulsating.

I eased the door open, and it yielded silently before I sidestepped into the hallway.

The corridor was dimly lit, a single bulb casting a weak glow. A man sat in a chair outside the bedroom door two meters away, eyes closed, head bobbing to whatever was playing through a set of earbuds. An assault rifle lay on the floor beside him, well out of his immediate reach.

I took two swift steps forward and came to a stop, paused a half-second, and then shot him through the temple.

His head lurched and he slumped forward, threatening to topple out of the chair. I removed a hand from my rifle and intervened, grabbing his shirtfront to bring him to an uneasy sort of equilibrium. A soft, metallic tinkling sounded behind me, the bullet casing of my subsonic round skipping along the floor after bouncing off the wall to my right.

But the muted sound of my shot seemed to have been swallowed entirely by the music in the kitchen, where I could now hear the low timbre of conversation. A pair of baritone voices seemed relaxed, unaware of my presence in the hallway.

Rotating my rifle to my back and letting it hang from the sling, I placed my other hand behind the man's neck and leaned him backward in his seat. His head lolled to the side and one of his earbuds clattered to the ground, blood draining out of the entry wound.

There was a fantail splatter of blood and gore across the wall and floor on his opposite side, and I made sure he was stationary before reclaiming control over my weapon and leveling it toward the only open door in the hallway: a bathroom. Its interior was dark, although either of the remaining guards could come to use it at any moment. I shifted my aim to the corner at the end of the hall, ignoring the closed doors of twin bedrooms.

After waiting for two breaths to pass, I continued moving, the music from the kitchen growing louder.

I paused at the corner ahead, letting my eyes continue to adjust to the low light from the kitchen that cast long, wavering shadows across the floor.

Listening intently, I heard two men having an exchange in Swahili. There was the clink of glass on glass, hopefully someone pouring alcohol. Then a muffled explosion of laughter wholly independent of the conversation, its noise barely discernible over the thumping beats of the music. It must have been from one of the guards outside the front door, I realized.

Rounding the corner ahead would lead me almost directly into the kitchen and dining room, where only the front door would stand between me and the guards outside.

I waited until the shadows on the ground stopped moving. The remaining men in the house were probably seated at the dining room table now, which would give me time to approach the open doorway, enter and clear to the right, and take them both down just as they were looking up.

Breathing a final sigh, I inhaled and spun around the corner.

A man was in the kitchen, leaning against a counter and cutting his eyes in my direction. I was already aiming at him, and some gut feeling told me to go for a headshot that would leave no chance of sound beyond his corpse hitting the floor—I somehow knew beyond all doubt that my bullet would sail true and smack him square between the eyes. Without the slightest hesitation, I pulled the trigger.

My suppressor made a hushed whiff and the milliseconds stretched out as I watched for the imminent spray of brain matter out the back of his skull.

The bullet struck him in the throat.

He dropped with a wheezing, gargling noise, landing on his back and flopping around like a fish out of water before I could so much as take a follow-up shot. Fortunately, I'd achieved a hit; unfortunately, the round clearly hadn't severed his cervical vertebrae.

I heard the scrape of a chair from the dining room, and when there was no corresponding cry of alarm I held my fire, instead stalking further down the hallway; the downed man involuntarily kicked and flailed as approaching footfalls were increasingly audible over the music. Whoever this unseen guard was, he was utterly confused—for all he knew, his comrade was choking on a chicken bone, although that would change as soon as he spotted blood—and my best move was to exploit the delay and continue moving.

My first glimpse of the newly arriving guard occurred when I was a meter away from the kitchen entrance. A massive shoulder and arm appeared at the right edge of the doorway, its owner facing his fallen teammate as he tried to comprehend what was happening.

I momentarily halted, taking aim at the exposed shoulder and firing a single shot that sheared through cartilage and bone as the man gave a hiss of alarm and vanished from the doorway. A scream was about to follow or, worse still, a radio call, and I entered the room and pivoted my upper body to the right to silence him before either could occur.

To my horror he had barely moved. I'd just begun my turn when an AK-47, wielded by the guard's good arm, smashed my weapon to the side. Dropping to a knee as I fought for control of my rifle, I brought my barrel up a fraction of a second too late.

The AK-47's buttstock cracked against the corner of my head, causing me to drop like a stone as the music was replaced by high-pitched ringing in my ears, blotches of color obscuring my vision.

My pain level was an 11 out of 10, arms and legs turning to jelly as I landed on my left side, straining to see what the hell was about to happen.

Neon flashes ringed the periphery of my vision. I felt like I was looking through a drinking straw, aligning my gaze upward to see my opponent hoisting his AK-47 high with one hand, buttstock aligned with my head as he prepared to swing it down. That would break my skull wide open without a doubt, and this sudden realization caused me to regain some degree of control over my limbs. The tip of my suppressor had come to rest just between the man's feet, and I managed to lift and angle it to the extent I could before firing a single shot.

The bullet tore through his right knee and he went down hard, the floor vibrating with his impact. The bizarreness of this fight wasn't lost on me—I didn't know that I'd ever shot out an enemy's joint before, and now I'd destroyed two of them within a single point-blank engagement. I swung my rifle toward his sternum, only making it as far as his groin before the effort caused my still-tingling hand to fire prematurely.

Now that we were both on the ground, I rolled groggily to my back to lay my rifle flat over my stomach, aiming between my legs. All I could see at present was an expanse of camouflage fatigues, but that was good enough for me. I pulled my trigger once, then twice more, before I could feel enough of my extremities to steady the weapon somewhat.

Then I ripped five more shots, halting the effort only upon seeing the mass of fatigues roll sideways.

I fought my way to my knees, lungs screaming for air. Looking down, I saw that I'd blasted a loose flurry of bullets through the man's abdomen just below his sternum. His head was rolled to the side, eyes staring blankly, either dead or fully paralyzed. Either was fine by me.

Finally I staggered to my feet, using one hand to brace myself against the wall behind me. I nearly fell sideways, shoulder hitting the wall and causing me to fire a subsonic round into the vinyl flooring a few inches beside my right boot—my second negligent discharge of the evening.

Fixing my eyes on the dead man, I stammered in a whisper, "You... fucker."

I almost stumbled forward and tripped over his body, finding my balance at the last second with a foot on his chest. My knees were weak, the sum total of my partially concussed movements akin to operating on the ragged fringe of drunkenness before a full blackout.

But I had a lot of experience in that state, and managed to rest my suppressor against his temple before firing again, this time intentionally.

I regretted the act as soon as I completed it. Blood spray coated the tip of my now scorching-hot suppressor, where it instantly baked into a dried crust that would be nearly impossible to clean off.

It was only then that my bleary mind registered that I was supposed to be in the middle of some grander clearance attempt. I looked up, alarmed, waving my rifle with one hand and finding that the rest of the small kitchen-slash-dining room was unoccupied.

Or at least, almost unoccupied.

The throat-shot man was somehow still alive, though previously frantic kicks had by now slowed to a lethargic scrape of boots against the floor. Was he still making gargling noises? Had his partner screamed after his 5.56mm vasectomy? Was the music still playing? I had no idea, still couldn't hear a thing except gongs ringing in my brain.

Staggering over to the throat-shot survivor, I aimed at his chest and fired a single bullet that ended his life—by then, he probably couldn't feel a thing—before suddenly recalling that there were two guards positioned out front.

Arcing my rifle toward the front door, I backed up slowly, looking down only to ensure I didn't trip over the man behind me. I cleared the doorway and moved back down the hall, tucking my body behind the corner and kneeling to address any guards that might enter. If I turned away now, I wouldn't be able to hear them if they came stomping through the kitchen banging cymbals.

I transmitted, "The guards outside the front door—did they hear? What are they doing?"

No response.

I wondered if my comms were down, nearly checking my radio before a more obvious explanation came to mind.

Keying my mic again, I whispered, "I'm deaf right now. Speak up, yell at me."

Then I registered Reilly's voice, tinny and distant against the ringing in my ears.

"*They're still sitting around.*"

"Okay. Good. Great. Three guards down, stand by."

Checking the hall behind me to find the first guard dead in his chair, I reloaded and moved toward the doorway of the main bedroom. The constant ringing in my head was only now beginning to subside, my balance and alertness slowly returning, but I couldn't afford to wait any longer.

I opened the door and made entry, breaking left with my rifle at the ready.

The hallway's light illuminated the room as I stopped and scanned for targets. A worn dresser stood against one wall, its surface cluttered with various items. A small, threadbare rug lay on the floor, and faded curtains hung limply over a window that looked out into the night.

I focused on the bed and saw a woman lying on her side, facing away from me. Her body was still, draped in a thin, worn blanket that had slipped down, revealing her wrists bound to the bed frame by rope. She was either sleeping or pretending to be asleep, although the kitchen massacre made me suspect the latter.

Before she could scream at the sight of a blood-splattered white man standing over her, I pulled out my cell phone and dialed.

When the display lit up with a connected call, I walked forward slowly and whispered, "Fatima. Fatima, it's okay."

But she didn't move, spurring me to continue, "Be very quiet, there are guards outside. Azibo sent me."

That caused her to roll over and face me, her eyes wide and glinting.

"Azibo?" she asked, the sound faint.

I approached and held the phone to her ear. If all was going according to plan, Azibo was on the other end telling her to cooperate fully—it was about the only insurance I had that she'd do what I said when I said it, and both were steadfast requirements for getting out of the neighborhood alive.

Once I saw her eyes well with tears I took the phone away, trading it for my Winkler knife. I cut the rope from the bedframe, then freed the knotted ends as I whispered, "We've got to go, now. Put your shoes on, we've got a walk ahead. Well," I said, quickly correcting myself, "probably more like a run."

Fatima sat up and pulled the blanket away. Her belly was swollen with the fetus but not terribly so, and she slipped on a pair of worn sneakers beneath the bed.

"You need to follow my instructions exactly, okay? We've got people in the woods telling us when it's clear to move."

"Yes," she acknowledged, rising to move toward the dresser—there was a silent understanding between us that she'd never enter this house again.

"Forget about clothes—"

But she turned with a rosary instead, a cross swinging in the center as she pulled it over her head and tucked it into her shirt.

I asked, "Do you need water? Bathroom?"

She shook her head. "I would like to leave now. Where are we going?"

"The cellar. I want you to go out the door and turn right. Don't look, understand?"

She nodded but I preceded her out of the bedroom anyway, stopping to the side in order to block her view of the dead man propped up in the chair.

Fatima averted her eyes as instructed, stiffly approaching the stairs with a surprisingly dignified air for a woman who'd spent days tied up. After reaching the cellar I'd take the lead once more, but first I had to send a formal update to my team.

Keying my radio, I transmitted, "Jackpot, jackpot, jackpot—we're coming out now."

Ian lay in wait at OP 3, surveilling the neighborhood from the southeast as Worthy responded to David's transmission.

"*Suicide, the route to my OP is blocked. A civilian went outside, and two guards are inbound now to deal with him.*"

"*Well, shit,*" David said. "*We can't afford to wait.*"

"*Concur. You can exit the cellar now, but you'll have to take an alternate exfil to OP 3 instead.*"

Ian continued scanning the streets ahead for any sign of movement, though a definitive unease came over him as he keyed his radio.

"Doc, you'll have to talk him out one block shy of the main road. I'll be able to take over once he reaches the bend."

Reilly answered, "*Copy, OP 2 has control. Suicide, head southwest from Azibo's house and move two blocks. I'll guide you from there.*"

"*Moving.*"

Cancer transmitted, "*OP 1 is cold. Doc, remain in place until I reach you— we'll move out together.*"

"*Copy,*" Reilly replied, quickly adding, "*Suicide, I can see you. Continue on your current approach.*"

David's new destination presented a significant issue—since the two western positions were farthest from Azibo's house, they'd been ceded to Reilly and Cancer. That left Worthy and Ian to cover the eastern observation points, with the pointman selected to station himself at David's point of departure and, according to the original plan, his return with Fatima in tow.

Azibo was located with Ian for precisely that reason: no one wanted to test the guards' hearing with a tearful reunion between husband and pregnant wife echoing from the woodline.

But now the tables had turned.

On the plus side, Azibo couldn't exactly race into the field at his first sight of Fatima. He was flex-cuffed at the ankles and wrists, the latter secured to a low-hanging tree branch that was thick enough to be unbreakable, even for him. The restraints were in place only in the event that he'd sent the team into an elaborate trap, and Azibo had willingly submitted to being tied up.

That was, however, before he knew his wife was headed for him.

And the fact remained that they'd left his mouth ungagged in case any questions arose as to the layout of his house or the neighborhood. Ian couldn't break his gaze from the neighborhood to remedy that, and if Azibo spontaneously called out upon Fatima's return, there was more than a passing chance that a guard would hear it.

"Hey," Ian whispered.

A crunch of leaves to his rear before Azibo said, "Is everything okay?"

"Everything's fine. She's okay, they're on their way out. But they have to divert to our position, so listen carefully. I don't care how excited you are to see your wife. You will not, under any circumstances, make a sound. If you get excited and call out to her, then we're all fucked, including Fatima. Got it?"

"Of course," Azibo replied, leaving Ian to hope that raw emotions wouldn't get the better of the man.

"*OP 4 is cold,*" Worthy transmitted. "*I'm heading to OP 3 to link up with Angel—*"

Reilly interrupted, "*Hold. Take cover.*"

The medic's voice was tense but controlled as he went on, "*Suicide, you've got a patrol headed northbound, one block west of your position.*" Ian couldn't make out either the guards or David and Fatima, and he held his breath until Reilly came back over the net.

"*Okay, they've passed. Move, now.*"

Gradually Ian could make out the faint outlines of two figures moving through the buildings ahead.

"Eyes-on," Ian transmitted. "Suicide, you're one block shy of the thoroughfare. Cut southeast and continue moving toward me."

The figures did just that, David in the lead with his rifle at the low ready.

They'd barely completed the turn, however, before Ian noticed a lone guard emerging from a side street twenty meters to David's front.

"Hold! Take cover, guard ahead."

The words left his mouth instinctively despite the obvious—there was nowhere for David or his freed hostage to hide, and no time for them to retreat to an adjoining street. The two figures ducked against the side of the nearest home anyway, getting behind a bush that was far too small to fully conceal them.

Ian took aim at the guard and tracked him, thumb on the pressure switch of his infrared laser in preparation to fire. David was surely doing the same from his current position. While they could easily conduct a dual takedown and probably do so before their target had time to cry out, the presence of his body in the streets would mean a full compromise sooner rather than later.

And if the guard force fanned out into the woods now, the team would find themselves in a firefight of the worst kind.

But the bogey continued his casual walk across the street, gazing southeast instead of northwest, where David and Fatima were more or less plainly visible. The lone militiaman passed out of view, oblivious to the prospect of imminent death he'd unknowingly strolled through.

"He's clear," Ian said. "Give him some time to get out of earshot before you continue movement, and clear to the right before you cross the next side street. If he doubles back, I won't be able to see it, and you'll run straight into him."

There were two bursts of static as David acknowledged the update, then a ten-second pause before he continued moving, stopping at the next house to angle his rifle in both directions before crossing the street.

"Two blocks to go," Ian transmitted, releasing his transmit switch to the sound of movement in the forest to his right. He peered over the vegetation to see a man patrolling southwest under night vision, then resumed surveillance before keying his radio again.

"Racegun, I've got eyes-on. Turn right 45 degrees and skirt the woodline."

Two bursts of static followed, and by then David and Fatima were clearing the next street.

"One block remaining," Ian said, scanning the clearing. "Open ground is clear at the moment, but stop before you cross it until I have a chance to confirm."

The neighborhood remained free of movement with the exception of David and Fatima, and moments later the team leader sent his first verbal transmission since leaving the cellar.

"*At our last covered and concealed position, need final clearance.*"

Ian scanned the buildings, paying particular attention to the main thoroughfare, before visually sweeping the open ground once more.

"You're good," he said. "Go, now."

Fatima broke into a run then, a heroic effort for a woman five months pregnant. Her current course would take her roughly ten meters left of the OP, but as long as she made it into the woods they could worry about the rest later.

David followed a few paces behind her, pulling rear security to engage any late-breaking threats.

Ian's focus was solely directed at the neighborhood—any guard who appeared at this point would have to die—and he heard a set of jogging footfalls that could only be Worthy, moving behind him to receive David and Fatima in case any pursuers appeared. Unable to break his focus on the neighborhood, Ian only vaguely registered the two running forms in his peripheral vision as he waited for one or more militiamen to stumble into view.

The next transmission was from Worthy.

"*I've got her,*" he said. Moments later he followed that up with, "*Suicide's clear.*"

After performing a final visual sweep to confirm that no guards were moving across the clearing, Ian rose and transmitted, "OP 3 is cold," before using his Winkler to slice Azibo's flex cuffs.

"Follow me," he whispered, leading Azibo between the bushes and trees until spotting his teammates in the woods ahead.

Azibo raced past him and locked Fatima in a tight embrace a few meters into the treeline, where they spoke quietly to one another in French. Worthy and David were posted next to the clearing, both men pulling security back toward the neighborhood.

Ian came to a stop just as Azibo and his wife separated.

He happened to be the closest American when that occurred, and Fatima grabbed him in a bear hug. Warm tears ran from her cheek down Ian's neck as she whispered, "Thank you, thank you. *Thank you*."

Did she assume in the darkness that Ian had been the one to rescue her? He couldn't be sure. Ian briefly returned the embrace and replied, "Welcome back."

Worthy swept past them, already leading the way to safety.

Stepping back from Fatima, Ian reached into a pouch of his kit and, without thinking, handed her a Snickers bar.

"Here," he said. "Let's go."

Azibo took her hand and led her in pursuit of the pointman, and David brought up the rear. Before any of them could transmit that they were on their way out, Cancer came over the net.

"*I just made it to Doc. OP 2 is cold, we're heading for the trucks. See you guys in a few minutes.*"

23

Meiling Chen awoke to the sound of a door swinging open.

A male voice said, "Ma'am, David Rivers is on the line."

"Get the light."

She swung her legs off the couch and sat up as the office illuminated in a blinding glare. Sleep shifts were rare during the course of a Project Longwing mission, but a lengthy drought of radio communications since the team arrived in Kavumu presented a prime opportunity for her and the staff to cycle through a few rotations of uneasy rest.

Any of which, Chen knew, could be interrupted at any moment.

She'd remained fully clothed including her shoes for such a possibility, squinting now as she rose stiffly to her feet. The man who'd awoken her was one of the J2 Intelligence desk's junior staff members.

"Team status?" she asked.

"All accounted for, they're in a village called Kaseke. Six hours south of Goma, so they need to be on the road soon to have any chance of making the diamond transfer."

Chen glanced at her watch—11:23 p.m., which meant the sun was rising over the Congo. She grabbed a lanyard with her identification badge from the desk, a space entirely devoid of clutter save for her computer, a secure communication console, and a single personal touch: a framed photo of her wife and three children that now faced away.

"Staff primaries?" she asked, pulling the lanyard over her head.

"Already alerted."

Crossing the spartan office to where he held the door open for her, she breezed past him and called over her shoulder.

"Results from the laptop analysis?"

"Nothing yet, ma'am," he responded, struggling to keep pace with her brisk walk.

"Follow up with the DA and see where they stand."

"Yes, ma'am."

She strode across a hallway lined with secure doors, any number of which were actively monitoring missions-in-progress. It was a far cry from the vast majority of CIA headquarters, most of which comprised offices dedicated to foreign intelligence collection and analysis, data interpretation, support functions, training, secure communication facilities, and archival storage.

But there was the Agency writ large, and then there was the Special Activities Center.

The SAC was a world unto itself. It contained two primary components; the first was a Political Action Group for influencing foreign governments through psychological operations as well as economic and cyber warfare.

Chen's purview, however, was within the second, far more direct section. The Special Operations Group was divided into four departments, including the Air, Maritime, and Armor and Special Programs Departments.

Ground Department, however, was the home of the CIA's paramilitary operations officers and contractors, the latter of which included her team. While all four departments were formerly titled branches, the name change hadn't quite taken hold among her current setting, where, with the exception of formal briefs, almost everyone still referred to the organization as Ground Branch.

Here, the hallways were alive with hushed activity nearly 24/7 as staff members for various operations moved to and from their respective OPCENs.

It was impossible for her to tell how many operations were underway at any given moment, although judging by the constant activity, a high global demand for covert and clandestine paramilitary operations was alive and well.

Many such missions involved providing support to case officers in the Agency's Directorate of Operations and the DoD's Tier One forces. Both required a correspondingly high degree of cooperation and crosstalk among organizations. A few others, however, were the sole purview of highly compartmentalized special access programs like Project Longwing.

And while that all sounded glamorous to the outside observer, the inside view revealed a far darker truth. When the president signed an executive order for something he couldn't risk being tied to—namely, authorizing assassinations conveniently retitled as targeted killings with the same evasive fluidity that caused the National Clandestine Service to suddenly become the Directorate of Operations—the secrecy became very high indeed.

Among politicians, only the chair and ranking members of the Senate and House, along with the lead Republican and Democrat in both the House Select Committee on Intelligence and the Senate Select Committee on Intelligence, knew that Project Longwing even existed. And of those select few, Thomas Gossweiler, Chairman of the Senate SSCI, was the only one in Washington who had direct contact with Chen as the program director. The remaining politicians received, at best, periodic updates on the program's successes—none of which, she thought, provided the slightest insight into the myriad complications and near-failures that each mission presented.

The end result was that the jobs of anyone in the Project Longwing OPCEN were as unattributable as the lives of the ground team, which meant they were considered expendable by anyone who risked potential embarrassment should anything go wrong, from the CIA Director to the president. Chen began her involvement with Longwing determined to protect her career at all costs; after the first mission she'd supervised, however, she was braced for a no-notice forced retirement almost every day that her team of paramilitary contractors was deployed overseas.

The thought hung heavy on her mind as she swiped her identification badge over a keypad beside the door, pausing to let the staffer push it open for her.

And then, she entered the Project Longwing OPCEN.

Chen was one step inside when she asked, "Have there been any new communications from Mubenga or his people?"

Lucios shook his head. "No, ma'am, not since we confirmed the time and place of the exchange."

He and all the remaining primary staff members were at their stations along the descending tiers leading to a front wall of screens. She glanced at a digital numeric stopwatch near the ceiling, its display now frozen to denote the total elapsed time since her team's last transmission.

Shaking her head, Chen approached her desk to find a fresh mug of coffee waiting there, steam rising from the top.

She pointed at it. "Who did this?"

Jamieson raised a tentative hand.

"If I could give you a pay raise," she declared, "I would."

Dropping into her seat, she lifted the mug with one hand and her satellite hand mic with the other.

"Suicide Actual, this is Mayfly."

Without waiting for a response, she continued, "It's been 17 hours since you notified me of your arrival in Kavumu, and shortly thereafter we had peripheral reporting of police and military activity. No explanation, and no reported arrests. Then everything went quiet." After taking a sip of scalding hot coffee, she added unenthusiastically, "I'm guessing you have a lot to tell me."

David didn't immediately reply; he knew there were times he could trifle with her and times he couldn't, and her tone after being woken up was firmly in the latter camp. To be fair, she'd have felt sympathy for him if one or more team members were dead. But as soon as the J2 staff member informed her that all men were accounted for, her patience went from thin to nonexistent.

"Yeah," David agreed. "*We've had some developments here, starting with a full cordon of Kavumu shortly after our arrival. We had to flee into the park—*"

"Park?" she demanded.

"*Kahuzi-Biéga. The KL Militia pursued us and we had a significant engage-ment in the rainforest. Doc got shot.*"

She took another pull from her coffee mug, then asked unsympatheti-cally, "And his status?"

"*He's, you know, stable. Good enough to walk. But Azibo ratted us out—he'd been reporting to the CLF.*"

Chen's initial response was disbelief—not shock, but actually not believing that the team leader was telling her the truth. If past experience was any indication, this was as likely as not to be one of David's elaborate ruses to cover some team indiscretion.

She decided to nip it in the bud.

"We've been monitoring for cellular activity that would indicate any communication from Azibo before, during, and since your linkup with him. There were none."

"*That's because it's not cellular. He had something exotic that used, I don't know, mesh networks or something. Angel can tell you what it was, want me to put him on the line?*"

"High dollar," Lucios called out, pre-empting her inquiry. "At least, if he's not lying. Definitely beyond the CLF's capabilities. It could have been provided by Mubenga's outside sponsor."

And that, she thought, raised the stakes considerably.

She keyed her mic and said, "No, that won't be necessary. Go on."

"*Azibo claimed the CLF came to his house a few days before our infil, took his wife hostage, and provided the device. Angel thinks they reverse-engineered our drop zone, had it surrounded, and emplaced that triple-A cannon based on the flight paths to Kananga Airport. But we know for sure that Azibo reported our activities just before the ambush outside Kolwezi, and again upon our arrival to Kavumu.*"

Chen struggled mightily with her next words.

The last thing she needed now was for any indications that her men had executed a local asset to come over the official mission transcript, and yet she needed the truth more than ever.

Then she relaxed somewhat, knowing that if anyone could throw smoke over illicit activity, it was David Rivers.

"Azibo's status?" she asked.

"*He, um, he's in Kaseke with us.*"

"With you," she noted dryly, seizing upon David's uncertainty.

"*Correct.*"

"As a prisoner?"

Chen felt stupid as soon as she'd said the words. No one would believe they'd hauled that man out of the rainforest while their lives were in danger, least of all her.

"*Well,*" David continued hesitantly, "*at this point he's more of a willing participant.*"

That didn't check out either. If something as sophisticated as a mesh network device was in play, then it had surely come with discrete protocols to indicate which transmissions were legit and which were sent under duress. Ian would have known that, which meant there was no trusting anything Azibo sent under his team's supervision, torture or no torture.

Something else was afoot.

After another sip of coffee, she replied, "And how, exactly, did you manage to gain his compliance?"

"*Here's the thing. They were holding his wife—his pregnant wife—hostage in their home in Mugenderwa. So we, you know, we just...we got her back.*"

"A hostage rescue?"

"*Right,*" he quickly supplied, "*that's exactly it.*"

"I don't recall you mentioning that your team had been compromised."

"*That's because we're not. It all came off without a hitch, so...we're good. Deception plan's already in place. Azibo's reported that we took casualties in the park and are carrying them to a ground exfil. He's back on our side now. We just need to take him and his wife with us, so if you could, you know, start working on their relocation, that'd be great.*"

"She's *with* you?" Chen asked, struggling to explain why the team would assume such an immense liability.

"*Look, there's no safehouses in the area and no time to reach one if there was. Ground Branch is stuck in Goma right now. There's only five of us and we need Azibo as a driver, so...yeah. His wife is with us.*"

"How long ago did you rescue her, exactly?"

"*Raid was complete by zero three-thirty local.*"

When she didn't immediately reply, he added, "*Over.*"

A delicate sort of anger was blossoming inside her now. Chen swept her gaze across the staff primaries, registering looks that ranged from incredulity to outright horror.

David transmitted, "*How copy?*"

She set her mug down and pushed it away, instinctively fixing her communications officer in her sights. "Is there any way to fix this?"

Christopher Soren was now pale. "Mubenga's people have already switched cell networks once that we know of, and given how long it took us to get so much as a *probable* fix on the buyer's communications in the first place—"

"Lucios?" she asked with a sense of mounting despair.

"The hostage's absence was probably noted within minutes. Maybe an hour if we're lucky. Either way, we're plus or minus three hours behind the power curve. At this point, it's a matter of how long it takes to reacquire the altered communications network relative to the time and place of the new exchange, because it won't occur in Goma."

"You're positive about that?"

"I am. A simple travel time analysis will assure the buyer that the team that rescued Azibo's wife are the same people that Mubenga attacked outside Kolwezi. And given a hostage rescue outside Kavumu less than ten hours before the exchange, he'll know the team was en route to Goma. The buyer won't fail to assume that Goma has already been reinforced with Agency elements to interdict the diamonds."

"All right," she muttered to herself. "Okay."

Then she pointed out the obvious to David, who was either blissfully ignorant or, far more likely, hoping she'd overlook the immediate implications until his next check-in.

"I was wondering why we didn't have any new intercepts—Mubenga and his entourage switched to a new communications network again the moment the CLF discovered their hostage was missing. That means the exchange that we knew the *exact* time and place for is going to be aborted in lieu of a *new* place and time that we most likely won't be able to anticipate. In case you need reminding, there is twenty-odd million worth of diamonds headed to finance international terror hanging in the balance."

"*So we don't need to drive on to Goma?*"

Chen said nothing.

"*What were we supposed to do?*" David asked, suddenly defensive. "*Azibo is a big guy. We couldn't carry him out of the rainforest, and executions are against the rules of engagement.*"

Now he cites the letter of the law, she thought. The only rule of engagement he'd previously followed was doing whatever he deemed necessary and lying to her as required for his team's continued employment. Sticking her with regulations was an entirely new tool in the team leader's acumen.

Lucios interjected, "The mesh network device, ma'am. If the team hasn't already destroyed it and relocated, they need to do so now."

Chen transmitted, "What's the status of the phone you captured from Azibo?"

"*After he phoned in the deception plan,*" David answered, "*Angel made us smash it into a billion pieces and leave it behind. Hope you didn't need it for analysis.*"

"No, we didn't. We need everything else in the world after you blew up the exchange, but not that device. So well done there."

"*Happy to help.*"

Without thinking, she blurted aloud, "Jamieson, what else is Rivers hiding from us?"

The former Marine shot her a pained look and pointed out, "He already used a legitimate compromise in Kavumu to take his team on an unauthorized hostage rescue, then came up on comms to give a full confession while citing legal considerations that we can't officially reprimand him for." He gave a resigned shrug. "If there's anything he's not telling us after all that, I shudder to think of what it may be."

Chen groaned and keyed her mic.

"Am I correct in assuming you're in a safe location in..." She consulted a screen at the front of the OPCEN, knowing by now that every location in the DRC sounded more or less the same to her. "Kaseke?"

"*As far as we can tell, yes. Azibo's happy with it and his word means something now that his wife is co-located.*"

"Good," she confirmed. "Stay there. I need you glued to the SATCOM and conducting a radio check every half hour until I tell you otherwise.

When we're able to make our best guess at a new exchange location, I'll need you ready to move within sixty seconds. Is that clear?"

"*Crystal*," David replied.

"We need to squeeze water from a stone over here. Give Doc our best. Raptor Nine One, out."

Setting the mic down, she started to reach for her coffee and decided against it.

Instead, Chen rose swiftly from her chair and announced, "Ladies and gentlemen, welcome back to square one. I'm going to notify Ground Branch that everything we knew about the exchange no longer holds and that they are now in limbo for immediate relocation. J2."

"Yes, ma'am," Lucios replied.

"I want a fresh assessment of possible exchange towns rank-ordered by likelihood relative to the avenues of approach, population density, and civilian activity at thirteen hundred local time that made Goma the chosen point of exchange in the first place. Chart these towns in concentric geographic circles from Goma outward per the travel times required to reach them and provide all information to the J3 as you acquire it."

"We're on it."

"J3."

Jamieson looked eager to get to work. "Ma'am."

"You and your staff will convert the imagery of those towns into possible meeting locations, and do so in real-time. If any correlations become too large to ignore, you will inform me first for a preemptive relocation of our team and Ground Branch because this will probably move too fast for us to react if we wait for definitive confirmation."

She cut her eyes to Christopher Soren. "J6, this is a five-alarm fire for you. You will pull in all outside support necessary to monitor every conceivable means by which we can follow Mubenga and/or the buyer's representative for the exchange through a total rework of the communications protocol. That includes cyber through the DDI and collaboration with the Five Eyes as required. Any restrictions on using my authority as program director in a crisis capacity are now lifted in full, and if anyone questions your need to know, I want their call transferred to my phone before you so much as inform me who I'm talking to."

After taking a breath, she asked, "Alibis, anything I'm not thinking of, let's hear it now."

Her legal counsel lifted a hand, although what an Agency lawyer had to weigh in on at this point remained beyond her.

"Yes, Gregory. Go."

Pharr lowered his arm and offered, "The relocation, ma'am. For Azibo and his wife. I can handle that, if..."

She sighed in defeat.

"Sure," she said. "Why not. Get the dossier from Lucios and put it into motion."

"Yes, ma'am."

Chen glanced at her coffee, thinking she was going to consume nothing else for the next few hours. Sleep would have to wait. Then she eyed her staff and concluded, "Let's get to work."

24

"Right here," Cancer said, peering out the rear windows of the Nissan. "Kill it."

Ian put the vehicle in park and cut the engine, leaving Cancer to groan as he stepped out, his boots crunching on the gravel and debris that littered the ground behind the abandoned gas station. The air was fresh, with a hint of dew, as the light of dawn began to seep through the horizon, casting a soft golden glow over the desolate structure.

The building itself was a relic of better times, its walls now weathered and graffiti-laden, telling stories of clandestine teenage escapades. With windows boarded up, the gas station had the look of a place forgotten by time, perfect for their current needs—inconspicuous and off the beaten path.

As the rest of the team disembarked his truck, slinging their weapons and squinting into the rising sun, and the Suzuki Vitara parked alongside them, Cancer scanned the woodline behind the building.

The trees stood tall and dense, and amidst the greenery Cancer's eyes landed on an enormous tree with a staggeringly thick trunk and sprawling branches.

He pointed at it and decreed, "Fatima gets the baobab. The rest of you animals use the woodline over there. You're allowed to piss and get back in the trucks to close your eyes, but that's it."

Reilly sauntered over, twisting his upper body in both directions to stretch. The movement hitched on his left side, the only visible indication that a bullet had entered him the day before. A tough motherfucker, Cancer thought, though he'd never voice that opinion aloud.

The medic asked, "Why bother trying to sleep? We're about to drive to Goma anyway."

"Goma," Cancer replied, "ain't happening anymore. Count on it. Off you go."

Worthy followed Reilly toward the treeline, then stopped to ask, "What about you?"

By then Cancer was shifting his slung HK417 to procure a pack and a lighter. "I'm fueled by nicotine, and you're not." He inserted a cigarette between his lips and spoke around it. "Burdens of fuckin' leadership."

Ian passed him without a word while David pulled himself atop the Nissan's hood, setting up his mobile satellite antenna on the roof.

Fatima glided toward the baobab tree with her husband in tow, until Cancer grabbed the man's sleeve and pulled him aside, delivering his next words in a harsh whisper.

"I don't need to see her," he said. "But I better be able to see you."

Azibo's eyes went wide, his posture suddenly erect as he advanced with the expression of someone who was about to throw the first punch.

Cancer didn't flinch, didn't move in the slightest, as Azibo hissed at point-blank range, "You know that I did not have a choice—"

"But you do now," the sniper cut him off, "so choose wisely. Everyone here but you put their life on the line to get her back. You better start earning this shit. Because if you try to run with her and take your chances without us, I can promise you that your kid will grow up without a father."

After letting the words sink in, Cancer added, "And I'll be the one to make that happen."

Azibo was a physically imposing man under the best of circumstances. In a fistfight, he'd be able to pummel Cancer into a coma or beyond without much effort.

And while Azibo had initially bowed up, his shoulders had quickly slumped as he transitioned to more or less passive acceptance. It was all in the eyes, Cancer knew; there was a petrifying gaze of sheer rawness that couldn't be feigned or even fully grasped by anyone who hadn't personally served as a Grim Reaper to countless human beings who were desperately trying to return the favor.

Besides, he thought, if the man tried anything now, the response would be well beyond a fistfight, and Cancer would be far from alone.

Azibo turned without response, following his wife behind the tree and, as directed, keeping his backside visible.

David clambered back off the hood, connecting the antenna's commo wire to his radio as he offered, "Bit harsh, don't you think?"

Cancer shrugged ambivalently. "He picked the spot."

Everything about their current setting seemed like Azibo's choice was a good one.

The derelict gas station was large enough to conceal their strategically parked vehicles from a rarely traveled dirt road. Azibo had said this place was a teenage drinking spot when he was growing up, and judging by the minefield of broken bottles and empty cigarette packs scattered across the ground, it still served that purpose during nighttime hours.

But Cancer's inherent sense of pessimism told him that while Azibo now had the team's best interests at heart—at least, now that his pregnant wife was under their protection—there was always that chance that he'd selected the location for some footpath or another that he could use to flee. There was no reason to, of course, so long as Azibo trusted the team to make good on their promise of relocating him and Fatima. But individuals in the CIA's employ weren't known for their trustworthiness in making promises, particularly in the Congo, and Cancer wasn't going to take any chances.

David spoke into his hand mic. "Raptor Nine One, Suicide Actual."

Reilly and Worthy were already shaking off the last vestiges of their urination, turning to make their way back to the trucks.

"Copy," David replied. "Where's Mayfly?"

Then, turning to Cancer with a furious expression, he muttered, "Sleeping. She's fucking sleeping."

"Must be nice," the sniper observed, checking that Azibo was still visible as David continued.

"Current location is Kaseke, Kilo Alpha Sierra Echo Kilo Echo. Everyone is accounted for, we're all still alive, and I need to talk to her...all right, standing by."

Cancer watched his men gradually returning to the trucks, each of them keeping their chin up but nonetheless moving in a zombielike shuffle. 99.9 percent of people in the world, he thought, couldn't grasp what it would be like to manage this type of exhaustion in any setting, much less in a foreign country full of bad guys trying to kill them.

By contrast, special operations guys were acquainted with sleep loss almost to a fault. David could certainly order the guys to get some rest, but he was too busy to do so whenever the opportunity arose; the remaining men on the team wouldn't want to ask because doing so could be construed as complaining or, God forbid, weakness.

So it was up to Cancer to fill the role of mother hen, lest anyone on his team push themselves to the point where they literally passed out on the job.

"Let's go," he called out, jerking his thumb behind him as Reilly and Worthy approached. "It's naptime in kindergarten, assholes. I better not catch anyone awake."

Even Ian appeared depleted to the point of collapse, his overworked mind finally free from analyzing the intelligence particulars after their hostage rescue had come off, for everyone but David, more or less without a hitch.

He walked slowly past, halfheartedly swinging an arm toward David and offering, "Wake me up if he needs anything."

Cancer slapped him on the ass. "Will do. Now find the 'off' switch on your thirty-pound brain."

Fatima was the next to approach on the return trip to the vehicles. Cancer gave her a deferential nod and said, "Sorry we don't have better facilities, ma'am."

"After a week in captivity," she responded, Congolese accent thick and cheerful, "that was the best piss I've ever had."

He grinned as she passed, finally lighting the cigarette in his lips.

For a woman five months pregnant who'd just endured more trauma in the past seven days than most people would in a lifetime, Fatima was surprisingly upbeat. She was younger than he'd expected, mid-twenties at most, and beautiful in a way that only African women could be, eyes dark and deep amid the glow of pregnancy. Her every movement was graceful, he thought, or else he'd just spent far too long seeing nothing but the masculine architecture of the gun-toting whackos he called his teammates.

"Do not talk to my wife," a voice beside him growled.

Cancer casually glanced at Azibo before looking away, unimpressed, and taking a drag. "How about *you* don't talk to *me*? Next time I need a rat, I'll know who to call. Keep your phone on just in case—and I'm talking about the phone we gave you, not the one you use to whisper sweet nothings to Mubenga."

When there was neither response nor the sound of footsteps, Cancer turned back to see Azibo standing motionless, face solemn, hands flexing into fists.

Rolling his eyes and turning to face him head-on, Cancer said, "Hey, Congolese Benedict Arnold—get in the fucking truck and go to sleep. Or," he offered, more politely this time, "you can take a swing at me and see how that works out."

Azibo walked away and then looked away, in that order, and David waited until the Suzuki door slammed before asking, "Can you at least try not to piss him off?"

"Shouldn't you be reporting right now?"

"Yeah," he said, exasperated. "I'm all for it as soon as—shit, here she is."

The pause that followed was sufficiently protracted to assure Cancer that the ass-chewing had begun.

He puffed his cigarette down to the filter, flicking it to the side. There was ample time to light another and hand it to David before the team leader finally spoke again.

"Yeah. We've had some developments here, starting with a full cordon of Kavumu shortly after our arrival. We had to flee into the park...Kahuzi-Biéga. The KL Militia pursued us and we had a significant engagement. Doc got shot."

The team leader took a nervous drag, quickly following that up with,

"He's, you know, stable. Good enough to walk. But Azibo ratted us out—he'd been reporting to the CLF."

This was going to take a while, Cancer thought. He had enough experience witnessing David's half of the updates to fill in Chen's unheard responses with fair to above-average accuracy. Striding between the vehicles, he squinted through the glare of the windows to make sure everyone was either sleeping or pretending to be in a convincing enough manner to satisfy him.

When he encountered Worthy with eyes open, casting a thousand-yard stare at the windshield ahead of him, Cancer rapped his knuckle on the window.

The pointman closed his eyes, giving a weary nod of compliance.

By the time Cancer rounded the Nissan, David was sitting on the hood with his boots perched atop the front bumper.

"...he reported our activities just before the ambush outside Kolwezi, and again upon our arrival to Kavumu."

Cancer's eyes steeled at the words—Azibo certainly had his reasons for the betrayal, but there was no universe in which the sniper would forgive anyone for the unredeemable sin of putting his teammates' lives in jeopardy.

Besides, of course, himself and David, the latter of whom was now stammering.

"He, um, he's in Kaseke with us...Correct...Well, at this point he's more of a willing participant."

Cancer grinned. "Go ahead and tell her what you did."

"Here's the thing," David explained. "They were holding his wife—his pregnant wife—hostage in their home in Mugenderwa. So we, you know, we just...we got her back." A pause, and then, "Right, that's exactly it."

Cancer pulled out his phone, finding the imagery of Kaseke and panning out until a larger portion of the eastern border was in view, Lake Kivu filling the right side of his screen. He tuned out David's update, swiping across the map as if doing so would reveal their next destination. The only city he could definitively rule out was the one they were supposed to be traveling toward at this very moment.

"Raid was complete by zero three-thirty local," David said.

That drew Cancer's attention. The moment of truth was drawing near. "Over."

After another pause, David said with frustration, "How copy?"

Cancer intervened, "She hears you, dickhead. Just needs some time to wrap her head around the fact that the Goma exchange is as dead as dial-up internet."

"I mean," David replied, "yeah, probably. Can I get another one of these?"

He impotently held up the remnants of his now-extinguished cigarette. Cancer found his pack and held it up.

"You'd be totally fucked without me."

"I know, man," David admitted.

"Say it."

"I'd be totally fucked without you."

Cancer opened the pack as David spoke again, this time into his mic. "So we don't need to drive on to Goma?"

"Told you," Cancer said, lighting a cigarette and holding it out.

"What were we supposed to do?" David asked, suddenly defensive as he snatched the cigarette. "Azibo is a big guy. We couldn't carry him out of the rainforest, and executions are against the rules of engagement."

Cancer sang, "Never stopped us before…" and procured a smoke for himself.

"After he phoned in the deception plan," David said, "we smashed it into a billion pieces and left it behind. Hope you didn't need it for analysis."

The team leader and Cancer took their next drag in unison.

"Happy to help…As far as we can tell, yes. Azibo's happy with it and his word means something now that his wife is co-located."

"Or does it?" Cancer asked provocatively.

"Crystal," David said at last, waiting a beat before lowering his hand mic and fixing Cancer with a look of mild dread.

"So," Cancer said with the intonation of a parent picking up their child from the first day of school, "how'd it go?"

"How do you think it went? She was pissed."

"Are you surprised?"

David considered the question.

"No, not really. Pretty standard at this point. New info on the exchange is that there is no info on the exchange—she's fairly well certain it won't be in Goma after we got Fatima back."

"Told you."

"Said we need to be ready to roll in one minute and then some nonsense about squeezing water from a stone."

"It's an idiom, you moron. Difficult or impossible."

"Yeah, well, let's hope it's just difficult. At any rate, that's her problem to deal with now," David retorted, his voice tinged with frustration.

Cancer flicked his ash to the ground. "If those diamonds make it out of the DRC, it's all of our problem."

David groaned, his head rolling back. "There's always something—rising militia shithead, hostages, new terrorist plot. The job never ends and never will. Chen's going to keep feeding us into the woodchipper until we retire or die, at which point the second team will step up and repeat the process. Right now I'm just happy all five of us have stayed alive, along with Fatima."

Cancer took a drag from his cigarette. David was a case study in contradiction, he thought. On one hand, he'd been surprisingly laissez-faire about accomplishing their stated mission set ever since announcing to the team that he was leaving the Agency once his contract was up, an unfortunate complication originating from the moment he found out he had a new baby on the way.

On the other hand, he'd recklessly flung himself into and out of Azibo's house with the deranged lunacy of a man with a death wish.

Shifting his gaze from the ember of his cigarette to David, Cancer said, "We're all in one piece, yeah. But you're luckier than the rest of us with the stunt you just pulled. That better be the last time you ever enter and clear a fuckin' building by yourself because if not, the next time will be. And not because you made it out, either."

"Stunt?" David asked, sounding offended as he put the filter in his lips. Interlacing his fingers, he rotated his palms out and extended his arms, popping all of his knuckles at once. "That was a one-man hostage rescue pulled off with skill and aplomb, thank you very much."

"Yeah?" Cancer asked, raising his eyebrows. "Then why's your head the size of a watermelon?"

The swelling on David's head had turned into a misshapen mass, bleeding anew at the slightest provocation.

David's victorious expression vanished and Cancer continued, "I've got smoother surfaces on my balls than you have on your head right now, and if that buttstock had come down a few inches to the side we wouldn't be having this conversation. Now get in the truck and close your fucking eyes —I'll take the first shift."

25

Chen hung up her desk phone, thinking that this was the second call she'd deeply regretted having to make. The Special Activities Center's deputy director had been tight-lipped about the chain reaction of events that began with her team's unauthorized hostage rescue, but she could tell easily enough from his tone that he was, in a word, furious.

Her previous call to the Ground Branch leadership who'd jumped through every conceivable hoop to forward-stage their men in Goma was only slightly more pleasant, likely due to the fact that they were just as accustomed to fast-moving changes and setbacks in any tactical plan as her ground team was.

She looked up to see two men approaching her desk. Leaning back in her seat and throwing her hands up, she said, "You both cannot have completed your assessment yet."

Lucios stood tentatively with a tablet in hand. "Ma'am, I think we've completed as much as we need to."

Behind him was Wes Jamieson, who by virtue of his resolute expression wasn't going to be dissuaded from his current viewpoint, whatever that was.

"Fine," she replied, waving a hand toward a pair of empty rolling chairs beside her. "Approach the bench."

Jamieson spoke before he finished sitting down.

"The first factor we need to consider is where they *won't* conduct an exchange, namely anyplace rural. That would give us ample opportunity to trace incoming and outgoing cellular traffic, not to mention conducting surveillance and fixing him in place. So we can rule out the vast majority of real estate along the eastern border, which leaves us with major urban centers. And the long and the short of it is—"

"Bukavu," Lucios said quietly, taking a single piece of paper from Jamieson and handing it to her. "They'll most likely conduct the exchange in Bukavu."

Chen accepted the page, still warm from the printer, and examined the map contained therein.

Lake Kivu formed an oblong body of water running vertically across the paper, its long axis divided into the Democratic Republic of the Congo on the left, and Rwanda on the right. Goma was on the north end, right along the border, mirrored by Bukavu at the lake's southern boundary.

"Gentlemen," she said, "given two major reasons that I shouldn't have to state,

color me skeptical in the extreme."

Jamieson countered, "So were we, ma'am, until we added up all the factors."

"Let's hear it."

"Both Goma and Bukavu are border towns with Rwanda. Both are major trade hubs with extensive cross-border commerce, which means a lot of human and vehicle traffic that both sides of the exchange can blend in with. Goma is the largest city in North Kivu Province, and Bukavu is the largest in South Kivu Province. Even the populations are similar: 780,000 for Goma, 870,000 for Bukavu. And both are highly conducive to foreigners of varying ethnicities to come and go without drawing attention."

Chen frowned. "Before we send our all-Caucasian ground team somewhere they'll be easily spotted, you had better convince me of that."

Jamieson went silent then, ceding his outspoken role to Lucios.

The intelligence officer consulted his tablet and supplied, "Goma is the gateway to Virunga National Park and the Nyiragongo Volcano, and hosts several NGOs conducting educational and humanitarian missions. Bukavu is the point of arrival for international visitors en route to Kahuzi-Biéga

National Park, along with a thriving tourist industry as a result of its history and colonial-era architecture. Both are the only cities large enough to host the vast majority of tourists on the shores of Lake Kivu."

Without looking up from his device, he continued, "We also have to consider the opportunities for exfil once the buyer has his diamonds. Ground: both towns have highway access due to trade. Air: both towns have their own airports and, more notably, they each have one on the Rwandan side of the border. Kamembe Airport is eight kilometers from Bukavu, and Gisenyi Airport is less than two from Goma."

Jamieson interjected, "Then we realized he's planning his meet based on Lake Kivu as much as anything else. It's literally wrapped by highways on both sides of the border, right?"

She examined the map as he went on, "You've got N2 on the DRC side, and NR11 in Rwanda. Goma's on the north edge of the lake and Bukavu on the south, and each town has extensive waterfronts. If the exchange goes bad, the buyer's representative can step on a speedboat and have access to a combined total of 400 kilometers of highway and four airports spanning two countries. And if he needs to lie low, there's a very high density of inlets, coves, and small bays, most of them heavily vegetated."

"Or," Lucios added, resting the tip of a pen on Chen's map, "he could go to Idjwi Island. It's the second largest lake island on the continent. Three hundred and forty square kilometers, population of a quarter million, and no law enforcement to speak of. It's entirely possible he's already placed an emergency recovery team on the island. He'd have unlimited opportunities to hide and ample early warning to relocate as needed until they could spirit him to the mainland, blending in with heavy boat traffic going to and from fishing villages on all sides."

"Is that it?" she asked.

Jamieson was getting frustrated now.

"Ma'am, you asked us to find areas that met the criteria of his initial Goma meet. We already told you that Bukavu meets all of them and then some, and now I'll tell you that the list of alternatives is exactly zero to either the north or south. Not one, not two, but zero."

"Point taken," she conceded, setting her paper down. "But I'll say it since neither of you have: Bukavu is a few hours closer than Goma to a couple major engagements by our team. One is their shootout in the rainforest outside Kavumu, and the other is a hostage rescue in Mugenderwa."

Fixing Jamieson in her gaze, she asked, "Why would the buyer possibly risk sending his representative closer to those points of contact rather than farther?"

"Because," he explained, "he's not worried about five guys who've already been shot up a few times. He *is* worried about the army of Ground Branch shooters waiting for him in Goma right now, which he anticipated as soon as the hostage rescue assured him that his first exchange location was burned. There's simply no other reason our ground team would be in the border region after being ambushed outside Kolwezi."

Lucios cleared his throat and frowned before speaking.

"That is also why we believe the buyer has already advanced the timeline for the exchange. He removes Ground Branch from his threats simply by holding the exchange a few hours earlier in a location they couldn't possibly reach in time. He is confident that he can do so given his refreshed communications network with Mubenga, and has every motivation for his representative to recover the diamonds sooner rather than later."

Chen considered the windfall of information.

They no longer had the luxury of waiting for definitive confirmation, primarily because they hadn't yet penetrated Mubenga's new communications protocol. At this point they were trying to predict the future, which was an unbecoming and highly unreliable play for any intelligence organization.

"Let's say you're right about this. What's to say the diamonds haven't already changed hands?"

"Travel times," Jamieson said firmly. "Or at least, that's our operating assumption. It stands to reason that while our team spent the night between the rainforest and a hostage rescue, Mubenga was continuing his journey—as far as he was concerned, his pursuers were left behind the second Kavumu was cordoned off. That would place Mubenga outside Goma as of zero three-thirty local, which is the earliest the missing hostage could have triggered a change of location.

"Transit time for Mubenga to travel from Goma to Bukavu on the Congolese side of the border is seven and a half hours, which means the new exchange could occur no earlier than eleven hundred. That gives us five hours' lead time as of this moment, and it's going to take Ground Branch five and a half minimum to get there on NR11 in Rwanda. Our team is still two hours away, and if they leave now they have about three hours to arrive in Bukavu and learn the lay of the land before we enter a possible window for the exchange. That makes this about as time sensitive as it possibly can be, especially for Ground Branch."

Jamieson concluded his last statement with a glance toward her radio hand mic, silently imploring her to make the call.

Instead she noted, "It seems like the buyer's in a hurry."

"It seems like that because he is," Jamieson said forcefully. "The noose is tightening around Mubenga. It's a matter of time until someone takes him out, and the buyer needs to gain control of the diamonds before that happens. Every hour he waits is one more for us to throw people and resources against him."

Nodding, she said, "Get on the line with Ground Branch. Have them direct their teams from Goma to Bukavu effective immediately. I'll fill them in on the way."

He was out of his seat before she finished speaking, jogging down the tiered levels to his workstation.

Lucios remained in place as she lifted her hand mic. "Ma'am, there's something else."

She kept the mic in her hand and said, "Don't keep me waiting."

He nonetheless hesitated before going on. "The abundance of getaway options makes it possible that the buyer himself will be physically present at the exchange."

She shook her head. "He's not going to risk that. Why would he?"

"It could be to reduce the possibility of leaks by intermediaries, or because he wants to personally verify the quality and quantity of the diamonds, or both. I can't say definitively, of course, but his presence doesn't seem outside the realm of possibility to me given the abundance of getaway options. I don't know if there are any atmospherics the team will be able to pick up on, but I believe they should be aware there's a chance."

Chen gave him a curt nod and transmitted.

"Suicide Actual, Raptor Nine One."

There was no delay in the response—the team leader had a tendency to take radio contact very seriously when his team's continued participation in a mission was contingent upon her say-so.

But it wasn't David who spoke then.

"This is Cancer, send it."

"Put Suicide Actual on the line. Now."

"Yeah, all right," Cancer responded dryly. *"I'll go get him. He's sleeping, sound familiar? Because the whole concept is pretty new to us. Is ten minutes a day enough, or are you supposed to get more than that?"*

Chen gritted her teeth and waited until an all-too-familiar voice came over the speakerbox.

"This is Suicide, send it."

"Your new destination is Bukavu," she began. "It's two hours south of your current location, which is the exact duration you're allowed to be off comms, no exceptions. Travel to the western outskirts and set up a mobile command post with continuous satellite communications so I can relay intelligence as I receive it. Forward stage the rest of your team in Bukavu proper. You are to remain low-visibility in the extreme."

"New exchange?" David asked.

"That's what we're banking on at the moment. I want to be informed the instant you detect any indication of Mubenga or his security entourage." She paused, cutting her eyes to Lucios. "We have reason to believe the buyer himself may be there; if so, your primary mission is to identify him, and if not, his representative. Secondary mission is disrupting the exchange at your discretion using all available means, recovering the diamonds if you have the means to do so. Tertiary mission is killing Mubenga, which shouldn't even be on your radar unless the first two are accomplished beyond a shadow of a doubt. What are your questions?"

"Time of the exchange? Pinpoint location?"

"Time: no earlier than 11:00 local. Pinpoint location: none known at this time. I'll follow up with a prioritized list of possible options as soon as my J3 is able to produce it. There will likely be a speedboat on call for emergency exfil, so the balance of probability is near the waterfront.

"Bottom line, Bukavu is our best guess based on known factors, but it's by no means a certainty. Ground Branch is relocating there, but it's going to take them five and a half hours to make the trip. Arrival time estimated at 11:30, half an hour after the earliest time for the exchange. In the absence of further information, I'm keeping both of your elements in play the only way I can."

"Copy, we're moving now. Suicide Actual, out."

26

Worthy maneuvered the Nissan Patrol with practiced ease, the hum of the engine a steady backdrop to the emerging plan.

"N2 merges with N3 in thirty kilometers," Ian said from the backseat. "Then we'll continue southbound for another twenty before hitting the city limits. Bukavu wraps the southern edge of Lake Kivu in a U-shape. N2/N3 follows the water's edge until the center of the city, then cuts due south."

David was riding shotgun, scrutinizing satellite images of Bukavu on his phone just as Ian was. "She said there may be a boat in play, so we need to focus on the waterfront."

"Yeah, hang on."

Worthy's hands were firm on the wheel, his right boot alternately accelerating and letting off as he maintained a tactically sound interval from the Suzuki Vitara containing Azibo, Fatima, and the remainder of his team.

The chaotic beauty of the Congo materialized through the windshield. They were on the N2, a road that meandered like a serpent through the landscape. The road was alive with activity, from rickety bicycles to trucks laden with goods, and they executed passing maneuvers whenever possible to continue making good time to Bukavu.

Lush green forest vegetation on either side was a stark contrast to the red dust kicked up by their two-vehicle convoy. Small villages dotted the landscape, the hum of daily life momentarily disrupted by their passing. Children paused in their play, looking up with wide-eyed curiosity, while market vendors briefly turned their attention away from their fruits and textiles.

Finally Ian said, "Western half of the city isn't going to happen; the highway runs a block away from the water, too much risk for them to get boxed in with only one way out. Eastern shoreline has a major peninsula on either side, and those are out too—limited road access in and out."

David nodded. "Concur. You think it'll be along that stretch between the two peninsulas?"

"Based on what I'm seeing now, yeah, I do," Ian responded, his tone analytical.

Worthy glanced briefly in the rearview mirror. "How far is that stretch?"

"Three kilometers," David responded, "straight-line distance, give or take. Probably five if we follow the curves along the waterfront."

"That's a hell of a lot of ground for us to cover."

Ian replied, "Better than trying to canvass the entire city, so it's a start. They'll need an isolated area to lay out the goods and inventory everything. Could be an abandoned store or home, or maybe the back room of some business or shop. There's no shortage of options along that stretch, and all of them would provide a few blocks to conduct the exchange between the waterfront and Avenue President Mobutu, which is the nearest major road running east to west. It comes within a few hundred meters of N2/N3 and Avenue Leopold, both of which connect to Avenue De L'Abattoir with direct access to NR11—that's the only major avenue of approach from Rwanda."

David was in agreement. "And since there's about a hundred local streets he could take to move between that stretch of shoreline and the highway, we've got minor and major road access, water access, and a dense urban area for him to hide in. This is looking good. How do we narrow it down—"

Ian cut him off. "Alfajiri College is a good start. See that athletic field? Plenty big enough for an emergency helicopter exfil, if the buyer has the means."

Worthy's response was immediate.

"If he can afford to bankroll a $20 million diamond heist, he's got the means. We need to look for tourist centers, someplace that foreigners can blend in."

"Way ahead of you," Ian said. "Eight hotels near that stretch of the shore, and if we're using the combination of boat and helicopter egress as a starting point, we can narrow that down to five. That dials us down to a one-kilometer stretch."

Worthy kept his focus on the road, but his mind was racing ahead to the streets of Bukavu, picturing the unfolding scenario as David transmitted.

"Cancer, we've got our sector. Starting point is—"

Cancer's response came quickly through their earpieces. "*The college?*"

"Damn, you're good," David acknowledged with a hint of admiration.

Cancer's voice was smug. "*What can I say, the man can afford a helicopter. Boundaries?*"

Ian answered, "Western would be Auberge Chante D'oiseaux Hotel. East, I'm thinking Horizon Hotel...scratch that, make it Lodge Coco. Pulls two more tourist attractions into the sector."

"*Lodge Coco sounds cooler,*" Cancer quipped.

Worthy followed the Suzuki as it accelerated past a motorcycle, listening intently as Ian continued, "And to the south...man, it's got to be Avenue Lumumba. I'd like to say a few blocks beyond that, but you see that imagery?"

"*Yeah,*" Cancer noted. "*Goes from residential to shantytown pretty quick. He's not going to risk going into any place that tight.*"

David then shifted the conversation. "Next up: task org."

Determining where each team member would be positioned was typically Cancer's domain. Aside from being second in command, his experience lent him an intuitive knack for coming up with a task organization plan without hesitation.

And as usual, the sniper didn't disappoint.

"*Pretty simple. We put Ian in the Suzuki west of sector, parked with satellite comms up and running with Mayfly. Fatima stays with him. That's our command post. Suicide, you and Doc will be dismounted on the west side, looking for Mubenga's approach. That gives us two shooters that can split up if needed. I'll be on the east side, solo, looking out for the buyer's rep.*"

Worthy, focused on the road, transmitted back, "Solo?"

"We don't even know what either of them will look like, so yeah. Slim odds require a lot of gut instinct, and that's my specialty."

David chimed in, "Fine. Racegun?"

"With Azibo," Cancer replied, *"right in the middle. They're either parked in the Land Cruiser or dismounted close enough to reach it in a hurry. That gives us a vehicle with long guns assembled, ready to reinforce whichever side needs help. Or, depending on where the exchange goes down, able to pick up and reposition the rest of our guys. Angel's vehicle stays fixed unless we're really in the shit."*

David was always considering the odds, and trusted Cancer's almost preternatural ability to predict how smoothly a plan would go—or not.

"What do you figure the chances of that are?"

Cancer's answer was blunt. *"Exactly the same as the chances that this exchange will go down in Bukavu at all: who the fuck knows?"*

"All right, fair enough. And I can't believe I'm relaying this, but she thinks the actual buyer might be there."

"Nope," Cancer said dismissively. *"Why would he stick his neck out by being on-site?"*

Ian quickly followed that up with, "He might need to check the payload himself before accepting delivery."

Worthy transmitted his response for Cancer's benefit. "But he wouldn't go through all that trouble unless someone was holding him to it."

Cancer's voice carried a note of concern. *"Yeah. That's what worries me, too."*

"Meaning?" David asked.

Ian hypothesized, "Meaning the buyer is accountable to someone who won't take kindly to delays."

David tried to rein in the speculation. "Is this the point where we diverge into wild conjecture?"

Ian pointed out, "Conjecture, yes, but not wild. If Erik Weisz were still alive, we wouldn't even be debating this. I'm just saying, we can't discount the possibility that someone new has already taken the throne."

"One thing at a time," David said firmly, staring hollowly out the windshield at the road ahead. "Let's worry about one goddamned thing at a time."

27

Raising the ceramic cup to my lips, I savored another warm sip. The Congolese, as it turned out, preferred their coffee strong and earthy. It was bold, just bitter enough to give it a sense of character, and the second cup was going down as smoothly as the first.

I sat at a small outdoor table under an orange and black umbrella. Across from me was Reilly, who'd more or less lost the power of speech ever since his food had arrived. He was in the process of ravaging an oversized bowl of Moambe chicken stew, shoveling spoonfuls into his mouth between bites of soft and doughy fufu from a heap atop the plate beside him.

"If you choke," I warned him, "you'll blow our cover. The Heimlich maneuver isn't exactly subtle—don't make me do it."

He was completely nonverbal at this point, managing only a grunt of indifference. I left him to his meal and took a bite of cassava bread, although my appetite by now was almost nonexistent.

Our table offered a perfect vantage point over a major roundabout called Place Mulamba. It was, as best as I could tell, the beating heart of Bukavu. Six streets converged here, and the surrounding area was accordingly filled with hotels, gas stations, religious centers, schools, supermarkets, and healthcare facilities. The air was filled with a blend of exhaust fumes, street food aromas, and the nonstop hum of conversations.

If there was ever a place for us to blend in unnoticed, this was it.

Power wires created a spiderweb against the sky above Place Mulamba, and I watched the traffic merge and diverge in a chaotic yet fluid dance. Yellow vans and car taxis dominated the scene, their horns blasting with short, sharp chirps. Civilian vehicles were only slightly less prevalent, a few covered in the unmistakable red dust of travel outside the city. The final demographic of vehicles were not-uncommon white Land Rover Defenders with brush guards, the calling card of NGOs working in this area.

The sidewalks teemed with a far more diverse array of people: multi-ethnic tourists and NGO workers with backpacks, local women in colorful dresses, and Congolese men in Western attire that ranged from practical to flamboyant. The snapshot of daily life in Bukavu was vibrant and unceasing, although none of the people swarming past us now had the slightest clue of what, if Chen's staff had been correct, was about to occur somewhere among their streets.

The city spread in a lively panorama before us. To the north, the landscape sloped gracefully down to the sparkling edge of Lake Kivu, while to the south, the terrain rose to meet the hilltops, partially shrouded by a cloud-speckled sky.

Reilly slowed his consumption somewhat, now focusing on the subtleties of his meal. He employed the fufu skillfully, pinching off pieces with his fingers and using them to scoop up the chicken and sauce.

"You okay?" I asked.

No response, not even eye contact. There wouldn't be much in the way of productive conversation, I knew, until he'd eaten his fill.

I looked northeast, across Avenue Lumumba. A notch of trees at one corner of the roundabout marked the edge of Alfajiri College, equally denotable by the youthful energy of students coming and going from the campus. We hadn't yet walked past the athletic field-slash-possible helicopter landing zone, but there was no need to; at best, it would serve only to support an emergency exfil for the diamond buyer's representative. Unfortunately for us, however, he wouldn't risk arriving in such blaring fashion. Barring an update from Chen or some Hail Mary sighting by Cancer, it was entirely possible we'd never catch a glimpse of him.

Still, I thought, the fact that we'd arrived here prior to the exchange going down—*if* it was going to occur in Bukavu at all—was no small victory for my team.

The transition from rural to urban Congo was stark. We'd traded rugged dirt highways for smoothly paved streets, remote villages for billboards and towering cell towers, and a literal jungle for an urban one. Trees and palms lined the streets here, their greenery a vivid contrast to the man-made backdrop of multicolored buildings.

I checked my watch—10:37. Reilly and I had been on foot in the city for the better part of an hour, and we were approaching the highest-risk time of the entire operation here: an approximately thirty-minute window between the earliest possible exchange time and the arrival of the Ground Branch shooters now speeding south toward Bukavu from the Rwandan side of the border. Soon my medic and I would have to begin a walking route to pick up any sign of Mubenga and his people in the not-unlikely event that Chen received no further intelligence.

But we couldn't exactly walk in circles for long without being noticed, which gave us a few more minutes to finish our meal.

Our team's first stop had been to procure nondescript backpacks. My rifle was broken into upper and lower receiver, buttstock collapsed and suppressor removed, in order to cram it inside. Cancer and Reilly had swapped weapons, allowing all our ground operators to pack an HK416 in backpacks along with ammo and supplies from the aid bag, while the two HK417s remained fully assembled with Ian and Worthy in their respective vehicles. We had, of course, shipped over H&K MP7s that were far more compact and therefore better suited for urban work, but they'd gone up in literal and figurative smoke when Mubenga's men rocketed our Sprinter van and Land Cruiser in the ambush outside Kolwezi.

My team's second stop in the city had been far more interesting than the first. Reilly had entered a pharmacy on the outskirts, where he'd promptly acquired a bottle of Adderall. All it took was a valid prescription from a doctor, which, in Bukavu, meant the pairs of giraffes printed on the yellow faces of 20,000 Congolese franc bills.

I took another sip of coffee, wondering if I even needed to bother. My previous fatigue was a thing of the past, along with any meaningful desire to eat. I was only on my second cup, yet felt like I'd already shot-gunned five or so without any corresponding jitteriness. My brain fog had long since evaporated, and I was wildly interested in everything around me: the sights, the sounds, the pores in Reilly's face.

"My God," I said breathlessly, noting Reilly was finally slowing down his inhalation of Congolese cuisine, "Adderall is amazing."

He watched me uncomfortably, swallowing another spoonful of stew before warning me in a stern voice, "Don't get too excited."

"This stuff makes it hard not to."

Reilly set his spoon down.

"You're taking government-approved speed. First time is the most intense and it's highly addictive, so you'll always need more. And the come-down is hell once it wears off."

I took another sip of coffee. "Sounds a lot like combat."

"Well—"

He stopped himself, cocking his head like a dog detecting a high-pitched sound. "Actually, yeah. I guess it does."

"Anyway," I said, switching gears, "let's finish our conversation."

"About Adderall?"

"No. Back in the rainforest, before your service as a human battering ram to take down Azibo. You wanted to talk about the senator's daughter, so let's talk."

"Her name's Olivia," he murmured, suddenly sheepish. "And it doesn't matter."

"Yes, it does. Out with it, Doc. That's a direct and lawful order."

Reilly looked conflicted, lifting a piece of fufu for another bite to steady his nerves.

"She wants me off the team," he said mournfully, his mouth half-full. "And she wants kids."

"Okay." I shrugged. "Great. So...?"

He was flabbergasted by my ambivalence. "I'm not sure what I should do."

I spun my ceramic cup, staring at him across the table.

"Look, man. Putting up with our bullshit requires a lot, and those women don't grow on trees. The second Laila told me she was pregnant, I knew my marriage couldn't sustain this job *and* a new baby. That's why I dropped my notice to the Agency. As soon as our contract is done, I'm laying down my sword."

"You don't ever think about it, though? About leaving the team behind?"

"Reilly," I assured him, "I think about it every goddamn day. It's going to hurt like hell to leave you guys, as tight as we've become."

After a moment of silence, I continued, "But that doesn't change the fact that leaving is inevitable. We can shrink away from that or face it head-on. You remember that Ward quote about Special Forces being a mistress?"

"Yeah," Reilly said, repeating the last line. "'...in the end, she will leave you for a younger man.'"

I nodded. "We're all getting older, Doc. My time's up; it's as simple as that. Maybe your time's up, too."

"But we've got six months left on our contract," Reilly pointed out.

"Well, yeah, I mean you've got to finish that up. Can't have you ditching me before I'm out. But after that, you know...just leave, man."

"I don't even know who I'd be without this."

His anguish brought a smile to my face. I'd wrestled with the same issue upon finding out that Laila was pregnant, and had since made my peace with it.

"You'll be the same person you always were. So will I. We've all lost sight of what that means because combat's become our identity. Once we get out, we'll have to figure out who the fuck we were this whole time."

"That's going to be hard."

"It'll be worse than we think, I imagine. But we're all going to have to turn around and face ourselves at some point. And if we—I'm talking about you and me here. If we wait too long to do that, it's going to cost us the poor women we've actually tricked into staying with us. You see how happy Azibo is to have his wife back?"

Reilly made a low whistle. "Yeah. 'Happy' is an understatement."

I lifted my cup and waved it toward him. "Marrying out of my league is the best decision I've ever made. Azibo would say the same. Don't screw that up by chasing the dragon any longer than you have to."

"All right," Reilly said, looking from the remnants of food on his plate to me. Then, with more determination in his voice, he went on, "All right, I'll do it. We'll leave together—I'm going to tell Olivia as soon as we get back."

I sat back in my chair, appraising the look on his face and determining at once that he meant what he said.

The status of the team after my departure remained unknown, and it nagged at me incessantly. Would the guys agree to work with a new team leader? It was statistically impossible for them to be assigned someone willing to play quite as fast and loose as they'd become accustomed to with me over the years. Far more likely was the assignment of a choir boy who would represent the very distasteful traits whose sirens' calls had always failed to seduce me: stoic professionalism, dedication to duty, and a grave respect for authority.

Cancer seemed the most likely to remain in this new era of the team's evolution. He'd put up with almost anything to continue his chosen mission in life, namely shooting people as often as possible. Ian had a similar dedication to the intelligence portion of the job, but Worthy was a wild card—he was far too pragmatic for blind dedication. For him the job was just that, a job.

But a medic's departure along with the team leader could serve to tip the scales for Worthy, and possibly even trigger a mass exodus of the remaining men.

I adjusted the bill of my knock-off Puma ballcap, procured to conceal the swollen lump on my head that neatly conformed to the buttplate of an AK-47 stock.

"Perfect," I said. "You and I will step into the great unknown together. Everyone's been complaining about how long it took us to get this mission, but to be honest my marriage has never been better. We'll all survive just fine without the Agency telling us what to do. I think you're making the right call."

"I hope so," he said mournfully.

"Don't worry about it. Married life will suit you. You'll be a good husband to Olivia."

"Yeah. I'll take care of her, forever."

"You're going to make a great dad, too. Seriously."

"Thanks, man. That means a lot—"

"And I stole your Snickers."

Reilly froze as if coming into contact with a sudden electric current; his eyes flashed a look of shock, then immense grief, before finally settling into a murderous stare.

He spoke in a low growl that I could barely hear over the noises of the street.

"You...*what?*"

"Look," I defended myself, holding up a soothing hand, "we gave one of those Snickers to Fatima." Then I seamlessly transitioned my tone to contempt. "What do you want me to say, that it's okay for you to hoard candy bars from a pregnant woman, a hostage no less? Shame on you, Reilly. Shame on you."

My bid to redirect his fury didn't have its intended effect; if anything, he'd grown increasingly livid.

"I would've given one to her. Maybe two."

"Well, you weren't there when she made it into the woods. Were we supposed to wait? I mean for God's sake, man, Fatima had been through hell and back."

He swung a massive arm over the table, setting his elbow down beside his plate and jabbing a finger at me.

"Don't you dare pin this on her. My bars went missing five days ago. You didn't even know she was a hostage then."

"All right," I stammered, "all right, fair point. For such a sensitive guy, you're pretty quick to cast judgment. But think about it, Reilly: would you be able to pass up that kind of chance to mess with someone?"

"Yeah," he said unflinchingly, "I would."

"Not everyone has your moral constitution. And besides, I'm telling you now for your own good."

His cheeks were reddening as blood rushed to his face.

"Yeah? Is that right, David?"

Leaning forward, he hissed, "*Is that right?*"

"Well," I assured him, glancing at the passersby to make sure I wouldn't be overheard, "I'm reasonably certain the exciting conclusion of this mission is going to require some physical movement. Now that would be a problem for you on account of your injury. But if you're pissed off? I've seen you in action. When you're angry, Doc, you can do anything you set your mind to. Do you feel angry?"

"Hell yes I do, and you're lucky we're in public—"

"Good," I interrupted. "Just channel all that hatred toward Mubenga and his people if this goes bad. Because given our team's historical record, it probably will."

28

"Raptor Nine One, this is Angel. Radio check."

"*Loud and clear,*" Chen replied. "*Keep standing by, we're still working on the new developments.*"

"Copy."

Ian was unenthused by her words; whatever the "new developments" were, Chen's staff had been "working on" them since shortly after he'd arrived at his current position.

He set his radio hand mic on the console of the Suzuki Vitara, eyes fixed on the construction site outside. It was unclear when or if the construction would resume—the structure before him was almost entirely covered by massive swaths of ragged blue tarp shredded with holes, pieces of exposed rebar protruding from the roof.

The ground behind the building-in-progress was uneven, a mix of hardened earth and gravel, with tire tracks from heavy machinery crisscrossing the surface. Mounds of construction materials from bags of cement to bricks sat unmolested and covered in dust, along with, of course, his satellite antenna. It stood on its tripod a few meters from the vehicle, connected to his radio by virtue of a long cable snaking in through the cracked window.

This location wouldn't win any awards for beauty, he thought, particularly compared with the vibrancy of Bukavu he'd witnessed on the drive in. However, it offered an almost ideal patch of seclusion from Avenue Lumumba at the front of the building, which extended a half-kilometer to David and Reilly's position at the western edge of their zone of interest.

"Do you need any more food," he asked, "or water?"

Fatima looked over at him from the passenger seat.

"No, thank you, Ian. I am quite fine for now."

There was a moment of silence, the hum of the city in the distance filling the space.

Then she asked, "Do you think we are in the right spot?"

"Sure. This is about as perfect as we can hope for. Doesn't look like anyone will come stumbling back here anytime soon—"

"I do not mean the construction site," she clarified with an air of concern. "I mean Bukavu."

He could certainly understand her reluctance. The options now boiled down to an imminent gunfight with her husband in the center of the storm, or no exchange at all. With a new life ahead for her, Azibo, and their baby, her preference between the two was clear enough.

And to be fair, Ian wasn't sure what to tell her.

The CIA had sent over their own assessment of possible locations for the exchange. The report, he noted with a mix of validation and disappointment, had so closely mirrored his team's own on-the-fly assessment while looking at phones from the confines of a moving vehicle that it was nearly useless to them. The staff's primary contribution had been a numbered series of named areas of interest, or NAIs, representing specific buildings most likely to be used for the handoff.

Ian checked his watch and saw that it was 10:50, a scant ten minutes away from the beginning of the potential exchange's time window.

"I'm honestly not sure," he said. "But whatever happens, we'll be on our way to Rwanda very soon."

Fatima said nothing. Ian, searching for a way to ease the tension, gestured toward the slight swell of her belly beneath her clothes.

"You must be excited about the baby," he ventured.

She smiled, a warm but weary expression. "Yes, very. But Azibo is quite nervous."

"About being a father?"

"Yes. Exactly this."

Ian chuckled. "I think every new dad worries about that."

"Oh?" she asked. "Do you have kids?"

"No."

"Why not?"

What was he supposed to say to that? Ian wasn't sure, and sided with a throwaway answer. "Just haven't found the right woman yet, I suppose."

"I see," Fatima replied. Then she probed, with a hint of curiosity in her voice, "And how hard have you been looking, Ian?"

Again, he found himself at a loss for words.

The truth was that the team consumed most of his waking hours. They were almost always on a mission or training for the next one, and in between he'd managed little more than a string of casual relationships. Some were more serious than others, but all, ultimately, were unable to withstand his frequent absences.

And yet he couldn't blame his CIA employment, either.

Before that he'd done largely the same job in the mercenary realm, the same shadowy underworld where he'd first met David and, later, Reilly, Worthy, and Cancer as well.

Was he suited for a domestic life, he wondered?

He mused aloud, "I guess I haven't been looking for the right woman much at all."

"There is always a chance for the future. New opportunities, new paths. For both of us. Yes or no?"

"Yes," Ian said. Then he changed the subject. "Azibo's going to be a great dad."

Fatima continued watching him as if she was about to force the conversation back to its previous trajectory, but ultimately allowed Ian his secrets.

"Yes, he will." Fatima leaned back, her hand resting on her belly. "We both want...how should I say...balance. A new life where we can be safe, where our child can grow up without fear."

"You'll have it," Ian easily replied. "Very soon."

She gazed out the windshield and asked, "Where will we be moved?"

"Where? I mean, just about anywhere you want."

"Wherever we want," she repeated softly.

Ian nodded. "Sure. My team will vouch for Azibo's cooperation, we'll tell them he saved our lives. They'll provide you with full relocation, stipend, residence and employment assistance. I mean, it's our fault you have to leave DRC in the first place."

Fatima clucked her tongue. "I am afraid the Congo holds little for us, anymore."

"And I'm inclined to agree. So, where do you want to go?"

"I am not certain," she said. "Yet. But I am thinking—"

His phone rang with an incoming call from David.

"Hang on," he told her, answering at once and putting his phone on speaker. "Go ahead."

"We're picking up from the traffic circle," the team leader began, "heading out on the prowl toward Avenue Muhumba, north side, eastbound."

"Got it. Cancer and Racegun are still holding what they've got."

"Angel, Raptor Nine One."

Chen's voice caught Ian off guard—he snatched the hand mic from the console and tucked it between his shoulder and ear.

"Stay on the line," Ian snapped, "she's calling."

Then he transmitted, "Raptor Nine One, send it."

Chen answered, *"I have an update for you. And before I give it, I want you to know that the effort required to gather it was nothing short of herculean."*

Ian manipulated the phone with his free hand, patching Cancer and Worthy into a conference call with David.

"The fact that we know this after Fatima's rescue threw everything off the rails is a literal and metaphorical miracle, so do not, under any circumstances, mess this up."

No shit, Ian thought. At this point, her theatrics were wasting precious seconds that his team desperately needed to get into position.

But he restrained himself to a respectful, "Copy all, I'm prepared to receive."

"The exchange will occur at NAI 3, the Belgian colonial administration building. We've intercepted traffic indicating 11:15, though it's not clear if that's for the exchange itself or the arrival of the buyer's party."

"Stand by," he said, then spoke into his phone. "Update: NAI 3, NAI 3, the old colonial administration building." He checked his satellite imagery. "It's on the north side of Avenue Muhumba, just across the street from the college, aligned with the northwest corner of the athletic field. Time provided was 11:15, no further information. Confirm."

"Suicide, check."

"Cancer, check."

"Racegun," the pointman began, "check. Moving into position to get eyes-on now."

Ian continued, "All stations, stay on the call."

Then he spoke into his hand mic. "Everyone's informed and relocating."

Chen replied, *"Excellent. Ground Branch is still southbound on NR11, twenty minutes from the border."*

"Stand by for guidance," Ian told her.

He spoke into the phone. "Ground Branch isn't going to make it in time. They're still twenty minutes out. What do you want them to do?"

Ian keyed his transmit switch and held the hand mic up to the phone as David provided his response.

"Unless we require an emergency intervention, they need to set up on the east side of Bukavu. If the buyer's representative flushes out of the city by vehicle, they move to interdiction based on our information or the Agency's, whichever comes first. Otherwise they need to wait at the border crossing and support our exfil."

"Mayfly," Ian transmitted, "did you get all that?"

"Confirm, will relay now. Keep me posted."

Then she added hesitantly, *"And good luck."*

Cancer listened intently to Worthy's voice on the conference call.

"In position, street parking on the south side of Avenue Muhumba, seventy meters east of the colonial building. No activity, looks abandoned."

Cancer replied, "Watch for the arrival of a bunch of guys to secure the exchange site, if they're not in place already. My money says Mubenga has been given a staging location somewhere to the west. Once he reaches it, they'll direct him to the building. Security will shake him down, confirm the diamonds are there, then call in the buyer's rep to check the haul and make the final payment. Suicide, where are you and Doc at?"

"Eastbound on foot," David replied, "south side of Avenue Muhumba, approaching the west side of the college now. There's twenty meters of woodline between the campus and the road—we're going to duck into it and kit up with long guns, then continue movement toward the colonial building."

Cancer checked his phone map and replied, "Good. Advise you proceed no further than the final side street before the exchange site. Chances of getting spotted by security once you get past it are too high."

"Yeah, will do."

The call went silent then, leaving Cancer to continue scanning local traffic for any irregularities.

A warm breeze filtered through the blinds, carrying with it the scent of fresh water. The smell brought back memories of shoreside camping trips at Greenwood Lake in Jersey, although Cancer's current settings—and his role in them—were a far cry from the childhood excursions with his father. He felt a deeply gratifying sense of satisfaction that far exceeded what his surroundings afforded.

Most of that, he knew, related to how miserable the rest of his team was.

With Ian and Fatima restricted to the Suzuki, David and Reilly soon to be fighting their way through the strip of woods north of the college, and Worthy and Azibo in their sweatbox of an SUV, Cancer was the only one whose surveillance position afforded him the ability to live large, however temporarily.

His corner suite on the third floor of Hotel Elila afforded him the closest thing he'd get to a God's-eye view.

In the blind spot to his east, Avenue Chantal merged with Avenue Muhumba, which channeled traffic from both roads into a single corridor to Cancer's front. Visible to the southwest was the juncture of a side road leading to Avenue Commandant De Kemmeter, and just beyond the trees lining the south side of the main street were the academic buildings of Alfajiri College. His westward line of sight even revealed an inlet of Lake Kivu, bordered by a resort that his map assured him was the Orchid Safari Club.

Anyone crossing the eastern boundaries of the team's zone of interest would pass by below, and all Cancer had to do now was sniper shit, which came more or less as second nature—minus the smothering ghillie suits, lengthy belly-crawls through thorns and anthills, and countless hours of waiting in position to survey a target.

Instead he'd opened all the windows, then adjusted the vertical blinds until they were separated just enough for him to peer outside without being seen from the street. His backpack was zipped up on the bed for hasty retrieval, while almost everything in it was on his person now—tactical vest stripped of all but the bare essentials like magazines and aid pouch, with his radio and Glock in their concealed configuration beneath his shirt. His HK416—actually, it was Ian's rifle, since Cancer swapped his longer weapon for something he could carry in a backpack—was fully assembled beside him, suppressor included. He had his earpieces in, phone at the ready, and could seamlessly communicate over the team net or cellular network as necessary.

It was 11:04 now, and the streets below were bustling with the midday rhythm of the city. The occasional burst of sunlight through the clouds cast a dynamic pattern of light and shadow across the room, playing over the sparse decor.

David transmitted, *"We're kitted up, transition to FM."*

Cancer dropped off the call, looking up by the time he noticed his first aberration in the flow of traffic below.

"Convoy inbound from the east," he said quickly, analyzing the vehicles streaming past him now. "Mitsubishi Pajero, black, Isuzu D-Max times two, gray and white, Toyota Prado, black, they look unarmored, westbound on Avenue Muhumba."

"Copy," Worthy replied. *"Stand by."*

Cancer had barely watched the final truck flow past when a new development caught his eye.

There was only one way past the brick wall surrounding the hotel parking lot below, and at that moment a charcoal Land Rover Discovery pulled through the port.

The vehicle's proximity to the convoy heading west caught his attention, and he watched closely as the driver reversed into a parking spot with its windshield facing him.

By then Worthy was transmitting, *"Convoy has stopped at the old colonial administration building. Guys are getting out now, carrying bags in the front door. Any sign of Mubenga?"*

"Negative," David answered. *"We're almost alongside that last side street, no sign of him yet."*

Cancer had his phone in hand as all four of the Land Rover's doors opened almost simultaneously. His focus centered on the individual exiting the back passenger side.

He was a heavyset man in cargo pants and a green plaid shirt with the sleeves rolled up to his elbows, wearing aviator sunglasses over a bushy salt-and-pepper beard. The other three individuals to exit were clean-shaven, no visible weapons, but they casually sauntered to a loose semi-circle perimeter around the bearded man.

Whoever he was, his departure from the vehicle suddenly made sense —he now held a satellite phone to his ear.

Cancer was in the process of aligning his phone camera and zooming in for a picture when Worthy spoke again.

"Convoy is pulling away now, everyone who exited the vehicles is still in the building. Looked like eight to ten guys."

Snapping his photo, Cancer transmitted back, "The convoy drivers are going to stage for emergency exfil, so keep an eye out for them. And check it out, I think the buyer's representative just arrived in the hotel parking lot. Texting a pic now. Angel, send it to Mayfly."

"Copy," Ian replied.

After sending the photo, Cancer lifted his HK416 from its resting position against the wall and deftly stepped atop the chair he'd positioned beside the window in the unlikely event that he'd actually be able to take a shot before this was all over.

"I know this cat," David said with disbelief.

"How? Who is he?"

"I don't remember his name. But after Yemen, Chen showed me the profiles of our Top 5 targets. Said they were all off the grid, but...yeah, I'm sure of it. This Santa Claus-looking motherfucker was one of them."

"Wonderful," Cancer said, pleasantly surprised at the development but chagrined that he'd denied that the actual buyer could or would show himself at the exchange. "I'm dropping him."

Their primary mission was to positively identify the buyer or his rep, and now that it was complete, he could move on to priority number two: disrupting the exchange.

But upon taking aim, he saw that he was already too late.

With a frustrated grunt, Cancer transmitted, "He's back in the vehicle."

As if to rub this in his face, Ian came over the net.

"*Mayfly has positive identification. The bearded man is Dominic de Lange, an international terrorist financier, missing for the last six months.*"

David asked, "*Racegun, can you hit him once he gets out at the target building?*"

"*I'm too close,*" Worthy responded. "*I step out of the car with a long gun and I'm dead. They're going to drop him off in front of the main entrance—you and Doc won't have an angle from the woods before he's inside.*"

Cancer shook his head.

"You're both missing the point. We've got a Top 5 target here so we take him now, before he has a chance to disappear. There's only one entrance to the parking lot, and it's surrounded by a brick wall on both sides. Racegun, get here now. Block his only way out—they won't be able to get up enough speed to ram you—and transition to a long gun. His vehicle is unarmored. Dark gray Land Rover backed into the fifth parking spot inside the entrance, north side of the lot. I'll cover you from the high ground. There's only three bodyguards, and we can hit them from both sides. Buyer's options are to die in place or make a run for it on foot, and if he chooses the second, one of us will drop him in the open."

Worthy, it seemed, approved of this plan. "*I'll be there in thirty seconds.*"

Cancer took aim once more as David transmitted, "*Angel, break down SATCOM and move to the street. Once this goes down, we need to exfil asap.*"

Azibo drove the Nissan SUV as fast as traffic would allow, tailing a taxi to their front as Worthy transmitted from the passenger seat.

"Ten seconds out."

He expected to receive confirmation from Cancer then, but it was David's voice that came over his earpiece. *"Eyes-on Mubenga, we're taking him. Side street west of the exchange—"*

"There," Worthy cried, pointing to the vehicle-wide gap in the brick wall outside the hotel. "Block it, hit the parking brake, and get behind that wall."

Azibo slammed on the brakes, steering the Nissan into a 45-degree angle in a journey that ended when the front bumper smacked into the edge of the vehicle entrance.

Worthy leapt out of the passenger door as the light jolt subsided, fully intent on using the quarter panel before him as cover while he opened fire on the Land Rover that he could only now make out.

But fate had other ideas, and it only took him seconds to realize that Cancer's plan, while well-intentioned given the available information, had one catastrophic flaw.

A steady succession of men exited other vehicles in the parking lot without warning, an equal succession of rifles appearing as a previously undetected security force made their presence known.

There were far too many for Worthy to engage, and the very attempt to open fire now would cause him to get shot more times than he cared to estimate. Nor could he race around the vehicle to seek cover—they'd take him down long before he reached the rear bumper, and any attempt to scramble over the hood would result in a similar outcome. He'd just gone from a two-on-three engagement against Dominic de Lange and a pair of bodyguards to a two-on-God knew how many opponents while he was caught, frozen, standing in the open.

Worthy dropped to the ground and executed a panicked crawl beneath the Nissan Patrol, immensely grateful for the vehicle's ground clearance—bullets popped into metal above him, glass shattering as he pulled himself on his belly toward the street. Judging by the sheer volume of gunfire, the situation was escalating rapidly.

He and Azibo had succeeded in blocking the lone vehicle exit, but nothing more; Worthy pulled himself free of the Nissan's undercarriage, emerging on the driver's side and looking up to see Cancer leaning out of a third-story window, firing vertically downward in a feverish attempt to save the teammate he'd ordered into a fight beyond anyone's imagining. The situation was totally fucked, and at this point all they could do was try to clear out enough opposition for Worthy and Azibo to drive away without getting killed—if, of course, their vehicle worked after absorbing an untold number of bullets.

Every second Worthy took to respond with deadly force exponentially increased the risk that Cancer would be shot and tip out the window in a flailing stuntman fall.

Assessing his options didn't take long. The brick wall, while a barrier to his visibility, also restricted the angles from which he could be attacked.

And, regrettably, narrowed his selection of a shooting position.

He ran toward the front bumper, stepping atop it and leaning against the hood to gain a narrow angle of visibility against the men shooting at him now.

Worthy engaged from right to left with calculated precision, not shifting to increase his field of view until he was certain the current target was down.

The first man he spotted was roughly ten meters away, taking partial cover behind a black sedan as he reloaded a UMP submachine gun. Worthy popped him twice before he could complete his magazine change, then angled further left to find another fighter spraying an Uzi upward, toward Cancer. Two subsonic rounds between his shoulder blades caused him to shudder and fall, the Uzi tumbling from his grasp.

The third target was more cautious, moving erratically between a midsize SUV and a pickup truck. He was relocating to acquire a more advantageous line of sight to the Nissan, and given a few more seconds, probably would have succeeded. Worthy tracked the man's movements, waiting to fire until he came into view again, now swinging his compact rifle into position—he suddenly collapsed on the ground, his killer transmitting a moment later.

"*Racegun,*" Cancer said, "*you're good. Get out of here.*"

Worthy scrambled off the hood, taking cover behind the brick wall and looking left to find Azibo, hunkered down as ordered, watching him with detached interest as he said, "So much for the plan."

"Get in," Worthy shouted. "We're leaving."

He threw open the rear driver's-side door, staying low as he pulled himself across the backseat and shifted toward the opposite window of the vehicle. The only way to find out if the Nissan was still functional was to crank the engine, which placed him and Azibo in a Catch-22 of the worst kind: if the vehicle started, they'd have to leave asap, and if it didn't, they'd need to get the hell out before they became a stationary target for any of the security men moving toward them now.

"*Suicide,*" Reilly said over his earpiece, "*he's headed south. Cover me.*"

The transmission served as a cruel reminder that Worthy was alone with Cancer out here, the remainder of his team dedicated to efforts that didn't involve turning the tables in the current fiasco.

Raising his HK416, Worthy took aim through a rear window spider-webbed with bullet impacts as Azibo cranked the engine. There was enough time to fire three rounds at a man crouching between cars, and he may or may not have scored a hit—auto glass had a strange effect on bullet trajectories, particularly when the rounds passed through at an angle— when suddenly the entire parking lot disappeared from view.

Azibo floored the gas in reverse to send them rocketing backward into Avenue Muhumba amid the blaring of car horns.

The Nissan jolted to a halt with a crunch of metal on metal, and Worthy looked behind him to see that they'd struck an oncoming van, the traffic in both directions coming to an abrupt halt.

Before Worthy could speak, Azibo had shifted to drive and was accelerating in a tight, careening left-hand turn that took them across the opposite lane, over a median, and onto the merger of Avenue Chantal beyond.

Once the front bumper was aligned with the road, Azibo accelerated, taking them west toward the exchange building and, to its south, Alfajiri College.

"Well," Azibo said, "it seems that went poorly."

David had barely finished his transmission when Reilly grabbed his shoulder and said, "There he is."

The team leader swung his gaze north, where a Subaru Forester was turning off the main road with a Toyota Hilux following a short distance off its rear bumper. Reilly couldn't be certain that either contained Mubenga, but the close proximity of two vehicles abruptly stopping a few hundred meters from the old colonial building was impossible to ignore. Checking his watch, he added, "It's 11:15."

Cancer had warned them not to proceed farther than the side street west of the target building, which turned out to be the exact location the two vehicles were stopping at now.

David said, "We've got a minute tops before they get to the exchange location. Follow me."

And that was all the advance notice Reilly had before the team leader rose and took off for the woods, approaching the edge of the treeline north of Alfajiri College.

"*Ten seconds out,*" Worthy transmitted.

Reilly followed David as quickly as he could. There was precious little preparation required: they were already kitted up in tactical vests over civilian clothes, now-empty backpacks cinched down over their shoulders, HK416s assembled down to the suppressors.

And while the medic was flabbergasted by the sudden change of plans, it made perfect sense to a certain extent. Worthy and Cancer were seconds away from hitting the buyer at the hotel parking lot, which meant there was nothing to lose by hitting Mubenga hard and fast—except a few pints of blood or, perhaps, their lives.

But he didn't know exactly what David had in mind until he swept left and transmitted on the run.

"Eyes-on Mubenga, we're taking him. Side street west of the exchange, we're flanking left through the houses. Angel, be ready for pickup."

There was just one minor obstacle the team leader didn't mention: Avenue Muhumba.

They broke cover in a near-sprint, darting out of the treeline and into the dirt road. Reilly half-expected to get T-boned by a taxi at any second, but traffic screeched to a grinding halt on both sides at the sight of two armed men, drivers and pedestrians alike staring in disbelief and fear. A few brave drivers laid into their horns, the sounds lost amid the constant barrage of similar blasts throughout the city.

And then they were across, moving between sand-colored houses in an increasingly bizarre journey toward Mubenga.

Twenty minutes ago, Reilly thought, they were sipping coffee beside Place Mulamba. But that was all a half-remembered dream in the midst of their current endeavor: racing through the dusty backyards of Bukavu houses, chickens scattering before them in a flurry of feathers, a woman who'd been hanging laundry freezing, eyes wide with shock, a wet shirt slipping from her grasp and splatting on the ground.

"*Jambo*," Reilly called to her, "*jambo!*"

It was the only Swahili he recalled off the top of his head, and he'd never know if his greeting of *hello, hello* had its intended effect. By now they'd breezed past her and were faced with a dog who stood its ground in howling protest, but ultimately didn't attack.

Reilly nearly stepped on a loose soccer ball, vaulting it at the last second as an electric jolt shot through his wounded left side. The sudden wave of pain caused fresh beads of sweat to form on his brow as he raced around a cluster of rainwater collection barrels, looking up just in time to see David pointing to his right before continuing to move.

Reilly's first thought was, *oh, thank God, I can stop soon*, as he cut around the house, raising his HK416 to begin slipping east toward the two stopped vehicles. He could only see the empty side street ahead but knew the bad guys were waiting to the left of the next house corner, with another possible threat from the security men in the old colonial building through the trees beyond.

A quick scan to assess his options for cover and concealment revealed that his luck had run out in full.

There was a goat tied to a stake in the ground—he wouldn't be much help—along with a handmade outdoor dining set and trash bins. A better prospect lay in the form of two mango trees ahead, until he registered that neither trunk was anywhere near large enough to conceal a man of his stature.

He'd struck out completely and could only hope that David had fared better on the north side of the house, the very thought causing him to pick up his pace. A simultaneous engagement would be ideal although virtually impossible to achieve; they were both winging it now, and each man knew it as well as the other.

Reilly heard car doors slamming ahead, followed by the unintelligible chatter of men. They were waiting to receive a call directing them to the final exchange location, and now that Cancer and Worthy were hitting the buyer, that call would never come—it was up to David and Reilly to hit them before they realized it.

Reilly slowed to a stop before the corner of the house, which represented his only available cover. He'd have to compensate for that with an excessive volume of fire to keep from getting shot, and dropped to a knee and angled himself just enough to see the tail end of the Hilux.

Just beyond it were two armed men, removing all possible doubt that he and David were in the right place at the right time.

Having beaten his team leader to the punch of initiating the engagement, Reilly exploited the element of surprise while he still could. He opened fire on one man, then the other, before lowering his aim to the Hilux windows and unleashing a salvo of bullets from left to right and back again.

He pivoted further around the corner, acquiring only the slightest view of the Subaru and, with it, a man aiming an AK-47 over the hood. David opened fire on him just before Reilly could take his own shots, but he did so anyway, although any chance of assessing his accuracy was lost amid successive volleys of automatic gunfire.

Reilly ducked behind the corner as bullets thwacked into bricks, then rose to a standing position before attempting his next engagement. He caught sight of Mubenga almost immediately, his face unmistakable as he wielded a Galil assault rifle, although Reilly had barely taken aim before the terrorist leader dropped out of sight.

Instead he fired four times at the slightest glimpse of a man behind the rear axle of the Hilux, then transitioned to a fighter who made the mistake of overexposing himself over top of the pickup bed. It was an opportunity for an almost certain kill, and there was time for five quick shots to seal the deal before incoming gunfire forced him back behind the corner, where he knelt and waited for the sound of bullet impacts to subside before exposing himself again.

Mubenga kept popping his head up to fire, though he never stayed in one place for long. He was a slippery bastard, and had two vehicles to use as cover while Reilly's options were only to engage from standing or kneeling firing positions around the corner, which he utilized interchangeably in the hopes that any incoming fire would veer high or low when he rounded the corner again.

Cancer transmitted, *"Racegun, you're good. Get out of here."*

And then, a very peculiar thing happened.

Unsuppressed gunfire broke out through the trees behind Mubenga's vehicles, and it only took him a moment to realize the shots were coming from the old colonial building, a new development that defied explanation. Did the security men at the exchange point think the gunfire was directed against them? Did they think it was Mubenga attempting to kill the buyer at the hotel, or were they simply trying to stop the two American shooters? Any explanation was possible, but the rationale didn't matter much to Reilly at present.

What *was* important was what happened next.

His magazine went empty, and he ducked behind the corner to reload. But he'd scarcely retrieved a fresh mag when there was a flash of movement to his front, an armed man with a slung duffel bag running past the gap in houses. Reilly faced the sobering realization that an intrepid militiaman had maneuvered and was about to pop him, but the runner didn't so much as slow down, vanishing from view and leaving no doubt that he was fleeing the gunfight entirely.

Reilly completed his reload before registering the significance of the duffel bag.

He transmitted, "Suicide, he's headed south. Cover me."

Whether David heard him or not was anyone's guess, but Reilly could reasonably assume that if his team leader had an objection, he'd be voicing it now.

He wheeled around and slipped past the goat and into the row of backyards, cutting left and making it around a house before breaking into a run at full tilt. There was no point clearing the spaces between houses and no time to do it—his best chance of nailing his target was at the open strip of Avenue Muhumba, provided he arrived in time.

If anyone was suited for a running pursuit of Mubenga, it was David. Reilly had taken a bullet less than 24 hours earlier, but the fact remained that he was closer to the fleeing target.

He didn't slow his pace until he neared the edge of the last house before the road, where a steady stream of westbound traffic had now resumed. But the cars in the eastbound lane were stopped entirely, his first prelude to the sight that awaited him around the corner.

Reilly pivoted around the house with his rifle at the ready, just in time to see Mubenga mid-carjack.

The black duffel bag was still slung across his back, and he was in the process of yanking a woman from the driver's seat of a Toyota sedan. Reilly took a breath and aimed carefully, waiting until the woman cleared his sights before firing four rounds that he hoped would drop the man his team had been sent into the Congo to clear.

But he narrowly missed, and while the shots were suppressed and the bullet subsonic, Mubenga couldn't fail to miss the attempt on his life.

The car's open door intercepted the rounds, one of which punched through the window, and Mubenga abandoned his theft and scrambled around the hood as Reilly lined up for another shot.

But his view was obscured when a taxi sped past—the driver was hell-bent on making it to his destination, gunfire or no gunfire—and by the time he had a clear line of sight, Mubenga was already slipping into the woods lining the campus.

Reilly lowered his rifle and ran across the road, transmitting as he moved.

"Mubenga's headed toward the college, I'm in pursuit."

Cancer's follow-up was so closely timed, and so closely mirrored the previous transmission, that Reilly almost wondered if the sniper was fucking with him.

"*Buyer's moving for the lake, I'm on him.*"

Cancer darted across Avenue Lieutenant Dubois, the final road in his path. All that lay between him and Lake Kivu now was a narrow expanse of trees extending along the shore and, with any luck, Dominic de Lange.

The financier wasn't alone, however, and there would undoubtedly be a group of bodyguards to contend with. Cancer had no idea how many, namely because he hadn't actually seen the financier leave the parking lot —it wasn't until he'd ended a particularly devastating three-target engagement against the security men directly beneath his hotel room that he'd glanced up to catch the sight of men running across the street, headed north.

De Lange and at least two bodyguards were slipping away, cutting behind a house and disappearing from view. By then Worthy and Azibo were on their way out, and Cancer set a land-speed record down the hotel stairs and out the side exit, bypassing the parking lot entirely before following his quarry.

Worthy transmitted, *"Doc, I'm headed for the college to reinforce you— vector me in."*

"Main building next to the athletic field," Reilly panted. *"Mubenga just went in the northwest entrance."*

"Copy, I'll be there in one minute."

Now that Worthy had committed to the school, Cancer was on his own, unless someone was available to reinforce him.

"Support," he transmitted on the run, approaching the treeline ahead.

David replied at once, "I'm on it—where?"

"Go north until you hit the shoreline. Follow it east until you see me or de Lange; he's on the run with bodyguards, two minimum."

Cancer entered the treeline as the air trembled with the shudder of a helicopter passing by overhead. De Lange wasn't making it to the athletic field and there was no spot for a landing along the shore; but if the pilot was either very good or had a rope ladder—both of which were extremely likely—he could easily recover the financier once the boat made it into open waters.

That meant the water egress was still in play, but the question remained as to whether Cancer should follow the woods to the right or left, east or west. To the east, the shoreline curved north for three hundred meters before the nearest house; at half that distance to the west, however, was the Orchid Safari Club and, more significantly, its long dock extending into the lake.

He went left toward the dock, sprinting through the stretch of trees lining the edge of Lake Kivu, his breaths coming in rapid, controlled bursts. The shoreline was to his right now, its waters gleaming under the sun, while to his left, scattered houses peeked through the dense foliage.

Despite the urgency driving him, Cancer moved with calculated caution. Each step was deliberate, his eyes darting between the shadows cast by the trees, searching for any sign that one or more bodyguards had detected his presence and decided to stop long enough to gun him down. The terrain was uneven, littered with roots and rocks, demanding his full attention to avoid a misstep.

Cancer heard the helicopter flying westward, a solid indicator that he'd chosen the right direction to move, and he could faintly make out the gentle lapping of waves against the shore. Then he caught the fragment of a man's voice ahead, just out of sight, further assuring him that de Lange was near. The presence of the financier urged Cancer to push his limits, particularly given his rage at the moment.

Many of the team's missions had gone to utter shit, but none quite so exquisitely as this: two simultaneous gunfights, two team members in pursuit of targets on the run, and precious little time to coordinate with one another.

And besides, Cancer thought, he was utterly furious with himself.

He'd made a grave error in ordering Worthy's plan of action, having failed to account for two factors that put his team in their current predicament. The first was the unanticipated presence of a major security contingent that had arrived well ahead of their primary—so early, in fact, that Cancer felt certain he hadn't missed their arrival at all.

And the second, equally heinous miscalculation was the perceived unimportance of a pedestrian exit in the brick wall surrounding the hotel.

The sniper had noticed it, of course, dismissing it out of hand for one simple reason: if the buyer made a move for it, he'd be an easy target, plain and simple. But he hadn't counted on having to save Worthy's life and, to a lesser extent, Azibo's as well. The security force that fought in place had only one reason to do so, and that was to cover the escape of their primary. At some point in Cancer's feverish shooting, a few bodyguards had rushed Dominic de Lange toward the gap in the wall, and with their escape toward the athletic field blocked by Worthy, ran him north toward Lake Kivu instead.

Cancer couldn't blame his sleep loss, currently mitigated by Adderall elevating his neurotransmitters, and he certainly couldn't blame anyone else on the team but himself.

Adding insult to injury, he thought as he ran, was the importance of his current target.

Dominic de Lange had been off the grid for some time, and risked exposing himself only after a half-year disappearance ended with a massive payload of diamonds backstopped by the availability of ground, air, and water exfil options.

Cancer heard the helicopter drawing nearer, helping to cover the sound of his movement.

But the chopping rotor blades were soon underscored by the growl of a speedboat approaching from the west. Then a new noise caused him to startle—a sharp, piercing whoosh that cut through the ambient sounds of his surroundings so suddenly that Cancer was certain a rocket was flying his way.

But an intense hissing followed, reminiscent of a firework being launched, that culminated in a sizzling crackle.

He caught sight of a bright, luminous streak soaring upward through the sky between the trees—De Lange's security detail had just fired a signal flare, and for Cancer, that was a very, very good thing.

He charged forward, desperately seeking a view of the dock and achieving it within seconds as an azure Eurocopter soared north over Lake Kivu.

The best piece of cover was a single tree that could protect him from an initial flurry of gunshots but not much more than that; if and when the bodyguards maneuvered on his position, he'd be done for.

But he wasn't going to get another chance to bring down Dominic de Lange, and driven by anger at having endangered Worthy almost to the point of total annihilation, Cancer dropped to the prone behind the trunk and angled his suppressed HK416.

Four men were silhouetted against the waters of Lake Kivu, all standing at the edge of the dock. De Lange was easily identifiable by his girth and the fact that he wasn't holding a submachine gun. It was a miracle that none of the security men had noticed Cancer yet, but that would change in seconds or less. He was at a disadvantageous position, taking aim after a frantic gunfight and the ensuing race to the coastline.

He set the bottom corner of his magazine on the ground to steady his shaking hands, taking a final breath and letting the air escape his lungs with a steady exhalation. The speedboat was ripping along the shore toward the dock, the helicopter orbiting in a loose turn over the lake's southern expanse. Cancer steadied his sights as a bright, glowing orb from the signal floated downward just beyond the target, and he broke his trigger to fire one precisely aimed shot.

Dominic de Lange collapsed to the ground, writhing as the sniper let loose a trio of additional bullets that ended the motion with a final sideways flop.

There was an almost immediate reaction from the bodyguards, who whirled and opened fire as Cancer slid behind the tree trunk, hearing its wood splintering as he fought his way upright to a kneeling position.

He braced himself for a fight to the death that could only end one way.

Cancer was about to lean past the trunk and open fire before the bodyguards could split up, when there was an abrupt break in the gunfire.

And when it resumed, no bullets were hitting the tree that he hid behind.

He peered left to see the men firing at a new threat, this one further down the shore to the west—David had arrived and dealt himself into the gunfight.

The bodyguards could pursue one of their assailants at the expense of taking fire from the other, or they could simply admit defeat and scramble aboard the speedboat slowing to a halt at the edge of the dock, waiting to ferry them to safer waters.

The security men wisely chose the latter, and Cancer didn't bother trying to gun them down as they leapt, one after the other, onto the boat.

"De Lange is down, I'm withdrawing," he transmitted, rising to move south as David replied, *"I'll follow you."*

At this point their sole priority was exfilling the area without getting shot, and with men from the exchange site likely flooding toward the boat pickup this very second, that may be easier said than done. Every remaining bullet was an asset they may well need to get out—particularly, he thought, if they made it back to Avenue Muhumba in time to back up Reilly.

Reilly slipped up the northwest staircase of Alfajiri College, moving quietly as he listened to the footsteps charging up the stairs.

His best effort at stealth paid off as he rounded the second-floor landing and registered a door clicking shut above him.

"Racegun," he transmitted, breaking into a run, "third floor."

"On my way," Worthy replied.

The thudding chop of rotor blades followed the pointman's transmission as a helicopter roared low toward the building, and Reilly reached the top step and placed his hand on the door handle.

Mubenga was making the smart play, he thought, by hauling himself and the diamonds as far as possible from the fight in the streets below. All he had to do was find a place to hide and call for pickup, which would flood the college with militia fighters or de Lange's men or both, and Reilly had to stop him before he made that call.

Turning the handle and flinging the door open, Reilly raised his HK416 and advanced.

A long hallway stretched before him, lined with dorm rooms and interspersed with open corners in either direction. He whirled right to clear the first one, finding a short corridor ending in a window. Through the glass he made out the form of a sleek blue helicopter soaring over the athletic field, its pilot initiating an arcing turn toward the lake.

He'd just resumed his movement down the main hall, thinking what a nightmare this place was to clear without support, when he heard the low tone of a man's voice from one of the corridors—Mubenga making a phone call to save his life.

And at that exact moment, the stairwell door swung fully shut behind Reilly, emitting a bang that reverberated across the floor.

The medic had just enough time to duck back into the side corridor when a partial silhouette emerged from another one further down the hall, and the deafening burst of a Galil assault rifle erupted as a cluster of bullet impacts blasted through the door that had just compromised him.

Dropping to a knee, the medic transitioned his rifle to a left-handed grip and edged around the corner in time to see Mubenga with the duffel bag across his back, making a break for the next side corridor.

Reilly fired twice, certain that both rounds found their mark before Mubenga vanished around the corridor, his movement unhindered beyond the slightest stumble. The sight was inconceivable until the medic realized that he'd aimed too high, his subsonic rounds grinding to a halt somewhere in the body of diamonds secured to his target.

He switched his HK416 back to his right shoulder, rising without a second thought and moving noiselessly down the hall toward his target. It was a risky move, but Reilly instinctively knew the terrorist had exactly three options given his current hiding place: he could expose himself again and get killed in the process, or hunker down in place to wait for his pursuer to appear. Finally, he had the choice of leaping out the third-story window into the courtyard, which would make Reilly's job immensely easier.

But Mubenga chose a fourth option, one that the medic hadn't anticipated in the slightest.

A dark sphere flew from the side corridor, bouncing off the far wall and ricocheting toward him. Reilly had only a split second to choose whether to retreat or advance, choosing the latter and sprinting four steps to fling himself into the nearest side corridor.

The grenade bounced off another wall, then skipped off the floor and visibly leapt a meter off his side before disappearing down the hall toward the stairs, leaving Reilly time to do nothing but key his transmit switch and whisper, "Racegun, *hold*," before the detonation.

A concussive force reverberated through the hallway, shaking the entire third floor. The shockwave hit Reilly like a physical blow, air pressure fluctuating wildly and pressing against his ears and chest.

The blast unleashed a lethal spray of shrapnel, razor-sharp metal fragments flying at deadly speeds. The hallway's walls and ceiling were pockmarked with shrapnel impacts, chunks of plaster and debris blown outward. The grenade's roar was accompanied by the splintering of wood and the shattering of glass, creating a total cacophony of destruction.

A cloud of dust, smoke, and pulverized debris billowed out from the epicenter of the explosion, engulfing the hallway in a choking, opaque fog.

For a fraction of a second, Reilly was a mere spectator to the raw power of the blast; he winced from the overpressure and waited for the shrapnel to subside before kneeling at the corner and taking aim down the hall.

Visibility had gone to shit, the air now thick with dust and smoke. The grenade had done its job with ruthless efficiency, its shrapnel tearing into the walls and doors, leaving them riddled with holes and jagged edges. Some of the overhead lights were out and others flickered erratically, casting eerie shadows across the devastation. The smell of burnt material and plaster dust hung heavy in the air.

Reilly scanned the hallway cautiously, fear pulsing through his veins. But he had to be ready to fire if the terrorist tried to run; another key consideration was that he damn well wanted to know sooner rather than later if a second grenade would follow the first.

But neither eventuality occurred and, fully unwilling to advance further given Mubenga's demonstrated propensity for unwelcome surprises, Reilly moaned.

"Uhhhhh," he said, doing his damnedest to affect the sounds of a mortally wounded man. Then, more quietly, "Uhhh-uhhh."

He went silent, suddenly feeling ridiculous at his ploy. It was a good thing no one else from his team had been there to witness it, because there would be no end to the ridicule—they'd change his callsign to Moaner or Groaner or Whimperer, if not Iron Wailer or worse.

Mubenga's rifle barrel appeared around the corridor, but nothing else. Reilly ducked behind the corner as the terrorist loosed a wild, unaimed burst, bullets skipping off the floor and walls.

When the gunfire subsided, Reilly took aim once more, not making a sound amid the echo of gunshots.

And then, impossibly, Mubenga appeared.

He moved warily, stepping halfway into the hall while waving his Galil in the medic's direction.

Reilly's first round hit Mubenga in the collarbone, and was followed up with another four shots for good measure. Most found their mark, and the terrorist leader collapsed with alarming speed, the duffel weighing him down like an anchor the instant he lost motor function.

Rising and shooting twice more, Reilly advanced rapidly until he could see Mubenga's chin, his head tilted back, eyes staring wide and uncomprehending in death. Reilly stopped and fired a final bullet through the bottom of Mubenga's jaw, the round skipping off the ground somewhere behind his skull and lazily tearing through his left cheekbone in a ragged exit wound that produced a small geyser of blood and bone.

He heard Cancer transmit, "*De Lange is down, I'm withdrawing,*" and David reply, "*I'll follow you.*"

Reilly put his weapon on safe, reloaded, and transmitted, "Mubenga's down, too. Racegun, you're good to proceed, link up with me in the third-floor hallway."

He knelt and flipped the body sideways to wrestle the duffel strap off Mubenga—it would be quicker to cut it, but then he'd have no feasible way to haul the bag out. Finally, he lifted it free only to gasp in alarm as he nearly threw out his back.

How had Mubenga ever run with this thing?. It must have weighed 150 pounds or damn close to it.

"*Angel,*" David said over the radio, "*me and Cancer are moving to Avenue Muhumba for pickup, just north of the college.*"

Ian replied, "*Copy. Doc and Racegun, get to the street. I've linked up with Azibo but we've got cops and bodyguards all over the place. It's time to leave, now.*"

The adrenaline was fading and Reilly's gunshot wound from the rainforest had turned into a piercing lance splitting his side, making any movement a concerted effort with or without the anvil of diamonds weighing him down. He had to leave the duffel behind, but was equally unwilling to do so out of fear that a responding terrorist would recover it as they searched for Mubenga.

He dragged the duffel to the corridor window instead, looking down to see the courtyard of Alfajiri College below. Its grassy surface was dotted with trees and palms and, he noticed, roughly fifty Congolese men, women, and children who'd sought sanctuary amid the gunfire outside. More students fled outside from the first-floor classrooms, likely after losing control of their bladders in the wake of the grenade blast and gunshots overhead.

Reilly dropped the duffel and unzipped it. A foam panel blocked his view, and he ripped it out and cast it aside to see what awaited him within.

The interior was divided by custom-cut foam panels for even weight distribution, and in between them lay the diamonds.

They varied in size and shape, their raw and unpolished surfaces glinting subtly in stark contrast to their immense value. He'd never seen a million dollars before, much less twenty, he thought, and never would again.

"Holy shit," a voice behind him drawled.

He looked over his shoulder to see Worthy standing behind him, HK416 lowered as took in the sight.

"Yeah," Reilly agreed, opening the window and squatting to deadlift the duffel to waist level before setting it atop the windowsill. "Holy shit."

Worthy grabbed his shoulder, stopping him to reach around and pluck out the largest visible stone before saying, "Go ahead."

With a grunt of exertion, Reilly tilted the bag to empty the contents.

The cascade of diamonds transformed into shimmering rain in the sunlight, glinting with an array of rainbow hues, rough surfaces reflecting the sun's rays like glittering stars falling from the sky.

There was a burst of movement as the civilians below initially scattered away, and then, realizing their unexpected good fortune, halted and reversed course.

A scramble to recover the stones ensued, bringing Reilly a warm feeling of utter satisfaction—it was the first time the Congo's resources would actually benefit her people, and he hoped it wouldn't be the last.

He tossed the duffel over the side in case any diamonds remained trapped in its creases, then turned and followed Worthy back to the staircase.

29

Ian gripped the steering wheel of the Suzuki Vitara as he led the convoy northbound on Avenue President Mobutu.

Behind him, Worthy announced, "One kilometer out—five minutes."

"Right," David confirmed, shifting uneasily in the passenger seat. "What's Ground Branch's radio handle again?"

"Skinwalker," Ian replied.

The team leader murmured appreciatively, "Badass callsign."

Then he transmitted over the joint FM frequency, "Skinwalker, Suicide Actual. Be advised, we are five mikes from your location."

Ian appraised his surroundings over the next twenty seconds of silence that the team leader spent with the hand mic pinned to his ear, listening to the return transmission. They were now traveling toward the edge of Bukavu's easternmost peninsula. Checking his rearview mirror, he saw the Nissan Patrol following two car lengths behind, driven by Azibo. The vehicle carried Cancer and Reilly, along with Fatima.

The trip from their gunfights to the border crossing was only three kilometers total, but it felt much longer given the reality of their situation.

They were exhausted, fresh out of combat, and moving with a pair of Congolese natives, one of whom was pregnant.

The linkup had been relatively straightforward: the Nissan was already parked in front of Alfajiri College with Azibo at the wheel, and all Ian needed to do was park his Suzuki there and wait for the rest of his team. David and Cancer had been the first to arrive, their arrival delayed by a short halt in the southern woodline to break down their rifles and stuff the weapons, along with their tactical vests, into the backpacks they carried. By the time they strolled across Avenue Muhumba, the men appeared as little more than two exceedingly wary civilians.

They transferred Fatima to the Nissan, which would serve as the trail vehicle during their exfil—but only after Cancer had taken a position in the passenger seat, lest Azibo speed away with his wife and one of the team's vehicles.

Reilly and Worthy, however, had no time to concern themselves with appearances.

They'd come sprinting out of the dormitory building in full battle rattle, splitting up between the idling vehicles that pulled away the second both men were safely inside. The first kilometer of the drive was harrowing to say the least, with police vehicles crisscrossing the roads in various stages of responding to an unimaginable number of civilian reports.

The second kilometer was largely uneventful, save the sudden appearance of two Isuzu D-Max pickups that Cancer recognized as part of the convoy. Both trucks were headed in the opposite direction, moving deeper into Bukavu in a probable attempt to recover de Lange's remaining security men, now scattered to the four winds by the chaos surrounding the death of their primary.

And now the team was in the final stretch, their destination and all the safety it represented so close that they'd be able to see it in the next few minutes.

"Good copy," David said into his hand mic, replacing it with another to transmit to his teammates.

"Immigration and customs will be on the left up ahead. We'll see Ground Branch's red Mazda pickup sitting out front, and they've got a guy with the border officers to wave us through to the bridge. Stay right once we make it to the far side; we'll follow the south edge of the inspection area and see the rest of their vehicles. Landmark is a white Iveco panel van— stop there and they'll provide all instructions."

"Damn," Worthy said from the backseat. "Would you look at that."

Ian slowed the Suzuki in anticipation of the curve ahead, a hairpin turn in the road that crested the north side of the peninsula before twisting back on itself.

Baie De Nguba Bay stretched into the southern expanse of Lake Kivu, now a vast, tranquil canvas mirror reflecting the sky. The sun cast a peaceful light across it that was so at odds with the mayhem in Bukavu that Ian almost felt like he'd entered an entirely new dimension.

Ian wondered how deep the lake truly was.

"Watch it," David scolded, and he veered right before drifting into the oncoming lane.

Worthy said, "There's the Mazda," as Ian rolled the steering wheel left, exiting the curve and proceeding along a straightaway heading southeast. The red pickup was parked beside a long two-story building with a flat roof, where a trio of uniformed Congolese customs officials stood beside a tall man in sunglasses and a khaki vest.

One of the customs officials frantically swung his handheld radio back and forth, directing the team vehicles across the open lane like an airport traffic officer trying to clear out cars from the arrivals area. Given the long row of stopped outbound vehicles that Ian drove past now, the urgency was, to an extent, fully understandable.

Ian held up a friendly hand as they passed, making out the Ground Branch man's radio earpieces before he and his Congolese partners swept out of view.

Checking his rearview again, Ian saw that the Nissan cleared the checkpoint with equal ease and was now hovering just off the rear bumper. Azibo was antsy to get this over with, Ian thought, and he didn't blame him.

The Suzuki's tires thumped over the concrete edge of a two-lane bridge that was completely empty, spanning the gap where the southern outflow of Lake Kivu turned into the Ruzizi River. They were halfway across when Worthy spoke.

"Welcome to Rwanda."

David glanced out the windows and replied, "The view is a hell of a lot better than what we just left behind."

The bridge ended at a huge oval of pavement, the entire left side packed with cars, vans, pickups, and cargo trucks waiting to transit into the Congo.

For Ian's team, the border crossing had been seamless, but he knew it belied a much lengthier process of greasing the skids. US ambassadors in both countries had leveraged diplomatic relations to achieve official government orders, and then the Ground Branch operators had to make their presence known while issuing cash payments to the actual border officials calling the shots on the ground, any number of whom would otherwise find a reason to create unwelcome friction.

In the end, the dollar—or the Congolese or Rwandan franc, as one preferred—held the ultimate sway.

Ian steered right, following the curve toward a white panel van parked facing away. It was flanked by seven other vehicles: whatever issues Ground Branch had faced since entering Rwanda, acquiring transportation wasn't among them. Ian pulled the Suzuki to a stop, momentarily startled by the fact that there were no Americans in view.

If this was a trap, he thought, it was a particularly elaborate one.

But a lean white man with a silver handlebar mustache stepped out of a Hyundai SUV, and when he approached alone, Ian realized that the man's fellow operators had opted to remain in their respective vehicles rather than risk having their faces photographed by occupants of the stopped traffic. Privacy didn't seem to be much of a priority in the open inspection area.

Cancer dismounted the Nissan and closed with the Suzuki as Ian rolled down the window.

"GFC's in here," he said.

"Right on," the Ground Branch man said. "Tony, Skinwalker Actual."

David replied from the passenger seat, "David. Suicide." Jerking a thumb toward the team sniper standing outside, he continued, "That's Cancer."

Tony asked, "Casualties? Anyone need medical attention?"

"Ironically," Cancer said with a smirk, "our medic's the only one who got hit. But that was a while ago, so he can wait until we're out of here."

"How about long guns—you guys have any assembled?"

"One in each truck."

"Keep them in the vehicles, I'll send a guy with a bag to collect. Your team's riding in the Iveco van. Two pax for relocation, right?"

David nodded. "Yeah, both in the other truck."

He gestured toward another van and continued, "They'll ride in the Peugeot for debrief. We'll have three vics on point and three in the rear, and a couple guys driving your trucks. Shouldn't be any trouble, but if there is, we'll handle it. Keep your team buttoned up inside."

"Gladly. What's our destination?"

"Kamembe Airport, five klicks north. We've got an Air Department bird on standby to haul your team to DJ."

Ian frowned. He'd been in some real hellholes across the planet, and Camp Lemonnier in Djibouti was one of his least favorite locations on that extensive list.

Tony continued, "Couple days' layover, then a C-17 to Germany and back home. Go ahead and load up—we've got a couple guys to drive your trucks, just make sure you've got all your gear with you."

"Hey," David asked, "what about our two locals? They flying with us, or—"

"No, they'll be traveling commercial with an escort. Better say your goodbyes now, because you'll never see them again."

Tony and Cancer departed in unison, the former back to his vehicle and Cancer to the Nissan to brief everyone else.

Ian pushed his door open and stepped into a sweltering inferno; the immense swath of asphalt had soaked up every possible ray from the sun, and was now radiating that heat back upward.

Everything happened quickly after that, the team shuttling their rucks and backpacks into the panel van in a flurry of movement. Four days had elapsed since the shootdown on infil, and everyone present was ready to relegate this mission to the history books.

Ian intercepted Azibo and Fatima on their way to the Peugeot.

He extended his hand, and Azibo shook it firmly.

"Thanks for the help," Ian said. "Sorry to put you and Fatima through all this, but I'm glad you're both making it out."

Azibo dipped his head in a short bow.

"So am I. Stay safe." With a wry smile, he added, "I wish you better luck with your next local asset."

Ian had barely turned to Fatima when she embraced him tightly, whispering in his ear, "Find the right woman, Ian. She is out there somewhere, waiting for you."

When she stepped back, he noticed tears in her eyes. Ian was speechless, nodding dumbly, when Worthy mercifully stepped in.

"Here," he said, reaching into his pocket. "Since we're going to miss the baby shower."

Fatima's eyes went wide as he held out a single diamond.

It was large, easily the size of a walnut, and its uncut surface caught the light in a myriad of ways, each facet reflecting a different shade of brilliance. She quickly accepted the gift.

"Thank you," she said breathlessly, composing herself before her eyes crinkled with a broad smile. "We will put it to good use...I have a nursery to build."

When the team's final farewells were complete—with Cancer merely shaking Azibo's hand as both men eyed each other with equally frigid glances that caused Ian to question whether a fistfight was going to ensue—the team loaded up in the Iveco van for the first leg of their journey out of Africa.

The barren cargo space was tight with five men and all their gear, each team member jostling for a seated position atop their hiking packs as Cancer slammed the rear doors shut, encapsulating his team inside.

No one looked at each other and no words were spoken; each member of the team was alone with his thoughts.

The van pulled away, taking its place in the convoy as the chain of vehicles threaded their way north out of the inspection area and proceeded at a swift pace to escort the team to Kamembe Airport and, within a few days' travel time, back to America.

And home.

30

Cancer broke the silence.

"Where's *my* diamond, you piece of shit?"

Worthy shrugged. "I only took one and, well, you're not pregnant."

I resituated myself atop my hiking pack just behind the cab, finding a pack of water bottles in the back and nothing else; for the sake of America, I hoped that Ground Branch was better at intelligence collection and gunfights than they were at hospitality.

Ripping the plastic covering open, I extracted the first bottle and passed it to Reilly—he was about to boil over, I could tell, his glances between the team members increasingly harsh and unforgiving.

A man in the passenger seat held out a hand mic and said, "Suicide, I've got her on the line."

"Give us a minute," I replied, handing out the water bottles. "We've got some team business."

Then I said, "Go ahead, Doc."

The medic thrust out his open palm toward the center of the van and snapped, "Hand them over, you pricks. Every last one. I'll know if anyone's holding back."

I opened a pocket of my hiking pack, extracting a Snickers bar that, from the feel of it, was already half-melted.

Reilly snatched it away, extending his hand again. "Keep them coming, assholes. Time to fork over your thirty pieces of silver."

No one moved, the entire team frozen under Reilly's withering stare.

"It's okay, guys," I assured them. "I already told him."

Cancer groaned and slid his hiking pack between his boots, followed in short order by Worthy as both men transferred the remaining candy bars back to their rightful owner.

Then, reluctantly, Ian opened a pouch.

"*Et tu, Brute*?" Reilly said accusingly, grabbing the final bar and counting the pile beside him: six out of an initial 19, the medic's stash decimated by my theft.

Worthy said, "Now that we've got that out of the way, the real question is whether Cancer gets a case of beer. I mean, he didn't get our main target, but he did kill a Top 5."

Reilly looked up with fear in his eyes.

"Well I'm not giving up my case, not after you fucks took my—"

"No," I assured him, "you're not. And I don't think it'd be fair to give Cancer a case."

The sniper drew his Winkler with an expression that said, in no uncertain terms, *I'll cut you.*

"Oh, stop with the drama," I chastised him. "All I accomplished during the fight was covering two withdrawals, Reilly's and yours. Both of you got to take down a target thanks to me. And besides," I added with a final decree, "a Top 5 kill is worth two cases."

Cancer sheathed his knife with a delighted smile.

I leaned toward the cab and announced, "Thanks for waiting, I'll update her now."

The Ground Branch officer passed me a hand mic, threading the coiled wire back until I could hold it comfortably.

Waving the mic at Ian, I offered, "Want to do the honors?"

"You're the team leader," Ian deferred.

I keyed the transmit button and said, "Raptor Nine One, Suicide Actual. Mubenga is dead, and the diamonds were distributed among the citizens of Bukavu so they're out of enemy hands. The bearded guy, the financier—what was his name?"

"*Dominic de Lange,*" Chen supplied, her voice emitting with a tinny echo from a speakerbox in the cab. "*He was tied to a network of shell companies and cryptocurrency trades. Along with gold and diamond exchanges in Africa and the Middle East, all to finance terrorism.*"

"Yeah, well, he's dead too. So you can cross him off the Top 5."

When Chen didn't respond, I continued, "This is where you say 'great job, team, the Agency and the United States are forever in your debt.'"

The line remained silent once more, and I glanced across the faces of my team—hollow gazes all around except for Ian, who stared up at the roof of the van. I felt my elated spirits fall.

"What happened?" I asked, feeling increasingly uncertain whether or not I wanted to hear an answer.

There was a pause before she finally replied, "*The Directorate of Analysis has been analyzing the laptops. We just got the results back.*"

"What laptops?"

"*The three you captured at the mine,*" Chen clarified.

Damn, I thought, questioning my own sanity—I'd almost forgotten about the mine entirely, much less the computers Ian had seized there, in the wake of what had just occurred in Bukavu.

"And?" I said expectantly.

She went on, "*The entire cobalt mine was part of de Lange's operation. All profits went to him and have since been transferred to places unknown...the trail ends in cryptocurrency, but all indications are that the funds went to the same place.*"

I couldn't stand the suspense.

"How much?"

"*The mining operation has yielded $103 million over the past eight months alone. Which begs the question of why he would risk sponsoring a comparatively insignificant diamond heist to begin with. Even at maximum retail value, the mine would have netted the equivalent of the fenced diamonds in an additional two months' time.*"

Ian said quietly, "He didn't have time to wait."

Chen went on, "*De Lange's presence in Bukavu links the mine profits and the diamond heist to a single—and imminent—terrorist attack. The cobalt money is already gone, and the diamonds were to serve as the final funding. That means the operation is on an accelerated timeline, and given the financial scope, disrupting the diamond exchange will serve to delay but not stop it.*"

"What about the attack," I asked. "When, where?"

Chen replied, "*We have no further information at this time.*"

Lowering the hand mic from my ear, I tried to wrap my mind around everything she'd just said.

Finally, I handed the mic back to the cab without signing off.

"Cancer," Worthy said. "The picture you sent, the one of de Lange. He was on a satphone."

"So?" the sniper asked.

"So who was he calling? He didn't need a satellite to communicate with his guys at the exchange site, and that tells us everything we need to know. The only reason he'd show his face would be to report to someone higher up the food chain."

Reilly offered, "De Lange was a financier. He couldn't engineer something like the diamond heist himself. Maybe he was just keeping *his* buyer informed."

Ian shook his head, leaning against the wall of the van. "Before the sale went through? No, he was accountable to someone. The question is, who?"

Silence ensued, my mind racing until Cancer spoke.

"We all knew the score," the sniper said dismissively. "It's terrorist Whac-A-Mole in this bitch. Knock one down and another pops up. You degrade a network long enough to save a few hundred lives before some new band of shitheads enters the fray."

But he didn't sound like he believed his own words and I wondered who exactly he was trying to convince, us or himself. We all knew now this was headed toward some apex of terroristic ambition, some calamity that we couldn't even grasp in that moment; we could sense it as surely as a sharp drop in barometric pressure.

All of us knew a storm was coming, and the only question that remained was what.

And when.

ROGUE FRONTIER:
SHADOW STRIKE #9

Elite CIA operative David Rivers leads his paramilitary team into rural Pakistan with a critical directive—neutralize Kamran Raza, a rogue general selling nuclear secrets to the highest bidder.

But when their mission is blown apart, the unit uncovers a devised plot with stakes far beyond their wildest estimations: a conspiracy to ignite a nuclear crisis between Pakistan and India. Raza's intricate plan, a digital charade of doctored communications, could convince both nations they're on the brink of war. Now, Rivers and his team must outmaneuver Raza on the geopolitical chessboard to prevent jeopardizing regional order.

With the specter of nuclear war looming, the stakes couldn't be higher. As David navigates the razor's edge between duty and disaster, he learns that a war between Pakistan and India is only the beginning.

Because Raza's true goal is something far more catastrophic.

Get your copy today at
Jason-Kasper.com

ABOUT THE AUTHOR

Jason Kasper is the *USA Today* bestselling author of the Spider Heist, American Mercenary, and Shadow Strike thriller series. Before his writing career he served in the US Army, beginning as a Ranger private and ending as a Green Beret captain. Jason is a West Point graduate and a veteran of the Afghanistan and Iraq wars, and was an avid ultramarathon runner, skydiver, and BASE jumper, all of which inspire his fiction.

**Sign up for Jason Kasper's reader list at
Jason-Kasper.com**

jasonkasper@severnriverbooks.com